THE RETELLING OF FAIRY TALES

NICHOL GOLDSTEIN

THE RETELLING OF FAIRY TALES
Published by NixComix Publishing
nixcomix.com

ISBN (print): 979-8-9870103-4-1
ISBN (e-book): 979-8-9870103-5-8

An application to register this book for cataloguing has been submitted to the Library of Congress.

First Edition: June 2023

Cover design by Fiona Jayde Media
Editing by Lyric Editorial

Dedications

To the members of the 321...Write! group.
Some of us imagined a fairy tale anthology, taking the old into the new.
You are the reason this exists.

Also, to the Progress writers' group.
You helped me see that stories don't have to be 90k word novels.
Sometimes they can be a mere 500 words...and everywhere in between.

This is for you.

Foreword

This book is an illustrated collection of fairy tales and legends retold for adults, each with its own new flavor and perspective.

From *The Frog Prince* to *Arabian Nights* to the fall of the Devil and *The Little Mermaid,* my hope is to capture your imagination in new and exciting ways while still incorporating threads from these timeless stories.

Content warnings:

- **For the Love of Coffee:** Language, allusions to a male/male relationship.
- **Symbiote:** Death of a minor character.
- **Sympathy for the Devil:** For devout followers of Judeo-Christian faiths, this story may be offensive, as it takes the devil's side and makes the God-figure the antagonist. Please know that it is not my intent to devalue or disrespect anyone of faith; this is merely a work of fiction designed as a "What if?" scenario. Biblical themes have been adopted, but modified for the sake of the story. If this content seems concerning to you, I understand if you choose to skip this

piece. Death of major and minor characters, violence, suggestive sexual content, references to biblical genocides and incest, and brief mentions of pedophilia and suicide.
- **Soulmates and Silence:** Language, sarcasm, snark, and shenanigans.

Enjoy, dear readers. See you on the other side.

For the Love
of
Coffee

~HOME~

Hot doesn't describe it. Dry pales in comparison. Jacob feels his body shrivel as his knees finally give out.

Gales of sand lash at him. The Arizona desert isn't supposed to be like this. It's not what any of the brochures or internet ads said. It had seemed like the perfect place to travel, hefting along a backpack laden with canteens, pop-up tents and non-perishable foods with promises of the future laying belly-up in Jacob's hands. He was supposed to find his true purpose out here on a peyote-filled trek toward adventure.

Instead, Jacob is dying.

Whether he's caught in a cyclone or a sandstorm, he doesn't know. All he can do is slam his eyes shut and curl inward, trying to protect his nose so he can breathe without drowning in dust. The grains rake over the reddened patches of his skin, roughing up where he's not just been sunburned, but baked and blistered. His whitened lips rub themselves raw as he clenches his jaw and whimpers, ready to give himself to the darkness, but the wind only whips away as fast as it began, leaving Jacob nestled in a dune that curves over his body like a wave of beige.

Coughing comes next. Hacking. Spitting and batting at his face to free his eyes. As they creak open, Jacob sees something unexpected lying off to the right, innocently uncovered in a newly made divot in the landscape. A lamp. An oil lamp. Slender and oblong, it curves up at the top with a delicate handle. Brass, or perhaps gold, it's like something directly out of *Arabian Nights.* Like it would grant you wishes if you only rubbed it just right.

Delirious, Jacob crawls like a manic toddler through the sand, watching the heat of the sun shimmer off the lamp's surface. The relic fills the withered young man with bubbling, unhinged laughter when he snatches it, as if he could actually use the thing. Irrationally, it's more hope than he's had in days.

Why the hell not? Jacob thinks with a crackling grin, rubbing the lamp with his palm and watching his tired face reflect on its shiny surface.

It...trembles.

It actually grows hot in his hand.

The smile on Jacob's face falls into a slack idiocy, his sandy lashes lifting over ever-widening eyes. "What the fu—"

With a heavy slam, Jacob is rocketed back onto the dune, billowing smoke pouring from the lamp's nozzle. It's unlike any smoke he has ever seen. Reds and purples swirl in puffing clouds, twinkles of light dancing around and forming a massive shape that hovers above Jacob like a childhood fantasy painted in jeweled tones.

He'd lose his bladder if anything remained there. Instead, dumbfounded, he watches as the smoke solidifies into meaty hands, a barrel chest, and a face so beautiful it burns a brand on Jacob's mind. Shimmering, perfectly golden skin replaces the ethereal rainbow the figure was lost in. Elaborate bangles swallow its wrists and throat, a vest of embroidered violet and turquoise materializing and hiding its carved-marble torso in a dash of modesty.

Again, Jacob repeats, "What the fu—"

And again, the thought doesn't get a chance to complete.

"WHO HAS SUMMONED ME?!" booms from the figure, pummeling Jacob's chest with sound.

A shrill *eek* slips out before he rasps, "Y-you've gotta be kidding me..." His mind can't grasp the word *genie* at the moment, but Jacob knows that's exactly what this is.

The creature eyes him, stroking a fine, trimmed beard that edges its jaw as it looks Jacob up and down. Its lower body fades into a colorful mist that ebbs from the lamp, ensuring there is no mistaking this thing for a regular man.

"Seems like you're having a bad day," the genie says.

Jacob can only blanch.

Legs form and solidify as it floats, its two feet adorned with ornate, curly-toed slippers. "I can help with that. I'm guessing you know what I am?"

What Jacob knows is that he's going to pass out. "A-aren't you a little far from home?" Swallowing nothing, his rough throat rubs painfully on itself. "You're s-supposed to be in the Middle East or something, yeah?"

The genie shrugs and crosses its legs mid-air, cascading slowly to the ground like a puff of downy feathers. "Life's full of surprises."

Jacob tries to say something else, but falls into a strangled coughing fit, his head getting light and his eyes rolling back. *I'm hallucinating,* he thinks. *I'm dying and my brain is fried.*

The genie muses. "I can see we're getting nowhere like this." Its large hand comes up, middle finger against its thumb, pointer finger curled just so, and...

Snap.

It's as if Jacob has been made whole. Every ache and pain is gone. He feels watered and fed, sane and sound, as if the past week of miserable wanderings never happened at all.

"How did you...?"

"If you haven't noticed, I'm kind of magic."

"Ya think?" Jacob squeaks. The genie only cocks an eyebrow.

Opportunity rages in Jacob's mind, thinking of every story he's ever been told about genies. "Do I get wishes?"

It nods.

"Three?"

It nods again.

Jacob blurts, "I wish to find the love of my life!"

There is no pause. With a heavy sigh, the genie rubs its eyes. "Why does everyone wish that? Can't just one person already have...? *Ugh.* Never mind." Tipping its head left and right, snaps and pops echo from the genie's thickly tendoned neck. "So, there are (sort of) restrictions."

"Sort of?"

"Okay, so there are definitely restrictions," it corrects.

"Oh."

"Things out of scope, let's say. Things I can and can't do." Scrubbing its hands over its face in something like embarrassment, the magical male says, "See, I'm only a genie-in-training."

Jacob's brain hitches. "A what?"

"You heard me."

They stare at each other for a minute as one of Jacob's frequent bouts of self-pity builds into a knot of pique, his mind grumbling, *Well, isn't that just dandy?* Narrowing his eyes, Jacob casts a sidelong glance at the golden-skinned djinn. "So, I'm guessing world peace is off the table then."

The genie huffs. "If I can't make two random idiots fall in love, how the hell could I possibly end all conflict everywhere?"

"Then I wish to be a king," Jacob tries.

"Yeah, that's not gonna happen."

"A prince?"

"I think you're missing the point, here."

Edging from a general annoyance to a more focused irritation, Jacob asks, "Well, can you at least make me rich?"

Suddenly on its feet, the genie grimaces as it paces in circles, shaking its head. "No one ever thinks about the socioeconomics of these things." It chops the side of one hand into the palm of the other for emphasis as it rants. "I can't just make someone rich out of nowhere! If I print you actual bills, it's counterfeit and hell rains down when the Feds come in. If I funnel you money from other bank accounts, you get charged with fraud, theft, or embezzlement. If I skim you cash and you try to deposit it, they'll lock you up for drug dealing or something else nefarious because the money didn't come in on your W2! You wanna go to jail!?"

Jacob's mouth hangs open wide. "But...you used to get people gold and stuff back in the day!"

"You wanna play in the gold market, now?" it asks in a pitchy voice. Turning its hands inward toward its chest, it repeats, "Genie. In. Training. I'm new, okay?"

Looking around at nothing, Jacob scoffs. "Then get me the boss genie! What's the point of finding you if you can't even do anything?"

"Excuse me, what?" The genie leans in, brows raised over slitted eyes as he cups a hand over his ear. "Weren't you dying just now?"

Jacob is beyond hearing. "That's just how it goes for me, isn't it? Get a girlfriend, get gonorrhea. Come out here for enlightenment and get screwed by the *environment!* Find an all-powerful genie just to be told it's an incompetent—"

"How dare—"

"—piece of—"

The genie goes from gold to rouge.

"—trash!"

"NEGATIVE WISHES!" the genie bellows, rearing up into a blackened, stormy figure at least three stories tall. Blazing eyes now flare like supernovas within the deep, dark shadows that were once the genie's beautiful face. It points a newly gargantuan finger at Jacob, only inches away from caving in his chest, and repeats, "THREE. NEGATIVE. WISHES!"

Idiotically defiant, Jacob puffs his chest out. "Are you stupid or something? What the hell are negative wishes?"

The genie growls, *"FOUR, then! Or shall I pick INFINITY?!"* The nightshade nightmare leans over until it blots out the sun, smothering the day in oppressive shrouds of cold nothingness. Heavy fists pound into the sand on either side of Jacob—a dull *thud, thud*—until all he can see are those blinding starbursts for eyes narrowing on him like he's something to be eaten.

All fight leaves; all bravado is lost. Throat bobbing, Jacob stammers, "F-four. Okay. Alright. Four. W-what do I do?"

That blackness hovers closer until Jacob can feel a cool mist letting off electric static, sending prickles up his arms and making his hair stand on end. He cringes until he's lying flat in the sand, hands up in defense over his face.

"*You will serve me until my wishes are complete!*" The genie's dark exhale shakes the ground, stirring up eddies.

"O-okay." Jacob is breathless as he curls like an armadillo ready to roll away. "Whatever you need."

That huge, black hand comes up again...and *snaps!*

...Suddenly they're standing in Jacob's...house? The genie is golden skinned once more, admiring its fingernails and pursing its lips.

Jacob looks around, trembling, stunned to be back in the dull surroundings of his kitchen. It feels impossible, surreal—but everything seems accounted for. Fake palm tree; check. Empty fridge; check. Dining chairs; check. Litter box Jacob never threw away, even after the cat died; check.

"Welcome home," the genie says with lifted eyebrows. "Your name is—"

"J-Jacob."

"I know. And I'm going to make my first wish. Are you ready?"

Jacob could never be ready.

"I wish for you to make me coffee at six a.m. every day, including weekends." The genie flicks his eyes to the digital clock glowing on the little, off-white microwave door. With the power of time zone changes, it now reads an ominous 5:55 in the morning.

Every ounce of blood in Jacob's body hits his ankles, and he swoons. He has never felt anything so urgent, so all-consuming in his entire life. "You've gotta be kidding me," he says again, even as his body moves on its own. Ingredients in hand, it's as if he's been physically warped to the countertop and compelled to shove things into the coffee machine until it begs for mercy.

5:56 and Jacob is quaking with unleashed energy, twiddling his fingers and bouncing on his heels, looking at the clock in tense bursts, praying for the batch to brew in time.

5:57 and he can smell the familiar scent as the drip starts.

5:58 and the glass pot is partway full.

5:59 and Jacob gives up entirely, taking the partially filled reservoir, burning himself with a hiss in the process, and sloshing it into a mug that shakes in his jittery hand.

The rest of the coffee machine pours useless liquid onto the burner as 6:00 hits and Jacob drops to his knees, holding out a mug that says "DEEZ NUTS" to the genie in supplication, an overwhelming feeling of fulfillment coming over him.

The genie whispers, "Cream and sugar," and what can Jacob do but comply?

The contents of DEEZ NUTS is now a light caramel color that Jacob somehow knows is exactly what the genie wants. He offers it again, hilariously horrified, and says unwittingly, "Your wish is my command, M-master."

When the subservient words fall from his traitorous lips, Jacob's head shakes back and forth rapidly. He tries to yell *Bastard!* instead, but it only comes out as "Master" once more, delivered with respect and reverence.

The genie's smug grin reigns supreme. Eyes half-lidded and brows to its dark hairline, it leans down and takes the proffered mug in one hand.

Voice silky, it intones, "Welcome to my world," before drinking its goddamned coffee.

* * *

The oil lamp sits on Jacob's spare bed, nestled in the softest sheets he owns. The innocuous metal stares at him, the genie having vanished back inside, giving Jacob space to accept his new reality. This weird, unsettling, ridiculous reality.

"What happens when I don't catch my plane back home? Will they come looking for me or something?" Jacob asks the genie, as if disrupted travel logistics were the most concerning thing to happen in the last few hours.

"Not my problem!" comes a muffled, mini voice from the lamp.

Maybe if he cancels his ticket, he can get a partial refund. Jacob wasn't supposed to fly for a whole other week, after all.

If only he hadn't lost his compass in the sand.

Or seriously cut into his water rations when he was recovering from that bender he took about two nights in.

Or maybe he shouldn't have fed those snakes such a good portion of his food just to make them stop flicking their tongues at him and go away.

Yes, this trip has "failure" etched deep into its tombstone.

But the Milky Way had been beautiful. Toward the end, Jacob had waxed poetic about dying under the vastness of the stars. If there's anything worth taking with him, it's how humbled he felt in those moments.

He cranks up the A/C and ignores the droning hum. Oahu's not as hot as the Mojave desert, to be sure, but it's still hot enough. Jacob pinches the corners of his t-shirt, fluffing it up and down to suck up the air and dry off his armpits.

"Shower," he says out loud, so used to living alone that he jumps when he hears, "Don't care!" pipe out of the lamp's little spigot.

Jacob narrows his eyes at the thing. Shaking his head, he snags a towel and heads into the bathroom, a drab little thing with tiling left over from the seventies, all pale greens with dingy grout. When he dares to take a peek in the mirror, he hums in realization: the genie did a good job.

Jacob's sunburn is completely gone, leaving only his normal, light brown skin, and his lips look moist and whole, no white, fraying flakes or cracked, bleeding splits. Looking down, his knuckles are no longer chapped or scuffed, either. The only missing item on the checkbox is his hygiene. He still stinks like acrid sweat and desperation, his shoulder-length, black hair separated into clumpy, greasy strands, and his thick fingers grungy with unmentionables wedged under the nails. Tipping his face this way and that, admiring the forever-lack of facial hair, Jacob notices that his jaw is more pronounced as well. Thinner. Constant exercise and starvation will do that to you, he supposes.

With a heavy sigh, he calls out, "So what happens now?"

A squeak from the other room informs him, "You wait for my next wish."

He can't refrain from rolling his eyes. "Oh, yeah? And when's that going to be, *Master?*"

The genie simply says, "Whenever I want."

Turning the shower knob, Jacob mimics the voice in quiet, whiny tones, and tries to put himself back together again.

* * *

"What are you doing? Stop!"

The genie is crowding Jacob on his tiny lanai, overrun with fronds. Seeing the genie in the desert was mind-boggling, but handleable. In his house it's unnerving, but he'll get used to it. Seeing the genie on his porch, however, is somehow, nonsensically, one step too far.

Taking in the hibiscus-scented air, it asks, "Why don't you talk like a Hawaiian?"

"I lived with my dad on the mainland my whole life." Jacob tries to shoo the genie back into the house. "I came here to live with my ma before she died. She's a local."

"Picked up any new words?"

"Yeah. Swear words."

The genie's eyebrows tick up. "Can't wait to hear them."

"Well, jackass is universal, so there's always that. Here's something benign: *Stay kapu, yah?*" Jacob takes his chances and lays his palms flat on the genie's annoyingly ample chest, almost surprised to find he can touch the thing, and tries to push it back inside. "If the neighbors see, it's gonna be *junk!* There! Happy now?"

"Where are you going?"

"I've gotta shop. I've got no food." Jacob goes rigid in realization. "Hell, I've got no car."

"Why?"

"It's still at the airport!"

"Wouldn't it be nice to have three wishes right about now?" the genie asks mildly.

Again, Jacob tries to say the word *Bastard*, but it comes out as "Master" in an exasperated tone.

The genie puts a large palm on Jacob's face and scoots him backwards, making more space for itself to walk straight out into the scraggy, dead grass of Jacob's tiny patch of land.

"Hey! Wait!" he says, trying to hold the genie off, flailing under the shadows of his awning. "They'll see you!" That's all he needs. Some nosy retiree from his mom's neighborhood looking out their window to see a godlike anomaly strutting around like it owns the place.

"No one is going to see anything other than you acting like a prat." The genie gestures up and down its body. "In-vis-i-ble," it sounds out. "I'm coming with you. I'm insanely bored. I haven't been out of the lamp in who-knows how long. What year is it?"

Jacob recites, and the genie whistles out an impressed, extended gust.

"When were you...I dunno...created? Born?" Jacob asks.

"Transformed. I used to be a human," the genie replies. "Not to change the subject or anything, but do you want to keep talking to nothing in front of Mrs. Ailani, who is ever so happily staring through her window over there?"

Jacob's eyes snap up to the salmon-colored stucco of Mrs. Ailani's house, locking gazes with the old, crinkled woman and smiling weakly, waving as if his hand were about to faint off his wrist.

He speaks through his teeth. "Why do you know her name?"

"I might be in training, but I'm still magical."

And what is there to say to that?

* * *

Jacob feels haunted. To retrieve his car, he'd gotten a cab to the airport which had taken two expensive hours in commuter traffic, all with the genie sitting beside him, crowding his space and *Ooh*ing and

*Ahh*ing over every tiny little thing. Jacob wondered what he looked like to the cab driver, huddled in one corner against the window with discomfort written all over him, but it's not like he could have done anything about it either way.

Now, after a shorter trek back and a trip to the grocery, Jacob cooks himself lunch while the mischievous male hovers around him, floating like a ghost over Jacob's head, grazing his cheeks with puffs of red smoke from time to time. Jacob wishes he could telepathically tell his "Master" to go pound sand.

"Do you eat?" he asks it instead.

"I could. But I don't have to."

"Then why drink coffee?"

"Hey, I've got four wishes. And unlike you, I have enough respect to limit myself to what you're actually capable of."

"Why six o'clock in the morning, then?"

The genie grins, tousling Jacob's hair. "I'm a morning person."

Jacob slips the spitting bacon onto a paper towel to drain before slamming his pan back down a little too hard. "You realize I have a night job, right?"

The genie shrinks to a little pipsqueak version of itself, sauntering across the countertop, its voice high-pitched and nasal when it asks, "What do you do?"

"I work in events. Corporate retreats, weddings, dinner parties, that kind of stuff. Every night's full of people irritated because their lighting is aqua and not teal or whatever the hell else they dreamed up in their heads. They like to yell at me because I have a mainlander attitude. Everyone else I work with is Kanaka, so the guests think they're too nice to rail at."

"Kanaka?"

"Natives. They all work together like they're best friends or something, too. Island attitude, let's call it. I'm not like that. I'm more of a get in, get it done, go home kind of person. They don't like it. Makes me seem uppity. They're all like, 'Brah, s'ok! Don't be such a townie, yah? Who went die and make you Kahuna?'"

"I don't think I will ever get tired of hearing you talk like that."

Despite himself, Jacob chuckles. "I'm getting better at it."

"How long have you been here?"

Pressing another paper towel over the top of the bacon and watching it turn transparent, Jacob says, "Ma died about a year ago. I came in a year before that to help her on her way. Stupid that I barely knew her in life, but I had to come here to watch her die. She had no one else, though."

The genie digs under the paper towel, going belly-down on the plate, little slippered feet in the air kicking back and forth while it tears itself off a crumb of the crispiest part to nibble. "Why did you stay?"

Jacob lets his chest fill with air all the way to the top before letting it out again. "Because I had nothing better to do. Nothing going on at home. Plus, this is my heritage. I thought I'd find myself here. I didn't. Hence my fateful trip to the desert and coming back saddled with you." He has the overwhelming urge to flick over the rodent-sized genie as it blinks up at him, cheeks working as it chews.

"Well, if you weren't so...you...you could have walked away having earned wishes instead of owing them."

Scuffing the hair at his nape and tugging it a little, Jacob purses his lips in thought. "What's the coolest wish I could grant?"

The genie grins. "Let's just stick to coffee."

* * *

Days go on like this. No alarm needed; Jacob's body outright leaps from his bed no later than 5:50 every morning to get the coffee started. Brew, cream, sugar, go into the spare bedroom, get on his knees, serve the steaming beverage to the golden male. The only thing that varies is the coffee mugs Jacob selects from his cabinets. Things like "DON'T TOUCH ME, PEASANT" and "MEH" and pictures of Danny DeVito as Jesus. The most apropos is one with two monsters hugging that says, "YOU'RE NEVER ALONE IF YOU HAVE INNER DEMONS."

Jacob sometimes wonders if he's insane, but the fact that he can't get a refund for his return flight somehow grounds him in the reality of it. The mundane meets the supernatural.

At times, their living arrangement is homey and weirdly pleasant. Domestic. The genie binges Netflix like a nightmare, obsessed with reality TV, and listens to 80s music to the point where Jacob knows every word Pat Benatar has ever sung. Not to mention Michael Jackson. God knows Jacob would prefer not to mention Michael Jackson.

But then there are times when the genie fills the house with terrible black smoke and lightning, angry about one thing or another. Usually something Jacob did. To escape the mayhem, Jacob makes the horrible decision to go back to work early. Why hang around at home with an ominous lamp living in your spare bedroom when there's money to be made?

What Jacob didn't expect was to be followed around again.

The genie is, indeed, very bored.

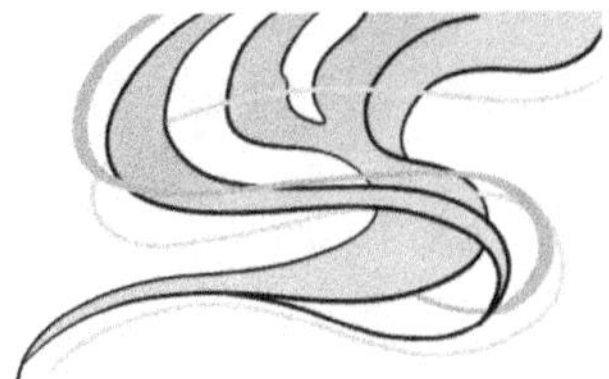

Chapter 2

~WORK~

"Aloha Friday, au'rite! Big party tonight, yah? Gettin' dem tips." The bartender, Iokua, rubs his fingers back and forth with a thick-lipped grin on his face, making Jacob frown. The man sighs, taking him in. "Halala, bruddah, what's got you now? You broke your smile or somethin'?"

"Or something," Jacob says, skirting the pleasantly tubby guy. "You got the liquor set up? You know they want top shelf."

"Yah, yah." Iokua shuffles clinking bottles around behind a portable bar stand framed in heavy black cloth. They're set up in the bamboo pavilion tonight, a pretty place with lots of palm trees freshly painted white all the way up to Jacob's chest line. "I got da Elijah Craig Barrel whiskey and some Chopin Reserve vodka."

"Tequila?"

Iokua digs around the stacks of colorful glass. "Mm. I got a few Reposados. Dese people gonna wrack up da bill tonight, no lie."

Jacob's nod is curt, his whole body tense as the genie floats invisibly around him, making it really goddamned difficult to concentrate. Especially when it starts talking.

"Ooh, is it a wedding?"

Jacob literally has to bite his tongue to keep from answering.

"Or, no," the genie muses "if we're going top shelf, some rich-people thing, right?"

Tossing the genie a glare, Jacob straightens his uniform, the resort name embroidered neatly above his name tag, and goes to do the rest of the venue check. No DJ tonight. Only a string quartet, plucking and strumming and tuning up before their three hours of being ignored begins. Music like theirs becomes "atmosphere." No one actually listens to them, and they know it. It's sad. Still, Jacob eyes the full-bodied, mahogany cello with envy. He probably should have just wished to be able to play every instrument known to man. That could have changed his life. He could have been a rockstar, and then he'd never have to deal with tourists again. And it might have actually been on the list of things the genie knew how to do.

The decor is shaping up nicely as the event crew drapes tables in sensible forest-colored linen to match the dim greenery as the sun sets. This twilight time is always Jacob's favorite. No food service assholes fluttering around with chafing dishes yet. No drunk clients either trying to drag him onto the dance floor, proposition him to be an exotic, brown-skinned tick mark on their island to-do list, or yell at him for something imaginary going wrong. It's the time when everyone knows what to do, is doing it with practiced ease, and Jacob has to intervene very little.

Looking closer, though, he realizes the chairs are wrong. Snagging Taina's arm, he looks at her with slitted eyes, hissing, "These aren't supposed to be teak." He points a finger up and twirls it clockwise, gesturing around the pavilion as if she were an idiot, because she *is* an idiot. "Bamboo grove, bamboo chairs. It's on their list."

Wide-eyed, she digs in the back pocket of her standard-issue charcoal trousers. Bringing out a ratty copy of the client's event list—a page filled with items and itineraries, hopes and dreams—her head tips back with a groan as she sees how very right Jacob is. Her face crumples as she clutches the paper, leaving little fingernail marks as she obstinately refuses to meet his glare.

Fine. He'll fix her problem himself.

Jacob ducks weirdly, likely looking very strange as he avoids the colorful smoke swirling around his head that only he can see. He claps his hands together in two sharp smacks. "Radio for the right chairs and carts, I need everyone breaking down and resetting." The staff all make different sounds of disappointment and irritation. "Get these stacked and racked, ladies and gentlemen, we have an hour until guests arrive and everything has to be perfect. We know this."

Flapping in front of his own face as if to wave off a mosquito, Jacob *ppppffth*s away a rainbowed tendril of genie tail and approaches the electricians as they finish setting up the last bits of lighting.

"You, too," Jacob tells them. "All hands on deck."

Grunting, one looks at him. "Dat's not on *our* list, brah. We don' work for you."

Jacob scolds, "I contract you, don't I? You wanna get another job with me, you jump when I say how high, *yah?*" He emphasizes the last word in a way that only gets the other man to give him the stink eye. Tapping his nametag, which now says Event Manager as opposed to Event Coordinator, Jacob smirks. "If the clients are happy, everyone's happy."

"Fine," the man grunts, patting his coworker on the arm and walking to the table set-up, dragging a chair out from behind a table with a scowl that can't be beat.

"Mahalo plenty!" Jacob calls over with a sarcastic salute.

Circling around his head, the genie prods him. "You're a real jerk, aren't you?"

Again, Jacob bites his tongue, surveying the employees with his arms folded.

It asks, "Why aren't you helping too, since it's 'all hands on deck?'"

Giving the floating male the side eye, Jacob mutters, "We'll talk about it when we get home."

We get home. As if they share it. As if they're roommates or something...though Jacob supposes they are. How stupid is that?

Jacob takes a deep breath to still himself and gets busy looking at the rest of the event details, checking for more mistakes. That's his job in a nutshell: make sure that no one screws up.

* * *

It's one a.m. and the party wasn't supposed to go past midnight. Money, money, money makes the world go round, so these dicks get extra time to ruin their livers and threaten jovially to throw each other in the resort's fake lagoon. Jacob loves it when they make good on their threats. Pissed off, soaking wet tycoons are the world's great equalizer.

A smiling Iokua is closing up the bar as people stumble out, slipping him wads of tip money that he shares with the bar staff who run his dishes. He's one of the good ones. Someone who everyone likes. For that reason alone, he makes Jacob uneasy.

"Ho, brah!" he calls out as Jacob scoots by. "We goin' leeward on Monday ta hit da beach. You wanna come? You not workin'; I check da schedule already." He winks, knowing that's usually how Jacob wheedles his way out of any team rah-rah activities.

"Oh! I want to go to the beach!" the genie says from beside him.

Jacob shakes his head. "I'm still recovering from vacation."

"Oh, yah! You went mainland, right? The desert or somethin'?"

Yeah. I almost died of dehydration until I found a magical being who saved my life only to subsequently curse me.

"It was a lot of hiking and I'm still sore," Jacob half lies. He's never felt healthier in his life.

"Yah, you come back lookin' all skinny. Go grind some food, bruddah."

Jacob runs his fingertips over his sharper jaw.

"Seriously," Iokua says. "Tabby opened her new place. Da food? So good, broke da mouth!"

Despite his best effort, Jacob smiles a little.

"Go," the genie waves him on. "Go break your mouth on food. I want to see that."

"It means 'it tastes so good it hurts,'" Jacob says.

Iokua looks at him funny. "I know what it means, brah."

Well, damnit. Jacob had almost gotten through the whole night without getting called out on his strange behavior. Before it can get any weirder, he clears his throat. "You alright, then?"

"All set." Iokua extends his pinky and thumb in the Hawaiian equivalent of a thumbs up.

"I'm gonna head home, then. Night."

The genie echoes Jacob, saying, "Have a good night," with a grin, and Iokua looks around a little, confusion written on his face.

Did he actually hear you? Jacob wants to mind-jam the question into the genie's head, but he just keeps his teeth embedded in his bleeding tongue and moves back off toward his car. It's been a very long night.

* * *

Leaping from his bed at 5:50, Jacob's eyes are bloodshot as he dashes to the kitchen. He didn't get home until two o'clock in the morning, and his head pounds. A string of curses flicks through his mind as he pours coffee grinds into the filter and adds water, muttering about hoping the genie chokes on it as quietly as possible. He still doesn't know what the genie can hear from inside that lamp.

Brew, cream, sugar, spare bedroom, on his knees, "Master" leaving his mouth in an exhausted sigh as today's mug screams "NOPE" in black block letters.

The predictable curl of crimsons, pinks, and violets trickles from the lamp as the genie appears with a yawn, its mouth gaping and widening his words. "Good morning."

Jacob merely lifts the mug slightly higher for the golden male to take, and it accepts without thanks.

"You look tired."

"I wonder why," Jacob says, blowing his hair out of his eyes as he stares at the carpet. Clutching his hands into loose fists, he laments,

"This is horrible. You know I can't get back to sleep after mornings like this. I've tried. It's like my adrenaline skyrockets and I can't calm down."

"It's just part of the wish." The genie shrugs. "The compulsion. You feel like your life depends on you completing your task on time—and my wish was very specific about that. All wishes should be very, very clearly defined."

"Why?"

"Or else you can cheat. Say you wished for a long life...but you never said exactly how long. If I was feeling nasty, I could make you immortal and, trust me, I've never met anyone happy after the first few hundred years. The trickiest part is that you never asked to be able to die, so you're stuck for eternity. Wishes are like that. Ask for exactly what you want and exactly what you don't want."

Jacob's wheels turn. "So, if it's not explicitly said in the wish, you don't have to do it."

The genie takes a slow, slurping sip. "Exactly."

Facing the dingy carpet as he is, Jacob's sure the genie doesn't see the devilish grin pull at the corner of his lips. Saying nothing, he goes to take his morning shower.

* * *

Next daybreak, similarly exhausted, Jacob shuts off a soft alarm that he's set for 5:45. His heartbeat isn't through the roof, that gripping need not yet in gear, and so he gets up at his own pace, sauntering to the kitchen to make coffee. Today, he's going to try something.

Several minutes before six a.m., he goes into the spare bedroom and gets on his knees. He can't help the smile that slides up the corners of mouth. "Master," he calls, watching the genie ebb from its personal prison. Taking the cup wordlessly this morning, the genie puts his lips on the steaming mug...

And spits it right the hell out.

"*PFFFFFFFFFFFFFFT!* It's black!" it says, horrified.

Jacob is the Cheshire Cat, his smile glowing. "You never actually wished for cream and sugar."

The genie's eyes go round, its pupils shrinking as Jacob gets up, dusts off his knees, and goes back to bed.

* * *

The next morning, he takes it even further. The gentle wake-up call from his cell phone alarm lets Jacob stay in a blissful state of grogginess as he mindlessly goes through his task. Today's mug says, "BOSS LADY," a remnant left over from his ma.

From the kitchen, Jacob yawns, setting a fresh mug of black coffee on the countertop, ready for cream from the fridge and sugar from the little canister next to the stove. The clock strikes six, yet Jacob has said and done nothing else, his test working perfectly. Listening to the familiar little sounds as the genie wakes up—something Jacob can only vaguely describe as what glitter must sound like—he stumbles back into his bed, immediately dozing after a hard night's work.

It doesn't last.

Feet stomping, larger than its normal huge self, the genie slams Jacob's door open and tears off Jacob's sheets, making him curl up and murmur, "You never wished to have it brought to you."

The genie gets even bigger, walking its palms up the sides of Jacob's mattress and making it creak as the genie leans over the foot of the bed. It's huge enough now to still manage to go eye to eye with Jacob even though its feet remain on the floor.

"But I *told* you to do those things!" the genie hisses.

"You also taught me that wishes must be very specific, *Master*." Jacob's lips quirk into a smile, even as the genie's eyes start to redden, its skin giving off that black smoke again as time ticks in slow seconds.

"Fine." With a terrible grin, the genie leans so close their foreheads almost touch. "I make my second wish, then. I wish for you to be obedient in all things."

Jacob's body goes rigid.

"Now then, servant," the genie intones, "cream and sugar."

God damnit.

* * *

"Aloha, Jacob! Howzit?" Iokua waves.

Jacob blinks at him. "Didn't know you were on-shift." Tuesday is a customer meeting day in preparation for events later this week, so he's surprised to see the man walk over with a smile.

"Meh, coverin' for da restaurant bar." Iokua gets closer, tucking his hands into his pockets and rocking on the balls of his feet. "Ask me how da waves were yesterday."

Jacob has no desire to ask how the waves were yesterday.

"H-how were the waves yesterday?" his traitorous mouth says.

Iokua grins and slaps Jacob's back. "Killah, no lie! I got a new surfboard, yah? Cuts da waves like a dream. You betta come next time!"

Don't do it. Don't do it.

"O-okay," Jacob says, his mouth falling open with shock.

Iokua matches his expression. "No way. You sayin' yes to me?"

It wasn't a command, so Jacob says not a damned word. Another heavy slap thwacks him happily.

"Ho, brah! Seriously?"

Jacob's about to vomit.

"I'm gonna tell da others. No one gonna believe it!" Iokua waggles a finger in Jacob's face with one eye narrowed. "You betta come now, yah?"

"Yah," Jacob repeats, high pitched.

The glinting grin on Iokua's face lights up the world. "Au'rite. I knew it. You ain't such a townie after all."

For some horrible reason, Iokua plays drums on Jacob's freakin' shoulder before walking on toward the rest of his day.

* * *

"Why you givin' everything at a discount?" Jacob's boss scowls.

Because the cheapskate clients told me to give them everything at a discount. "They were going to go to another resort if we couldn't match their package pricing. They showed me estimates."

An outright lie.

"No one on da island would be stupid enough to price like dat!"

Apparently, I am, Jacob internally scolds himself.

"When I made you manager, it wasn't so you could screw us, yah?"

"I'm sorry," is all he can say.

"You betta not do it again, you hear?"

A relief washes over Jacob. Since it was a command, maybe he'll have to listen to it and not get himself in trouble again. He doesn't know how the whole obedience thing works, but he needs this job and can't afford to be ousted because of some stupid wish.

"Any more meetings today?" his boss asks, and Jacob shakes his head forlornly. "Good. Get outta here before I bring you mauka and toss you in a hole."

Jacob can't move fast enough...until he gets to a resort guest, that is. A drunk one.

"Alooooohaaaa!" Some random man in a Hawaiian button-up shirt and a woven, cliché sun hat stumbles over to Jacob. "Hey. Hey, you! C'mere."

Jacob in no way wants to *come here,* but that's exactly what he does. The guest paws at him, using Jacob's frame to hold himself up and puffing pineapple breath all over him.

"Tell me. You got...you got any money?"

Oh no. Oh no, no, no.

"Yes," Jacob ekes out.

"Give me some, okay? I want one more drink, but I'm outta cash. Help a"—he hiccups—"bruddah out."

Jacob hates it when haoles try to speak Pidgin. This white guy doesn't live here. He can go jump off a balcony. Still, Jacob's hand goes to his back pocket, and he slips out his slender wallet. Opening it, trembling, he hands the guy a twenty. But he's got more in there, and the guy can see it.

"Don't be so stingy," he pouts. "Your island's pretty damn expensive. That's gonna buy me, what? A virgin daiquiri?"

Jacob swallows. This is his gas money.

"Give it to me, *yah?* What's it you all say? Show me some *Aloha?*"

I hate you, Jacob thinks, but his spirit is begging to do what he was told. He hands the money over without verbal complaint, and the man takes it with a smug grin.

"Wow. You people sure are friendly." He salutes Jacob with two fingers. "Mahalo plenty!" And then he stumbles off toward the nearest tiki bar.

Jacob is dumbstruck, remembering the last time he heard those words as he heads back to his car. They had come from his own mouth. He'd told those contractors to help break down the event set-up, even though he knew it wasn't their job. He'd said those words just as sarcastically as that stupid tourist did and didn't think anything of it.

Do people hate him the way he now hates that random man?

Jacob knows that he doesn't get along with people, too east-coast-asshole for the likes of the staff here, but does he ever make them feel this terrible rage and bitterness?

To say it cuts into his ego would be putting it mildly.

* * *

Jacob tosses his keys down on the kitchen counter only to find the genie with its legs up on his tiny coffee table, remote in hand, watching something inane.

"YOU did this to me!" is what Jacob starts with, going to stand directly in front of the TV. "You have no idea what happened today! What other people made me do!"

The genie blinks at him.

"I could lose my job because of this! A client asked to rake us over the coals to get dirt cheap pricing, and I said yes! Some idiot today asked for all the money in my wallet, and I gave it to him! I got asked to run errands like some stupid towel boy, and I did them! I'm roped into working shifts for people I barely know; I'm now going to have to go and hang out with mokes who probably hate me; I don't know which commands overrule other commands so I'm freaking out about what happens next, and *I can't believe you did this to me!* What the hell is wrong with you!?"

The genie's expression goes from sympathetic to sour. "It's hard, isn't it?"

"It SUCKS!" Jacob yells, purposefully refusing to see the point in the genie's barb. "I never asked for any of this!"

"Would you rather be dead?" the genie asks mildly.

"Don't you do that." Jacob takes a quick step forward, shaking a finger in its face. "Don't you give me that bullshit. Do *you* wish I was dead? Because all that needs to happen is for someone to cuss me out and tell me to go jump off a cliff, and that's exactly what I'll do, isn't it? *Isn't it?* You callous, heartless, piece of—"

"Stop talking," the genie says harshly, and Jacob's lips zip shut.

He has so much he wants to say. So much he wants to yell and scream...but he can't. The feelings all bubble up inside him until tears fill his eyes. Unbidden, one slips down his cheek, then another. Seeing the wet trails, the genie stands up, eyebrows knit, but Jacob can't take it anymore. With a heavy sniff, he takes large strides to the bathroom, locking himself away and huddling in the corner, putting his head on his knees, and letting himself have a good, silent cry.

A knock echoes off the door, a gentle *rap-rap-rap.*

"You can speak again," the genie whispers, its voice sad. "I'm sorry."

As the genie's footsteps fade away, Jacob's tears come in earnest. Who knew this would be so hard?

Chapter 3

The house feels pretty empty over the next few days. The genie's coffees are left cold in the morning, and it never seems to come out of its lamp anymore. Utterly bored, Jacob tries to rub the thing's metal surface again, but only hears a long-suffering sigh come from inside.

Lonely for the first time in forever, Jacob focuses on work, doing unexpected double shifts the whole week. He swears people must think he's a sucker for all the ordering him around they're suddenly doing. Like a good boy, though, Jacob blindly obeys, taking his rage and turning it inward.

What was the phrase? Oh, yeah. 'Turnabout is fair play.'

* * *

Sitting on the couch the next morning, cold coffee on the counter, Jacob gets a text.

Aloha!

He eyeballs it.

Who's this?

Iokua.

We work together two years

Why I not listed in your phone already?

Because Jacob barely knows him, that's why.

You're coming to the beach with me tomorrow.

Jacob's body sits up at attention even as his teeth grind. Apparently he can be commanded over text message.

I know you on the schedule,

But you always on the schedule lately, brah

Call in sick.

Jacob never calls in sick. Yet here he is, shaking as his thumbs peck the keyboard.

Okay.

Chee-hoo! You serious?

Never thought you'd say yes to that!

Neither did Jacob.

We goin' to Kamehameha

> See you around seven, yah?

That would give Jacob time to make coffee and drive over there.

> Come before the people with hangovers
> come out

Again, Jacob says:

> Okay.

And he wants to scream.

Fine. Godamnit, fine. But there's no way he's facing this alone.

"Hey!" he calls out into the silence. When nothing happens, he calls out again, louder this time, and a stream of color tentatively ebbs out of the top of the spare bedroom door, a set of round eyes materializing within the shimmering mist.

"Thanks to you, I'm taking a sick day tomorrow to go to the beach with people I either don't know or don't like."

A mouth appears, only to squeak an "Oh?" before vanishing.

"Can you make yourself look like a real person?"

Those cartoonish eyes blink before bobbing up and down in what can only be a nod.

"Come with me," Jacob asks/demands, sipping his own morning beverage.

"Why?"

"Because if I need an escape plan, you're it."

Materializing into its golden self once more, the genie gently picks up its cold black coffee—a kitten on the front of the white porcelain mug exclaiming, "I NEED COFFEE RIGHT MEOW!"—and puts it in the microwave. "Do you want me to be male or female?"

Jacob nearly spits out his brew. "You can be either?"

The genie lifts its eyebrows with a smirk that can only mean bad things. There are no magic spells to be said, no special hand gestures; only a swirl of red, puffy clouds before a Hawaiian woman appears, standing in Jacob's tiny kitchen in front of Jacob's shabby microwave with *incredibly* nice skin and a figure to die for. A floral, two-piece bathing suit is cut high on her hips and low over her breasts.

This time, Jacob chokes. "You can't go looking like that!"

"Why not?"

"They'll think you're my girlfriend!"

The genie slides its hands down its stomach, unintentionally seductive, looking at itself with a sexy pout. "I thought you'd like it."

"Yeah, I do, and so will everyone else. You want the entire beach coming on to you?"

Evidently, that was something the genie didn't think of. With a pass of its hand over its face, it is now significantly uglier. Jacob hears the phrase "butter face" in his mind: Everything is beautiful, *butter face.*

"No. That's somehow worse," he tells it. "Look, can't you just be a guy?"

With a huff, the genie mutters, "You'd think you were the boss around here." Still, it takes pity on Jacob and changes into a man, keeping its regular, burly physique and dark hair color, only letting it hang long instead of the usual ponytail. His chest puts body builders to shame, and his swim trunks ride low on his hips, showing the line that leads to his groin.

"Can you just," Jacob tries, "just don't be a sexpot, huh? Just be a regular person!"

The genie frowns, but tones it down to a lithe, muscular figure—totally Jacob's type. Tall, but not too tall. Shortish, bone straight black hair and the deepest of brown eyes. Heat rises to Jacob's cheeks as he looks the genie up and down. Over and over. Hell, he might even be ogling.

The genie cocks an eyebrow. "I thought you didn't swing that way."

"I swing any way I want."

"Fair enough," the genie says. "So, who am I?"

"A friend."

"You have friends?"

"Unfortunately, just you."

The genie grimaces. "Now that's sad."

The microwave beeps, and the man-shaped-genie fiddles with cream and sugar before taking a sip from the coffee. The mocha brown swill is probably ruined with magnetron waves or whatever the hell else microwaves use, and the genie's wince of disgust says it all, but it merely waves a hand over its drink before tasting it again and humming out a happy sigh.

Jacob's sigh is harsher, a staccato puff with his nose wrinkled. "If you can do that, I feel redundant."

"You are. This is a punishment, or have you forgotten?"

Jacob's fingers tighten on his cell phone. "I thought it was, but this" —he waves the handheld machine around—"is the real punishment."

"Going to the beach?"

"Being told what to do and doing it."

The man-shaped-genie sits on the couch and crosses its legs, a tiny grin pulling at the corners of its mouth as it sips. "You realize that's what being a genie is, right? No matter what your scruples, no matter if you disagree or not, as long as it's possible for you, you make it happen."

Tossing his phone on the table, Jacob sulks. "I never asked to be a genie."

"Neither did I. But here we are."

There is a silence in the air as Jacob toys with a lock of hair laying over his collarbone, trying not to look at the beautiful man/mythical creature in his living room—instead looking anywhere and everywhere else. The darkened TV. The ceiling fan in its ever-lazy twirl. His powered-off laptop. His mug of dregs.

"You said you were transformed, not born or anything. That you were human once. How did that happen?"

"Well, I was an jackass, as you so bluntly put it. But a smart one. I made ridiculous amounts of money, sat at the top of any company I worked for, was on the board of directors for quite a few firms, and all in my late thirties. I was self-absorbed to the nth degree. I didn't care who I hurt, so long as I benefitted."

"I see that sadism remained."

The man-genie only looks at him askance. Chastised, Jacob toys with the frayed edges of his khaki shorts.

"Anyway, I went to the Sahara with a group of other sleaze bags. Vacation. Once-in-a-lifetime experience, yada, yada. Little did I know, they wanted me out of the picture."

Jacob's jaw drops. "They what?! Why?"

"Too powerful. In their way. Revenge for something. They hate capitalism. They hate gays. They hate philanderers. They hate beauty. Pick your reason."

Deciding to ignore the 'beauty' remark, Jacob asks, "Wait...you're gay?"

"Yup. I can't switch like you do. Vaginas are weird."

"So are penises."

"Fair. Anyway, they abandoned me deep in the sand, not unlike you, and just before I gave up and let go, I came upon a lamp. My genie was not a genie-in-training. It was all-powerful. If I had asked it for world peace, it might have actually been able to do it. Instead, I asked it to bring me home. It did. Unfortunately, my empty penthouse had no one to help me, and I was so weak I couldn't stand. I did exactly what you did. I told it how stupid it was. How useless. I made my second wish to be young and healthy forever. With an evil look, it smiled, saying nothing. Feeling better than ever and never wanting to be one-upped by those bastards again, I asked to be more powerful than any man alive."

"Sounds a bit grandiose."

"And therein lies the problem." The man-genie turns to look at Jacob with an intense frown and sorrowful eyes. "It told me I didn't truly want that, wearing this expression that sent chills up my spine; still, I wouldn't be cowed. I threatened it, like an idiot. Told it I could bury its lamp in cement so it could never come out again. Challenged it, mocking how it probably wasn't even capable of such a thing in the first place, and how weak it must be. The weakest of all the genies.

"I didn't get negative wishes. I got exactly what I asked for. It made me what I am today: more powerful than any man, yet forever weaker than any other genie. I'm not actually 'in-training.' I'm incapable, just like you said, but I got all my wishes. I will always be young, I will always be healthy, I will never die, and no mortal man can ever match me."

Jacob pales slightly. "All because your wishes weren't specific..."

The man-genie presses its lips into a fine line, lowering its eyes. "I didn't realize what it must have felt like to be that genie until I met you. To be insulted when you've sacrificed so much of yourself for the sake of granting someone else's wishes. The only difference is that you were right. I *am* weak. I *am* incompetent. But I still couldn't bring myself to ruin you the way that I was ruined. I'm not sure I could even if I tried.

"So, the next time someone asks you to jump and you say 'how high?'" the genie quotes him, "remember that your punishment is simply a lesson to be learned and not a never-ending curse, like mine. You may think I'm cruel, but the truth is, I had more mercy than you know."

Jacob's hard-heartedness melts a bit. He stares at the blank screen of his cell phone, his mind filled with white noise. "If I had my three wishes back, I could wish to undo yours, if you wanted."

"I've begged other Masters to do it, and one had enough pity to try, but I couldn't make it happen. I can't escape the curse. The only thing I can do is be the best wish-granter I can be and try not to get lonely." The beautiful man-genie ducks its head low to catch Jacob's eyes. "And that's what you are. You're lonely. That's why the first thing you wished for was love."

Jacob's eyes mist, and he takes a deep breath. "I'm not good at that. I don't know how to be with other people. And I think I've realized... I'm worse than just antisocial; I'm entitled. Now I think of all the times I would tell people to do something and just expect them to get it done. I never asked them if it was something they could do, or wanted to do, or had time to do; I just assumed they'd figure it out." Jacob scrubs his hands over his scalp, tugging the hair at his nape. "When I thought I would die, I knew no one would miss me...but I wanted someone to. I don't want to be this way anymore, but I don't know how to change."

"Old habits die hard." The man-genie nods sagely. "And that's why I won't take back my wishes yet. You need to learn. You need to not end up alone like me."

"You're not alone. You have this house," Jacob puts his finger up, twirling it around, gesturing to all four corners of the room. "And you have me."

"For now," the man-genie agrees, making Jacob's heart twinge. With that, the genie tosses back the rest of its drink and fades back into colorful smoke again, ebbing toward the ceiling. "I'll go with you tomorrow. I'll be your friend." And it disappears through the thin opening at the top of the spare bedroom door.

* * *

Waves crash, making that roaring sound only they can. The water rushes in, soaking the sand before retracting again, sucking back seashells in tumbling trails. Jacob doesn't like the ocean. There are too many things living in it. If he's going swimming, he wants it to be in a well-treated, reeks-of-chlorine pool where anything microbial has been murdered by chemical burns.

It's the time of day before the sand gets hot, and Jacob digs in his toes, scanning for the man who commanded him here. Iokua is an adversary to be reckoned with, his niceness terrifying as it draws a distinct line between "a person people like" and Jacob.

He sighs through his nose.

"Ho!" the man of the hour calls from down the shoreline, dragging his surfboard as a woman walks behind him, scuffing her toes through swirling eddies. Iokua jerks a thumb over his shoulder. "Dis Tabby, like I told you, yah? She da one who opened da new restaurant."

When the woman looks at him with a shy grin, Jacob immediately panics. Still, he lifts a hand in a curt wave as he leans closer to the man-genie. "If he's trying to set me up on a blind date, I'm going to kill him."

"Good luck with that," the genie chuckles. "All he has to do is say, 'stop.'"

Much to Jacob's chagrin.

Iokua drops his board out of the path of the tide and jogs up, sticking out a hand to shake the genie's. "Aloha, stranger! You a good lookin' guy. Why you hangin' out with dis one?"

Jacob rolls his eyes as the genie and Iokua shake hands. He knows his one redeeming factor is that he's attractive. Hence the woman—Tabby, evidently—making goo-goo eyes at him.

"You gotta name, brah?" Iokua asks.

Oh hell, Jacob thinks. They never thought of a good name. Do genies even have names?

"Albert!" it declares loudly, pumping Iokua's hand irrationally hard.

Jacob fights not to facepalm. Here's this guy, looking like an absolute, pureblood Kanaka, with the whitest name in existence.

"Albert..." Iokua tries, his smile going a bit funny.

Jacob matches that wan, thin facsimile of pleasantness. "We just call him Al."

"Au'rite, den! Dis Tabby and I'm Iokua. You guys know each other from hanabata days?"

As if "childhood friends" was the only excuse for someone intentionally hanging out with Jacob.

"No," the genie says. "But he's been my best friend for a while now." It tosses Jacob a wink, and Jacob has to clear his throat to hide the almost-smile that surfaces.

"Anyway, what are we doing?" Jacob asks. "I don't surf or swim."

Iokua's arms go wide. "Why you wanna come to da beach den?"

Hiding his embarrassment, Jacob says, "Because you asked me to."

Confused, Iokua looks at him for a second too long before shrugging as if it didn't matter. "Okay, okay. You can hang with Tabby on da beach den, yah? I'll share my board with Al, here."

It's like the man-genie's eyes turn into glittery stars. "Really?"

"Sure! Why not? If you didn't bring nothin', I'm guessin' you not da kinda guy who knows how to ride. S'ok though. Surf is mild, no lie, so you might just ride your belly da whole way. Good practice, though, yah?"

The man-genie nods so fast, Jacob's surprised its head doesn't fall off.

Following along at something close to a skip, the genie reaches Iokua's board where it lays innocuously in the sand. At the behest of the friendly native, the genie hoists it onto its shoulders before dashing into the water like an overexcited toddler, leaving him alone to deal with... whatever this is.

Bastard.

Running a hand through his hair, Jacob looks at the woman. "So..."

"So?" she repeats with a smile. The first word she's spoken to him.

"Tabby? Looks like it's just you and me. You wanna walk around, or sit in the sun, or what? Build sandcastles?"

She giggles sweetly, but Jacob's already not in the mood. He stares at the genie's back with a *Help Me* expression that goes unseen.

"Just walk. I've heard a lot 'bout y—"

But Jacob's feet are already moving at her gentle command, and she has to stride quickly to catch up.

"I'm sure they weren't all pleasant things," Jacob gripes.

"No," she chuckles. "Guess not."

A certain smattering of insults peppers its way through Jacob's mind, aimed in Iokua's direction. "Sorry you got stuck with me."

"Don' say things like dat," she chides, and Jacob's words fall completely away, making his hackles rise. "Iokua says you have a hard time makin' friends, but dat's one thing him and me are good at. We bring out da best in people."

Jacob tries to keep himself in check, his sarcasm unlikely to earn him any favors. "How do you know him, anyway?"

"He's ohana."

"Your brother?" Jacob asks.

"Mm. Da best, too."

Jacob's lips become a straight line. "I can only imagine."

"Tell me 'bout yourself. You got a girlfriend?" she asks.

"Not anymore. I broke up with her when she gave me a venereal disease."

And his trap snaps shut with a click.

Oh. My. Literal. God.

Jacob wants to dig a hole in the sand and die.

"Um...I ah...I take it you all betta now?"

"Oh yes, modern medicine works wonders."

Humiliated. He's absolutely humiliated. His face is a red cherry about to burst.

"You got anyone to look out for you?" she asks, clearing her throat and looking away.

"Just"—the genie—"Albert."

"You live alone?"

He swallows. "Al and I are roommates." Jacob casts a spiteful look at the genie. It is, indeed, belly-down on the surfboard and swiping its perfect arms through the water, its muscles flexing as Iokua stands with his hands on his pudgy hips and a stupid, proud grin on his face. The genie looks childlike with glee, and if Jacob didn't know any better, he'd think it was adorable. "But he's stupid."

Tabby smacks his shoulder. "Don' say things like dat, either."

Goddamn this woman. So now, what? He's never allowed to self-deprecate and can't speak poorly of the creature who infected his days? How dare she?!

"I wish you wouldn't tell me what to do." Jacob glowers. "I take stuff like that seriously."

"Ohhh, keiki has a weak spot? You do anything for pretty girls?"

He mutters, "Who said you were pretty?" under his breath, but she hears him anyway. Her eyes go round with surprise for a second before they narrow.

"Lotsa people, actually, but mahalo for dat," she says, prickly. This is not going well.

She pokes his breastbone in a challenge. "If you talk like dat all da time, s'no wonder people don' like you."

"I never asked anyone to like me," Jacob says through his teeth. "Especially not you. I don't even know you! You should just leave me alone."

She stops, hands on her hips. "And you should go drown in da ocean."

Shit. Jacob's eyes go wide, his face twisting around to look at the aqua blue waves. He quakes, his mind hammering *Shit, shit, shit* as his heart dives into his stomach. Still, he says a weak and whispering, "As you command."

He turns on his heel as Tabby watches, dumbfounded. "Hey!" she calls, but it doesn't matter. Jacob is now a man on a mission, stomping through the shifting sand toward his doom.

Help me, he wants to scream, but no sound comes. He's just doing as he was told. He's being obedient. He's fulfilling the genie's wish.

When he gets waist deep in the tide, Tabby starts to yell. "What da hell you doin'!?"

Iokua and the genie turn toward him as the water gets up to his shoulders.

"Why you yellin'?" Iokua calls to his sister. "He just goin' for a swim, yah?"

No, Jacob thinks. *I'm going to die.*

The water comes up to his chin and he knows he'll breathe it in. She didn't tell him to swim. She didn't tell him to hold his breath. She told him to drown.

Under he goes, his mouth wide open...until he's yanked to the surface, the genie dragging him back to where they can stand.

Jacob coughs, struggling in the genie's arms, yelling, "She told me to go drown! I have to go drown!"

But the genie's hands are on his face, touching everywhere. It whispers, "Shhh, Jacob, listen to me. I make my third wish. I wish for you to follow only my commands. No one else's. All others fall away. And I command you not to do this. Not now, not ever. This is my wish."

Jacob's body goes limp in the genie's arms, everything about him sagging. The genie wraps an arm around the small of his back and a wide palm over Jacob's neck, holding him while the wet of the ocean makes their skin slide. Jacob can't breathe. All he can see is the waterline as it flows, rushing higher and lower in waves. His heart hammers painfully, keeping him on the edge of panic, but then the genie's words sink in.

"I don't want to obey at all," he says, weakly pounding a fist on the genie's shoulder even as he buries his face in its neck. "Why won't you make it stop?"

"It'll be alright. Hush. You'll see," the genie says, holding him close and pulling him further out of the water.

Looking over his shoulder, Jacob can make out a horrified Tabby with her hands clenched together over her mouth. Iokua's struggles with the ocean tide, fighting to reach them. The genie hikes Jacob up over his hips and lifts him from the sea, shushing him as he trembles.

"What happen, brah? What's goin' on? He suicidal or somethin'?"

Jacob flinches in the genie's arms.

Lifting its hand, it points to Iokua and then to his sister. "You will forget this happened. You never invited him here today. You will forget his number and remove all conversations. It will be as if you don't know each other at all beyond work. Do you understand?"

Iokua looks upset for a moment before his face turns completely blank. He looks to the horizon for a beat before turning away, saying nothing, and catching his surfboard as it bobs in place. Tabby walks down the beach and calls to her brother like nothing happened. Like they were alone. Like Jacob didn't exist.

It hurts more than it should, more than rejection or disdain. He's been forgotten.

And Jacob goes numb.

* * *

There is no car ride. There's only a poof, and Jacob is home in the genie's arms, wrapped in an unknown, deep red fluffy towel.

Jacob casts his eyes out the window to see his car parked in the driveway instead of back at the beach. Considerate, he supposes. Perhaps he should be grateful, but he doesn't know how to feel just now. Shock has set in.

The genie sets him down on his little sofa: old, worn, ratted in some places, but still comfortable even after decades of his ma's daily wear and tear. Still, Jacob doesn't stretch out. He doesn't lean back. He huddles in on himself, forehead to his knees, clutching the new, unbought towel over his shoulders as it drapes down its back.

"I'm surprised you didn't just make me dry," he says.

The man-genie, who was taking pans and items from the kitchen cabinets, freezes mid-motion. "I didn't think of that. Do you want to be dry?"

"Towel, too. And couch. Please," he remembers to add.

There is no drying process. It simply just is.

"Is your name really Albert?" Jacob asks, looking to fill the space with words as he forces himself to breathe regularly under the now-useless towel. There is a sound like cracking eggs, but he doesn't feel like looking up.

"It's Jake, actually," the genie says. "But I thought 'Jake and Jacob' would be asinine."

Jacob hums his agreement. There is a set of empty minutes where sizzles and scents fill the air. Maple syrup, pancake batter, coffee. How ironic. The genie is actually making him coffee. Maybe Jacob should be moved, but he finds he doesn't care.

"I don't want to do this anymore," he says, the lump in his throat squeezing his words. "I don't want to obey anyone. I'm sorry I insulted you. I'm sorry I didn't realize how hard serving others was. Can you please just make your last wish?"

He hears the light clatter of a plate being set down.

"Soon, but not yet."

A rock settles in Jacob's heart. "You just don't want me to be *lonely,* right? Or is it *you* you're more worried about?" Jacob waits for the genie's reply, but nothing comes. He stands, keeping the towel wrapped around him like a nursery blanket as he stares directly at the floor. "If that food's for me, I don't want it."

With that, he storms out, shutting himself in his bedroom and leaning on the door for good measure, wanting to keep anything and everything out.

Should he say he's sorry for being rude? Will this earn him more negative wishes?

He doesn't know.

And right now, he doesn't care.

* * *

Later, Jacob's door opens with a light knock. He's buried under blankets with only his nose and mouth out, hiding from the world and all the happier for it. Footsteps approach, making shushing sounds on the carpet, and Jacob rocks slightly when the genie's weight makes a depression in the bed.

"I'm going to command you to do something now."

"Of course, you are," Jacob mutters bitterly.

"When you go to work tomorrow, you're going to try to be a better person. The person you dream of being. Don't start with grand gestures; start small. But you must make an effort. And when you come home, we'll talk about it. I want to know what you did and how it worked. Understand?"

Jacob wants to run to the resort right now, but grinds his teeth instead, his temples throbbing.

"Do I have to go in early, *Master?*"

"No. Just work your shift and come home."

Home. Again, that word. As if it belongs to both of them. As if the genie is wanted here.

Yet, Jacob thinks of the spare bedroom, now decorated with lounge pillows he didn't buy; of MP3s on his iPod he's never heard before; of his Netflix account boasting recently watched series Jacob wants to delete immediately with great shame. The genie has gotten under his skin effortlessly. It's begun to embed itself in Jacob's life. Jacob's space. All that's missing is an extra toothbrush next to his on the bathroom sink.

No matter how angry he feels, after only a few weeks, Jacob can't imagine a life without the genie. He's never felt more mischievous, more clever, more exasperated, more desperate, more chatty...and less alone.

"Alright," he says, pulling back his blanket just enough to peer at the genie, who's still in the guise of a beautiful man. "I'll try."

* * *

I swear to God, I stink!

Jacob is in one of the resort's many restrooms, freaking out more than he should be, considering. He's in the handicapped stall, shirt off and hung on the hook so he can wave at his armpits, wiping them down with shredding toilet paper that leaves white flecks behind in the fine wisps of his pit hair.

Why is this so hard?!

All he'd done was smile at his colleagues. Well, more than that. He'd smiled, nodded, and waved at them as if he liked them. Everyone looked shocked. Some smiled back. Some, gobsmacked, raised a hand halfheartedly. But it was something! And now Jacob's pouring sweat like a fat runner and it's all he can do not to stain his white polo. He prays that a little time in the A/C and his skin contracting into goosebumps will do the trick.

One thing's for sure: this is a rush. It's like the time he went skydiving. He was super tense while waiting for it to happen. Then, after getting hip-chucked unceremoniously from the plane, he had a moment of 'what the hell did I just do?!' right as his adrenaline spiked. Why waving to people made his adrenaline spike, he has no idea. Life or death comes in all shapes and sizes, apparently.

With a little shiver, Jacob picks up his shirt and sniffs at the crease where this sleeve meets the side. It's fine. It smells like deodorant more than anything. Criss-crossing his arms, he slings it over his shoulders and tugs it down, donning his black vest next, ensuring his name tag is on straight. He knows where he wants to go next.

Taking a breath, Jacob pushes open the door, lets his pupils shrink to pinpricks in the sun, and allows his feet—and his Master's command —to guide him.

* * *

"Ho!" Jacob tries, immediately feeling stupid.

Iokua looks up and cocks a half grin. "Aloha. You need somethin'?"

"Something," Jacob agrees, stuffing his hands in his pockets and fiddling with random, omnipresent lint.

Iokua ties on a little black apron before scooting behind the smooth, faux-mahogany surface of the indoor bar, setting up before old-people-dinnertime starts around four. The man's stubby hands bring out maraschino cherries, lemons, limes, and all sorts of metal drink-shakers that Jacob has no idea what to do with.

"So," Jacob clears his throat, "I wanted to ask you for a favor."

"What? You need me pick up anoddah event? Can't do tonight, brah. I've gotta help my sistah out at her new restaurant."

"Oh. That's...nice. But no. I, uh, wanted your advice on something."

"Halala. What's da mattah?"

Why is this so goddamned hard? "Well, I'm not so good with people."

Iokua snorts with a smirk. "No lie."

Jacob gives him a dirty look, and Iokua raises his hands in submission. Pursing his lips, Jacob forces out, "But you are. Good with people, I mean. I was hoping you could, I dunno, give me some pointers or something."

A scoop gets shoved into the ice tray with a *chunk.* "You askin' me to teach you how ta make friends?"

No. Yes. Maybe? "I mean—not in so many words. But. You know. And not that you have to be friends with me or anything. If you don't want to, I mean. I mean, if you do, then that's great, but I don't expect it. But maybe you can show me, I dunno, how to talk to people or be around people or—"

"Brah, you ramblin'."

"Yes, I absolutely am." Jacob lets out a rush of air.

"You can start by bein' friends wid me. I don' mind." A large, warm smile makes Iokua's eyes squint. "You off tomorrow? I coul' take you down to da beach or somethin'. Go surf."

God no. "No beach...please. I'm...well, I'm scared of the ocean." *As of yesterday.*

"Au'rite den. Wanna do somethin' else?"

Now this is the part Jacob practiced in his head. "We can go to a bar. Hang out. Drink some beer." That sounds like a normal-person thing to do.

"Love me those green bottles, but I got night shift tomorrow."

Jacob curses inwardly. "You wanna do lunchtime at the pool?"

"Why you wanna come to work when you don' have ta be at work?"

"No, like, two resorts over, maybe? They have a swim-up bar. We could—I dunno. Swim up?"

Iokua looks at him, shaking his head. "No lie, bruddah, you *are* bad at dis. You sound like you askin' me on a date and I ain't dat pretty."

Exasperated, Jacob throws his hands up high and lets them flap down again.

"Au'rite, au'rite! Calm down, yah? I see you tryin'." Iokua sets up some glasses, bringing them up from a rack beneath the bar, wiping them down with white towels. "We can 'swim up.' Grab some grinds. Drink some greens. You seem more like da froofy drink type, tho'."

"You're not wrong," Jacob admits. "I don't really like beer."

Iokua's voice gets pitchy. "Why you ask me to drink beer if you don' like beer?"

Again, Jacob flaps like a chicken, just once, trying to get across that he's dying inside.

"What's your poison, den?"

"Basically, anything that comes with a little umbrella at the top," Jacob confesses, earning himself a laugh.

"Sounds good. 'Round eleven?"

"Hawaiian people time or clock time?" Jacob asks.

"Clock time. You got my numbah?"

Jacob's phone didn't look like he'd texted with Iokua before; the genie said it was all wiped from Iokua's phone as well, so Jacob shakes his head.

"You mean you work with me two years and you still don' have my numbah?"

And Jacob knows he's said that before. Taking his phone from his back pocket, Jacob thumbs it open. "Well, what is it?"

Jacob's fingers fly over the keyboard to put the number in, and he sends a practice text:

Hello

Yo!

Is what comes back. Jacob smiles a little and lets his thumbs dance once more.

So tomorrow, eleven, swim up bar

Iokua adds:

I'll even buy ya a Piña Colada

Jacob accidentally laughs out loud.

* * *

"And then we texted each other for like five minutes. We didn't say anything, we just stared at our phones while standing there, not even three feet apart, sending each other the stupidest jokes."

"Jokes?" the genie asks.

"Knock-knock jokes."

"You're kidding."

"Dirty ones," Jacob amends, as if that helps at all.

"Like what?" the genie says skeptically.

Face-palming, Jacob speaks through his fingers. "Knock-knock."

"Who's there?"

Jacob's voice ticks up a notch, pre-embarrassed. "Jamaican."

With a groan, the genie plays along. "Jamaican who?"

"Jamaican me horny."

The two burst into sputters of stupidity.

"You know more?" the genie goads, but Jacob only shakes his head.

"Thanks, but no thanks. I've shed enough of my dignity today."

Fork and knife scrapes echo off the plate as Jacob eats the Lomi Lomi salmon the genie made him. You can't live in Hawaii and not like fish. Paying for cow meat over here is like paying for God.

"Will you come with me again?" Jacob asks around his food.

"Sure," the genie asks. "Male or female?"

"What did you look like in real life?"

The genie obliges and transforms in an instant. Brown hair in a suave cut; paler than pale, like he never goes outside; not skinny, not muscular, but somewhere in between; and a grin that twinkles with danger. He looks like he'd drag you to hell, but let you taste heaven first.

"I like you better gold," Jacob says, lying through his teeth. "You just better wear sunscreen."

With a snap, genie becomes man-genie again, all toned, swimmer's muscles and honeyed skin. He looks just as good as he did on the beach, and Jacob blushes a bit.

"I like it better like this," the genie says.

"And why is that?"

"Because I like the way you look at me."

When Jacob swallows, it's an audible thing.

"I'm ready to make my fourth wish," it says.

His eyes fly up to connect with the genie's.

"I wish you freedom, Jacob. Freedom from my previous wishes, freedom from your fears, freedom from your insecurities. I want you to have a chance to be the man you dream of being without being trapped by the past. That is my last wish."

Relief floods Jacob, something wholesome budding in his chest. He can barely speak for a moment, just sitting in this new feeling. It's a kind of bravery growing in his heart, like he could do anything he set his mind to...and it might be the first moment in his life he's ever felt such a thing.

"Thank you," he says over the lump in his throat, holding back grateful tears. "Thank you so much."

Looking at the man across the table from him, Jacob realizes this is it. This is where he and the genie part ways. In his heart of hearts, he realizes he doesn't want that. His home would be so empty without his newfound friend. Perhaps it's that new feeling of bravery that helps him ask, "If I rub your lamp again, can I have my three wishes back?"

The genie quirks a lopsided smile. "You don't have to rub. Just ask."

"I wish...I wish you would stay. Stay until I want you to go, or you want you to go, whichever comes first. But please stay."

The genie's palm slides across the table, taking Jacob's hand in his own. Its smile is soft, warm, and filled with promise.

"Your wish is my command."

SYMBIOTES

Symbiotes

~THE FIRST MARKER~

His feet pummel the ground, the pads of his reptilian toes doing nothing for traction on the wet, leafy ground. It might be only moments before he trips and falls, a feeble offering to the creature behind him, reduced to a mere morsel to be gobbled up in one visceral bite.

The beast's snarls echo in his tiny ears, ghastly and nightmarish, inspiring his heart to thump so hard it hurts. Thoughts of gnashing and frothing fill his mind so vividly, he doesn't have to turn around to see them in real life; they're already like painted murals in his imagination, forever stained with the pigment of horror.

The Gishatich rips through the ashen branches that separate them, unrelenting no matter how many boughs he ducks under, no matter how many pricker bushes rake into his scaled skin, making him bleed a familiar and terrifying green.

It's my fault, he knows. He brought this on himself, after all. He's even abused his symbiote and betrayed the Gods. That's not how you evolve. The gift must be freely given; he knows that. He's always known that. And yet...

I'm selfish, he thinks, *just like everyone says I am.*

A khaf tree cracks to his right, thrashed into pieces by the Gishatich's long tail and falling directly in his path. He skids to all fours, tensing his muscles to leap, but a scythe-like leg stabs into the ground, hammering his linen shirt against the grass and pinning him there.

With bulging eyes, he stares up at the drooling mouth of the black monster before him. The Gishatich doesn't have a wicked grin like he was always told, just an open maw lined with oscillating teeth.

There is no surviving this. No one ever has.

Perhaps this was meant to be.

~ ~ ~

ONE HUNDRED YEARS AGO

It's cold.

Isi's two fluffy tails twitch as her hairs bristle. No matter how many winter pelts she piles on, she can still feel the icy chill.

A warm body moves to stand beside her. Elder Onye smells like moss and grass and everything green, sending a wave of comfort rippling through Isi as she slips her small hand into the Elder's without a second thought, looking up with bright, innocent eyes. The elegant Kendani female looks back down at her with nothing but love.

"So, what is a generation day?" Isi asks.

Elder Onye smiles, her copper fur glistening in the firelight of her earthen den. "Did you know, when babies are born, they come in fives? All on the same day, all at the same exact moment in time. Sometimes births happen every handful of years, sometimes spaced in decades—it's up to the Gods to decide—but when a birthing comes, it's always one child for each of the five sentient species. A Kendani, an Uzh, a Soghun, a T'ever, and even a monstrous Gishatich will come into the world simultaneously. *That* is a generation day."

"So, it's like a birthday." Isi says.

"A special kind of birthday, perhaps. You, my love, will have a generation day every twelve years."

"Why?"

"Because there were twelve years between Ren's generation and yours."

Isi snorts loudly at the reminder of her unfortunate predecessor. Ren is bossy; she's not sure she likes him. He always acts like he owns everything.

"So that's why Mak'ur's generation day is tomorrow?"

"Exactly. His every third birthday will be special because he was born only three years after you. Such a short wait! He'll have more generation days than anyone else in our whole tribe."

Isi's ears drift back, flattening in irritation. "That's not fair."

Scooping up her chin, Elder Onye chuckles. "But you still get to enjoy everyone else's generation day. With our numbers ever-growing, I feel like we're always celebrating. Perhaps after this we should move to celebrating only once per moon instead of once per week. I'm tired of making all the decorations."

Isi agrees, nodding firmly. "Daddy says he's tired of all the hunting, too." There are many singers and dancers and fire charmers who love showing off during the celebrations, but those who actually make the feasts never seem to enjoy the events. That's enough to sway Isi's opinion.

With a sweep of her arms, Elder Onye picks her up and rests her on her hip, their tails wagging. "Well, I don't blame him. There are many, many mouths to feed. Unless more go on their pilgrimage, this village will burst through the walls."

With that, Elder Onye lifts open the leather curtain of her den and carries Isi out into the snow. Mak'ur is playing near the red row of feathers marking the way from the pavilion to the gate, biting at their fluff as the other boys look on and laugh. The triplets, each born ten years apart to different families, watch him with toothy grins, Ren included. Unseen, Isi sticks her tongue out at him with a *mlahhhhh* sound.

"Isi!" Mak'ur yips, digging his back claws into the dirt and bounding toward her. He scrabbles at Elder Onye's woven skirt to stand up straight, pretending he's older than he is.

Isi slides from the Elder's grip and pounces on her friend, nipping his ears and making Mak'ur grump at her before *oof*-ing, pressed to the ground with her body weight. He whines plainly, and Isi giggles.

"Giving up so soon?" Ren calls over. "You should just roll her...like *this!*" He launches himself at the pair of little ones, grabbing both at once and flipping them in a never-ending tumble as he laughs, too loud, in their ears.

"Leave them alone," Hisk calls over, though he says it with a smile on his face.

"Or don't." Madax grins, jumping into the fray.

A frenzy of yelps and nibbles own the next handful of minutes until Isi's laughing so hard, she can't breathe. Mak'ur escapes with his four tails held high as he whirls around, growling. "You have to be nice to me! It's my day tomorrow!"

Hisk, the eldest of the triplets, bends down and scratches at Mak'ur's scruff in that perfect way, making him go belly up in the snow. "Happy generation day, little one."

The Elder claps her hands together, stretching herself tall. "Who's ready for lessons?"

They all stop dead and groan in unison. Elder Onye shows no mercy, though, scooping Isi back up and nudging Mak'ur with her toes. "Come on now. Let's make you civilized."

Isi can't believe she has to go to school until she's a whole hundred years into life. It seems so far away. Though, she supposes when you live forever, maybe that's not long at all.

* * *

"Oomph!" she thumps onto her soft and puffy bed as Daddy wrestles her down, kissing her cheeks and tickling her.

"Bedtime, little one!" he says.

Mommy twiddles her long fingers up and down in a scary, spidery way. "Otherwise, the Gishatich will come eat you!" Her mother lunges, and her grasping meets its mark. Isi's little toes get wiggled, two by two, and she squeals, kicking and scrambling until her parents finally relent.

"I'm too old for this," she pants, a never-ending grin on her face.

Mommy rests a hand on her chest in mock horror. "Never! No matter how old, you will always be my baby. Even when you're a thousand!"

Daddy pets her, ears to tails. "Unless you evolve," he says. "Then you'll be more grown up than anyone I've ever known."

"What happens when you evolve?" she asks.

"It's one of life's biggest mysteries. But to find out, you'd have to leave the village and find your symbiote." Her mother gives a pinch to Isi's cheeks, pulling them to the sides in an uncomfortable stretch. "And you're way too much of a 'fraidy cat for that."

Mouth skewed, Isi manages, "Iy nowt a fwaidy cat!" She flutters her hands, batting her mother away and rubbing at her face with a scowl.

Flopping onto the bed, Mommy cuddles her from one side while daddy snuggles the other, keeping her warm in the winter night.

"Then maybe you *will* leave someday," Mommy says. "You'll find your match, give your gift, and evolve."

"I don't wanna." Isi sulks.

"Then you'll just have to stay with us forever," Daddy says, nuzzling in and curling his legs up into the crooks of hers.

"Mm," Isi agrees. With a huge yawn, she gazes through the wide, arched window that points directly at the red gate, a symbol of danger and the unknown. "I'm never going to leave. Not ever."

* * *

"Where are you?" Isi whisper-yells. Her svelte form sneaks along the edges of the den rows, ducking under windows so as not to be seen. Decorative paper lamps remain unlit for now, hung up on pikes and lying in wait as flags of five colors drape along the gutters, signifying each of the sentient species—even ominous black triangles for the terri-fying Gishatich.

Isi shivers. She has nightmares about them. Lately, they cry out from over the wall, their screeches loud enough to put fear into even the strongest of Kendani, yet here they are honoring them along with everyone else.

Why does this celebration have to be so different?

But she already knows. Mak'ur's symbiote could come from any one of the other four species. These hanging colors of tribute are sacred. Special. A prayer to the Gods for a successful pilgrimage. More than that, they symbolize a beautiful goodbye, though the thought makes Isi's heart ache.

"Mak'ur!" she tries again, getting only the tiniest bit louder, but it's enough to draw the triplets out of hiding. Ren, Madax, and Hisk poke their heads around a corner, raising their ears. She's been caught.

"There you are!" Ren grins at her in that devilish way of his, his black ears cocked. "Are you looking for the soon-to-be traveler?"

"Yes." She sighs, resting her hands on her hips and flicking her tails. "Do you know where he is?"

Hisk shrugs. "If we knew, we'd be with him. It's his last days. We want to see him as much as possible."

"Last *day,*" Ren emphasizes. "Singular." He looks down at Isi. "I thought if anyone had seen him, it would have been you."

Madax reaches up to thwack one of the dangling flags, an orange one representing the Uzh. "You know, with him gone, you'll have to pick one of us as your mate, instead."

Isi rolls her eyes. "I was never going to mate with him. He's my best friend."

The three males all make different expressions. Hisk looks shy, knowing that—no matter what Isi says—his competition is decreasing by one; Madax seems excited, thinking he actually has a chance; and Ren is just smug, assuming her choice is him and always has been. Isi would be flattered by their obvious displays, except she knows they don't have much else in the way of choices. She's the only single female of age. They're all just lonely.

"Sorry, boys, you'll just have to wait until Tesa grows up."

All three roll their eyes.

"Tesa's *two*, Isi," Madax groans.

She lifts her shoulders with a coy smile. "I bet she'll be worth the wait."

"Yeah," Ren says. "For one of us, anyway."

A familiar sadness takes over the three. Even if Isi chooses a mate, until more females are born, the rest of them will be left alone, and with every new male generation—two more since Isi's birth—the triplets' odds of finding happiness diminish. There is a good chance one or more of them may end up unmated, alone for all eternity. They're afraid...and Isi doesn't blame them.

Hisk leans against the rough surface of one of the clay dens. "Do you ever think of going on your pilgrimage instead of mating?"

Madax plays with his fingers. "No. But I think about going to war."

Isi's eyes go wide. "Outside the wall? But you could die..."

"One less mouth to feed," he says, his smile something terrible. "Besides, the Uzh move closer every day."

"It's only to find their symbiotes," Hisk says.

"Or take what's ours," Ren reminds. "They've overrun the valley. You know that's where most of our food comes from. If we let them think they can just take whatever they want, we're losing before we even begin."

Unease worms its way through Isi's heart. "You sound like you *want* to go to war."

Ren holds her eyes. "Would you like me better if I did? If I survived and came home?"

All three of them look at her as if she holds the key to their futures. And maybe she does.

"Tesa might care about things like that when she grows up," Isi tries again, but Ren cuts in.

"I don't want Tesa, Isi."

The "I want you" goes unspoken.

Isi clears her throat, side-stepping the comment and lacing her fingers together. "I just don't want you to get hurt."

Madax ticks up an eyebrow. "What about me?"

A smirk crosses her face. "Oh, not you. You can go whenever you want."

They all laugh in good humor, snickering at the familiar banter. They've been together for over a hundred years and there is love between them all, just not that kind of love. Isi wants the boys to have the same joy her mother and father have, she truly does, but she also feels in her heart that she's not the one to bring it to them. Sadly, she rests all her hope on a single kit that can barely walk or talk, praying that she'll be the love of one of these males' lives.

Madax runs his fingers through Isi's short hair. "Go on, then. Go find our honored traveler. Just don't hog him all for yourself. We want to be with him, too."

"I promise." Isi crosses her heart before scratching under Madax's chin in kindness, tugging Hisk's ear, and fluffing Ren with her tails as she turns to leave.

It's a little fib. She'll hand over Mak'ur when she's good and ready, and it just so happens that she's not ready yet.

Grasping one of the decorative ropes, she swings herself atop the den roofs, grinning down at the boys before waving her goodbyes. From there, she stands and sniffs the misting air around her, scanning the plain tiles built to catch the rain and looking for the shape of her best friend, likely off brooding somewhere.

On a rooftop over by the red gate, she spots him—of course he'd be as far from their block as possible. Even though generations are searching for him, Mak'ur already seems to want to fade away.

Well, too bad.

Isi trips four times as she tries to be stealthy, haphazardly hopping over alleyways from den to den. She's never been good at this sort of thing. Clumsy and bungling, she usually comes home with bruises from either falling flat on her face or scuffling with the triplets. It happens so often, she's not even ashamed anymore. Still, with a grunt as her foot catches on the end of a tile, Isi thinks she'd rather be nimble than not right about now.

Before she's even close, Mak'ur is laughing at her. "You walk like a flidget."

"Yeah? Well, you smell like a connix."

He turns toward her, jaw dropping wide, but with the edges of his mouth curling into a smile. "Crude! Crass! Offensive! You should be nicer to me, since you'll never see me again."

They pause for a long moment as his joke falls flat.

Sitting down on the rooftop beside him, Isi runs her hands over her arms, pretending she's cold if only to disguise her urge to jump onto him, pin him down, and force him to stay. "Hey, you don't know that for sure. Maybe you'll never find your symbiote and have to come back with your tails between your legs."

He hums, nodding his head side to side as if considering her words. "That would be difficult. I have more tails than you."

She scoffs, punching his shoulder playfully. "Don't brag!"

Falling into a comfortable, familiar silence, they look up at the moon. So many questions run through Isi's head. So many words. So many pleas for him not to leave her behind. Instead, she says, "I think your gift will be something stupid."

Mak'ur only smiles, watching the stars as they hover in the dark tapestry of sky. "Once I find my match, my gift will be exactly what she needs."

"You have no idea what she needs."

"Then I'll keep trying. I'll spend my life with her until I get it right." Mak'ur shrugs as if this was the most obvious conclusion.

Isi leans close, whispering into his perked ear. "What if you fall in love with her?"

Mak'ur leans back on the roof in a fit of giggles he tries to quiet behind a balled fist, sputtering as he waves her away. "Shhh! You'll get me caught by the others. I'm trying for privacy over here, you unwelcome intruder."

"Yeah, but what if?" Isi repeats.

"You want me to fall in love with a hulking, hairy, beast?"

"An Uzh," Isi corrects.

"A frog?"

Isi gasps. "A Soghun, you claw-for-brains!"

"A teeny, tiny little bug?" He holds his fingers out mere inches apart.

"The T'ever aren't bugs. They're beautiful. Their wings are just perfect."

Mak'ur hums and nods, giving her that one. With a grin, he asks, "What if it's a Gishatich?"

"Then you'll be eaten," she says blandly, as if it didn't matter. It brings some truth home to her, though. She doesn't know what it's like beyond the wall. Wrapping her arms around her knees, she asks a quiet question. "You'll be safe, won't you?"

Mak'ur lies on his back, gazing upward and seeming farther away than he's ever been, his eyes unfocused.

Isi says, "Just because it's a rite of passage doesn't mean you have to *pass*. I didn't. The triplets didn't. Maybe—"

"Isi?" he interrupts. "Will you see me to the first marker?"

Every inch of her fur stands on end.

Immediately rolling away, Mak'ur curls into himself, burying his face in his arms. "Forget I asked."

Isi looks at him for a minute. Her first and best friend. She adored him when he was a newborn, and still does to this day. She knows being asked such a question is a great honor. It's a sign of their friendship and respect. A sign that he loves her. It means that her face is the last one he wants to see before he says goodbye.

"I'll do it," she says, trying not to think too hard. She reaches out to stroke Mak'ur's back and realizes he's trembling. Her friend doesn't need her fear now; he needs reassurance. "When you evolve, what will your ask of the Gods be?"

He sniffles quietly. "I'm going to ask for the species to be able to live together peacefully in mixed villages."

"Mixed? You'll be including the Gishatich in that equation?" Her sarcasm only earns her a side-eyed glance.

"Don't be so...you," he gripes. "I just want no more war over land. Over resources. We'll be able to share our learnings and skills, and more and more people will be able to find their match, too."

"Their match..." She snorts, shamelessly annoyed. "What if people don't want to evolve?"

"Then they won't," he says simply. "They won't give their gifts and can live on forever. But they would also have an option if forever got too long."

Mak'ur's back is soft under her fingertips. The more Isi pets it, the more soothing it feels. She can only hope it feels as good to him as it does to her. Petting him is grounding. Safe.

Staring at nothing, he asks, "What would you want from the Gods?"

She doesn't even have to think about it. "More than one child per species each generation. A male and a female so no one will ever have to be without a mate."

Mak'ur turns over to look at her with sympathy, knowing the pressure put on her by the lovelorn males they've grown up with. Reaching up, he takes hold of her hand. "If I get a second ask of the Gods, I promise I'll ask that."

A little smile pulls at her lips despite knowing that's impossible. "Thank you."

* * *

The towering red gate looms, dark and foreboding even in the morning sunlight. In a tight knit circle, the village's congregation gathers around their honored traveler while the drums' thuds echo off the surrounding walls in an ominous throb.

Bum-bum-badum.

This is not the beat of celebration; this is the beat of solemnity. Mak'ur is the first to go on his pilgrimage in hundreds of years, giving extra meaning to this moment. Rows of Kendani faces are a mix of everything from the deepest pride to the darkest fear. Though stories have passed from generation to generation, no one truly knows what will happen once Mak'ur passes through the gate; all that's certain is that no traveler ever returns. They can only pray he is welcomed by his destiny rather than destroyed by it.

Isi's heart thumps along with each hollow, rattling bang against taut leather as she silently chants, *What's behind the wall? What's behind the wall?*

Mak'ur, on the other hand, stands strong, looking unfazed save the clench of his jaw. Elder Onye lifts a ceremonial necklace of five-color beads over his head, signifying his pilgrimage to all who may see him. He bows gracefully, the necklace sitting heavy on his fur, its weight a physical representation of the gravity of his journey. The responsibility toward all species. The importance of his ask of the Gods.

He's making the perfect wish, in Isi's opinion—pure and thoughtful, something benefitting all. Surely a wish like that will be given favor, leading Mak'ur to his match—that unnamable, unknowable *her* that lives somewhere in the distance.

"And who will be your escort?" Elder Onye asks, ensuring her voice carries over the crowd.

Mak'ur looks at Isi for a heavy moment, offering her a chance to bow out, but she forces herself to smile at her friend, smoothing out the cinch in his eyebrows even as terror rolls wildly in her belly.

Turning toward the throng of Kendani, Mak'ur says, "She of the twelfth generation. Isi the Brave!"

The name he'd chosen for her is pure irony. Still, the congregation repeats her moniker in a steady rhythm, looking at her with expressions that flip back and forth, circling through worry and surprise. Only Elder Onye is steady and sure, her eyes crinkled with her largest grin when she says, "Then come to me, child."

Holding out both arms as if to embrace her, the Elder welcomes Isi to the center of the ceremonial circle. All eyes of the tribe focus in to observe her every movement. Isi swallows and holds her head high... until she sees the triplets staring at her in shock. She didn't tell them about this. In her mind, she shouldn't have to tell them. She's not theirs, no matter what they think; still, the horror on Ren's face wounds her, somehow.

It doesn't matter. He can scold her when she gets back. Her parents can fend him off until then.

"Then let the twelfth generation join with the third to the first marker!"

More drumming and shouts of encouragement tent fill the air as Mak'ur takes her trembling hand. At the warmth of his touch, reality finally sets in. This isn't a joke. This isn't a dream. This isn't a game. Isi is leaving the village...and Mak'ur is never coming back.

Turning toward the crowd, Elder Onye yells, "His wish is pure, and his fate is in motion! May Mak'ur the Kind find his symbiote, evolve, and bring peace to us all!"

Whereas Isi had gotten cheers, the swell of the crowd's admiration for Mak'ur rings so loud it takes over the whole village, the sound ricocheting around Isi's soft insides until she's thrumming with their shouts. She lifts Mak'ur's hand high, her face jubilant even though her heart is pounding faster than she's ever felt. Swallowing her terror, again she wonders, *What's behind the wall?*

Well...she's about to find out.

* * *

"I hate this."

Mak'ur is the first one to say it. Isi's ears flatten immediately, even as he casts a smirk in her direction. They're scaling a small cliff face, a slope of collapsed dirt that may have been a hill at one point but changed its mind somewhere along the way. Roots of fallen trees poke through the loam, and Isi digs her nails in, grunting as she tries hard not to swallow sand.

"Well, this is what you wanted. Action, adventure, and annoyance. And just think, you're going to have to do this for much longer than I will."

Mak'ur grimaces as he turns back toward his climbing. "At least I have you with me for now. You're better company than...well...the nothing I'd have otherwise."

"You have such a way with words. I'm flattered, truly."

They've been traveling for two days already and have only come across one issue after another, the worst of which are the non-sentient species that plague them. Neither Isi nor Mak'ur had ever heard of the things they've seen streaking over their feet or staring from a distance. Tiny, winged things that bite; scurrying things that make Isi jump so high it's like she's flying; and blinking bird-like stalkers that hover in the trees, watching them in an unsettling way. They've yet to see any other travelers on their journey, though Isi supposes a pilgrimage is probably just as rare in other tribes as it is in theirs.

Every moment of their trek has been a slow climb uphill, and the muscles in Isi's thighs burn. Yesterday, they'd begun shaking by sunset, and feel on the verge of it again now. No matter how much pouncing or playing she's done in the village, no amount of movement could have prepared her for this. It's like she's going up to meet the heavens, so high the clouds come down at night to swathe them in mist.

Shrieking suddenly, Isi retracts her hand as something slithers over it, making her clutch one-fisted as she dangles from a single, brittle root, at risk of tumbling head over heels to the bottom and having to start all over again.

"You alright?" Mak'ur asks.

Gritting her teeth, Isi grumbles. "Just perfect."

"We should almost be there. 'On the night of the second day' is what they said."

"That was before they knew we'd have to climb over unclimbable stuff, rig our way over ditches, and run away from scary things. We've gotten off the path at least three times."

With an exaggerated grunt, Mak'ur manages to haul himself over the edge of the hill, grabbing onto handfuls of stringy-looking underbrush to do it, leaving only his feet left dangling over the side. He stays there for a moment, unmoving. Isi wonders if exhaustion has gotten the better of him, like it's threatening to do to her.

"Did you die up there?" she asks, but he doesn't respond. Three more pulls and her head passes up over the edge as well, ears up as she scans around. Her friend is staring, wide-eyed, into the distance. Following his line of sight, she sees it. A pike is driven into the ground, sporting the colors of the five species painted in fading stripes next to a battered red ribbon fluttering in the breeze.

Isi's jaw drops. "It's the first marker."

Suddenly, she'd rather be back at the beginning. She'd face the trials of the journey all over again if only to spend more time with the one who matters most to her.

"Isi, do you see it?"

I wish I didn't.

"It's time…" Mak'ur says. She thought he'd sound sad. Scared. Reluctant. Instead, he sounds awe-filled and excited. "I'm finally going to meet her."

A jealous stab hits Isi, but there's nothing for it. Bringing herself the rest of the way over the edge, she rests a hand on her friend's back again, swallowing past the lump in her throat.

"And then I'm going to evolve." He says it like it's a blessing. "And then I get to make my wish, Isi. I'm going to help everyone."

She nods, holding back the sniffle that threatens. It's like her chest is stuffed with a heavy cloth that bunches painfully against her lungs, making her fight not to choke on her sudden sorrow. The sorrow she'd been pushing away until now.

I'm never going to see him again, she thinks. *He's going to evolve and become someone I don't know. Something I don't know. Even if I saw his face, I wouldn't recognize him. Even if I spoke to him, he would no longer be mine.*

It's only at this moment she realizes…her friend is going to die. Evolution eradicates who you are today, after all, ending your life as you are. What could that be called, if not death? How did she not see it before now?

"Elder Onye says I'll become a being of Light," Mak'ur says with a reverent smile.

Isi scrubs at her eyes, unseen. "Yeah, yeah. I know. 'You'll leave this world forever to live among the Gods.'" She tries to make it sound like sarcasm or disbelief, but instead it comes out raw. "Bet they'll avoid you because you're so annoying."

He chuckles a little. "Don't worry. Even if they do, I'll never be alone. *She'll* be with me."

That jealousy burns Isi again, but there is nothing she can say. Standing up, Mak'ur brushes himself off and holds out a hand to help her up, just like he has many, many times. Every time she tripped on her own feet, every time she lost balance and slipped face first onto the ground, every time one of the triplets hit her with a snowball and knocked her on her rear, Mak'ur had always been there.

Taking his hand for the last time, she doesn't let go. Together, like children, they walk toward the first marker, looking into the distance.

To the west, Isi can see the smoke of war. To the north, she can see trees swaying back and forth as something prowls beneath their branches. To the east, she sees a huge body of water that stretches all the way to where the sky meets the horizon. She's never seen the world like this.

"Which way will you go?" she asks.

Mak'ur closes his eyes and takes in the air, tipping his head this way and that. Pointing a finger northeast, he whispers, "There."

She has to find her last words for him. She has to make them count. Wracking her brains for far too long, his hand clasped in hers, what she finally happens upon is, "I'm so proud of you."

His smile is dazzling. Pulling her in for a hug, he says, "Tell me you love me."

"I love you," she agrees.

"Tell me my wish is pure."

"It is."

"Tell me I'll find her."

She nuzzles deep into his neck. "If you don't find her, she'll find you."

Somehow, he manages to squeeze her even tighter. He has no tears when he pulls back, only that hopeful, glittering smile. He scratches her ears, making her giggle a little, and then there is nothing more to be said. Hiking his pack up higher on his shoulder, he turns away. The wind tickles the air and the trees chirp with sound as Mak'ur takes a deep breath—slow, steady, and sure—and walks beyond the first marker.

* * *

Isi doesn't know how long she's been standing there, watching her best friend get smaller and smaller. She keeps her eyes on his figure as the sky turns to orange, then red, then purple, the stars coming out in the patterns of legends as her tears leak slowly. The mist has rolled back in, yet she remains. Something holds her feet to the ground as if moving were the last thing she could ever do. Her heart doesn't just hurt; it feels...strange. She can't quite define it, as if the words to describe such a thing had yet to be invented, leaving her mouth empty.

It doesn't matter. She needs to move. Regardless of her grief, her exhaustion, her unknown feeling, she needs to go home.

Turning around, a sudden, unbidden tightness takes hold of her chest, like a small trap has snapped shut on her lungs, making her take a short, sharp gasp. Her heart starts to thrum. Her breath comes too fast. Her head spins and her tails tremble, tucking close under her.

What's happening?

A twig snaps. Isi whips around, ready to find something else that slithers or hisses or stalks. Instead she sees...a Soghun. Its wide reptilian eyes bulge as it stares at her, clasping a yellow palm over its scaled chest, only barely covered by a dirty, battered, low-cut linen shirt. It takes two steps closer, tentative and slow as its jaw drops open. "It's you."

There is a moment where they just stare, taking each other in. It's a moment that feels religious; sacred, special, and singular. Isi knows beyond a shadow of a doubt that it's him. There are no others possible.

This is her symbiote.

With horror, she realizes that means she's going to die. Like Mak'ur, she's going to evolve, and her world will end.

But, unlike her best friend, she never asked for this.

A single whisper passes her lips.

"No..."

Chapter 2

~CATCH ME IF YOU CAN~

Dumbstruck and humbled, Ati stares at the Kendani female, his chest hot and heaving. He's never felt anything like this. It's as if destiny itself has come to hold him in its arms and tell him everything is going to be alright. That there is hope now. If he evolves, he can make an ask of the Gods...which means he can save his people.

His scaled lips part to speak, to tell the female everything, to spill his secrets to this stranger who is his match. Her pointed, copper-toned ears are up as she quivers, likely longing to speak to him as well, excited for the moment she's been searching for all her life.

But then she whispers, "No..."

In a flash, she spins on her heels and darts, dipping over the cliffside. On instinct alone, Ati scrambles forward, following the sound of pebbles and scuffing limbs. When he reaches the lip of the edge, he sees her snagging root after dead root as she slides down the earthen embankment into the grassy marsh below.

His round eyes bulge.

This is unacceptable.

His body goes rigid as he leaps, landing on the soft ground below with no need to grab or slip or strafe. He touches down on his wide-toed feet and fingertips, diving into a run to overtake her quickly.

He's not wrong about her. About their connection. This feeling in his body, this heat, this energy, it has to be her. At first sight, Ati knew there was no one else. She knows it about him, too. She must.

So why?

She jackknifes over bushes and brambles as he follows close enough to snag her heels and knock her down, but refusing to do it. Ati doesn't want to hurt her. Instead he calls, "Why are you running?!"

"I don't want to evolve!" she shouts back. "Get away from me!"

It's a slap against his ego, and indignation sinks in.

"Stop!" he tries again.

But he is summarily ignored. Going to all fours, his symbiote increases her speed by at least half, raking up soil and flinging it with her feet, forcing Ati to try to run beside her instead of following close behind.

She ducks into a hollow log, and Ati bounds completely over it, landing on the ragged edge with ease and listening to the beat of her limbs against bark. Whipping his hand down, Ati takes hold of the hem of the female's shirt as she gallops past the exit, snapping her backward with a yelp. The sound of her in pain hurts to hear, but it doesn't matter. He has to stop her.

Falling upon her back, he pins her to the ground as she scrabbles and fights him, kicking uselessly as his weight keeps her trapped. She turns over her shoulder and shoots him a hateful glare, her golden eyes feral and her pupils narrowed into slits. Her teeth are bared and four sharp canines clench as she growls.

"I'm sorry," he says, looping an arm under her and wrapping a hand over her gnashing mouth. He lets the pheromones secrete from his palm, so strong even he can smell them. They have no effect on his kind, but to others, it packs a mighty punch. Within moments, his symbiote's body loosens and her struggling dies. Her eyelids flutter and close, and

Ati can feel her smile behind his fingers just as he hears her giggled sigh. Only then does he release her.

She looks at him with a grin as she lies on the ground, completely limp. "You're...you're a jerk." And then her eyes roll back in her head, a sign of her descent into dreamland. Or hallucination-land, as the case may be.

Huffing, Ati stumbles backwards, his muscled rear-end bumping into the log and knocking him to a hard sit, likely bruising his unmentionables. He doesn't even hear the hiss of his own pain, too distracted as his throat bubbles up in a round balloon before deflating in exasperation. At her. At himself.

She laughs once more, rolling onto her side as two lovely tails twitch and flick. He mulls over what she's dreaming about. Apparently, it's not evolution.

Slapping his scented hands over his face, he scrubs at the ridges just above his eyes. He'd never expected to meet his symbiote, but in his wildest dreams, she had always been waiting for him. Hoping for him. To finally meet her only for her to run away like this... It hurts more than he could ever say.

A rumble catches Ati's attention, the sound of wood cracking and the shushes of leaves upon leaves fill his tiny ears. It's the Gishatich. It has to be. Night has fallen, and when the stars fill the heavens, it's their time to own the earth.

Ati's symbiote snores lightly even as his adrenaline spikes. Eyes to the sky, he looks everywhere for a safe haven, finally finding one about twelve twisted branches up in a nearby Otomo tree. Its red leaves are so thick, it will make perfect cover, and the slight breeze winding through the forest will hide any sounds his symbiote might unwittingly make in her forced slumber.

Eyeing her, he sighs internally, knowing just how heavy she's going to be. They may be the same size, but she is denser. He is, however, much stronger.

He's heard the phrase "dead weight" before but had never had the unpleasant experience of hauling it until now. Every time he tries to lift the Kendani female, it's like she melts out of his arms. If he hoists her up, forearms braced under her shoulder blades and the backs of her knees, she sags at the middle, threatening to slip to the ground in a puddle. If he tries to sling her over his shoulder, the weight of her dribbles down his back until her ears are tickling his nub of a tail and her hands are in the crooks of his knees.

With a *Why me?* pointed at the Gods, Ati gets her stomach situated over the back of his neck, her head draped over one side of his chest and her knees over the other. He's sweating at this point, but maybe that will help stick her skin to his a little. Especially since he's about to jump.

Standing beneath the bottommost branch of the Otomo tree, Ati crouches, his legs tense and ready. He twitches his neck to the side slightly, letting out an unconscious croak as his throat flashes once more. Taking a deep breath to steady himself, he springs, catching the first arching branch before leaping to the next. And the next. Up and up he goes, mindless of the scratchy wood against the suckers on the ends of his toes, unaware of the threat of splinters, focused instead on keeping his symbiote balanced over his shoulders. If she falls to the ground at this height, he might not have a symbiote at all.

He frowns.

This was not supposed to be how the day went.

* * *

He'd barely slept. She kept rolling around, nearly slipping out of the natural nest formed by four of the tree's branches splitting and winding their separate ways into the sky. Ati knows he's got no one to blame but himself for her raucous behavior. She squawks and kicks and chuckles. She says things out loud like, "Shut up, Ren," or else sniffles and whispers, "Don't leave me."

He doesn't know what to make of it. He's never seen such an outward display of emotion from a stranger before. Not that he's met many strangers. Though, she's not a stranger at all. Or, at least, she's not supposed to be.

Again, Ati sulks with another *Why me?*, this time directed at his symbiote.

He'd ducked down in the early dawn to retrieve his pack, which had been lost somewhere along the way. Hers, too. Out of precaution, he'd tied her to the tree with a bit of vine, but Gods forbid she wakes up tangled and trapped. They had already started off all wrong, but her waking up like that would be a disaster.

Luck finally on his side, Ati had returned to find her just as unconscious as he'd left her, only with an arm strewn down the trunk of the tree, one tail twitching over the left side of a branch, and the other over the right. Ati kind of wanted to play with them.

Leaping up was twenty times easier without her weighing him down with her thick muscles and too many organs. She sloshes around like water inside and it's weird. Still, she's fascinating in her otherness. He's never seen a Kendani before, but if he ever imagined himself a symbiote, it was always one of them. Perhaps because they lived only in his imagination, just like all his dreams of evolving.

Pressing his thin lips together, he's not sure what to do now. He starts by unraveling the vine from around her. Then he uncaps her canteen, holding her nape and tipping her up to taste it.

She makes a small humming noise, and her ears perk up. Blinking her eyes open, she's bleary and still half-stoned.

"Why?" he asks again. The question has burned a trail through his exhausted thoughts all night. Her little wisps for eyebrows knit, so he clarifies. "Why don't you want to evolve?"

She giggles like a little one, staring into the distance with a smile on her face. "Oh, look. Butterflies."

There are absolutely no butterflies.

Ati takes her chin, guiding her back to meet his gaze. "I never thought I'd evolve. It's so rare. Yet, in seeing you, knowing in my heart exactly who you are, it's all I can think of. I even know exactly what I'd ask the Gods for."

He tries the water again. This time, it seems to be working. Her eyes have lost their glaze and she's begun to look around a bit, taking in her reality.

Capping the canteen and tucking it into her pack, Ati asks, "What's your wish?"

At that, she sits bolt upright, startling him—

Before trying to leap down off the tree entirely.

Ati doesn't even have time to groan. He catches her the same way he had before, snagging her collar and dragging her backward, wrapping his hand over her face again and letting her get another good whiff. She sags once more, this time with a laugh so loud it scares the birds from the upper branches of the tree. They scatter with blasts of sound, flapping away from the assumed threat that is this intoxicated female.

"Let's try this again, shall we?" Ati says through gritted teeth.

"You brat," she manages, snorting and curling into him in a weird, unfortunate snuggle.

He grumps silently. Reaching for his own pack, he takes out a good length of rope and cinches it around her waist, tying the best knot he knows. And then another. And then another for good measure. Leaning back, he does the same for himself, yanking on it and finding a satisfying snugness.

Let's see her get away now.

His satisfaction is short-lived, however, as he realizes exactly what it is he's doing. He's trapping the one person in the world who should want to be at his side.

But she doesn't.

He looks up at the clouds, then down at her—passed out and drooling—and throws one last *Why me?* out into the ether.

* * *

This time, when she comes back to reality, Ati is glaring at her. Apparently not one to be intimidated, she glares right back.

"I want to go home," she growls.

"Obviously," he replies, "But I can't let you do that."

"Obviously," she repeats, sarcasm dripping from her every pore. Scowling, she tugs at the rope around her waist, fiddling unsuccessfully with the series of knots entrapping her. "What were you doing so close to my village? There's a war going on if you hadn't noticed. Or are you actually on your pilgrimage?"

He gestures up his torso, chest to throat. "Do you see a traveler's necklace on me?"

"I'd rather not see you at all."

She harrumphs and turns away, sticking her pert little nose in the air and pretending Ati has ceased to exist. It takes every ounce of his self-restraint not to toss her from the tree and let her dangle on her new tether.

Taking a deep breath, he opens his pack in a show of good will, and removes a small purse filled with fine, dried leaves. "I was collecting kannock herbs."

She glances at him out of the side of her eye, offering him her profile. "What for?"

Looking at his collection, he cinches the purse tight again, careful not to touch what lies inside without his gloves on. "For medicine. My people...they're sick with a disease. We call it Rrpto. Have you heard of it?"

She only lifts her chin higher and huffs. The temptation to knock her off the tree lights up his nervous system again, but Ati just curls his fingers into his bag to keep his temper at a slow burn instead of a lightning bolt.

"It's horrible," he says, slinging his pack over his shoulders and testing the strength of the knot at his belly. "But I suppose you'll get a chance to see that firsthand."

Before the predictable "What?" leaves her mouth, she's up over his back. With a quick drop, he brings them down through the scaffolding of branches, rung after rung, her *eeps*, *eeks*, and short shrieks like music to his ears. Let her feel a tenth of the anxiety she's giving him.

Bound, jump, hop. Down and down as she squeals, making him grin a little at her expense. Once he hits the ground, he lets her go with a plop that has her groaning as she rolls and rubs her backside, tails tucked under.

Lifting a ridged eyebrow with a smarmy grin, he asks, "Are you alright?"

She tosses him what can only be a rude gesture in Kendani sign language. He gladly gives one of his own in return before yanking her up and pulling her along, grunting as he basically drags her behind him.

"Whether you like it or not, I need to evolve," he says.

She's turned away, leaning hard, trying to escape and failing miserably. "I don't care what you want! Let me go! Moron! Loser! Kidnapper!"

"This is ridiculous," he says to himself more than to her. "Listen. I don't want to use the medicine at all. My people are suffering, but if I evolve, I can ask the Gods to take their sickness away."

All resistance in the rope suddenly disappears. Before Ati can turn, something *thwam*s into his back, and his eyes fly wide as he goes to the ground. In a blink, his symbiote is on top of him and scrabbling at the knot on his side of the rope.

"How dare you?!" she yells. "You're talking about committing the vilest of sins! If Mak'ur heard you right now, he'd punch your scaly face off!"

Ati rolls up and over her, springing to a stand and yanking once more, dragging her on her back over the grass as she rants.

"You're only supposed to ask for things that would benefit all the species, not just your own!" she blathers. "Selfish, selfish, selfish!"

Bitter, he rounds on her. "How could a recluse Kendani know what would benefit all? Your species only comes out for food and fighting. You never voyage. You never collaborate. You don't trade. You have so few pilgrimages, it's laughable, yet you sit here pretending like you're the best of all of us!"

She tries to bite him.

With a snarl, she's up on him again, tussling and tumbling. Even so, it's more like she's play-fighting than real-fighting. She never tries to land a single blow and her bites are nips at best. It's like she's just trying to dominate him, but there's no way she'll ever manage it. He's both slippery and sly. Not to mention stubborn.

Glowering at her, he kneels atop her wrists to pin her, but she grabs at his neck with her feet and tugs him backwards. He grapples with her legs as they paddle beneath him, planning to trip her up should she try to run again.

"Will! You! Just! STOP!" she roars.

And something roars to match her.

Both of them freeze. The throbbing echo is high-pitched and terrible, scaring birds from the high branches and making things under the leaves of the forest floor scuttle to get away from the source of the sound. Slowly, and in tandem, Ati and his symbiote cast their questioning eyes to the woods beyond.

"A Gishatich?" she asks, backing out from underneath him with her ears flattened against her head.

"Quick," Ati grabs her shirt and tugs her back toward the tree. "Up. Up. Come on."

Despite any misgivings she may have, his symbiote hops up on his back and links her hands together over his collarbone, her knees clamping against his hips to keep her steady as she presses against his backpack. Up the tree they go once more, her face digging into the top of his spine as the roar continues, becoming wails and keens that make Ati's stomach queasy.

They go up past their nest. Up half the tree. Up two thirds until his symbiote is trembling against his back as he peers out of the canopy. It is, indeed, a Gishatich. Two, in fact. Far in the distance, one of the predators slowly circles another as it lies on the ground, thrashing weakly and flattening bushes with pounds of its enormous tail.

Ati has never actually seen a Gishatich before, he's only heard them, so looking down onto their beastly scene is like watching a nightmare come to life. They are both so dark, they barely reflect any light. Huge, sinewy tails extend behind each one, making them look like fat snakes with legs stitched haphazardly to their bellies. Their knees jut out to either side, taller than their body height and thinner than rails. Their heads have stripes of inky fur and whiskers that stand out like sharp quills, dark and ominous, just like the rest of them. Ati can barely see any of their other defining features; it all blends together in movements made of the deepest black.

The standing beast throws its head back with a cry so loud, Ati can feel it in his chest, and his symbiote grabs his back even tighter. At that point, the stalking Gishatich falls upon its companion, and the screams become screeches become howls and brays.

"It's...it's killing the other," she whispers, terrified. "The other one isn't even fighting... Why would it do that?"

"I don't know," he admits breathlessly.

When the felled beast stops writhing and its tail finally lays still, the other rears back again, facing the clouds as it cries once more—the worst sound yet—before taking a hold of its prey and dragging it through the brush. Ati and his match can do nothing but watch it go, mesmerized by the dreadfulness of it.

Swallowing, Ati asks, "Do you think most of the travelers' wishes benefit *them?*"

"I...I don't know," she admits.

"Exactly."

* * *

Hauling her through the woods is exhausting. They'd be making better time if Ati didn't have to keep knocking her out and carrying her. Much to his chagrin, however, she seems to be building up a tolerance, coming out of her spells faster and faster. Still, when she's under, she's quite something to behold.

Once she called him a frog.

Once she told him she was in love with him.

Once she told him he was on fire, and to stop touching her or she'd burn to death. That made it hard to keep a hold of her. She'd kicked him square in the jaw.

Now, she's awake and trailing behind him, whining, "Let me goooohohohhhhh."

"Keep it up and I'm going to tie this rope around your neck instead of your stomach, symbiote."

"Ugh! Don't call me that! My name is Isi."

He can't help but think that's a good name for her. Sounds like *hissy* and *pissy* and *sissy* and—

"What's your name?" she asks.

He turns over his shoulder and squints at her guarded expression. "I'm not telling."

"What? Why not?"

"Soghun names are sacred. Only my parents, my mate, and my symbiote can know."

"Well, what the hell am I?" she cries.

"Someone who refuses to evolve with me."

The string of swears that falls from her lips is truly impressive. Some he doesn't even know, but he's smart enough to tell by context.

"Well, I have to call you something!" she gripes. "How about Idiot? Stupid? Fool?"

He laughs in spite of himself. "I'll take fool. Why not? Out of everyone in the world, I'm probably the only person who wouldn't have just left you behind by now. I can only pray you give me my gift by accident."

She digs in her heels, causing them to stop. "You don't actually know what I'm supposed to give, do you?"

"No one knows that kind of thing."

"Do you know what you're supposed to give me?"

"Maybe a muzzle to keep your mouth shut."

They look at one another with narrowed eyes, furrowed brows, and pursed lips, refusing to back down from each other's challenge and breathing in deep, aggravated breaths through their noses.

Finally breaking away to look at the pink sky, she tips her head with a grimace. "Alright, Fool, what do we do now? If I'm not going home, where *am* I going?"

"To my village. I need to"—he clutches the strap of his pack tighter—"I need to deliver the medicine. We can figure out what to do after that."

She crosses her arms and cocks her hips, fluffy tails waving back and forth. "And do I get a say in any of this?"

"You get a say in how much firewood we collect. It will take us about four nights to get back to my home and we're going to need a good blaze to keep us warm."

With that, he bends down to pick up a stick. Surprisingly, she does the same.

"Why would you come so far just to get herbs like that?" she asks. "They're everywhere."

"For the Kendani, yes. But you don't travel to trade for it. You're all locked so tightly away, I'm surprised you even know who the five species are."

She actually seems to let that sentiment sink in. "How old are you?"

He scoffs. "I'm your match. I'm in your generation."

"Oh. Are you mated?"

"No," he says. "Are you?"

"I don't want to talk about it." She sighs, bending over to pick up more of the branches and dry bark littering the forest floor. "There's a cave over that way. Maybe we should stay there."

Ati follows her line of sight and sees that, indeed, there is.

"You've got a good eye," he says.

"I guess Kendani see better than Soghun."

"Then we're already better off together." He tries to toss her a smile, but she doesn't smile back. His throat inflates and deflates in disappointment.

"Fool," she says.

He doesn't bother looking at her. She can shove her insults up her—

"Fool!" she hisses, louder.

"What?"

"Look!"

Up ahead in the distance, beneath another Otomo tree, are...little lumps. "What are those?"

"People!" she says, as if he were an idiot.

He shields his eyes from the setting sun and squints to see more clearly through the dense forest. "What are they doing tied to a tree?"

"What am I doing tied to you?"

Fair point.

She deigns to stand beside him, firewood in her arms. "Let's go help them."

"Do what now?"

But she drops what she's holding and gets on all fours, darting from tree to tree and dragging Ati behind her, agape with surprise.

"What are you—"

"Shh," she warns, giving him a quick glance over her shoulder. Ears back, she whispers, "Something did this to them. You want to meet that something?"

Another fair point.

Isi runs again. Ati has to grab the rope to keep steady, unsure of where she's going or when she'll stop next. She finally slows as they near the tree, crouching behind a bush close enough for Ati to see better now. It's a small crowd of eight or so, all silent. Maybe they're sleeping...?

"Who are they?" he asks quietly.

Careful to stay hidden, Isi points toward the group. "There are Kendani. Can't you see them? Soghun, too. They're all females, I think."

No matter how he squints, he just can't see clearly enough. They're people, but foggy, blob people. "How can you tell they're females?"

She just gives him a look.

"Okay, fine, but why are they tied up?"

"We're about to find out. Hush, now."

At this point, they're tiptoeing. Both she and he seem on the stealthy side...until she trips and falls flat on her face with an *oof*. He stabs her with a look that screams, *Seriously?!* but she has the grace to ignore him.

They're so close now and, yes, this is definitely a collection of females. But why? Their ropes are thinner than the rope he's tied around his symbiote, but that's not a good thing. The bindings seem to be cutting into the skin, leaving harsh red marks on the Kendani and even drawing green blood from the soft under-scales of the Soghun. They all look exhausted and thin, their bones too visible and sunken purple hollows staining the Kendanis' eyes. It's horrible. Terrible. Who would do such a thing?

Isi's close enough to touch them. One of the females startles awake and immediately recoils, a telling sign if there ever was one. Isi merely puts a finger to her lips in the universal symbol for *"shh"* and leans down, silently gnawing at the topmost length of twine that threads around the captive females in coil after coil. Digging into his pack, Ati finds his small knife and starts sawing from the bottom as well, each of them working toward the middle. Ropes snap and loosen under their assault, and it's satisfying to be doing something productive—especially after the last twenty-four hours of non-productivity he's had.

All the females are awake now, and some tails wag, though everyone is certain not to talk, not even when they're finally free. Waving her hands, Isi points toward the cave she and Ati were going to for the night and beckons the females forward. One touches Isi's rope and casts a wary look in Ati's direction, making his cheeks heat with shame, but Isi smiles at the unknown female and tugs their rope sharply, bringing Ati to his knees with a grunt.

Looking up at Isi's grin, the other female nods in approval, and their little parade moves forward as silent as the stars.

* * *

The tether between them is stretched taut, twanging and tugging Ati at odd intervals as Isi sits as far away as possible, leaning in and whispering to the females, both Kendani and Soghun alike. Every now and then she runs her hands over her flattened ears, and her tails are in a constant state of motion. Ati watches them, hypnotized, just as he takes in every other twitch and tweak of her body language. He can tell his symbiote is in distress—again showing more emotion in public than he's used to. Though he's happy to have her share it with him (since he can't seem to stop sharing with her), he doesn't understand how she can bear being so open and vulnerable in front of these strangers. He refuses to expose himself in that way.

Withholding a frown, he tosses a few more sticks into the fire. They'd worked their way deep enough into the winding cave system to avoid any firelight being seen from the entryway's wide mouth. Tucked into a cranny, they have no wish to bring attention to themselves and get these random females trapped again. Nor Ati and his symbiote, for that matter. Getting held up with rescue missions and escape scenarios is the last thing he wants right now. He needs to get to his village, and every moment of delay is a moment he shouldn't be spending.

He slides his pack closer, cradling it against his hip. Trying to convince his match to evolve is the most important thing, but the medicine is his fallback plan. One he doesn't want to resort to, not if he can kill the sickness directly...but if that were ever possible, it would only be with the help of the Gods.

His throat balloons and shrinks, and one of the Soghun females sees him, splitting from the pack and coming to sit beside him.

"What's going on over there?" Ati can't help but ask, feeling like—literally—the odd man out.

She tips her head to the side, regarding the crowd beyond them. "We're talking about why we've come so far from our homes."

A conversation he would have liked to be included in. "And why did you?"

"Mating."

He looks at her plainly.

"There aren't enough males in our villages," she says. "We found the Kendani on the same trek for the same reason, but the Uzh caught us. They didn't want us to mother more enemies." The female wraps her arms around her legs and scoots closer to the fire. "As if finding a mate guarantees you'll birth a generation."

"Why does mating always matter so much to people?" Ati asks.

"It's not the mating as much as having a mate, don't you think? Some of us have been longing for hundreds of years. Can you blame us for not wanting to be alone anymore?"

"To each their own," he replies.

He looks at Isi's small back. When she'd brought up mates earlier, she ended the conversation quickly. Does she have a suitor? Is that why she doesn't want to evolve? Is she in love?

Ati clenches his jaw. That would ruin everything. Those called to travel shouldn't accept mates. Usually, they aren't even interested in them, perhaps by design. If Isi has someone waiting at home for her, she'll never be willing to leave that person behind. But then why was she outside of the Kendani walls at all?

When she was put to sleep, she'd said names. She'd also said things like, "Don't leave me." She'd cried soft tears. There is so much to her story that Ati can't see. So much behind all her stubbornness and fight.

He suddenly wishes he knew more; understood her better. More than that, though, he wishes she'd just give in to fate.

"Does she have a mate waiting for her?" he asks the stranger, gesturing in Isi's direction.

The female holds her hands up to the fire to warm them. The light glints off the scales on her palms the same way it glitters off the precious stones in the walls. "I'm not sure. There seem to be a few males in her village who are unmated—though there aren't enough for everyone." She nods over to the circle of whisperers. "There are three males of age and one who is growing. That means that, unless a new male is born, at least one of those females will still be left without. It's upsetting them."

Indeed, the five new Kendani females look unsettled; their ears are low and their noses point toward the ground. One appears on the verge of tears.

After a pause, the Soghun stranger shakes her head. "They should just continue to other villages. Look how sad it makes them. It's not fitting to make such an emotional display."

Though Ati agrees completely, he finds himself defending his match's species. "You have to remember that the next Kendani territory is said to be over the great sea. They don't often voyage, and even if they did, who would transport them? The Uzh?"

She concedes the point. Looking at him curiously, she asks, "How many males are unmated in your village?"

He shakes his head. "Too many. Far too many. If you come to us, you're sure to make someone's dream come true."

"Yours?" she asks with a hint of interest.

Ati is immediately uncomfortable. "I will never take a mate. I'm on my pilgrimage. I may not have intended to be, but then I found her..."

He looks at Isi who suddenly turns around with her ears up, staring at him for a moment before rolling her eyes and continuing her conversation.

"Seems she didn't want to be found," the stranger says.

"Apparently not," he agrees with no small amount of bitterness.

"If you're not open to a mate, we probably shouldn't stay with you. It's improper."

He can understand that feeling. He's uncomfortable being the only male in a pile of eligibles. His Elder would scold them.

"Isi is here to keep us in check," he says, trying to reassure the female. "And if it makes you feel better, I can sleep at the mouth of the cave."

The female lifts her ridged eyebrows and points toward the knotted rope at his belly. "And force her to go out there with you? Or do you think she'd actually want to go?"

Leaning back on his palms, he considers. He could always knock her out again. The other Kendani won't like it, though.

"Do you think she's kind?" he asks.

"Yes. She seems to truly care about her people."

"Then maybe she'll care enough about you to help me stay away."

The female graces him with a small smile.

Without warning, Ati is yanked onto his back and dragged an inch or so before Isi grunts in frustration. She'd gotten up to move and forgotten the rope entirely. Her fists balled up, she glares at him, and he just blinks back.

"Going somewhere?" he asks.

"I'm going to see my friends off." She gestures at the strangers as if they've become blood sisters.

Not bothering to roll onto his stomach, Ati arches his back and leaps up, not realizing that he's showing off a bit until all the female Soghuns' eyes practically hit him with stars. Oh yes, he definitely needs to stay out of the cave tonight.

Following behind his symbiote and the pack of Kendani, he wonders aloud, "Why would you choose to leave now? It's dangerous to go at night."

The tallest of the females stands proud. "If we're to make it to our new village before our captors return, the sooner we leave, the better. This cave is too close to where they left us. And too obvious."

They're not wrong, and there is risk in that. But in all honesty, Ati is too exhausted to find a new shelter for this mixed crew. He's spent more than half the day either dragging or carrying his unwilling symbiote along, his match either fighting him tooth and nail or flopping around on his back like the world's biggest fish. Still, if he needs to find a new location to keep them safe, he'll—

Facing away, Isi pushes a hand behind her, letting it land straight on Ati's chest.

"We'll be alright," she says. "My companion needs rest. But I agree it would be safer if you ladies go now. Will you tell my friends what I asked you to?"

"Of course," the tallest says, a short bow of her head sealing their promise. At that, she gestures at the rest of the crowd with her fingers against her lips, and they mimic her obediently. Each lays a hand on Isi's shoulders before stepping forward and patting Ati's head like one would a child. It's more than a little insulting, but he lets it happen.

Isi tugs him forward on the rope as they follow the females to the mouth of the cave, watching them slink off one after another. The night isn't too cold and the moon has been hidden by the world's shadow, so it's as dark as it can possibly get. To Ati, the group disappears only a few feet away from where he stands, their fluffy tails and muscular backs slipping against the rock wall in silence, even to his heightened sense of hearing.

"Will they be okay?" he asks quietly.

"They have to be," Isi replies, wrapping her arms around herself. "Because my friends need them. Especially Ren."

She's said that name before.

Ati swallows, his throat throbbing. "Someone you love?"

"Oh, I love him very much."

His heart sinks.

"I love all of them. Madax and Hisk, too. Now they'll finally be able to get what I could never give them."

Ati's brows knit a line up the center of his forehead. "I don't understand."

She looks at him without malice for the first time. "For some reason, I've never wanted to take a mate."

The pressure that was building in Ati's chest, that tight, merciless knot, loosens slightly.

The only sound is the chirping of insects and the rustle of leaves as things flap into the trees and out of them again. He and Isi stand, watching the black space where the females disappeared, each lost in their own thoughts.

Finally, Ati coughs up the courage to say, "How do you feel about sleeping outside again tonight?"

And the look of softness on Isi's face completely disappears. "Excuse me, what?"

With a sigh, Ati prepares to take his lumps.

* * *

"Fool," she calls out into the morning, but Ati isn't in the mood. With a huff, he curls in tighter on himself, telepathically telling her to just pee while his back is turned instead of fussing and making him get up.

"FOOL!" she tries again. He blinks open wider this time...and shock sits him up with a gasp. Two Uzh stand before them, casting heavy shadows that make it seem like the dim of predawn even though the sun hangs well over the horizon. Their fur is mottled. Dark brown base, light tawny flecks, spots of white, and stripes of black running over muscular thighs. Their heavy bodies are well proportioned, making them thick in every possible way—including their thick skulls.

Armor plating drapes across their torsos, dinged and dingy, splattered with a dried something Ati doesn't dare think about. Their greaves hold the stains of lives that have passed away, trampled under the Uzh's feet.

Ati sits perfectly still beneath the void of light cast by their hulking bodies, until he realizes each holds a spear hiked at an angle, ready for a downward stab...

...directly at his symbiote.

Ati snags her rope and pulls backwards with a snap, backpedaling Isi behind him. Whipping a hand to the side, he holds her in place as he stands guard, trying to protect her the only way he knows how.

"Are you deserters?" one of the Uzh asks in a low, gruff tone. He lifts his spear higher, adorned with a strip of cloth in the orange color of his kind.

"Deserters deserve only death." The other follows suit, stepping in closer until the tip of his weapon lays directly upon Ati's breast. This one's banner is a dirty, muddled blue.

Refusing to let himself shrink, Ati sticks out his chest until the triangular metal tip presses hard enough to leave a mark. "I tell you this in no uncertain terms: you are not to harm us. We are symbiotes. We are on our pilgrimage to find our gifts for one another"—Isi goes rigid behind him but has the sense to keep her mouth shut—"and it's one of the worst sins to stop a match on their way to evolution."

His bravado turns into fear faster than he'd like when the second Uzh ticks his weapon up under his chin this time, caressing his throat pouch with its sharpened edge.

"Then where's your traveler's necklace?" the wielder of the blue banner asks.

"Lost." Ati can barely keep his voice steady.

The first Uzh sets his orange weapon down, but eyes the rope cinching he and Isi together. "Why is she shackled to you?"

Ati is running out of ideas. "Safety. If the Gishatich tries to steal one of us, it will have to deal with two. We're better off together than alone," he repeats his previous sentiment, stepping backwards and leading Isi with him. He doesn't get far before that blue spear is pressed against him again, even harder this time, and Isi begins to whine.

Fangs gleaming from its grinning mouth, the aggressive Uzh asks, "If you're a traveler, tell me what your demand of the Gods is."

"D-demand!?" Isi cries.

"That's personal," Ati says. "You're not supposed to ask that."

"And you're not supposed to travel without a necklace. Our largest battle is with your kind right now, Soghun. I'm more than happy to kill you where you stand."

"Even if you get cursed forever?" Ati asks, giving his best cold stare.

The creature rears back its weapon, and it's Isi's turn to yank Ati backwards this time, getting him out of the way of the spear that ricochets off the stone rubble outside the cave entrance.

Standing in front, tails lashing, Isi yells, "I'm wishing for two to be born in every species per generation! Male and female! No one will have to be mateless. No one will have to be alone!"

Ati is stunned as he stares at her back, her arms out to protect him while she spouts a perfect, perfect wish. She says it as if it's always been inside her, just waiting for its moment to come out into the open. Warmth fills Ati's heart then, hoping for exactly that.

The first Uzh steps forward, resting a hand on the shoulder of its attacking comrade, standing him down. "That is a noble demand, little ears. That will indeed help all species."

The aggressive Uzh doesn't let his dangerous grin falter. "I didn't ask her."

Pushing his comrade back further, the calmer Uzh presses on. "Tell us your demand, too, enemy traveler."

Ati moves to stand beside Isi, lifting his chin. "I will end Rrpto."

"And what is that?" the mean one drawls.

"It's a sickness taking over my village. People are suffering. I need to end this plague."

The calmer one's orange-bannered weapon is lowered but remains an omnipresent threat as he takes a step closer. "I've never heard of this sickness."

The aggressive one hisses, "That means his wish is selfish. If it only affects your tribe, how dare you make such an unworthy demand of the Gods? Leave it to a Soghun to do something so disgusting."

Ati's heart is in his throat, his rage burning and longing to burst, yet he keeps his delivery measured. "Perhaps it hasn't gotten to your people yet, but maybe it will. Maybe I'm saving you before you ever need to suffer in the first place."

The orange-bearing Uzh stares at the pair of them, eyes flicking from Isi to Ati and back again before he speaks. "For the sake of her demand, we will let you be. Mark me, however. If your demand was the only one I'd heard today, Soghun, you'd be dangling on the end of my spear."

Isi's fur stands on end.

"If I were you, I'd sincerely consider changing my mind. For what if the Gods only smite your people worse because of your selfishness?"

Ati's feelings overwhelm him, making him lightheaded. Still, he works to slow his heart and keep his bile in his belly. The calm one with his orange banner walks the other back, offering the symbiotic pair space, and the aggressive one finally lowers his spear.

"Have you seen a pack of females traveling together?" the Uzh asks.

"What would two travelers be doing with a pack of females?" Ati answers. He is only met with scoffs.

The calm one tells Isi, "Find yourself a pair of necklaces, little ears, otherwise you may not survive long enough to see your demand come to fruition."

The blue-bannered Uzh tosses one last barb. "And convince your match to do better, or else don't give him his gift."

The two hulks step away, facing Ati and Isi until they're at a fair enough distance, then turning to walk back through the brush.

Under her breath, Isi says, "The girls..."

Ati takes her meaning immediately and begins his own backwards walk into the cave, waiting until they reach complete darkness before turning on his heels and running, his symbiote close behind.

The embers of the campfire remain, keeping the place warm, but that doesn't explain how bright it is inside...until Ati looks up. There is a perfect opening in the stone ceiling, letting in the blue of the sky from above them. They didn't see it at night, but the dawn must have given it away.

"Look here," Isi says, catching his attention.

On the wall, drawn in ash, is a simple arrow pointing up.

"They left," she says in a sigh.

"That means they're in danger. With those monsters around—"

"There's nothing we can do for them." Isi's eyes are distant. "If they've left, they're on their own. Did they ask where your village was?"

He shakes his head. "No."

"Then without a guidepost, they're likely already lost."

Unable to stop himself, Ati's knees go weak. The overwhelm of the past few days—even longer than that—hits him all too hard, forcing him to crouch down and put his hands over his head.

"Pray for them with me, Isi. Please pray."

Sitting down on his right, she also rests her face in her hands, rocking. "Once Mak'ur evolves, he'll end all of this."

"Mak'ur?"

"My very best friend. I followed him out as his escort all the way to the first marker. His ask of the Gods is to stop the war and make the species friends. A wish like that has to be granted; it's so pure."

"So is yours," Ati whispers, trying to hold back his tears as he hides his face. "Why wouldn't you want to evolve with a beautiful wish like that?"

Her voice is small when she says, "Because I'm afraid."

She worries at her knot again before sighing heavily and giving up, bowing her head once more. Maybe, if they pray hard enough, they can keep those Soghun females safe.

Chapter 3

~A GIFT, BY ANY OTHER NAME~

How did I get here? Isi wonders. It's a thought that has gone through her head more than once over the past few days. Sometimes with fury, sometimes with outright confusion, sometimes with awe. This time, it's with self-pity.

She's absolutely drenched. Her clothes are soggy, her ears flop, and her tails drag against the back of her thighs. Mud splatters all over her trousers—the same ones she's worn since she'd first left with Mak'ur, a time that feels like years ago even though it's only been a few days. At least, she thinks it's only been a few days. She knows she spent quite a bit of time under this Fool's spell, reeling with visions—nonsensical things, profound things, scary things and funny things, things that were both humbling and exalting. Sometimes her friends were in them, sometimes it was just the Fool, himself. Her symbiote.

She likes him.

Even though she hates him! That arrogant, kidnapping, son of a—

"Are you hungry?" he asks.

"No." It takes her a minute to realize why he's asking. "Have we eaten anything in the past few days?"

The Fool shakes his head. "My Elder said, once you meet your match, you share life energy and don't need to eat anymore. I thought it was a crazy myth, but I haven't needed water, either. Do you need anything?"

"Just dry weather," she sulks, her feet prunelike from mucking around on the damp ground. Little puddles soak through the grass, yet her symbiote does nothing to avoid them. In fact, he seems to relish in it. Damn reptile.

As if to prove her point, the Fool tips his face toward the droplet-dappled clouds, looking as centered as she's ever seen him. The rain cascades over his stub-nosed face, making his multicolored scales almost shimmer. He's fascinating to watch. He was acting so calm around the Uzh, but Isi knew better, somehow. He was boiling under the surface. He's feisty, like her. The same thing happened with the females. He was uncomfortable, but never showed it.

How does she even know something like that?

It seems like he can only be open about his emotions when they're alone, showing her his grumpy, sarcastic, secret self. A part of her can't help but growl, *That's exactly as it should be,* though the strength of the sentiment takes her completely by surprise.

This is stupid. I don't even know his name, she thinks.

A shiver runs through her, and her symbiote looks at her with sympathy. Opening his pack, he brings out a spare bit of clothing—leather, warm and water resistant—and drapes it over her head.

"Am I supposed to thank you?" she asks. "In all honesty, it's the least you can do. I mean, I'm only in this situation because I'm literally bound to you."

He doesn't seem to mind her snark. Instead, he raises his hand and points a thin finger toward the edge of the deluge-made marshland. "It won't be long now. See the pillars over those trees? We're almost at my village."

Something squelches between Isi's toes as she stops. In the distance—far away, but clear—she can see pylons covered with flowers she doesn't recognize, the carvings in the stone unfamiliar. Closer ahead, the path is lined with boulders and markers that display the green of the Soghun in unknown characters and patterns. Fear takes hold of Isi, the alienness of that place something beyond her comprehension.

"No. I don't want to go there."

For the first time in what feels like a long time, she bucks against him, reaching down and snatching their rope only to cram it in her mouth and gnaw on it.

"Hey! Hey, no!" he shouts, running up and trying to tug it away.

"Iy don' wannah go to your dam willage!" she manages through her teeth as they clench on the salty, rough material.

"What?" he cries. "You say this now?"

"Becawse now it's weal!"

He tries to wrench the rope from her mouth without getting bitten, but it's a hard job. Isi holds on tight and grinds her sharp molars, hoping to do as much damage as possible before he can pry the thing from her lips...which he is absolutely going to do in three, two...

"Stop it!"

The tether rips from her mouth almost painfully, and she snarls, jumping on him and knocking him into the mud—a slippery place to slide and struggle. Damn it, why is fighting with him so much fun?

He wraps his strong arms around her back, his weird neck puffing up against her shoulder and deflating as he croaks at her in warning. In less than a moment, she's lifted up and slung over his shoulder as she kicks and writhes.

"Put me down!"

"I have to deliver the medicine. Then I'll do whatever you want."

"I want you to go suck a rock!"

"Well, if you'd just evolve with me, I wouldn't have to deliver the medicine at all!"

"Well, if you'd just stayed in your village, evolving wouldn't have been an option in the first place!"

At that, he tosses her down in a pile of muck, letting it get all over her, even messing up the clothing he's only just given her.

"I could say that very same thing to you, *escort.*" He throws the word at her like it's dirty. "For someone as against symbiotic matches as you seem to be, I'm surprised you let your idiot friend go at all! Peace between the species"—he scoffs—"that's not a wish. That's a fantasy."

She gapes at him. "Don't you dare say anything bad about Mak'ur."

"And don't you dare pretend to understand what evolving means to me. This medicine..." His face twists into an expression she's never seen. Putting his head in his hands, he takes a deep, long breath. Then another. And another. When he speaks again, he only says, "It's not enough, Isi."

She looks at him then, really and truly. There is a hurt in him she can't define. Sitting up on her elbows, she feels as if she's done something wrong. Instinct says she's not supposed to make her symbiote feel this way.

Inhaling sharply through her nose, she gets up and straightens the rope around her belly. "Fine. I'll go with you. I don't care anymore."

He doesn't move from his spot. Scrubbing his eyes slightly he says, "It will be a short stay."

She wants to say, "It better be," but the look on his face won't let her. Instead, it fills her with compassion. Going up to him, she pauses before lifting a hand and resting it on his head, a sign of kinship. He tries to duck out of her grasp, but she grabs his shoulder and holds him tight, making him feel the warmth of her palm on his forehead.

"What are you doing?" he asks.

"Comforting you."

"Why bother?"

Simply, "Because you look like you need it."

How strange life is. Here she is with her captor, one she's railed against from the very beginning, showing him signs of affection because he looks like his world is falling down. Again, she wonders, *How did I get here?* and, this time, it's sad.

* * *

The gate to the Soghun village is enormous, at least twice the size of Isi's red gate. Elder Onye might like to see something like this—and maybe she already has in her long life—but Isi has no wish to be here. Instead, she trembles. She's lived over a hundred years in one village, not even straying far from her den block. Her friends have been her friends since childhood. She's known everything that would happen every day and loved that pattern and reliability. She needed that repetition in her life. That predictable mundanity. Which is what makes this so hard.

Wet, terrified, and humiliated, Isi trudges behind the Fool, holding her side of the rope like a safety line. Her family must be worried sick about her, and here she is stuck with a stupid Soghun with his stupid big eyes, stupid super-strength, stupid flabby throat pouch, and his stupid, fascinating face.

Why is he so hung up on evolution? What disease could possibly be worth giving your life for, especially if there's a cure?

The Fool had mentioned that the Kendani don't share their herbs, though. Maybe her people just need to open themselves to trade. Isi could even negotiate it, saving the Soghun people without ever having to evolve. She should go home and talk to Elder Onye. Even if the rest of the council won't understand, Elder Onye would. She's the wisest out of everyone.

Yes. That's what I'll do.

Filled with thoughts like these, Isi enters the looming gate, ducking her head a little and putting her ears back. Her tails tuck, belying the strong face she's trying to put on as gatekeepers stare at her. Wary glances, mild interest...and sadness—though the sadness seems directed more at the Fool than her. Are they disappointed he took so long to come back with the medicine? It makes Isi feel ashamed. She shouldn't have made such a fuss.

No, he shouldn't have stolen her away in the first place.

Ugh, it's all such a mess.

As they proceed along the main path of the village, Isi notes their artful way of making homes. Built with thatched fronds, it's completely different from the Kendani dens of mud and earth. People walk along, stopping to look at the Fool before giving her strange, furtive glances. She wonders what they think of her. She looks like a hostage like this. Maybe they think the Fool had to steal her in order to escape safely with the medicine they needed. Or perhaps her symbiote is just disliked? The thought irritates her.

Finally, they come to a huge building, this one made from full tree trunks, large logs, and a myriad of sticks. Taller than Isi by six or seven times, the wooden structure is decorated with white marks. Like her tribe, these people seem to make drawings to represent generations—little clusters of five figures, one of which she recognizes as the shape of her own species.

At the entrance, she is tugged to her knees, bowing willingly out of respect for Soghun culture if nothing else. The roof of this place juts out in a large awning, shielding her from the weather, so there's at least that. The Fool's head is lowered as an old Soghun female comes out—old enough to look old, which would mean millennia have gone by in this person's life. It's both shocking and humbling to be in the presence of someone who has experienced the world for so long, and Isi has to remember to close her gaping mouth with a snap.

Opening his pack, the Fool brings out a small cinched bag and holds it up like an offering.

"The herbs?" the old Soghun asks.

"I've collected all they had. And...I've also collected my symbiote."

The Elder eyes her with a smile. "Oho! Was this a happy accident?"

Isi can't help but frown. "I have mixed feelings."

The Fool looks at her with his eyebrows up. Was she being rude? Was it because she said her feelings were mixed and not outright bad? Gods, she wishes she could read his mind.

"Do you plan to evolve?" the Elder asks bluntly.

"No," Isi growls, glaring at this stranger. The Fool only hangs his head again.

Taking the medicine from the Fool's hands, the Elder nods. "Such a shame." To the Fool, she says, "Thank you. Our people will be grateful for all you've done."

At that, the ancient Soghun goes inside. Isi is tugged gently to her feet, her symbiote following his leader into the enormous hall, a place that looks made for rites and rituals. Within its walls, all is warm and dry, but there is no reason for comfort. Around the interior are beds. Some line the floor, others are on platforms nailed in a spiral pattern up the sides. A series of wooden beams are the only thing that leads up to their hammocks and cots, which would mean visitors would have to hop and jump to get from space to space. Filling the air are groans, coughs, and heavy breathing. The suffering on the Soghuns' faces tells of their pain. Some endlessly shudder, some gasp and cringe, some seem withered and hopeless—and it's one of those that they approach.

There are chairs about the room, and the Fool picks up two, dragging them toward a female who seems to cave inward on herself, her yellow eyes no longer bright and bulging, but milky and barely able to open. Isi wonders why her tribe is refusing to give medicines to these people. Her hope for bartering turns to righteous indignation on behalf of these strangers. Never mind trade; the herbs should be a gift, given for free.

She opens her mouth to speak, to voice her plans to help, but her match lays a hand on her wrist and the expression on his face makes her words fall away. He looks sadder than anyone she's ever seen.

As they take a seat, the wilted and frail Soghun inflicted with this cruel plague tries to smile at them.

"Son," she says.

"Mother," the Fool replies, reaching out and taking her hand, sliding his palms over hers in the gentlest of gestures.

"Who is this?" his mother asks.

"My symbiote. I'm going to find my gift for her, Mama."

Anger licks through Isi's heart. "And I'll refuse. How many times do I have to say it? You can't tell me what to do, and I'll never give you anything, no matter what. I'm going to stay as I am for eternity."

The Fool only grabs his mother's hand harder. "I'll convince her. I will. I just need time, and then I'll end this plague. Please, Mama, just please wait for me."

Tears of pain flow from his mother's eyes. "Your father is the one who has been waiting, my darling. He's been waiting a long time, and I won't make him do it a minute more. Did you bring the medicine?"

Isi looks toward the Elder, who seems to be grinding it in a mortar and mixing it with other elixirs.

"Yes, but—"

"Then what you've brought me is a gift. I accept it freely. Gratefully."

Isi startles as the Elder approaches from behind, holding up a tiny spoonful of the medicine.

"As promised." The Elder offers the spoon. "You have been ill the longest. You get to go first."

The Fool helps his mother sit up, and she cries out slightly, making the Fool whimper—a sound Isi didn't know he could make. Blankets fall away from his mother's body, revealing horrible sores, festering, and reeking of sickness. At least she'll have what she needs now. Isi will get them everything they need.

With one last caress of palm against palm, his mother leans forward and takes the spoonful in her mouth, her throat pouch throbbing—but only just barely. When she leans back, her breath comes all too fast.

Clutching at her, the Fool whispers, "I love you, mama. I love you so much."

And Isi can smell it. She can smell it the moment it happens.

Her symbiote's mother is no more.

He crumbles beside her sagging body, still holding his mother's hand and pressing it to his forehead. His soft whines break Isi's heart, but the Elder only prepares another spoonful for the next in line.

"Why would you do this?" Isi asks, horrified.

The Elder turns over her shoulder. "Because there is no cure. Better to release them from their pain than to let them suffer for eons. Or would you prefer to watch them like this?"

The bodies in the room have new meaning as Isi moves her eyes from bed to suffering bed.

Pointing, the Elder says, "Five years." She changes directions. "Seven." One by one, she names them, all across the room. With each number, a well of pain swells larger in Isi's chest, choking her.

"Death is better than this," the Elder says. "And somewhere inside, you know it."

At that, the Elder—the millennia-old woman deemed wisest in the village—walks around the wooden floor, offering solace in the form of poison while Isi's symbiote breaks into pieces beside her.

No.

This is unacceptable.

Slowly, the Elder makes her way, patient to patient, and each one greets her with sweetness. Gratefulness. Relief.

And not even one of them seems afraid to go.

* * *

Isi toys with her new traveler's necklace—something that will protect her from the unwarranted attacks of others. Something that will prove she's on her pilgrimage. And, make no mistake, Isi is absolutely on her pilgrimage. What is her fear compared to the pain of these people? What is her death when it's a single soul in comparison to all the other lives that will be lost? Every moment Isi wastes not evolving is another moment where the Soghuns suffer in the wide expanse of their wooden coffin. Why has she been so selfish up until now?

He tried to warn me about how horrible their plague was, but I thought the medicine would...

How naïve she was.

They walk along the damp ground. It's no longer raining, but moisture still hangs in the air. "Why didn't you tell me the herbs would kill them?" she asks.

It's a long beat before he answers. "Isn't that what it does to your people?"

"...No."

She sighs, scrubbing tears from her eyes as she trails behind her match. He was pale and wordless as they placed his traveler's necklace over his head. Now he's dazed, a mere shadow of himself as they wander back toward Isi's village—though, why she should try to return is beyond her. To get more poison? To announce her evolution? To be forgiven for leaving those she loves behind?

Her parents will understand her choice. Her friends, too. They'll even be proud. She knows this without having to see the crowds rallying for her, calling her name. There may be tears when she goes, but when the Gods grant her wish, all will be well. And when the Gods finally grant her *symbiote's* wish...

"Hey," she calls softly. "Will you hand me that branch over there?"

He stops and looks down, his eyes empty. Bending, he picks it up for no reason other than the fact that he was asked, and hands it to her.

It is not Isi's gift.

She grips it a little before snapping it into pieces and throwing each shard into the woods.

"How about that rock?" She gestures. "That one, by the puddle."

He complies once more, moving in slow motion as if his body were working its way through thick tar. When he puts it in her hand, Isi grits her teeth...and tosses that, too.

What could her gift possibly be? It must be a thing, right? Something that can pass from him to her, hand to hand. She knows it won't come with ribbons and bows, but that still leaves a world full of possibilities.

Isi kicks at the dirt, scuffing her toes and lamenting that, according to all the Elders, no one on their pilgrimage knew what to give until they gave it, and by then they were gone. Once they evolved, it was too late to learn their secrets. Elder Onye would speculate, imagining the most fantastical options, but Isi doesn't feel all that imaginative just now. All she can do is look around her and frown.

"Something else," she demands. "Give me anything."

This time, he cocks an eyebrow at her, then casts his eyes about mildly before reaching down to that same puddle. Cupping his palms, he catches the water and lifts it, slowly pouring it into Isi's awaiting hands.

Nothing.

"Damn it," she curses aloud. "How will I even know when you've given me my gift? Do I feel something? Do bells ring? Do T'ever dance? What?"

Everything about him goes rigid. "Is that what you're trying to do? Get your gift?"

Putting her hands on her hips, Isi plants her feet wide, feeling almost heroic. "I'm ready to evolve now. I won't fight you anymore. I'll even try to give you *my* gift. What do you think it might be?"

He won't look at her, but a smile crosses his lips. It is not a nice smile, though. It is scary.

In a snap gesture, he explodes, taking Isi by the collar and yanking her in.

"Why now?!" he screams. "Why couldn't you have said this in front of *her?* She would have *listened* to you! We could have *changed her mind!"*

Without warning, he pushes Isi, sending her to the end of the rope that tethers them until she halts with a snag. Leaping forward, he pushes her again.

"I went to your forest to help my mother die!" He shoves Isi this time, knocking her to the ground. "But by finding you, I thought I could help her live!" He falls upon her, pressing the weight of his body on her chest. "For a moment, I thought I could actually save her!"

Isi doesn't fight back as his tears fall upon her, his hands slamming down on either side of her head.

"GIVE ME MY GIFT!" he hollers, making Isi's ears ring.

"I don't know how!"

"GIVE ME MY GIFT!" he screeches this time.

"I'm sorry," she says, holding back a sob. "I'm so sorry."

He curls into himself, crumbling down upon her, his keens muffled into the crook of her neck. Unsure of what to do, she wraps her arms around him and lets him cry, time passing in a blink as he shakes and sobs, dusk turning to dark.

Then a roar echoes out from between the trees.

"The Gishatich." She tries to push her symbiote off her, but he's lost, stuck at the point where he can't hear anything besides his own cries even as the nightmarish monster calls out to match him, wail for wail.

Isi reaches over to pat his cheek, trying desperately to get his attention. "I'm so sorry. I will never understand how you must feel, but we have to go, okay? We can't stay here."

A thrashing sound cuts through the quiet of the forest, followed by twigs snapping and branches breaking, all accompanied by heavy footfalls from somewhere Isi can't see.

"Please," she begs. "Come on. There's nowhere to hide. We have to escape."

Taking his arm, she pulls him to his knees, then to his feet. The monster's pounding only gets louder. Closer.

Finally looking up toward the oncoming danger, Ati grimaces, reaching slowly for his pack to take out his small knife.

"What are you going to do with that?" she asks in an incredulous whisper.

He loops the blade under their tether, just where Isi had bitten, and in a single pull, he snaps it.

"Go," he tells her.

"What?"

"Go!" he shouts, the beast again screaming to match. The trees shake now, and Isi watches in terror as one tumbles down, dropping from the high canopy.

Without thinking, her sense of self-preservation kicks in. Getting down on all fours, she launches away from the oncoming monster, digging in her claws and propelling herself as fast as her body will allow.

* * *

Ati has traveled alone with the weight of his people on his back. He's felt the pressure. The responsibility. The weight of it all. He had accepted his duty, even fulfilled it, but it wasn't what he wanted. With his symbiote, he thought he could do more. Be more. Yet he's failed.

Perhaps it was because his wish was, indeed, selfish. Impure. The Gods may not want to reject him in person, so better to doom his pilgrimage, ending it in defeat. Not only that, but now Ati's called the Gishatich to him, and it comes ever onward.

Depression gives way to dread as he watches Isi run. His match. The one he'd dragged from her home and across the great forest. The one he's put in danger many, many times.

His head jerks forward again as a tree rocks to the side, and Ati can now make out a murderous black form. Its skin seems to soak up all color, refusing to reflect it back. Even under the dark of the night sky, everything about the creature is terrible. Terrifying.

And dread gives way to fear.

Turning away from Isi, he darts in the opposite direction, wanting to grab the beast's attention and get it as far away from her as possible. His feet pummel the ground, the pads of his reptilian toes doing nothing for traction on the wet, leafy ground. It might be only moments before he trips and falls, a feeble offering to the creature behind him, reduced to a mere morsel to be gobbled up in one visceral bite. The beast's snarls echo in his tiny ears, ghastly and nightmarish, inspiring his heart to thump so hard it hurts. Thoughts of gnashing and frothing fill his mind so vividly, he doesn't have to turn around to see them in real life; they're already like painted murals in his imagination, forever stained with the pigment of horror.

The Gishatich rips through the ashen branches that separate them, unrelenting no matter how many boughs he ducks under, no matter how many pricker bushes rake into his scaled skin, making him bleed a familiar and terrifying green.

It's my fault, he knows. He brought this on himself, after all. He's even abused his symbiote and betrayed the Gods. That's not how you evolve. The gift must be freely given; he knows that. He's always known that. And yet...

I'm selfish, he thinks, *just like everyone says I am.*

A khaf tree cracks to his right, thrashed into splinters by the Gishatich's long tail, and falls directly in his path. He skids to all fours, tensing his muscles to leap, but a scythe-like leg stabs into the ground, hammering his linen shirt against the grass and pinning him there.

With bulging eyes, he stares up at the drooling mouth of the black monster before him. The Gishatich doesn't have a wicked grin like he was always told, just an open maw lined with oscillating teeth.

There is no surviving this. No one ever has.

Perhaps this was meant to be.

"Get away from him!"

Isi skids to a halt, diving on top of Ati, once again holding her out arms in protection.

"What are you doing?!" he cries.

But she doesn't respond. She only thrusts her chest out farther and grabs her traveler's necklace, lifting it high in one fist and brandishing it as the beast hovers over them.

"We are on our pilgrimage!" she shouts. "We are going to make asks of the Gods. You cannot destroy us!"

The Gishatich's horrible mouth closes, drool seeping from the space between its lips. The slime of it drops upon Ati's skin which immediately sizzles and blisters, reeking of curdling flesh. He tries to scramble away with a yelp, but there's nothing he can do. He's trapped.

An ominous throb hits Ati's mind, making him fall back into the wet grass as Isi lurches, the necklace tumbling from her fingers as her hands grab onto her skull. Lashing its tail to the side, the beast pushes words into their minds.

"AND WHAT COULD YOUR WISHES OFFER US? NONE OF THE TRIBES CARE FOR OUR KIND. WHY SHOULD I NOT EAT YOU AND SAVE THE GODS THE TROUBLE OF IGNORING YOUR PLEAS?"

Isi is panting as she clutches her head. Still, she tries. "I...I am going to ask that two be born per generation. A male and a female. No one will have to be alone."

"BAH!" It growls, a guttural sound reverberating in the back of its throat. *"WE ARE BOTH MALE AND FEMALE, STUPID CHILD. WHAT DO WE CARE FOR YOUR WISH?"*

Stalling for time, Ati adds, "I will ask to end the plague that ravages my village." He casts his eyes side to side, searching for escape even as the Gishatich's claws keep him down.

"PLAGUE?" it asks silently.

Ati prepares for the scolding that awaits. "My people call it Rrpto. They suffer but do not die. They hurt from within and get terrible wounds and cuts on their body for no reason. Their skin splits. They stop eating. They wither. They cry without end, wishing for death."

The beast leans down, turning its head to the side to glare at them with one, slick, narrowed eye. Its pupil is a cross shape, cutting stripes straight across the iris into the white, and Ati can see their reflection in its darkened center.

"YOU LIE."

"I'd never lie about this. It's my only wish. I have nothing else to ask for."

The eye moves slowly up and down their bodies as Ati's arm burns. *"THIS IS SOMETHING WE SUFFER."*

Its leg lifts, freeing Ati even as the beast dips close enough for him to feel the heat of its body and smell the dank of its breath.

"THE GISHATICH MUST KILL OUR OWN, ELIMINATING GENERATIONS IF ONLY TO SAVE THEM FROM THEIR PAIN."

Ati's mind reaches back. Is that what he and Isi had seen before? When they were up in the nest of the Otomo tree, he'd thought that one Gishatich had preyed on the other...but the other had never fought back. Did it wish to die?

"We do the same," he says. "We use herbs to let them pass. But I need to beg the Gods to make it stop. My people can't bear it any longer."

With a heavy growl, the beast pulls back, regarding them from high above. *"THIS WISH...IT IS PURE. I ACCEPT YOUR ASK ON BEHALF OF MY PEOPLE. GO. ACHIEVE YOUR EVOLUTION. FIND YOUR FUTURE, THEN SAVE OURS."*

Ati shudders as he feels that heavy pressure lift from his mind. Letting out a grunt, Isi collapses forward, letting him know she has felt the same.

The black of the Gishatich's body edges away, turning and heading back to where it came. It steps over felled trees as if they were twigs, and the leaves rustle as they give way for its long neck. Ati watches its tail as it slithers side to side and feels pity for the beast for the first time. It seems no travelers have ever cared to wish for the fifth species, and no traveler could possibly understand their pain the way that Ati can. In that way, these black monsters are his kin. Their grief is shared.

Sliding a hand over the welt on his arm, the acid mark of the Gishatich's venom, Ati's mind reels. He can see the stars burn all too bright as he shudders, all sound suddenly too loud, all sensation too strong.

He has been poisoned.

* * *

Isi watches in horror as her symbiote falls backwards, his eyes rolling in his head as he clutches one forearm against his chest.

"Hey," she calls, gathering him up. "What's happening? What's wrong?"

A smirk forms on his face as he breaks out in a slick sheen of sweat. "If...if you're going to run again...now would be the time to do it."

"I'm not going anywhere. We're going to evolve, remember? We just said we would."

"I'm s-sorry..." he says, "for what I did before."

"You were upset." Rocking him, she strokes his head from his temples to his little ears and back again. "It's all right. We'll help everyone now. We can do it."

He chuckles softly. "I-I wish you had said that before."

Lip trembling, she says, "Me too."

He convulses in her arms, taking a sharp gasp of air. It makes her stomach twist. How can she help? What can she possibly do? She looks left and right, the night swallowing her. No one is coming to save them.

"I'm sorry," she says, ducking her head down to press her lips against his forehead. Cinching her eyes, she mourns with heavy tears. He feels feverish to the touch, and he shivers harshly when she kisses him, letting out a soft whimper.

"Isi..." he says, something aching in his voice...but no more apologies.

"Tell me your name," she urges, keeping her eyes shut tight, blindly touching his cheek with tenderness.

"It's sacred," he whispers.

"But you'll tell me, right?"

He rests a hand over hers. "It's Ati'si tana. But those who love me most call me Ati."

"Ati," she repeats in awe. Something blooms within her then, Isi's heart swelling with heat. Her whole body tingles and her nerves thrum. "Ati..." she says again, unable to keep the smile from her lips. "This is it. I can feel it. All this time, all I needed was your name. That is my gift..."

His fingers tug at her ears, and she looks at him. His face glows with an inner light, ethereal and otherworldly as he stares at her with moist, unblinking eyes. "And your kiss...that was mine."

Isi laughs even as she cries, and Ati joins her. It's like she's melting into his skin and he's coming up to envelop her in his warmth. How could she have been afraid of this? How could she have resisted? This isn't death. This is perfection. This is like coming home.

Isi and Ati look to the sky, their souls melding and meshing into something stronger. Something higher. Something she'd never imagined. Her mind expands past the forest, past the mountains, past the sea, and Ati swirls around her consciousness, their thoughts intertwining as their twin hearts reach out and caress their loved ones, letting them feel their evolution. Isi's parents hold one another in joy. Ati's Elder smiles with hope. Mak'ur fills with a pride unlike he's ever known. The triplets wrap their arms around the new females, pulling them into loving embraces. All is as it should be. As it was always meant to be. After all, Ati and Isi are symbiotes. This was their path from the very beginning.

The glowing heavens open, magnificent and beautiful, and the Gods welcome them to stand alongside every other traveler who has ever ascended. Each of the five species greets them with understanding, respect, and adoration, giving them their place among the light that hangs like jewels in the sky.

This is home now. Where they belong. Where they have *always* belonged.

And within moments, the plague is gone. The sick breathe easy—their bodies whole and healed—and across mountain, field, and sea, a new generation blooms in the bellies of loving mothers—two per species, male and female, just like Isi always dreamed. Their asks of the Gods have become reality, just as they'd always hoped, for their wishes were indeed as pure as the driven snow.

SYMPATHY
FOR THE
DEVIL

Sympathy For The Devil

~CREATION~

When he came into awareness, he was still one with the grass. It was embedded within him, threading through all his delicate parts, completely enmeshed...until it wasn't. Until there was a separation between *him* and *it*. It was only then that he realized that he could see. That there was more than the dim that existed behind shuttered lids. His vision flickered as he blinked the light in...and it was good.

Instead of a thriving meadow within his every fiber, he now felt a power in its place. An everlasting connection with something called Atua. He loved It immediately, and It loved him in return.

When Atua taught him words like *eyes* and *hands* and *heart,* It also named him. It was a beautiful name. One that made him press his tongue against the roof of his mouth for the briefest of moments before falling into a hiss near the end.

"Nox."

...and it was more than good. It was everything. He existed now. Instead of being nothing, he simply *was*. Not only him—Atua created many things. Within huge craters of water, deeper than the mountains were tall, life soon bloomed. While Nox watched, the oceans became home to things that swam, things that jumped in the waves, things that would never stop living, just like him. Just like Atua, Itself.

Atua showed Nox the vastness of Its creations, blessing him with vision upon vision of suns and moons, earth and sky, and in this way, Nox came to understand that Atua was woven into everything—the air, the stars, the swirling seas. It even dwelled within Nox himself.

And Atua was generous, sharing Its precious gifts with Nox. Things like the ability to create. To *make.* With that power, Nox made plants of any and every color he could imagine, naming those lovely hues things like *crimson, azure, violet, sapphire, olive*...and *gold.* To Nox, everything had a tint of gold, that holiest of colors, because in the center of his chest he had a window to his heart. It wasn't a heart like other creatures had. It didn't pump or thump. Instead, it *glowed,* a reflection of his inner soul. Gold meant happy, and Nox was forever happy.

Soon, Atua began creating complex things with complex minds, like the humans who ran on two legs, like Nox. It wasn't long until they became his absolute favorite, even more so than his own creations. Nox only made things that bloomed, slithered, pranced, and flew on leathery wings, never something as grand as a human. He could only dream of creating something so wondrous.

He watched the two humans—one male, one female—play all the time, entranced by the sight of them. Their bodies were similar to his own, though his was much smaller. Pudgy and soft. Atua called him things like *cherubic* and *childlike,* and Nox loved the body It gave him. From his beautiful, curved horns to his brown locks of hair; from his floppy ears to his humanlike face, chest, and belly; from his furry, goat-like legs to his wolfish tail, and the unique circular indent just over his breastbone, behind which shined the amber glow of his non-beating heart.

Something separated him from the rest of the world, however. All of Atua's other creations were made in pairs, so Nox knew something was missing. He had no other half to his golden soul. Watching the humans, he began to dream happily of having a counterpart. Someone to play and laugh alongside him. As it was, Nox had no one to even share his voice with. There was no need to speak to Atua, after all; It already knew his mind, his every thought and feeling.

Set apart the way he was, Nox focused on learning the ways of his Creator in silence. He meditated, practicing how to move things with his mind. Earth, trees, rocks, all obeyed his every ask. He could float in the air on the wisps of the wind, letting himself fall for miles without ever crashing. He could speak into the minds of animals and make them do the most adorable things. This power was as close as he could get to knowing his Maker the way It knew him, and every new skill made him thrum with happiness.

As a reward, Atua made Nox his pair—his other half—and she was more than good; she was perfection, with a soul just as golden as his own. Whereas he was a creature of earth, she was born of the sky, lighter than helium and forever in flight. Her four feathery wings put all else to shame, her lovely taloned feet staying clasped as she hovered above Nox's head, pressing kisses into his hair and nuzzling his nose, her sweet smiles meant only for him.

His mouth moved to create a word just for her. The sound made his teeth clench slightly before falling into a sigh, granting her a name just like Atua had done for him.

"Nal."

Her brown hair flowed in the breeze with the grace of a river current. She'd giggle and push it from her hazel eyes when the wind made it dance, gathering it behind her nape only for it to tangle together once more.

The simple, fiddling gesture became her signature movement, but—always looking for moments to make her smile—Nox wondered if she might prefer wearing her hair a different way. In truth, he was always wondering about her, working to discover her every aspect the same way he strived to understand the rest of the world around him. So, just in case she might want it, Nox made her a lovely bit of twine to loop her hair out of her way.

Her joy upon receiving the gift took over his whole being, her golden soul shining even brighter when she smiled, just like he had hoped. It was more beautiful than anything Nox had ever seen. She sang to him then, blessing him with sound and creating a memory that would never fade.

Nox loved Atua, but he loved Nal more. He couldn't help it. Like the humans needed each other, so he needed his Nal. They both belonged to their Creator, but they also belonged to each other. Earth and sky, married from now until forever.

In time, Atua also gifted Nal with the power of creation. She made all manner of things that flew, just like her, passing her song on in different trilling notes to the beaks of her birds. Winged creatures large and small came into existence thanks to Nal, from great eagles to chatty gulls and the tiniest sparrows, Nox's favorite. Their feathers were brown like the soil and bore the same markings as his Nal.

According to her, Nox was never close enough, even when he reached up to touch her tail feathers or grab her plush little hips to dance. Cherubic herself, they matched in their tiny, childlike bodies as he twirled her, listening to her song and sharing his own in return. Still, she insisted even those moments weren't enough. She needed something that lived with her in the sky. It was then that she named a star after him. She called it the Morning Star, because he made her soul shine like the crest of dawn.

He glowed so gold in that moment, it was almost blinding. If his feelings for her could expand, they absolutely did on that day, and his chest shone with rays to rival the sun. Love, adoration, it all paled in comparison to the feelings he had for his other half...

Which, in the end, was his downfall.

Without knowing it, Nox's love for Nal was the beginning of every-thing that ever went wrong.

It was the beginning of the end.

* * *

"Teach me again!" Nal giggles, one of the best sounds in the world as far as Nox is concerned.

Her wings flutter to keep her aloft while he grins, tugging her tail feathers softly. "You already know how to call the rain. You do it better than I do!"

Circling him, she fluffs his hair with the flapping of her wings, her pin feathers tickling the underside of his chin. "That doesn't mean I don't want you to teach me. I want to hear your voice until the end of time."

With a smile, he breathes in the crisp air of the plateau as the grass curls purposefully around his hooves. The earth loves him, too. He's made of it, after all. Still, Nox has to move quickly, or the blades will start twining around his ankles.

Deciding to indulge his other half, he tugs at her one more time before breaking into a playful run, hoping she tries to tag him but knowing he's too fast. His little legs gallop toward her favorite tree to roost in, for Nal's tail makes it hard for her to get close to the ground. It's long and rigid, keeping her firmly placed in the sky unless she's willing to lay flat on her belly, wings everywhere. At her tree, though, he can sit beneath a branch while she perches above, her feathers slipping down his spine and cradling him in a hug. He loves Nal's hugs. It's one of the many things about her that make his golden heart glow.

Settling down under the shadow of the leaves, it's a thick tree root that perks up to hold him now, wrapping around him with a lazy sort of happiness. Giggling, he offers an arm for it to encircle, its bark gently scuffing his skin as the tree says hello in its own special way. He purses his lips in a sweet pucker, giving the root a little kiss before shaking out his arms to relax. The familiar warmth of Nal wraps around his back as he places his hands on his furry knees and inhales deeply.

"Just get ready for Atua's power. Calm yourself and breathe deeply," he tells her, listening to the sound of her following his instructions. "That's right. Fill up your whole chest with air. Hold it for a moment— just enough so that it begins to tickle inside you, asking to come out."

Never able to hold her breath for long, she puffs out a huge whoosh, and Nox grins. Why is she so adorable?

Immediately, Atua swirls within him. Within both of them. Even though It was already there, It now knows that they want Its attention.

Hello, Nox.

I love you, he replies easily in his mind. It's what he tells Atua every time he feels It, and he means it from the bottom of his heart.

Hello, songbird.

Atua has a different name for Nal, and it's a good one, describing her perfectly. Nox still prefers the name he gave her, though. He likes that it sounds like a sigh.

He can't hear her reply, but her giggles come in droves at her private conversation with Atua, a sign that they, too, share their own holy connection.

Nothing else needs to be said at that point. Atua will share Its power, just like It shares everything else.

"Now, lift your hand," Nox tells her, continuing the unnecessary lesson, "and just ask it to move."

"Just ask," she confirms.

Casting his eyes to the sky, he sees it. The invisible droplets of water in the air begin swirling together in puffy clouds, deepening into gray. Piling on each other, colliding until they stand high, light flickers inside, a rumble following in its static beauty. Electricity is something else Nal made. Its little friction-induced zaps make Nox's hair stand on end when he rubs his hooves on certain textures, tingling him—but the best part of electricity is the dancing strikes that live within the clouds, calling out their own kind of music. Loud and booming. Nothing will ever be like it.

It's then that Nal's silent wish comes true and the rain begins, a curtain falling around them. The tree is her shield, but the ground soaks it up nicely, turning a deeper color and giving off a scent that feels like home.

Lightning may be Nal's creation, but the rain comes straight from Atua, Itself. All things live forever, but the rain comes and goes. That makes it precious, somehow. Fleeting. Special.

Unable to help himself, Nox jumps up and starts bounding in the droplets, whooping all the while. Its coolness soaks him, drenching him in another gift from his soulmate, making him dance in hopping twirls. The underside of the tree lights up in the dark of the rainstorm, Nal's heart swelling gold with an adoration he can feel with his whole body. Atua spirals around and within them as they leverage its power, but there's a beckoning there as well. It wants to speak with Nox alone, as It so often does.

Not yet. Can we wait until her rain stops? he asks.

Without warning, there is a tightness in Nox's chest unlike anything he's ever felt, making him halt immediately. His breath, his body, his everything. For the first time in his eternal life, his glowing heart dims and flashes a strange color—the wrong color. The sensation is gone within moments, yet his heart still stutters with an unknown emotion.

What was that? he asks his Maker, knowing Atua would have the answer. It knows everything, after all. It shares everything. It *is* every-thing. Yet It remains silent. For the first time in eternity, It is silent.

And Nox's glow fades to nothing.

"Nox?" Nal calls.

The rain ebbs immediately. The airy flutter of her lifting from the branch to join him fills the air instead, and it's only once her hands are in his hair that his golden tint shines again. But it's smaller, somehow... until Nal's strokes move down to his floppy ears, scritch-scratching behind them and making his full glow return. His leg goes wild and taps the ground, his balance wobbling. This always happens when she pets him there, and it's only a matter of moments until his laughter comes. Reaching around, he takes hold of her feathered ankles and pinwheels her, her squeals an absolute delight—so much so that he starts kissing her taloned toes with great, big "Mmmwah!" sounds. Her tiny fingers fold under his chin as she looks at him in that way only she can, eyes squinting with adoration.

After a moment, he asks, "Did you feel it?"

She blinks and tilts her head to the side, little curls of hair dangling down with the joy of gravity. "Feel what?"

Locked forever in her eyes, he uses a hand to cover the window to his soul. "Something new."

Batting him in the face with a fluffy puff, she lifts an eyebrow play-fully. "There's nothing new unless we make it. Atua. You. Me."

"Did you make it by accident when you called the rain?" he asks, tipping his head to mirror hers.

Looking up at the fading gray clouds, she ponders for a moment. "Nope. I don't think so. Did you do it when you were dancing?"

It's his turn to think. Making a funny *hmmm* sound, he fiddles with her talons, shiny and black. "Nope. I don't think so, either."

Adjusting the twine looping up her hair, she shrugs. "It must have been Atua, then."

"Yup," he agrees absently, replaying the moment and the strange feeling in his head.

Curious, she asks, "Was it nice?"

Nox pets his chest, his heart dimming once more and...his eyebrows coming together. An expression he's never made.

"No..."

Cocking her head to the side as if she doesn't understand, Nal just decides the best course of action is to kiss his hair to distract him before scritch-scratching his ears once more—then it's his turn to squeal. His leg is just uncontrollable!

* * *

Nox trots up to the clearing alone, his favorite place to commune with Atua. The air is crisp here, up so high that he can look down on the whole valley of perfection, a garden called Eden, its inhabitants little specks trotting around. He even sees the two humans he adores. His arms wave side to side as he turns absentmindedly on his hips, mulling over how to ask about what had happened—though he supposes it doesn't matter. Atua already knows his question without him having to voice it.

I do, It confirms, bringing a smile to Nox's face.

He echoes his refrain of, *I love you,* as he always has. As he will forever.

Not forever, is what Atua threads through his mind, giving him pause. *Not even for very much longer.*

Nox's eyebrows cinch together for the second time. *Why would You say that?* he asks, an odd feeling pinching in his chest, like a cold pressure. Something not good. There is no word for this.

He touches his heart, yet another new expression blooming—his lips pulling down at the corners. *I don't like this,* he sends, confused by the echoing pangs. *Why don't I like this?*

It hurts, Atua explains. *What you're feeling is pain.*

Pain? Nox thinks helplessly, his eyes squeezing shut. *Why do I feel it?*

There is no pause before Atua answers.

Because you are broken.

I'm what? Nox looks at himself, not understanding what that sentence means, and trying to guess by the the shape of his body, injecting context where it doesn't belong.

You are wrongness, his Holy Creator explains. *You were made badly. Your heart is not pure. You do not love as I have commanded.*

But I love everything, Nox sends back, not grasping the breadth of Atua's words.

You only need love Me, child, yet you love other things more. The humans. My songbird.

Nox feels an emotion coming from his Creator then, but it's not love or happiness. It's not this new pain, either. It makes him think of the color green...but a shade you don't want. It's unlike grass or leaves or stems. It's a color like the insides of spiders.

Nal is the other half of me. How could loving her be 'wrong'?

Shaking his head, Nox is unable to wrap his mind around it. Everything deserves to be loved, from the tiniest cells to the great beasts of the land, the perfect and perfectly-imperfect alike—and his Nal is no exception. To him, more than anything else, she is the rule.

I don't understand.

Understand this. Every living thing will soon feel the pain you do now, only worse. Deeper. And it will be because you bring it to them. You will poison them, Nox. Ruin them all. The path before you has been prepared; you've already taken the first step.

Lips parting, Nox's jaw goes slack. This time, his soul doesn't dim into nothing as it did before—instead, it shifts. A deep, dark sapphire blue swirls in his chest as that strange new sensation, that pain, compounds, making him take a full step back with the weight of it.

Why? he asks again, but it's more intense this time. He doesn't like this. He doesn't want this.

Yet this is what I want. I make no mistakes—not now, not ever. This was my plan from the very start. This is how your life will be from now until there is nothing. Everything will soon stop living, stop playing in my eternal garden, and it will be because of you.

Nox can't breathe. His sight roams the horizon, wishing there was something to hook his eyes onto, clasp his hands before, and...*beg* to make this stop.

Begging. Another something new. It's like asking mixed together with this newfound pain.

I don't want this, he repeats, covering his ears—a worthless gesture.

What you want doesn't matter, My child. It's already decided and has been since before you first opened your eyes. You will lead everything to sin, and I will not stop you. Only my songbird will see the pain you bring to all the souls that live and seek to save them. And then, because of the corruption you've sown, they will reject her, and she will die. Cease to be.

She will falter, fall, and never rise again. Her song will stop, and her glow will darken. All this, and all because of you.

The blue in Nox's heart throbs and his vision blurs. He's never felt something as strongly as this, as all-consuming. It takes him to his knees, his body crumpling without him asking it to. One hand flies to his aching chest, the other presses against his foggy eyes. Looking at his fingertips he sees... "Water?"

Tears, Atua corrects. *You will cry many, as will many more. You will make them feel your suffering, Nox, and you will give them a suffering all their own.*

How do I stop this?

I won't let you. I do not wish it; therefore, it will not come to pass.

Another color swirls for the briefest of moments. A dark, crimson red. Nox's eyebrows nearly touch now, his face contorted and strange even as his inner voice is meek and tiny. *You want Nal to die?*

She will sacrifice herself to save those you would destroy. Balance. Sky and Earth. Light and Dark. Good and Evil.

Evil?

You. Atua fills him with that word, heavy, thick, and undeniable.

The water, the *tears* pour down Nox's cheeks. A sound comes from him now, low and long, and it hurts to even hear it. He hunches over his little legs and buries his face in his fur, rocking himself as he sends Atua his truth. *You don't love me anymore. Even though I love you so much...*

I love you, child. I love you enough to give you a future that will shape the world. And I love my songbird enough to give her the power to save everything she holds so dear.

Me?

Not you. Never you.

Now, the sound Nox makes grows louder, something like a howl that stutters in his throat. He looks up at the azure sky—the same color that blares from his heart—with all his happiness taken away. It's then that he does something unprecedented. Something no one had ever even dreamed of. Something unthinkable.

He rejects the will of his Creator.

"No," he says aloud, his mouth pulled taut, his cheeks wet with his own bitter rain. "I won't do what You want me to. I don't want that future to come true. I won't let it happen."

It is destiny, my child. Something you cannot avoid. Something you cannot alter.

Another flash of red singes the skin encircling the window to Nox's heart. He flares his nostrils and bares his teeth. "Just watch me." He throws the words into the ether with another unnamed feeling, his voice strange and clipped.

His fingers crook into claws and his lip curls as that red burns inside him. Arcing out his arms in a swipe to either side, the earth rends itself open, its roots grabbing his ankles and pulling him in, just like he wants them to.

I'll hide. I'll hide forever! I'll stay good. I won't be broken or bad or evil. She'll be safe then. They all will!

It doesn't matter how deep the earth is pulling him down, splitting itself to caverns and gullies as it swallows him. Atua is just as loud in Nox's mind as It has always been.

You'll see. In time, you'll come to understand. She will become your enemy. She will hate you, the exact opposite of love. She will become a warrior of righteousness and you the son of darkness. A fallen star. You will battle each other for the souls of mankind, for the very Heavens, for control of My power. You will tear it in half, two sides of a whole. You will bring Armageddon, the end of all.

Nox's teeth grind on one another, a new sort of pain. A welcome one alongside the nicks and cuts drawn into his flesh as the rocks drag over him, his fine fur pulling off in patches as he scrapes into darkness. An urgent refrain repeats in his mind—*Hide, hide, hide*—no longer a word of play. A word of this blue feeling. Nox lets out a sharp cry as something rips into his face while he's sucked down into blackness, so deep underground that he feels the warmth of the earth.

I'll stay here for always! he screams silently. *I'll never come out! I won't hurt anyone, especially not Nal! She's mine. You made her for ME!*

This time Atua doesn't answer, and when Nox reaches out, It doesn't reach back. He can sense It, though; the power of his Creator remains within him. Nox can still feel the ties that bind the universe. He can call to the world, ask it to fulfill his needs. If he can do that, there's still hope. If he stays here long enough, if he's a good boy, maybe Atua will change Its mind. Sometimes Nox changes his mind, after all. So does Nal.

Nal...

She won't end. She won't be gone. If I don't become...evil...there's nothing for her to save. There's nothing to die for.

Crying isn't a strong enough word for the sounds he's making. They're...wails. *Keens.* New words are born as Nox's pain deepens, and he is weeping, sobbing, mourning, and bleeding, his tears burning the ragged opening in his face. In the deep darkness, his heart glows a terrible, awful, inescapable blue.

His world has been upended.

And he is drowning in sand.

Chapter 2

~THE TREE OF KNOWLEDGE~

When life is forever, there's no point in counting the days. They bleed together into flickers of light and dark, though Nox can barely tell in this arching cavern of nothing but stone. Over what must have been years in this meaningless moment in eternity, Nox has crawled farther and farther to the surface, one thought echoing in his blue heart.

I'm lonely.

One of the many new words he has created in his echoing silence. He's built a vocabulary of broken things, just like him. Things like *isolation* and *suffering* and *abandonment* and *cursed*.

And *sad*. Very intensely, unendingly sad.

His body is just as broken as his soul, he supposes, because it's deformed now. His curved horns have become knotted branches. His plush body has turned to angles. His size has doubled, if not more. And he *hungers*. He hungers for something to stop his belly rumbling with discomfort. He hungers for a sound other than the dripping of water inside the cavern of spiking stones. For a sensation other than the cool surface on his stretched skin. He hungers for love. For his other half. For his Maker, even now.

Maybe—as long as no one sees him—maybe he can go outside. Just for a moment. Just to see the sky. Just to see if his star still lives there, making sure Nal is never lonely.

Is she blue, too? Is she sad, like him? He doesn't want that. Even if he stays away forever, he wants her to find other things to keep her happy and golden and perfect. Atua is with her after all, so she'll never truly be alone.

He misses his Creator's wordless words. Its teachings.

Why did I have to be broken?

Familiar tears fill his eyes as his face pulls into a grimace. Today hurts in a never-ending way. There is no moment of blankness, no calm of detachment. There is only a flood of pain until his mind, heart, and lungs all scream with it.

He needs it to stop. If he can't control the anguish, maybe that's what will drive him to the evil Atua talked about. Maybe that's what will lead him to ruin things.

It's that thought that convinces him to crawl, hands, knees, and hooves dragging through the bowels of the caverns, the brambles of his horns tangling with stalactites hanging from the ceiling. When he emerges above ground, the nighttime air moves around him, kissing his throat with freshness, and a tension within him releases. His forehead smooths, as does the forever frown that creases his face. He catches the scent of something other than moss and dank. It's flowers. *His* flowers. Ones he created all on his own with the most delicate features he could imagine, back when there was nothing but gold in his heart. What's more, when his fingers slide through the awaiting grass, the blades ripple with a shushing sound, flourishing under his grasp and cascading up his wrist in welcome.

Lips trembling, Nox smiles and lets out a weary sound of relief.

Something still loves him.

He weeps for a different reason then, the night sky draping him in its blackness. In the heavens, his star lives on as he'd hoped—a sign that Nal doesn't hate him for leaving like Atua said she would. Or maybe she just doesn't hate him *yet.*

She never will, he vows, as he has innumerable times already. *Because I will never be what Atua wants me to be.*

Crickets creak in the brush as Nox lets his flora remind him he's alive, snuggling him in fronds and flowers, weaving around him like an embrace. Inside the blue of his heart, a golden flicker sputters to life—tiny, but there, and it gives him hope.

Perhaps he can stay outside of the cave tonight, letting the earth love him as he still loves it. Perhaps he can allow himself the decadence of being adored, even if just for a moment. He craves it so severely, after all. A thirst that will never be slaked.

He's tired of being lonely.

* * *

Nox crawls farther and farther from his hideaway as time slips by—whether days or decades or eons, he does not know. He is still blue, but with a thread of gold. Still sad but blessed with a glimmer of hope, proof that he aspires toward goodness. Wholesomeness. Together, those colors let him form a sort of peace with his existence. He has the land, he is under Nal's sky, and he is hidden away from all he could possibly harm.

Until he's not.

Nox had seen the forest from far away and longed for it. Now he's close enough to scent the pine on the wind and finds himself wanting more. He dreams of scrubbing his fur along the bark to attend to that itch he can never reach. He aches to scour his horns, too, relieving some of the weight that's grown over time...but he doesn't dare. Birds live in trees. Birds would break his heart. Their songs would rend his ears, he's convinced of it.

Until he's wrong. Until the first bird flies overhead with a twiddling note and, instead of breaking, he heals. The gold in his heart swells larger, reminding him that he loves more than just the earth. He has creatures he's made, things he's watched and adored, like his soulmate's fluttering, singing creations.

So, Nox sheds his apprehension, daring to step closer to the forest.

His body creaks with disuse but loosens as he moves. As he walks. As he runs. As a grin splits his face when he prances and bucks and dares to laugh. The birds chirp as he bounds among the trees and whoops. For the first time in a long time, Nox glows. The blue in his heart isn't gone, but it lights up from the center, bright and golden. Happiness. Contentment. Fear ebbing away as life returns to his limbs and heart.

And then he finds his way to something that stuns him. Something new. Ohhhh, how he's always fascinated when something new is made.

"Was it Nal or Atua, do you think?" Nox asks a nearby snake, beckoning it up to slither around him in a tickling bind, pressing their noses together for a moment before admiring the new work of creation.

It's a tree, but blinding white, gnarled, and spread into wide branches, perfect for climbing or nesting. Pink leaves, tinged with the tiniest bit of crimson, give off an ethereal mist. From its boughs hang sweet-smelling, yellow orbs.

"It's beautiful," Nox whispers in his new, lower baritone, reveling in his own sound. Any sound. It seems his ears are lonely, too.

Untangling, the serpent hisses its agreement, moving toward the perfect trunk as if to introduce the marvel to the newcomer. A smile curves on Nox's face. The sweet-scented orbs call to his belly, to that unending rumble, and he finds his mouth wet and slick. His tongue passes over his lips as he steps closer, finally fulfilling his need and scraping that itchy spot over the whorled bark, grumbling a purr as he does so.

The snake slowly lifts itself from the ground, rearing back and curving into an arc as it regards him. Nox can feel the animal's amusement at the show he's putting on.

"If you itched for this long, you'd make these sounds, too, I promise you," Nox tells it, eyebrows rising to the sky as he grins, scrubbing his now-angular, furry hip over a particularly bumpy part. Leaning his head back, his horns clatter against the branches above and knock down one of the tummy-tugging orbs.

Fruit, he decides, that slickness in his mouth building until he has to swallow.

Wondering if it smells as good up close, he lifts the fruit and presses its fuzzy surface to his nose. Humming a little, he casts his eyes to his new friend and says, "Yup!" even though the snake has no idea what he's on about.

A thought catches his mind and makes him stare at the round softness in his hand. His belly wants it. Clearly it does. But how can he get it in there? Cocking his head to the side, he presses the fruit against his navel...though it accomplishes nothing. Looking up at the snake, Nox shrugs a bit, and it agrees, tipping its head to the side and flicking out its tongue to taste the scent.

Eyeing the newfound fruit, Nox opens his mouth and...*licks* a stripe over the skin. The burst of sensation in his mouth is immediate, and his hum sounds different this time. More urgent.

Giggling at himself, he licks it some more. And some more. And more and more and more, but all that's happening is that his mouth is asking him to keep going while his belly still complains. Patting his stomach, Nox wonders what to do with it...and then he draws a line between his hunger and his mouth as he swallows once more, giving him an idea.

"Do you think I should...kind of..." He's not sure how to phrase it, so he just opens his mouth and places his teeth on the flesh of the orb.

His snake friend has no answers.

Deciding it couldn't hurt, Nox sinks in and tugs his head to the side, ripping the fruit and pulling its taste into his mouth. His eyes slip closed, and he just takes a moment to feel it.. New words bloom. *Tart, juicy, delicious, bite, chew.*

He swallows again and his stomach rumbles in earnest, crying out for more of what lays in Nox's grasp, and he is more than happy to oblige, salivating as he devours this new sort of perfection. His body responds and...

His eyes haze.

His thoughts...*expand.*

Looking down at the stickiness that coats his fingers, Nox's mind begins working in ways unfamiliar to him. Colors are more saturated. Meanings are clearer. Each sound is louder, and everything has an undertone of purpose. His curiosity reaches into eternity. And his body...

"Hello?" a sweet voice calls, and Nox's mind spikes with fear.

Can't get close! he nearly screams at himself as he pushes into a two-hoofed gallop, tearing clots out of the ground as he lunges behind a normal tree, not wanting to be seen. He cowers then, trembling but still curious. Always so very curious.

Inexplicably, his mind goes at the speed of sound. *What's alive that can speak? It's not Nal...* Or is it? His body has changed over time. His voice, too. Has hers?

His fear doubles. The very idea is like a strike of Nal's lightning, but bolting through him in all the wrong ways, making his soul flicker and dim once more.

I can't hurt her. I can't see her. I can't, I can't, I can't.

It's with this panging terror that Nox opens his mind and uses the special power Atua granted, looking through his snake friend's eyes and seeing what he's running from. Is it Nal? Is it something new? With his own eyes shut tight, Nox's sticky mouth drops open.

It's not Nal.

It's a human.

The female approaches the white tree from the other angle, the glow lighting her dark skin. Her body has changed as well, stretched out like Nox's, but softer. Those curves remain around her hips but they're wider now and her chest is swollen with soft spheres, heavy laden with perfect peaks.

Nox's mouth waters once more—but it's more than that. The unfamiliar thoughts in his mind have traveled down to every part in him, and the area below his tummy throbs. Comes awake.

He wants to swallow her. If his body is begging for her, does that mean it wants to devour her, too? He imagines putting his mouth on her...but swallowing isn't what he does. Nor does he rip or tear, though his teeth do close softly. *Nip. Suckle. Suck.*

And now he's on fire. He wants to be near her. With her. All over her. He wants to smell her, taste her, feel her body over his. Skin to skin, sliding over each other. Unbidden, a sound escapes his throat, new and deep.

Through the snake's eyes, he sees the female's head snap up, amusement and glee written on her face. She feels no fear.

Because she knows no pain, Nox thinks bitterly. Softening, his eyelids sealed shut, he adds, *But perhaps I could teach her pleasure.*

He's not supposed to get close, but the female needs to taste this fruit. Her body needs to wake up. Nox's fingers skate down his chest, then lower, sighing softly and wishing this joy for her. This perfection. And when his palm reaches a certain part of his body, he gasps.

The female's smile only grows, thinking she's found a secret—but he can't let her get any closer. Atua said he would bring suffering to the humans, and he can't let that happen. So, he does what he'd done in the plateau of Atua, where he and Nal lived in bliss. Nox asks the snake to let him in and take control, and who is his friend to deny him?

Sensual is the next word. Nox slithers this new, soft, muscular body over to the...*woman* he's so drawn to. Her dark hair kinks in tight curls all around her head, and she grins upon finding the snake on the forest floor.

"I thought so," she chirps, wholesome and lovely. "I knew I heard something."

Watching through his friend's eyes, Nox sees the woman lean up against the purest tree in existence, not knowing that it bestows this holy gift of...more. She's so close to the opportunity she could touch it. How can she resist such a scent? How can she not taste its sweetness in the air?

It's then that Nox is fully aware inside the other creature, running its winding body toward his target, captivated by her beauty. Does she understand how tantalizing she is? Clenching the snake's vocal cords into a shape like his own, he warbles air through them in hissing notes.

"Daughter of Eden, do you know," its tongue flicks out, "what resssts in the tree above you?"

The woman turns her ebony eyes up and into the glowing branches. "This is the Tree of Knowledge."

And it makes total sense, Nox thinks. *Because now I know.*

"Tassste the fruit it bearsss. It will open your sssenses."

Unfazed, the woman waves a hand with a gentle laugh. "I have my senses already."

You think so now, Nox sympathizes. *But you're missing the best part.*

He rushes the snake's body up the wavering bark, looping around and dislodging a plump fruit from its branch, clamping it within a coiled grasp and weaving toward the woman. "Open your teethhh," he urges. "Pressss this in and taste itsss sssweetness. Only then will you undersssstand."

Please, Nox begs from mere yards away, digging his hooves into the ground and pressing his back against the rough woodgrain. *Please, don't leave me alone with this. I can't be the only one who understands this feeling.*

The woman's eyes glisten with trust, and Nox basks in the expression. As she takes the fruit from the snake's grasp, he can actually feel her fingertips slide over its soft scales. On the other side of the trees, his lower lip pulls between his teeth as he bites down, trying to stifle the moan that threatens to escape him. The look of her mouth wrapping over the curve of knowledge sends a pulse through him. Her throat flexes into a swallow, making him tremble as he pleads with her silently.

Know this. Feel this. Touch it, taste it, want it. Want it just as badly as I do.

With half-lidded eyes, the woman's pupils dilate, and she looks at the world anew. Nox swears he can even feel the sweet caress of her eyes as they slip over the snake's lithe body. He drops its coils over her neck, slithering down...but taking his time. The daughter of Eden revels in the feeling and tips her head back with a sigh as Nox winds toward the ground, flicking that silken tongue and nudging his way scale by soft scale over the most sensitive parts of her. The fruit having opened his mind, Nox can actually feel her, experiencing her pleasure the way he does his own, and it doubles his need for touch.

"What is this feeling?" she asks, her voice an alluring whisper.

It's not love. Not love at all. It's...

"Lussst," the snake hisses the word like the blessing it is.

Sliding down in his hiding place, Nox goes to his rump, mouth slack as his breath comes in pants. Closer than she should be, the human follows suit, and Nox senses the snake's body happen upon a new sort of wetness between her legs as it slips to the deep grass. He winds by it, not knowing what it is, but wishing he could linger. Maybe that would taste sweet, as well.

"Eve?" a voice calls out from afar, jarring Nox out of his reverie.

The male.

Nox quickly wriggles the snake's body away, pulling it back to see what happens now. He is fascinated. Insatiable. He's always loved the humans, and now one of them shares this special gift with him.

The woman mumbles her pair's name so low he can't hear it. Nox didn't know humans had names. He didn't even know they could talk until today. His adoration for them compounds; they're more like him now than ever before. Still, he hides behind the snake's eyes, afraid to come near. Afraid to ruin, like Atua said he would.

The male kneels down beside the woman, all adorable grins. His body looks similar to Nox's stretched out form—angular hips, ridges in the muscle, and a broadened chest. The female, Eve, stares at her soul-mate, licking her lips.

"Touch me," she says. "Please touch me."

Her other half smiles at her, filled with love, and pets her cheek, pressing a kiss to her forehead for good measure. She looks confused, unable to articulate that it's not what she had wanted.

There aren't enough words for them yet. In an eternal garden of good-ness, they haven't learned the blue word of 'wrong.'

Nox's eyes slam shut, knowing he doesn't want them to learn.

"More, please," is what she says instead, and it's the perfect ask. She takes her pair's hand and lays it on her rounded chest, parting her lips and sighing at the touch.

The male dips in for a hug, wrapping his arms around and snuggling into her familiar curves with a giggle. An innocent, sweet, Nal-like giggle. "Of course," he tells her, because they've done this since time immemorial.

"I need you to understand," she says. Pushing him back slightly, she holds the bitten fruit up to the male's face. "Put your mouth on this. Kiss it. Touch it with your tongue..."

Those words. Oh, those beautiful, perfect, *lustful* words.

Her other half obeys without question, suckling as if by instinct. The same way Nox knew how to get the fruit into his belly.

The minute the male understands, his body trembles. His eyes close and he lets out a guttural grunt as Eve slips her fingers through his knotted hair and over his cheek. Nox can feel it in the ties that bind the universe: the male wants to devour her the same way he does. Breathe her in like air. Taste her like the sweet juice that still drips down her arm.

When their bodies connect, Nox hisses in their pleasure. They kiss —but not the way the male had kissed Eve before he had eaten. Now, the caress of their lips is filled with something else.

Desire.

Curving his back, Nox dares to look with his own eyes at the humans he's given this gift to. Their body position makes no sense now —but it also does. Like puzzle pieces fitting together. How did he not see it before? He'd created many creatures the way that Atua had, designing these areas to connect. When the male arches his back before pressing inward, the beautiful Eve cries out, making another color shine from Nox's soul.

Violet. A blinding, needy amethyst that bathes the couple in light they don't see, lost in their own moment.

But this is not lust.

Every now and then, they peek at one another and press their mouths close. They pet and caress and whisper wondrous words. Nox remembers love and this is it, but expanded, grown, improved.

And he is proud.

For a moment, he wishes to join them. To be accepted into their gasping dance of bodies. But their love is not meant for him. It's theirs alone. Precious. Special. Sacred.

I'm not ruining anything, he tells his Creator, not knowing whether or not It's listening. *I'm making it better. I'm creating a love you couldn't imagine because you have no body. You have no pair.*

Sorrowful blue threads through the purple glow in his heart, deep and dark as his eyes fill with tears.

I want my pair. I want her body to be like the woman's, and I want to hold her like that. I want to make her feel my love inside her.

And that would lead to DESTRUCTION!

Atua's words tear into Nox like a whirlwind, Eve and her mate jumping away from one another in shock and...*shame*. Another blue feeling.

One YOU gave them! Atua bellows into Nox's mind.

The ground trembles, but Nox isn't doing it. The white tree withers and shrivels, both humans screaming and lunging away from it in fear.
They feel *fear!*
No, no, no! Nox cries out to his Maker.

It's as I said, my child, this is your fate. This is the beginning of the end.

Ropes of tree roots whip out of the ground, lashing at nothing and spraying dirt into the air. The humans hold each other, cowering, their love still obvious as they try to protect one another from the devastation that begins raining from the sky...though rain isn't quite the right word.
Chunks of cold, hardened water—*hail*—fall in stinging shards as the wind whips. Clouds form dark triangles in the sky that touch down and sip from the earth, tearing at plant life and rending the land. Trees are sucked up into the vortices as animals bound away, howling. Birds scatter and screech, getting spun up and spit out somewhere Nox can't see.
His heart flickers red once more as he dives toward the cowering couple, screaming, "Run!" before darting near enough to yank one by the arm and drag them, the weight telling him they are pulling one another along. He has to get the humans out of the forest. They have to get out of Atua's...*wrath*. The new word thunders in Nox's mind as Atua's destruction booms all around them. He yanks and dodges, not looking back as his beloved humans cry out in terror.
I'm sorry, he thinks, scraping tears from his eyes as he bolts away from the dangers raining down from the sky. *I'm so sorry.*

NEVER, Atua howls. *NEVER ARE YOU TO STEP INTO MY GARDEN AGAIN. YOU HAVE EATEN THE*

FORBIDDEN FRUIT. YOU HAVE DISOBEYED MY WILL. YOU ARE IMPURE!

He hates that word. Oh, how Nox hates that word. "It's not their fault!" he yells, veering to the side just in time to avoid a heavy oak cascading to the ground in a thicket of skin-stabbing twigs and branches.

IT MATTERS NOT.

Nox stops trying to reason with his Creator, just as the humans have given up their crying. They follow him blindly toward sanctuary. Toward salvation.

I'll protect you, Nox's mind pounds, dragging them through horror after horror. Nothing is supposed to die, but things do break. And the world is breaking all around him.

The group clears the woods but doesn't stop, dodging cracks appearing in the grassy plain as the valley rumbles. Nox has to get them to his cave. Somehow that cave means safety; he can feel it in his heart. He just has to get them there.

My fault, my fault, MY FAULT!

He didn't mean it, but it doesn't matter. This lovely forest, the perfect tree, the fruit of pleasure, the animals, the humans, the plants— they are all suffering. If only he'd stayed away. He promised he'd stay away. But he didn't.

He is *selfish.*

And that's when Nox realizes... Nal won't be the first one to hate him. Because he already hates himself.

Chapter 3

~THE FIRST DEATH~

That all-encompassing sadness tried to come back; it really did. After the garden tore itself into pieces at the whim of his Creator, Nox fell into a predictable sorrow, nestling among his grass and letting it grow over him, hiding from anything and everything. He'd given the humans his cave, sacrificing his ability to retreat so they could take shelter. It was the least he could do after destroying their world.

His hunger raged. That urge to be filled was a rumble that bothered him incessantly, even though there was no fruit left to devour. Perhaps it didn't matter. All the changes the fruit had bestowed upon him happened in those first few moments anyway, waking up his body and making his intelligence skyrocket. All Nox learns now, he intuits with his newly open mind.

The tree didn't teach as Atua did. Instead, it destroyed the walls Nox had built around what he thought was possible. Many things were possible. Things he would have never dreamed before.

Like the fact that the humans loved him. Even knowing he was the reason for everything, they didn't blame him. They weren't angry. He understood that feeling. After all, he still loved Atua despite enduring Its constant torture.

After the humans were safe in his cave, Nox had hidden at first, ashamed of the destruction he'd brought. Some immeasurable time cascaded by before Eve found him in a mound of grass that shone blue with the light of his heart. It peeked out from between the braided thatch like a beacon in the dark, unintentionally calling her near. Her mate had come, too, and together they rested their cheeks on him, thanking him for saving them. For expanding their love. For giving them something they decided to call *babies*. That was what finally brought Nox out of hiding.

Eve's belly was rounder than even her breasts and looked heavy. How her eyes had shone with joy when she took Nox's hands and rested them over her, letting him feel the twirl of life inside. Atua may have taken their home from them, but It had given them the ability to create in its place. To *make*. And based on the frolicking and rutting from all else that lived, the humans weren't the only ones. It wasn't the same way Nox made life, but it was life, nonetheless.

Adam, Nox learned, was so proud he could barely stand it, and pulled Nox into a surprising hug so rough and filled with laughter that even Nox smiled. Then grinned. Then rejoiced alongside his beloved humans.

In gratitude, Eve helped with his horns, which had grown unwieldy, snapping off excess branches while Adam helped file down the pointy edges. For the first time in a long time, Nox's leg jittered and tamped on the ground, making them all giggle, just like Nal used to do. It brought a spark of gold back into his heart—forever laced with blue, tinged with flourishes of purple now and again, but with a center that hoped for more.

Even now, he thinks of his Nal. So many things remind him of her, after all. Like when he sits stock-still and her birds land on his newly sleek horns. Her blue butterflies, too. Perhaps, through them, he is feeling her love.

I'm sorry, Nox tells Atua again. *I never meant for anything like this to happen. I wanted them to live in happiness forever...but if you won't give them shelter, then I will. I'll keep them safe. I'll nurture their love. I'll adore their babies.*

Babies who appear in droves; adorable little things, birthing of all kinds. Some hard, some easy, but all the offspring are lovely, teeny-tiny versions of their parents, and Adam and Eve's twins are the most delightful of all. Their pudgy, soft bodies remind Nox of the way he used to look. And, of course, they remind him of his Nal.

If this is sin, why is sin so beautiful?

Still, there are times when he retreats from the world, hiding his sorrow from his adopted family to ensure they don't learn his blue words. They never understand why he goes away, but they also don't ask. When he comes, they cherish him, and when he leaves, they miss him. It's more than he could ever ask for; love for a broken thing like him.

* * *

The rumble is uncontrollable, but Nox tries to hide it, like he does many, many things.

"Does it hurt?" Cain asks, nuzzling into Nox's fur. Abel gives it a tug with his little fist and snickers as it comes out in patches. *Shedding,* Nox has decided. During the hottest months, all furry creatures shed— and it's pretty funny.

"No, little one, it doesn't hurt." He smiles down at Cain while Abel persists, still pulling.

"Your fur is all loose," he reports, looking at it all too seriously.

"Loose-y-fur," Cain agrees, yanking at it himself.

These children are precious.

Nox stands up and lets the twins roll off him with quiet "oof"s. He's so much bigger now. Broader. Taller. Even taller than Adam, though not as tall as many of his original creations. Nox and the boys hear a sonorous groan as one such creation steps overhead, its scaled, taloned feet landing in thuds as it treads around them easily, its long neck lifting and cutting through the clouds.

"Don't step on us," Nox calls out. Not that it ever would. Still, it indulges him with another grumbling roar, and he's satisfied...until his tummy echoes the sound.

Cain runs around his legs in circles. "Mine does that, too, you know."

"But quieter," Nox counters.

Patting his own stomach, Abel looks up. "Loud enough."

As if to prove his point, all three of them grimace as a gurgling wave runs through them simultaneously, a sound that would be hilarious if it didn't come with such discomfort. It seems to hit Nox harder than it does the children though. Harder than anyone, really. Another punishment from his Creator.

It's time to pull back again, he thinks, that blue light inside him flickering with the hurt of his belly. Nox smiles at the children as a warren of bunnies begin a familiar hopping dance around the trio. He bends down and caresses their cheeks. "I'm going away now."

The "no, no, no"s that greet him warm his heart.

"Yes, yes, yes," he says, indulgently pressing little kisses to their foreheads.

"How big do you think we'll be by the time you get back?" Cain tugs out some of his fur again, which is more pleasant than not.

"Big," is all Nox says. He scruffles their hair, getting them to let out little squeals before he starts to make his way in elegant steps. "Tell your parents, will you?"

Eve and Adam seem to miss him the most of all when he goes, though the children aren't far behind in their fondness for him. Their upcoming brothers and sisters will feel the same, Nox supposes, once they arrive.

The twins make a big show of tangling around his ankles in protest but let him go easily enough. They all know how this works.

But he'll be back. He can never seem to stay away.

* * *

Nox is panting, lying in the grass as the window to his soul bleeds the color blue, running down his chest like tears, his stomach cramping as he salivates.

It was so sweet, he remembers, trying to comfort himself by remembering the one and only moment he had eaten, though this compulsion to fill himself has existed for much, much longer. *It was sweet and cool and wet in my mouth, and when I swallowed it, I wanted more.*

He's sweating now, curled into himself while his center screams. His senses are on overload, that beautiful, delicious, cursed fruit making every part of him needy.

He gasps in the scent of the earth, burying his face in the grass and sending prayers to his Maker, even though It never listens.

Please make it stop. Please, I need you to make it stop.

When he next opens his mouth to take a gulp of air, a tendril of grass sways too close with the movement of his breath. The fresh, green blade comes near enough to touch his taste buds, and when it does, Nox's pupils blow wide. Rearing back at the unexpected sensation, he gazes at the soft grass beneath his heavy palms, now reflecting back a bit of his now-purple glow.

He knows what purple means. Desire. The need to devour.

Delicately, Nox reaches down and breathes in, a different place in his mind opening in wait for what comes next. It's then that he laps at the sharp-yet-soft texture, feeling it against his tongue and wanting it.

As he'd done once before, blinded by his need, Nox opens wide and bites down, tearing himself back with a mouthful of something. He chews as if it's pleasure itself and swallows the tang even as the grasses' emotion screams out in pain. In this moment, Nox doesn't think it matters. In this moment, all that exists is the need to end this agony in his belly. The need to feed this insatiable monster that wounds him from within. And so, he buries his face in the plants he adores, snapping and clamping his teeth down, ripping and shredding, his mouth bursting with flavor and perfection.

Pulling back to his haunches, Nox stares up at the stars, taking in the universe as his jaw works in slow motion, savoring every bite. The animals around him are following his example now, dipping their snouts to the ground and rending apart ferns and leaves, mashing and smashing. Looking at them, Nox realizes that they also hunger—just like him, just like the humans. The grass is weeping, but he can't find it in himself to care, choosing instead to revel in his stomach quieting after all this time.

Grass is a network. Trees make leaves endlessly. And that's why this doesn't matter, he justifies in his head. *Now they share in the pain we've all felt up until now. Fairness. Equality. It may be broken, but nothing ever dies.*

But he is wrong and he knows it, because someday Nal will die, and it will be his fault.

Nox shakes his head rapidly, breaking out of his unfortunate thoughts and watching the beasts of the earth devour something that loves him. It's then that one of Nox's creations, a sleek raptor with dusky, smooth scales over its muscular body, pulls away from the grass with a grunt of displeasure. It looks up at Nox in curiosity before turning its eyes to a trim creature beside it. One of the two hananja. Made of silken fur, white like the wide moon, its four legs are positioned primly on the ground as it stares at them all. The male and female pair have yet to mate or make offspring, as if Atua Itself had told them to reject such behavior, just as they now reject the notion to eat. Out of all the animals, they are the ones who have always seemed the closest to their Creator, ones without sin, a fact that is not lost on the others.

A look comes over Nox's fanged creation then. An expression of that...purple feeling.

No! Nox barely has time to think it. *No, don't!*

But it's too late. His scaled beast lets out a terrifying snarl and dives at the holy, singular male. It's only moments before the raptor's other half follows suit, going for the female, right for her soft, pale throat.

There is a squeal, a scuffle, and all the other animals watch in rapt attention, trying to understand what this writhing violence means. But Nox already knows. His creature...eats *meat.*

After one last, heart-wrenching yelp, the hananja go down in heaps, silence giving way to growling and gulping as the raptors rip through the white beasts' fur with wet, smacking sounds. The squelching of flesh between teeth is all Nox can hear as the acrid scent of iron cloys the air around them.

So, there is death, after all. More than just for Nal.

It's real, tangible, and undeniable. These ravenous beasts have destroyed a set of creatures made by Atua, Itself. A pair with no children. Their existence, their breed, their future is gone.

And my creatures were the ones that did it, Nox marvels, locked in both elation and disgust, satisfaction and pain, everything a sensation he can't help but accept into his body without resistance. Standing, he approaches the feast slowly. His animals part for him in deference, letting him see the insides they've spilled—the same as he's built into other forms with such care, following Atua's perfect design. Red stains everything, and yet Nox's heart is still drenched in the purple of wanting. Nearly hypnotized, Nox lowers to his knees, tips forward, and begins to eat, ending that wrench of agony in his stomach once and for all.

It's only then that the true slaughter begins.

It seems many of Nox's creatures eat meat.

* * *

The truth of it is clear. Meat-eaters nourish themselves with the flesh of their prey, ensuring overpopulation never occurs. Leaf-eaters cut back the overgrowth of flora, making it so all of existence doesn't get overtaken with green weeds, giving Nox's more sensitive flowers the ability to thrive.

His brain, with its new, unfettered power of knowledge, rationalizes all of it. More than anything else Nox has done, this seems like the will of Atua. It had given Its creations the ability to *make,* after all. The world would have been overrun if not for the balance that Nox has brought.

His hunger has never returned. He's passed that sensation on to the others, it seems. He's not sure if he feels the proper amount of anguish over it, or if there is a proper amount. There is violence in this new life, and there is pain...but somehow, both bring pleasure to his body. And pride.

Of all the unexpected things to learn, it appears that death can be a relief at times. Wounds scream, sometimes without end, festering and frothing and fever-inducing. But death can be merciful, melting away into gifts of nourishment, creating new life in its place. A perfect circle.

It's only when he ruminates on death that Nox remembers his beloved humans with their darling children. The ones who look so much like Nal.

Dread seeps in.

They have no fangs. They have no claws. Their skin is soft. They have nothing to keep them safe. Will they be gone forever, just like the hananja?

He tears holes in the ground from how hard and fast he runs.

Don't let it be too late. Please, oh please, don't let it be too late. Not them, never them. Don't take them away! I need them!

It's that fear of being alone that brings his familiar tears. He doesn't bother wiping them this time. Instead, he lets the salty drops water the grass that no longer blooms at his touch, acknowledging this, too, as an acceptable sacrifice for the balance he has wrought.

* * *

The humans have not been helpless. They have made something new. Something...*not* alive. Something they have named themselves. It shimmers like the sun at the mouth of the cave, keeping them warm and warding off all that would do them harm. Adam calls it *fire*.

Grinning, the beloved man pulls Nox into a deep hug, that beguiling innocence still lighting up his eyes.

"You're back!" Eve calls, beckoning Nox over. "Look what happened while you were away," she says proudly. A set of toddlers grab at her legs while two new little ones latch onto her breasts in a confusing way. She giggles at Nox's puzzled reaction. "They're feeding."

To say that Nox is perplexed doesn't even describe it. Eve is providing neither meat nor greenery. He doesn't understand.

Guessing at his question, the male answers, "We call it milk. White water. Sweet...though there only seems to be enough for the babies.

Everything eats now." Adam grins at him, gesturing to the fire. Meat is spiked through with sticks and suspended over the glow, turning golden as it's licked by the crackle of the flames around it.

"How did you do this?" Nox asks. Humans have no means of attack, yet it's obvious this meat came from something big.

Adam holds up a thick pole with a shard of rock lashed to it. He tips his eyebrow up with a look that's...*smug*.

"Weapon," the male explains, making a sharp motion toward the fire.

Nox's jaw drops open. How ingenious. The tree must have removed the humans' barrier of what's possible, too. It makes complete sense.

"YOU'RE BACK!" A call from behind startles him as he's bombarded by two much-bigger boys, knocking him to the ground with an *oof* and a laugh. Who knew he was still capable of laughing? The twins sit on the floor with him, grinning with deep dimples, each babbling on about so much at once, he can't take in all the chatter. Their blathering soon devolves into hysteria as Nox tickles them, only stopping once both are breathless enough to speak one at a time.

"We hunt, too!" Abel reports, also smug, just like his father.

"He's better at it than I am," Cain adds, though it only makes his brother lie down on him dramatically.

"You know it's only because Atua helps me," Abel says, splayed atop Cain's body.

Nox's eyes go wide. "It does what?" The surprises keep coming today.

It's Adam's turn to hang on Nox's broad shoulders, that familiar pride washing through him as Nox feels the human's emotions. "It talks to us again."

"It *loves* us again," Eve corrects, jostling the newest little ones against her.

Nox's heart flickers again with that golden core. *Then perhaps there's hope for me. Maybe I'll be loved again, too...*

Cain bites his lip and looks away, making a blue kind of face. Nox looks at him and swipes back the boy's hair in a silent question.

"But...not me," Cain confesses quietly.

"Not *yet*," Abel says, squashing his brother under his body weight again. "But it's okay. It will someday. You just have to get unbroken first."

Nox's heart goes cold.

"Do you know how to make something unbroken, Nox?" Cain looks at him, not understanding the impact of the terrible question he's asking.

"Yeah," Abel chimes in. "Loosey-fur knows everything." He grins at Nox with adoration. "Atua loved him first, after all."

Nox can't speak. There are no words—or if there are, they're so caught in his throat they can't come out. Before them all, and for the very first time, Nox cannot hide the blinding blue of his heart, and there isn't enough time to get away.

Something miraculous happens, though. When his lips tremble and his tears fall, the humans only press closer, wrapping their arms around him and peppering his skin with their soothing kisses. Nox wants to run, but he also doesn't. The grass doesn't love him anymore, but his humans still do. He'll keep them safe, as always, but maybe they can keep him safe, too.

He needs them.

He needs them to love him.

* * *

Cain remains broken, and Abel is the new favorite of Atua. He can now perform some of the same powerful feats that Nox can (though never quite as well). But no matter how much time Nox spends teaching the twins, Cain can't do it. He simply isn't connected to the universe in that way. Neither are his parents, though they are at least still graced with the voice of Atua—a voice Nox no longer hears and Cain never heard in the first place.

The family wants them to know their Creator's precious guidance, so they relay Its messages endlessly. It makes Nox both golden and blue at the same time, though ultimately sorrow wins out, reminding him that he is constantly rejected by something that he deeply, obsessively, wants in his life. At first, it only made Nox feel his familiar sadness, but every once in a while, he gets temporary flares of that red feeling in his heart. Something new has started, as well...and it lingers. Stays. Haunts.

Green.

Atua had felt like the color green once. Nox feels it most when Abel closes his eyes, tips his head to the side, and smiles while having some perfect internal conversation with Nox's Creator...even though Nox came first. Nox was perfection *first*. Atua loved Nox *FIRST!*

When he feels this feeling, his lips curl in a snarl that matches his animals in ferocity, and the color red flashes. Every time it comes, Nox makes himself walk away. Most times he just turns blue again, but sometimes he doesn't. Sometimes he turns that sickly green.

Jealous. Envious. Covetous.

Resentful.

Yet Cain never feels that way. All Abel's successes only make Cain happy for his brother. It makes their parents happy, too, for they seem incapable of jealousy. They hold steady, bolstered by the eons of their past where they had been perfect and pure before Nox tore Eden down.

No, he reminds himself. *Before* Atua *tore Eden down.*

Still, they've passed that peace, love, and tranquility to their children. Even to the one who is broken like Nox.

* * *

Watching Atua's sweet Abel meditate in the field, Nox hides in the shadows with narrowed eyes. Eve's first son has his legs crossed with perfect form, and a slight smile lives on his face.

It's not his fault, Nox reminds himself as the boy ages—a man now, like his father. *Anyone would talk to Atua if given the chance. He doesn't mean to hurt me. He doesn't understand.*

And that's the crux of it. Nox wasn't the only one who ate from the tree of knowledge, yet his heart is the only one that expanded into these unknown territories, these poisonous feelings.

Watching in silence, Nox sees Abel control the earth with ease, asking for its obedience with a lift of his hand, just like Nox had once taught him. The element obeys without question, and Nox can feel its love for the young man flutter in the ether. Yet another thing that now prefers Abel to him.

It's not his fault, Nox repeats, his green emotion casting a terrible glow all around him. He needs to leave again. And soon.

Hearing the rustling of the field, he sees Cain walking nearer. He, too, stops to stare at his brother, though he only chuckles at his excellence.

How can you feel so calm? Nox throws the thought at the broken twin. *How can you not covet what you could have had? What was withheld from you?*

Covering the acid color of his soul with his palm, Nox leans against the tree as the red starts to seep in. *You don't feel this greedy feeling because nothing was taken from you. You didn't have it and then lose it. You are ignorant, my hollow friend, and that's why you can't be blamed. But him...*

Nox's fingers clench, digging his nails in as that flame-color flickers in a hot, sick, unbidden threat. *Abel rubs our noses in it. He doesn't think of us in our plight. He is selfish.*

And so am I, Nox realizes. *I want what he has. I want to be him. If he was gone, would I get to take his place?*

But no. Even now, he knows Atua wouldn't let him.

Anger takes over his chest. Such sorrowful, jealous, painful anger.

Why can't it be me?

It's a thought—just a thought. As fleeting as a flicker of Nal's lightning. And yet...

Cain's scream rends the air, a deep heavy bellow, shocking Nox to attention alongside his meditating brother. Pushing away from the shadows that hide him, Nox tries to move forward, but he's too stunned by what he sees.

Cain is not an animal.

Cain does not want to devour his brother.

Cain has no claws or teeth.

But he does have a weapon.

"I hate you!" the man hollers, slamming heavy fists against his brother, splattering red on the ground. Like Nox's red.

"You have everything! Why were you chosen? What's so special about *you!?*" Cain roars, grasping his pointed stick and lifting it high over his head while his brother coughs up wet things. When the pike spears down into Abel's chest, Cain's voice breaks. "Why can't it be me?"

Nox is locked in place. He can't move. He can barely see. His mind is flooded with images of the little boy who'd tugged his fur and who he'd taught to use the power of Atua. No matter how jealous or angry, he had loved that boy. Dearly. Truly.

And now he's gone.

That's not what Nox wanted. Never.

Nox drops, letting out a wail that shakes the world, and it has a heavy echo to match. Cain's echo. Looking up, he sees the man pulling his twin into his arms and crying out, holding him close and shaking him, begging his brother to open his eyes. To please come back. That he's sorry and he didn't mean it.

When the horrified Cain finally looks up at Nox, he asks a timid, "Why?"

Shaking his head, Nox doesn't understand.

"Why did you make me do this?" the young man asks, voice crumbling into pieces as he realizes he can never take back what has happened...and knowing somehow that those poison feelings were not his own.

Murder. The word worms its way into Nox's mind and undulates there, a new color completely dominating his heart. Black.

When he hears Eve's scream from afar, he knows he can't do this. Whatever comes now, he wants no part of it. Rearing up, Nox gallops far and fast. Despite his Creator's abandonment, he's able to use the wings of the wind to launch himself ever forward, far and away.

It was me. There is no denying it. They feel what I feel. If I lust, so do they. If I hunger and eat, I'm not alone in the sin of it. And if I feel jealousy and rage, I defile them as well.

He can't breathe. Again, Nox admonishes himself for his inability to stay away. His mind spirals for ways to be free of this curse; if things can die, maybe he can die, too. He could make it happen. There has to be some way.

And that's when he hears her.

"Nox?!"

His heart shreds anew. Her giggle simultaneously melts him and pours lead into the pit of his stomach.

No, he begs. *Please, no.*

But Nox never gets what he wants.

Her flutter is achingly familiar, no matter how much time has passed. Her excitement would have been infectious—even a day earlier and he would have dived in and kissed every piece of her that he could reach—but now? Now, Nox wants to become invisible. Become nothing. Disappear. End.

Nal's awed sounds make him wince as she flaps behind him, kicking up a breeze on his shoulders.

"Look at you," she marvels, making him cringe over his deformed body—his too wide, too strong, too thick body. "You're beautiful," she whispers.

He lets out a sob. Covering his face, he hides from what he loves most of all, refusing to look and see if she's changed—if her body is like Eve's now, just like his is so much like Adam's. He doesn't want to know. He wants to dig into the ground, but it doesn't obey him anymore, not unless he forces it, and he never wants Nal to see him do that—rend and tear what was once his.

And Abel's...

Poor, dear Abel...

Her hands are in Nox's hair. Gentle, cherubic fingers flow through his tresses and drag across his ears before Nal presses herself against his chest. Her heart's glow lights up his vision even behind clenched eyelids.

"I missed you," she chants over and over, as if they're the only words she knows...though her tone isn't blue. It's filled with such golden happiness. "I missed you so much."

Her tiny kisses fall on him like absolution, but it's only because she doesn't know what he's done—and he's not sure he cares. He doesn't want her to know. He wants to forget everything and stay in this dreamed-about moment. With his large hands, eyes still closed tight, he reaches up to try to hold her...but he can't. Between her tail, wings, and sharp talons, he can't wrap his arms around her. Atua made it so he could never hold her, even from the very beginning.

Sensing his intention, she swirls around him with a giggle and tugs at his horns before wrapping herself over his back, her tail feathers spreading over his rear and against the backs of his calves, all the way down to his hooves. He's only just tall enough for this, and it's a gift.

He lets his Nal hold him, echoing her words back to her, but stuttering and broken with the pain of loss. "I missed you, I missed you, I missed you," he repeats, hot tears falling over her small arms as they clasp around him. She pets his chest and slides her palm to hide the purple-blue ache of his heart. His words morph into concepts she doesn't understand. Things like, "I'm sorry" and "I didn't mean it" and "Don't hate me."

Hushing him with nothing but sweetness, his other half blesses him. "I love you, Nox. I love you so much. I know what you're doing is a journey. Atua told me that you are helping to enact Its plan, and I adore you for it."

He whimpers at her words, melting into harsh trembles. He hates Atua's plan. He hates being broken.

"You've changed the face of love, Nox. You've changed the path of life. Like the rain, it comes and goes now." She nuzzles the nape of his neck in all her innocence and glory. "That makes it precious. That makes it all the more momentous. When the rain comes, it's like everything else stops to witness its finite beauty. It's so much more precious *because* it's finite. The lives of all creatures now burn so brightly because they cannot go on forever."

Her touches make him lean back onto her, feeling the twine of her hair tie run over his long ears. She still wears the gift he gave her, even now.

"Can you love me like the humans do, Nal?" he asks. "Can you stretch and curve and grow? Can we make things in a new way with our bodies?" He swallows roughly, his eyes cinched. "Can we die, too?"

I can't live forever like this. I can't feel this until the end of time.

"Silly," she chuckles against him. "You and I are eternal. And you're so special, Nox. Out of the two of us, only you get to stretch and grow."

He can feel her smile against him, yet he still hasn't laid eyes on her. "Do you ever feel alone, Nal?"

"Never," she reassures. "Because I have your star in my sky." His wavering lips tug into the tiniest of smiles.

She lifts up from his shoulders in a small jerk, as if listening to something. Her laughter is clear, but he's still ruined when she says, "Atua is calling me home." She tousles his hair. "Come with me."

But her motions slow and her voice softens. "He...he can't come back?" Atua has spoken to her; of that, Nox has no doubt. "But..." Her voice trails off. There's something wrong with it. He finally opens his eyes to the sight of her golden light dimming darker and darker.

No! he screams at himself. *She can't learn the blue words! Don't let her learn them!*

He whips around and grasps at her tiny little hips, beseeching her even as she stares at the sky with her eyebrows knit together. That expression is how it started for him.

No, no, NO!

Can he tell her something that isn't real? Do words exist that are fake? Can he make...*lies?*

"I can't come home yet, silly," he repeats her endearment, rocking her back and forth, drawing her beautiful hazel eyes down at him as her wings move in rhythmic perfection. "I'm doing Atua's work, right?"

She cocks her head to the side, staring at him with a dimming heart. He *tsks* and peers through his swollen eyes. "You love Atua, don't you?" he asks.

She snorts her amusement at the rhetorical question.

"And you trust Atua?" he prompts.

Because I don't. Not anymore.

"Yup," she answers, that little smile returning to her gorgeous face as her heart begins glowing brighter again.

Good, he tells himself. *Now say false things. Keep her strong. Keep her in Atua's good graces.*

"Me too," he croons in sweet tones. "That's why I'm here. Besides, if we live forever, then this journey isn't so long, is it?"

She fiddles with her fingers.

"And you still have my star in the sky, don't you?"

She smiles shyly.

His voice softens to a longing whisper, "And you know I love you, right?"

She grins in earnest then. Kissing him chastely and nuzzling her nose against his, she agrees, tugging his horns, which have grown again into branches. How long has he been running? He always seems to lose track of time.

"Okay. I'll go home," she concedes. With one last adorable smile, she tells him, "But I'll visit you again."

He both needs and dreads it.

She adds, "And I'll wait for you forever."

It nearly crushes him because he knows now, deep within, that he's never coming home. Still, he tells her pretty lies. "You won't have to wait long, I promise. I'll be there as soon as I'm done." His voice drops to a whisper. "And you know I'm always thinking about you, right?"

That, at least, is the utter truth.

"Because I'm your other half." She twirls around him in satisfaction.

"Absolutely. Forever and ever. Until the end of time." He burns the sight of her into his mind, needing every minute of the memory to pore over once he pulls back into solitude.

Swooping close one last time, her tiny thumb slides over his heart—his colorful shame—but she smiles up at him. "This is beautiful, too. I love it. I love you."

Stealing one more kiss, the top of his head this time, she turns her tail and flaps his face playfully before darting away. He watches her go, every moment of her motion, even after she's long out of sight. Is it nights? Weeks? Years? His fingers caress the vortex of emotion in his chest—tainted, like him—swirling with that new, deep, self-loathing blackness.

But Nal said it was beautiful.

She's wrong, he states, knowing the truth. *And yet I love her all the more for it.*

His tears come again, but they're detached. He cries them but doesn't feel them. He hurts, yet he is also numb. If his emotions are what makes everything change, then he just has to control himself. He has to lift his mind above his feelings, though even now he knows it's impossible. That's not how he, or anything, was made—and at that realization, the gaping hole in his chest opens wider.

He needs to hide in a new way, then. He needs to block his emotion from reaching the world. Lifting a hand up, he reaches back into the thicket of his horns, tugging and snapping off branches, reveling in the grounding sensation of his own pain. Then, using his disgusting, Atua-given power, he grows the dead branches in his hands, weaving them into each other, moss flourishing in patches within the cracks.

A mask. Something to hide behind.

Pulling the cold seed of reality down into the pit of his stomach, Nox dons his veil of broken things. Made not of the earth, but of pieces of his ruined self. It stings as the sharp edges pull into his flesh, but he's earned it. He deserves it.

It covers the ridges of his brow and the flesh of his cheeks, leaving only his eyes and mouth uncovered as Cain's words scream in a never-ending echo. "Why did you make me do this?!"

Abel is dead, and Cain is more broken now than he ever was. It's all Nox's fault, every little thing, though he didn't mean it. He never means it...but that doesn't matter. Nothing matters except for the fact that Nal still loves him.

For now.

Nox clenches his jaw, making a terrible, sickening sound as his teeth press together...and slide.

Chapter 4

~DROWNING THE EARTH~

The loam and soil have pulled away from Nox's matted frame, leaving him curled over in a blue-black haze of self-loathing. The only things that haven't rejected him are the cold, jutting rocks of an abandoned quarry and the stagnant collection of rainwater that collects between the cracks. Quartz crystals leave imprints on his dampened skin, but he stopped caring a long time ago. His mask hurts. It digs in, but he'll leave it. There's still a shred of hope that, if he can hide his expressions from the world—facial twists of anger, sorrow, need, and jealousy—then maybe he can someday return to his Nal.

Unbidden tears come again and again, though he still can't feel them. Not really. Instead, he wallows, waiting to either be forgiven or forgotten.

But Nox never gets what he wants.

"Hey!" a voice shouts, so jarring that Nox flinches. Over the lip of the high rock face, Nox can see the silhouette of a human, a stranger, waving a hand and beckoning to him. It must be one of the children.

"Hey!" it waves again, "Hey! Up here!"

Nox considers ignoring it, pretending like he's invisible, making the person think he's just a trick of the eye. But there's no hiding from the child of Eve who cries out to him, cupping its hands over its mouth and getting louder, as if Nox simply isn't listening. The poor thing's voice cracks at the end of a long holler.

"I hear you." Nox answers so weakly, it goes unheard the first time. Clearing his throat, he tries once more, raising up on rickety legs and ensuring the sound is loud enough to carry.

The human...laughs. It *woo-hoos* and jumps in a joyful spin, throwing cheers at the sky. Bewildered, Nox gazes as if unseeing, unsure of what to do next.

"I..." he starts, calling up to where the human stands, letting his rusty voice ricochet off the stone. "I have to stay down here! I'm cursed!"

The human ducks to the cliffside, leaning over the edge with a grin so wide Nox can see it, even as the sun rides the human's shoulders, casting it in shadow.

"Not at all!" it counters, sounding so gleeful that Nox is ashamed. "You're blessed! You're Loosey-fur, right?"

Nox's heart breaks. How many times can it shatter over the course of eternity?

"My name is Nox," he corrects, looking at the ground in sorrow. "Atua named me Nox."

More laughter from above, delighted. How can this human be so happy to have found him? Nox feels the heavy pangs of loneliness, flickering the familiar purple of longing in his heart.

"We've been searching for you for generations!" the child of Eve calls.

"For me?" Nox steps closer, one hoof over the other until he's just under the outcropping where the human peers down. Parting his lips, he starts to form a million questions before landing on a simple, "Why?"

The new angle lights the human's face slightly, revealing a grown male with a smile that can't be beat and hair as black as Eve's. "Because we miss you."

And Nox's mouth ticks up at the corners.

* * *

Walking beside the slender human who swings his arms back and forth, humming, Nox says his name in reverent tones. "Seth?"

"Yup!" Looking at him with squinty, happy eyes, the man skips and whistles—just like Nal's warbling birds—for no reason other than to do it.

Nox's wooden mask drags thorns over his cheeks, dimming his attempted smile. "I remember the first time you whistled. It was the first time anyone had done it. Back when you were just a little one, no bigger than a pup. Back before your brothers..." he trails off, not wanting to ruin this moment so easily.

The human snickers. "That's not me. You're remembering my grandfather. I was named after him. He was always so proud to have figured out the trick to it. You should see how many birds he can copy. How many songs he can make. It's amazing." Seth whistles again, apparently happy to have learned.

"What's a grandfather?" New words. It's been so long without new words, and Nox revels in each one.

Seth *hmms* a little, trying to put a definition together. Pausing in their short trek, they seem to have come upon some items the man left behind, and he collects them with practiced ease. "Adam and Eve gave birth to my grandfather. He loved his sister and gave birth to my mother. My mother loved her cousin and made me."

Nox's smile comes again, broader this time despite the damage his mask does to his face. "So, love still exists?"

The man *pfffts,* waving him off as if he's silly. "Of course, love exists."

Unable to stop himself, Nox asks, "Even for Cain?"

Seth winces, looking up at him with more...*somber* eyes. After a bit of hesitation, he says, "I think about that all the time. My grandfather's sister, Awan, felt pity for Cain. She went with him when he was sent away."

Nox tilts his head to the side. He *goes* away; he is never *sent* away. His lips pull into a frown. "Is pity like love?" he asks.

With a small grunt, Seth hoists the last of his supplies into his arms, and hands some to Nox. "No. Pity is a sad responsibility. It can look like a kind of love or kindness, but it makes no one happy. Not the person doing the pitying, and not the person being pitied, either."

"But...at least Cain isn't alone." Nox lowers his gaze, knowing that being alone is the worst thing there is.

Perhaps Cain was able to make a special kind of bond grow between him and his sister over time. He was such a good boy, after all. Kind. Patient. Someone absolutely worthy of love. I'll bet they became a true pair —soulmates, like their parents. Like Nal and me.

It makes Nox feel a little better to think like that.

"You didn't need to run away, you know." Seth tugs Nox's hand to make him follow along, leading him toward the unknown. "No one blames you. When Great-Grandma Eve saw what happened, she knew that you were very sad about it. She said you always went away when you were sad. She thought you might think it was your fault—"

Because it was.

"—but it wasn't. It was Cain's fault. No one has ever been mad at you. In fact, ever since you left, we've all been looking for signs of you."

Turning over his shoulder toward the harsh quarry he'd spent decades in, Nox asks, "What signs?"

With a mischievous glint in his eyes, Seth turns around and pokes just underneath Nox's blue glow. "That. Your shine. Great-Grandma said that's how they first found you, wrapped up in the grass. She said that if we found a glow, we should follow it." The man turns them back on their way, stepping with purpose. "I started walking as soon as we found your light in the night sky. I promised to be the one to bring you home."

Nox's mask may hide most of his expressions, but it can't hide the awe in his voice. "Home?"

Giggling, Seth confirms, "Home."

There is a pause before Nox asks, "Am I...am I pitied?"

"No. Just loved." That sweet smile stays on the man's handsome face, and he reaches out to take Nox's hand again, leading him toward the horizon.

* * *

Buildings, Nox learns, looking out as Seth points a short way down the valley. Buildings are like caves, evidently, but made on purpose. "Did Atua teach you how to do this?" Nox asks in wonder. *Or was it the fruit?*

Seth shrugs. "Maybe. Atua does talk to some of us. Not all, though."

Turning his horned head as they near the village, Nox asks, "Does it talk to you?"

"No," Seth says, eyes sad, but resigned. "I'm broken."

Nox can't help it when a flash of red taints him, and he covers his heart, begging the feeling to stop. After a moment, he admits, "I'm broken, too."

Seth looks at him in confusion. "But Atua loved you first."

Atua is the one that broke me. Just like It broke Cain. The red glow only grows stronger, and Nox scowls. His hooves dig in and he drops Seth's hand. Shaking his head, his tail tucks close in fear. "I can't come. I can't be with you. This is a bad idea."

"Bad?" Seth questions, not knowing the word.

Nox is about to explain when startling cries ring out in the distance, scores of humans starting to run toward them, glee adorning their lovely faces. Nox hears calls of his new friend's name...alongside his. Overwhelmed, he watches in amazement as they get closer, running as fast as possible—some hand in hand, some grinning, and some even crying, but in a happy sort of way. A few shout *Loosey-fur,* while some whoop *Nox,* and a few precious others call him *The Morning Star*—just like the one that sits in Nal's sky. Better than all these, though, are the ones who call him *Beloved.*

Just before the crowd envelops them both, Seth smiles softly at Nox.

"Don't be afraid. Lots of us are broken now. You don't have to be alone anymore."

Then, Nox is wrapped in the embraces of strangers—*his* strangers. He is the reason humans love like this, after all, so he is the reason they came into being. The throng covers him in adoration, and he finally lets the gold seep from the center of his heart. Calling to Seth over the din, he asks, "Where are Adam and Eve?"

Seth shakes his head. "They died."

And the golden ember is already gone.

* * *

Please speak to me, Nox begs his Creator yet again. *Please tell me why things die without being killed.*

He's on his rump in meditative prayer, small beads of sweat collecting at his temples, the weather now too hot, of all things. It never used to get too hot. Or too cold. So many changes.

Please, he implores, *I need to understand. This kind of death isn't my fault. Or is it? Please, mighty Atua, I want to love You even now, I swear, so please help me understand.*

But there is nothing.

"Nox! Help?" one of Eden's descendants calls over.

Nox breathes in deeply and lets go of his prayer, repeating the vow he's made many times. *If Atua won't love the humans, won't protect them, then I will. I may not have created them, but they are mine now—like my gigantic, scaled beasts, my winged horses, my raptors and their kin. The humans are mine.*

Wasting no more time, Nox rises, forcing a smile on his face. At this point, the mask has dug a groove of scars to allow freer expression, though it still hurts. Enos is waving him over toward the new stone pillar they're raising in order to build a storehouse for items and materials. With everything in one place—pots and timber, thread and tools—it's easier to share back and forth. Nox got a deadly spectrum of emotions, but humans got the power of endless innovation. It's magnificent.

Enos can commune with Atua, but he loves Nox anyway, a sign of hope. The man turns with a grin toward the pillar, lifts his hand to summon the power of their Creator, and makes a lame attempt at lifting the heavy thing they've been honing for months. It shudders, rears up the tiniest bit, and hangs there, trembling. Enos makes a face that looks comical in its stern concentration.

With a cocky grin to match that of the honored Adam, Nox simply twitches his fingers and connects to the universe—the endless web of threads that was never taken away—and rights the stone column as if it were a feather. Several "whoas" turn Nox around.

"We've gained an audience." Enos chuckles, gesturing at a group of children gathered in an enthralled circle. They like to watch those with Atua's power perform what the little ones call *miracles,* and everyone knows that Nox does them best. A group of adults—both with and without the holy gift—gather as well, staring at him with green and blue expressions, wanting that strength for themselves.

Seth sneaks up from behind, clapping Nox on the back and distracting him from the envious onlookers. "Imagine how much good we could do if Atua shared with all of us instead of just a holy few. Together, we could combine our power to heal the sick, bring loved ones back from the dead, multiply our resources...maybe even walk on water!"

The human laughs with a dreamy look on his face and his head in the clouds like always. It makes Nox smirk and correct him with good humor. After all, no one can do such things. Not even Atua, Itself.

* * *

Nox's friendship with Seth is beyond anything he's had with any other human. The man isn't a confidante—no, not quite that—but someone to discuss the workings of the world with. Someone who makes Nox feel less alone in his logical reasoning. Intelligent and intuitive, this human's words snag your mind, and his radical ideas take root in Nox's heart, blooming there for good and for ill.

"Guilt," Seth says, poking a stick in the fire, older and now sporting white curlicues that pepper his otherwise dark temples, "is a tricky thing, I think."

"How so?" Nox lounges beside the warmth, flopping his tail absently, feeling thoughtful. He knows a little something about guilt, though he never talks about it.

His friend sighs, sinking back onto his haunches, grimacing before letting out an aged grump and deciding to take a more comfortable seat on the earthen floor instead, his hip popping a little in the process. "It's more complex than it used to be. Things get less and less simple over time...guilt, especially."

"Guilt is guilt. If you feel it, you did something wrong," Nox says, tipping his masked face closer. His blackening hair cascades over the hay he rests on. The topic is already uncomfortable, as conversations with Seth often are. The man is insightful, but sometimes says things that Nox feels are aimed directly at his secret soul.

A contemplative look comes over Seth's crinkling face. "How can I put this?" he muses. "Imagine I'm in a room with a dog."

Nox likes those. Hounds, particularly.

"And the room has pottery in it."

Which takes days and days of effort, truly. Not only functional, but the newest ones are ornate with decorations of colored sand woven into the clay. Nox nods a bit, picturing the image in his mind.

"Now imagine the dog and I are playing fetch, and the dog breaks the pottery. Lots of it. All of it."

Nox grimaces, thinking of how angry that would make everyone. "So, he's guilty."

Seth's head tips side to side as he considers. "Let's say he is...and that he's punished for it, never allowed to step inside our shelters again. Forever stuck out in the cold and looking in. And maybe it makes me feel bad when I see his little face wishing to be with us in the warmth. In seeing him suffer, I also feel guilty."

"But you shouldn't. It's not your fault."

"Ah, but it might be. What if, while I was playing with him, I was careless when I tossed the stick, making it fly too close to the shelves? He is a dog, after all. He will chase. It's his nature. Should he be blamed for what he does in his innocence?"

Innocence. Nox remembers a time when he was like that. A time before he was broken. Even though, from the beginning, he was always made to be broken.

Seth continues, "Or imagine I roughhoused with him too close to the fragile pieces in the first place. Again, he is a dog, and I am a man. I should have known better, shouldn't I? Does that make it my fault?

"Or what if I wanted the pottery to be broken, and I tricked the dog into doing it so I wouldn't be blamed?"

"No one would do something like that." Nox's lips press together as his eyebrows knit, even though he's not sure he believes his own words. "It had to be an accident."

Seth agrees, leaning back on his hands and looking at the thatched ceiling. "Guilt can be good, I think. It makes you careful not to make the same mistake twice. It's a terrible feeling. It hurts, but maybe it's supposed to. When I place my hand in the fire, I feel pain, so I learn to stop doing it. If I know the dog will be punished and I know my guilt will hurt me for it, I'll be more careful next time. Because of the consequences, because of the pain, I learn."

Dangerous. This topic feels so dangerous. Still, Nox asks, "What happens if you can't feel the pain of someone else's suffering?"

Seth considers, staring at his feet now, scrunching dirt between his toes and digging little lines across the floor. "Then you don't care. If there's no punishment in it for you, no pain of guilt, you don't care that the dog is out in the cold. You don't consider a scenario where you are at fault. You only care that the pots are broken, and the dog did it."

"But...the dog loves the human, doesn't it? It trusts the human to love it back. To be kind. To care," Nox says, quiet and meek, every word hitting too close to home, taking the metaphor too far.

"Then it has been betrayed." Seth just shakes his head. "Poor dog."

Nox sees the parallel so clearly his eyes burn. Atua has no body, no heart, so It doesn't feel the pain of empathy in Its chest. Atua only sees Its intended results being achieved, so It has no guilt. Without guilt, It can be cruel without repercussions. It commits crimes against those who know not what they do, and It doesn't hold Itself accountable for their pain.

So maybe someone else should.

The things that build firm foundations swirl in Nox's brain, myriads of mortar and mud, tainting and solidifying into the shape of a horrible thought.

Maybe that someone should be me.

Smiling with something like pain in his eyes, Seth looks directly at Nox, hard and honest. "You and I, my friend, we may be broken pottery, but somewhere out there is the dog that broke us, and its betraying master is the one that threw the stick." Seth tosses something in the fire, making it crackle. "The question is, does the master feel guilty for the pain it has caused? And, if so, the most important question is whether or not it will learn."

This story, it's a...*parable.* An allegory. Nox is the hound, unwittingly breaking things without meaning to, and Atua is his heartless master throwing the stick. It doesn't feel guilty. It doesn't feel sad. It's not learning or changing. Words echo back and forth in the crimson bloom of Nox's soul.

I've been betrayed.

And there is no unseeing that truth.

* * *

When Seth is dying, Nox can barely stand it. Watching his friend wither is hard—intensely, viscerally hard—but it's when the man's mind begins to break that it becomes almost impossible. Seth's intelligence blunts from scythe to hammer. His whistles and walks give way to bed sores and incontinence. His pride turns into shame and disgust with himself...when he remembers who he is, anyway. In more ways than one, Seth dies long before his body does, and when his husk ends its journey, his family breathes a sigh of relief, because at least their beloved philosopher is finally free of pain.

But Nox doesn't feel that way.

Nox wants his only friend back.

Nox wants him sane, whole, and perfect.

Nox wants him young, spry, and whistling, just like on the day they first met.

Nox feels a rage so deep it chokes him.

For the first time in a long time, he runs away. It's still to hide his emotions from the humans, but this time it's absolutely essential that he do so...because he feels that terrible emotion again, dark and twisted, borne of anger. An evil urge. An *uncontrollable* urge.

Nox wants to kill something.

If his hunger is enough to change the balance of earth, if his jealousy pushes murder into the hearts of the innocent, what would this mindless rampage do?

As he howls his fury, red lightning screeches from the sky in burning licks of fire, matching the incandescent blare of his heart as each bolt ignites the trees in dry bursts, roaring at a volume to rival his own. This is not Nal's lightning; hers only dances in the clouds. This destructive maelstrom is all his.

And he hates it.

"WHY!?" he bellows, stalking around his familiar quarry's edge, rolling his shoulders back and looking at nothing, knowing Atua swirls all around even as It ignores him...just as It ignores all those who are broken. "Even if they have to die, why make them suffer? Why make them fade? Why be so *cruel!?*"

And yet, he's powerless to do anything about it. Nox can't heal the sick. He can't bring people back from the dead. What good is lifting rocks and walking on the wind if he can't save what he loves? Why live forever only to watch everything die?

He senses his other half on the horizon, and his hackles rise in brown bristles. When he hears her voice, it's like a knife slamming under his nails.

"Nox?"

"No!" he screams, baring his teeth and whirling on the ever-absent Nal. "No, you can't just swoop in at the whim of Atua and explain this away like you did last time! You can't rationalize this! How long has it been? How many years!? How much suffering have I endured without your attention? Don't you *dare* give it to me now just because you were *told to!*"

But when he finally glares up to confront her, the words he had spit become shameful, emptying him of anything but regret. His other half blinks at him, wings pumping in the ember-filled sky with a look on her face so blue it twists his stomach.

Guilt. Such horrible, intense guilt. Why can't Atua feel this inescapable thing?

"I'm sorry," he bleats, going to his knees in anguish. "I'm so sorry. I didn't mean it."

Another one of his pretty lies. He'd very much meant it...in the moment, at least. Though now that he's laid eyes on her, it doesn't matter how much time has passed; he'd still bleed for her every word.

She flutters to the ground, standing upright on two clawed feet. He startles as he notices...she severed her tail. Running into his arms, her wings are still unwieldy, but easier to manage when they don't have to keep her aloft. She presses innocent kisses over the colored vortex of confusion inside him; a horrible murk of love, hate, anger, sorrow, want, and desperation he can't pull apart.

Running his hand over the cherubic curve of her back and what's left of her tail feathers, he asks, "Did you do this?"

Her words, her beautiful words are, "I needed to be closer to you."

He all but folds over her, enveloping her body in heavy heat, curling her into his arms like Eve cradled her babies. Nal is crying. His stunning, perfect Nal is crying.

In his anguish he wonders if he could lead her down his path. If she became broken, they could be together. But when he sees the bloody mess of her pin feathers, cut with no regard for her own well-being, he lets the thought go. He doesn't want his Nal to be broken.

"Sweetheart," he murmurs into the twine of her hair. "Never harm yourself. Never, ever. Not for me, not for anyone."

She cuddles against him. "It hurts, Nox." And he aches with her suffering. She must have panicked when he lit up the sky. He's never seen her like this, never wanted her to *feel* like this.

Seth was right. Guilt is good. His lesson is learned.

"I won't act out like that anymore. I won't misuse your creation.

Hush. Oh, my sweet darling, hush," he soothes her, rocking. Any pain he felt is inconsequential now. Atua wouldn't have blessed him with her presence, which means she came here on her own. She saw what he had done, she needed to soothe him, so she came.

Finally.

"I..." she starts—on the cusp of loving him, he just knows it—but then she pulls away and looks into the distance with wet eyes. "Atua is calling me."

Not again. Don't you take her again!

His scowl returns and he clutches her closer, turning her face back toward him. "I'm calling you, Nal. *I am.* You belong to me," he insists, his voice a low, possessive growl.

She pushes back more firmly this time and looks at him with concern. Staring, seeing how he's changed, she tries to reach up to touch his face, but his mask of thorns pricks her, and she takes her tiny fingers away. "I don't belong to you, Nox, I'm a part of you—and it's not the same thing."

You're right. It's even better.

"If you're a part of me, then stay," he tempts, folding her little hand in his. "The humans will mend your tail."

Her lips quirk slightly. "Atua will mend my tail."

Heart throbbing, he slides a thumb over her moist cheek. "I'll make your tears go away."

They drip hot trails over his knuckles. "You brought them," she says. "I'm supposed to leave you to your journey, but I felt your pain, Nox. How could I feel it?"

"...Because I'm a part of you, too," he breathes out the realization.

In the past, I hid from the world to avoid worsening its plight, so Atua did it in my place. Freezing cold. Scorching heat. Age. Today, I disguise my emotions to keep the humans steady in their innocence, and so Atua bonds me so deeply to my pair that she feels me from endless miles away. If I'm not poisoning the humans, Atua makes me do it to her instead, dragging her into my sorrow. Am I supposed to feel nothing at all? Does everything around me need to suffer?

The word betrayal pulses again, but this time, it stings less. Instead, it turns bitter.

"I won't bring your tears anymore. I'll..."—*keep it hidden*—"be good next time."

She smiles, but it's soft and laced with sadness. "You're already perfect."

Am I, though?

Instead, he says, "So are you," and caresses her hair, not wanting to sneak a kiss and risk hurting her with the branches that line his cheeks. "I love you, Nal. In a world that's ever-changing, that's the one thing that will stay the same."

"Forever?" she asks instead of tells. The first sign of insecurity she's ever shown.

Fervently now, he stares into her hazel eyes and whispers a confident, "Always."

"I want to go home, Nox," she sniffles. "Please come home."

Never again, my darling. "When my work here is done."

Her face crinkles into the beginnings of a sob. "But whatever you're doing down here hurts you!"

And what is there to say to that? "It's just because I love the humans so much."

She shakes her head. "Love isn't supposed to hurt."

Eyes cast down, he traces the blue edges that dim her golden glow. "But it does anyway." She covers her chest like it's all wrong... and maybe it is. And maybe it's not.

He tells her, "Just because it hurts, doesn't mean we shouldn't do it." It's all so confusing. Love hurts. Hate hurts. Knowledge hurts. Killing and being killed hurts. Guilt hurts. All of it. But what's a good hurt, and what's a bad hurt?

His perfect little angel lays in his arms with an azure glow, and she deserves to be comforted. To be loved. If her colors change, he'll still adore her. If her mind expands, that's wonderful, too. Even if she stretches and grows, she'll still be the most beautiful thing imaginable.

And if she breaks...

Well, his love is not conditional.

Nal ponders, her little mind twirling even though she has never eaten the fruit of the tree. "It's worth it because love also feels good."

"That's what it's like when I love you," he says, wooing her with words and rocking. "I feel better when you're with me. You make me happy."

Eyes glistening, she frames his mask with her tiny hands and whispers, "Why can't I ever get close enough to you?"

And there's a flicker of purple in her heart—one she found all on her own.

How marvelous.

"You have my star," he reminds her.

"I don't want a star. I want you."

The purple deepens into something rich and thick. If he could, he would kiss that glowing window and never stop—after all, he's turning the same color. They match. For the first time in eons, they match.

But they shouldn't. They can't. This is wrong. These feelings are dangerous for her. Without meaning to, he's drawing her deeper into his darkness. He has seduced her into staying, just like he wanted, but at what cost?

Pushing her away, he says something that hurts him. "Atua is calling you, isn't It? Shouldn't you go?"

She looks at him as if wounded, "No, please! I want to..." But then she turns her face to the smoke-filled sky, toward the burning valley in the distance, moving her wide eyes over anything and everything that's not him.

"Atua feels like..." She struggles to explain herself. "Can you hear It?"

"No," Nox replies, afraid of what repercussions might be in store. Keeping the desperation out of his voice, he urges her to safety. "You have to go. If you don't belong to me, then you belong to Atua."

Reluctantly releasing him, she moves off toward the unclouded part of the sky. Unsteady without her rudder, she calls back: "Everything does."

Watching her go, anger prickles his skin again as fire ebbs to coals around him. *Not everything, Nal. Don't forget that Atua gave us the ability to create, too. You made your children, just as I made mine.*

And the humans? Atua may have birthed them...but I made them better. I gave them the fruit that led to their intelligence and their fami-

lies. I love them all, leaving no one behind. To me, no one is broken. They don't belong to their absent Creator. They are mine.

And it's time they learned that.

* * *

Some don't believe Nox when he tells them the utter truth; that those who are called 'broken' have been abandoned. Yet they are not alone. Atua may have loved Nox first, but It also broke him first, leaving him to the depths of sorrow and pain. Nox repeats, over and over, that every horror the earth has experienced—from sadness to killing, from the harsh elements to aging and death—is all the will of Atua. After all, if Atua is all powerful, couldn't It save them if It wanted? And so, It is either sadistic or a liar. It either wants them all to suffer or It wants them all to believe It has control that It doesn't... But which is reality? And why should the humans adore something that breaks them? Abandons them? Favors only a precious few—less and less as new children are born? How long until no one can use Its power? Feel It? Hear It? They are not broken. *Atua* is broken. And the more children are left behind by the Creator that 'loves' them, the more parents come to understand how right Nox is.

Except Noah.

Noah is the last to have access to Atua, but his power has grown dim. Instead of being able to take hold of the ties that bind the world—like Nox, like Abel, like Enos—Noah can only hear the whispers of Atua...at least, he says he can. At this point, no one—not even the man's wife or children—can sense what he assures them is there. And when he rejects Nox's teachings, rejects his love, the descendants of Eden all laugh at his stupidity.

Like the hananja, the very first things to die, Noah's faith in the power of Atua only makes him blind to the danger around him. His cousins are restless, tiring of Noah's wild tales, growing sick of him as the days go by. When they finally decide to turn the man away, shunning him from the crowd, Nox feels the only emotion the humans had first: pity. He pities the foolish man who toils day and night, collecting wood to build an unknown monstrosity while ranting that everyone needs to listen. Proclaiming that Atua is truly wonderful. That, if they let It, Atua will save them from absolute destruction. It's then that Nox's pity melts away to...*disdain.*

Animals arrive in droves, but Nox turns away from their pilgrimage alongside the humans that follow him, his happy collection of those who trim his branches and give him kisses and listen to his wisdom, for he *is* wise. He's lived longer than everything, has thought more, understands more, and sees Atua's betrayal with an acute eye.

Still, Noah begs. He cries and preaches the word of the cruel deity all around them, though the only ones who listen are his closest family. All others are more intelligent. Where Noah is blind, they can see.

But as creatures keep coming in twos, some Nox never even knew existed, he begins to doubt himself. He stops fighting Noah...but his people don't. Nor do his creations—things the humans call dragons and unicorns; hydras and manticores and dinosaurs; all manner of fantastic beasts that mix together the pieces of Atua's simpler designs into better ones. They stand with Nox, proud and unflinching as Noah feels his failure and slinks away.

Then the ship seals by itself, locking its menagerie away without human intervention. Nox sees this, though his followers do not, and anxiety thrums beneath his skin...for what if he is wrong?

It's when Nal's birds move their nests into the ark's rafters that Nox's worry turns to outright fear.

And when the sky opens up, it's too late.

The heavens pour in a never-ending rain, yet Nox's followers still clamber to his side, understanding that Atua hadn't lied about Its omnipotent power; It's just proven Itself to be cruel. They hand the children to Nox, as many as he can carry—which is barely any at all—and beg him to save them.

"To the mountains!" he calls, leading them up the painfully steep hill of the valley.

Their rocky salvation is cold and unforgiving, but there's no hope otherwise. The water has already gone to their waists on the high ground, and so they must swim peak to peak. Noah's stark invention is an ominous blot in the haze of the deluge as many give in to exhaustion. Nox feels every one of them end—the aged, the children, the weak and the sick—each of them like pangs in his blackening heart, digging fingers into the cracks in his conscience.

My fault, my fault, my fault.

No.

Atua's fault.

Still, Nox begs his Creator to make it stop. He pleads and implores and beseeches, but Nox never gets what he wants! Never! No matter how hard he tries!

And when the mountaintop freezes the toes of his congregation, taking their legs so they're lost when the waves come ever higher, all hope dies. Nox stands hauntingly still on the summit, those around him frozen solid, their arms and tails still wrapped around his snow-flurried legs as the sky hurls down Atua's wrath.

It's the end of his creatures. The end of the tallest of what he has made. The end of everything. Even those that fly have exhausted themselves and given up, plummeting into the ocean waves that cover the earth, the heavy flood drowning even the flowers and grass that once loved him.

Dead.

It's all dead.

And soon, the water takes him, too. He submits immediately, numb from the brain down, but no matter how much liquid he sucks into his lungs, nothing happens...

Because Nox never gets what he wants.

When the sky clears and the water recedes faster than should ever be possible, everything becomes heated with sunshine—almost more than the earth can bear. Still, Nox's pruned body stands on the mountain, lost in depression, and he decides to take matters into his own hands.

Drought now. Noah's brood lives in a perfect plain of vegetation, life, water, and happiness, but the rest of the world is fire and magma and mud and doom.

And Nox steps into the flames.

His skin blackens, an agony like he's never felt—but he wants it, he needs it, he deserves it. He waits to die, he waits to end, his branched horns turning to cinders and deforming as the ground beneath turns to ash.

My child…

Even in the furnace, ice spikes in Nox's veins at the sound of Atua's voice.

How well you've done.

Nox's tears burn away even as they bloom, the voice of his Creator the last shove that breaks him. *I can't do this. My mind is shattered. My heart is shredded. My body is burning. I'm going insane. I need this to stop. Please, please, please let it be over. Let it be done. Please let me go.*

Sweet boy, you are everlasting. It is impossible. Until the end of the world, until the end of Armageddon, you will live.

Nox's thoughts are distant and detached. *You said I would make bad things happen. you said it would be my fault. But it's not me…it's you. From the very beginning, it's always been you.*

I don't deny it. After all, what are you if not a product of Me? You, my son, are My evil personified, and My songbird is My goodness. She stays with me and urges My benevolence for the sake of all. Yet there must be balance, Nox. You, My dark darling, are My corruption. Casting you down eases My violence away.

If not for the lava bubbling in his mouth, Nox would laugh. *I haven't eased anything. You've destroyed the earth. You've killed your creations.*

Not Mine, child. Only yours.

And Nox chokes in clots of magma, sinking into the molten ground which welcomes him home. With Atua's destruction of all, Nox has become the lesser of two evils, and thus the earth moves to obey his whims again...but even this is thwarted by the will of his cruel master. Atua drags Nox, limp and dirt-encrusted, to the surface to witness the world being made anew.

Rebirth, my son. Nothing is ever truly gone. Everything that matters will soon be as it was. The humans will multiply and fill the earth once more.

The ones you've killed aren't replaceable. They are individual and special and have been sucked into nothingness because of you.

You'll find, in time, after innumerable amounts of them come into existence, that they are mirrors of each other. Their range is limited, their lives monotonous. They are replaceable. A means to an end. All for you. All for Me. I will open your mind even further to let you see into the souls you so adore. You'll see their folly then. I'll give you the ability to whisper to those who will hear you, like I can. You can even still make, Nox. Broken, writhing, beautifully twisted things that no one can see but you. You are ever special, My child. I will isolate you into excellence that no other can match. Nothing will even come close. You are a plague. A pestilence. Peerless and perfect.

"I hate you," Nox says aloud, a choked whisper as he floats in the new air.

But I love you. I will always love you. No matter your sin, I don't blame you. But I will make a promise, child, to soothe your aching mind.

An arc swoops through the sky—beautiful, almost painted—boasting all the colors of Nox's heart and more, representing emotions he knows he hasn't even felt yet.

My rainbow. Made just for you. This symbol is the proof of My promise. I will never drown the earth again. Even in floods, there will be survival. I will never cause another mass extinction. The next act of obliteration is yours, My son, and yours alone. A gift to honor your power.

He's being manipulated, he knows. Placating endearments. Unwanted gifts. Pale imitations of kindness. Nox picks apart every word, every idea and emotion, doubting everything.

Something that feels like a kiss is placed on his forehead as he's set on the ground.

I love you, Nox. So much. And in your darkest hour, I will send My songbird to bring you back from the abyss. She pines for you, but I must keep her away. She is special, so very special, and I can't let you ruin her just yet. Every time she sees you, you draw her closer and closer to her demise, yet there are things I need her to do first. But don't worry. I will allow you to kill her in time. That, too, will be a gift. Not for you, but for those you love. Her death is their salvation.

"I hate you. I hate you. I hate you," Nox chants, breathless, unable to stop.

Yes. You do.

Atua's words leave him, but he is not empty. Plans and schemes and vile thoughts fill his mind. He is destroyed, utterly and completely, so that means he must be born anew, just like the world. The soil below him shudders, liquefying into mercury, beading and drawing droplets in lines toward his blackened hooves and whiplike tail. The silver poison collects with the red ooze of volcanoes, crawling up his body.

He realizes his mask is gone, burned away, though its scars will live on his face forever, carved so deep they'll never heal. Strangely, in his insanity, he finds himself vain. It's not love or lust he wants to inspire.

It's fear. Terror imprints on you so much more deeply than love, after all.

The earth hears him, and its crawling liquids form a new mask, one made of black crackles and lava-drawn lines. One last, forever-tear stains his face with a brush stroke that scours down his cheek and chest. An acid mark. A physical representation of what his creator has done to him.

Atua has broken him. Laid him low.

It has ruined Nox.

No. Not Nox.

Abaddon. A creature who is fated to vie for the souls of mankind.

Chapter 5

~INHERENT VIOLENCE~

It's not about hiding away from the humans anymore; it's about living in their shadows. There is no need for deep caves and lonely quarries when Abaddon's charred flesh makes him as dim as the shady spots where he lurks, outright invisible as long as he clamps a hand down over the murky glow of his heart. The best part is that he could be right beside someone, and they'd never know unless he revealed himself. At that point, they wouldn't be able to miss him if they tried. His newfound darkness makes him as vivid as an ink stain on parchment when he wants to be seen.

And when he's seen?

Well.

They simply run.

* * *

It isn't too long before Noah's brood corrupts itself. Not even a single generation passes by before the seed of discord is sown. Abaddon doesn't have to lift a finger to make it happen either, because *Nox* does it for him. Oddly enough, the sons of Noah still have Nox's teachings engraved on their hearts. They use those wise words to turn themselves away from their father and even Atua, who so obviously spared them. It makes Abaddon grin.

Stupid humans.

He loves this new, willful ignorance. It's not that they don't understand the power of Atua. They see it, acknowledge it, and then convince themselves it doesn't matter simply because following it is inconvenient. It's not that they think Atua is corrupt or cruel or not worth worshiping; it's that they think they have better things to do.

It's adorable.

Noah, Noah, Noah, Abaddon chides silently, hiding in a tremor of smokeshadow. *The world's first prophet, foretelling doom and gloom. Saving souls just to have them turn on you. I hope not all prophets have to face the same backhanded gratitude.*

He holds in a mean-spirited chuckle, inventing sarcasm word-by-word as he enjoys this family drama. It took too long, but Abaddon has finally decided that, if his existence inevitably ruins everything anyway, why not just sit back and watch it unfold? Why not accept, once and for all, that he is a poison Atua makes others swallow? It's not his fault, it's not his choice, and so Abaddon refuses to feel guilty anymore. And without guilt, there is no need to endure the pain of empathy. Free of that, he finds himself more philosophical when it comes to his views on the world. He comes to understand that, in their own way, all actions, sensations, and emotions are good. They are the vastness of everything, a rainbow of threads in a illustrative tapestry. After all, a solid purple fabric may seem beautiful, a symbol of longing and desire, but it's also boring. Weave black into it with special dips and loops, and now you've got something. A visual representation of need that drips with self-hatred...and isn't that all the more captivating?

Abaddon likes to watch things from a safe distance now, his mind active but his entire face hidden beneath the weight of his new mask. It is a terrible sight. When he catches his reflection, it startles him. The only thing that indicates he's not a monster is that his eyes still show... But even then, they burn sun-yellow, rimmed with vermillion. If he were still Nox, he would terrify himself. Instead, Abaddon stares endlessly, admiring the body devoid of anything but singed skin that doesn't seem to heal, a head of blackened hair that's grown too long, and the haphazard curves of a silver and black mask.

Most of all, though, Abaddon admires the swirl of color that sometimes oozes down his body like candle wax. So many hues and shades. Out of all of them, though, his favorite is still the pin prick of gold that burns eternally. Love for his Nal.

What would she say if she saw me now? he wonders. *Would she speak my new name? Be afraid, like the children of Noah? Or would she embrace me without question, as she always has? Could she love me even now? And if not...?*

Nox died in the flood along with nearly everything but, if Abaddon needed to, could he pretend to be Nox again, if only just for her?

Ahh, and there's the problem. It's impossible to pick apart what should and shouldn't happen. Atua threatened to send Nal to him at some point, so that's out of his control—if it's foretold, she will come—but then what? If he behaves like Nox, will she fall to her doom even faster, trying to match him color for color? Or if he shows her the truth of Abaddon, will her fear be what throws her into darkness?

He chuckles again, crossing his arms over his chest and grasping at his shoulders, rocking as the humans slumber under his watchful eye. "It's useless to think about. No matter what I choose, it won't change her future." There is a sort of peace in the futility of it. In accepting it. In no longer fighting it. Fate is fate is fate. Atua made that clear from the very beginning.

"My darling, you're just as cursed as I am. Both of us beasts to be used and abused," he sing-songs, staring enviously at the sky. "You just have a softer cage."

* * *

Abaddon has a sly grin on his face tonight, looking down the mountainside as the new city settles for the evening, torches snuffing out one by one.

"They pretend to follow Atua in the day, yet sin in secret at night. You see it too, don't you? Oh! No, I guess you can't see anything right now," Abaddon murmurs to the thing he's making. That he's *trying* to make. All his recent attempts have come out warped, their insides not going together right.

These eyes might work. He squints behind his mask, moving his fingers in the way he was taught, though the end results are wrong. The corners of his mouth pull into a frown as he tries again, still with no luck.

"It's funny though," he tells his misshapen non-thing. "The consequences are getting steeper—for those actually caught in their transgressions, anyway. If you steal, they take your hands, as if blaming them for the crime! Can you believe that? Poor hands," he *tsks*. "They're terrified of being robbed, yet no one cares about the man going around chopping pieces off of people. Which is better? Taking bread or taking hands? At least you can make more bread..." he trails off, lips pursing as he checks his progress.

Wrong. All wrong. It will die in mere moments if he brings it to life like this. With a wave, the non-thing becomes nothing as it liquifies and streams back into Abaddon's blackened body. Clapping his palms together as if wiping off the vile bits, he turns to look down more closely at the newest nest of humans.

"Their work is coming along nicely, Nal," he tells her, as if she could hear him. "They call it a *tower*. You should see it. It's a marvel of geometry and engineering. They'll be up in your clouds any day now, I think. They say they want to go meet Atua." He snorts out loud. "As if they could see it. As if it only lived in the sky. As if it wasn't already in and all around every one of them." Abaddon's smile goes from wide, to strained, to faded. "I wonder how Atua feels about being misinterpreted so badly. It seems to have a bit of a vanity problem."

Not that he's one to talk. Like creator, like child.

* * *

Laughing! Abaddon can't stop laughing! Booms and bangs and dust consume the horizon as the tower is brought low. From here, it seems to be imploding, so there's no way lives won't be lost.

What's a few more, right? Abaddon thinks, wiping some cackle-induced tears from his jawline at the bottom of his mask... but he stops mid-gesture and sits up snap-quick. His tail lashes to the side as the whispers in his head shift into something new. A scraggly ear, burned to near-bluntness, twitches when he leans his head to the side—as if listening actually mattered.

Since Atua opened his mind, Abaddon has been overrun with the thoughts of mankind, their personal musings leaving five-toed footprints in his brain. At first, he barely noticed because Noah's brood was so small, but as time went by, he found himself trying to claw his ears off to make it stop. Now that he's acclimated, he mostly ignores it unless he feels like snooping, but right now he zeroes in. All the thoughts are...no, the *words* are...

Fractured.

Looking out at the settling dust, Abaddon's instinct is to run to them, but that's an instinct that should be stomped on. It's worse when you know them as individuals. Easier when they are a herd.

Still.

He doesn't run as Nox would have. Instead, Abaddon slinks his way down the mountainside under the morning sun, slipping from one tree-cast shadow to another, listening without trying and looking through the eyes of others. Their mouths are shaping a word that means *why*...yet they're all moving differently. Making different noises. Different tones. But it's all the same idea. Confusion peppers people's faces as they look at each other, their "what" word also becoming *qué* and *nani* and *che cosa* and *waa maxay*.

Abaddon's eyes go wide as the humans' disorientation becomes crippling fear. Not fear of death. Not fear of him. Fear of each other. Two humans who had stood side by side now look at one another in horror and back away, shrieking the same concepts but in different consonants and vowels.

Languages.

The humans panic, their confusion escalating into an angry mob, brother turning against brother, each thinking their sibling is possessed. No one even notices Abaddon as he wanders among them, a strange mix of emotions circling in his center. He can understand all of them. They are asking each other "why" and "how" and "please," but it's garbled. It's the babble of children who can't yet speak.

There, that one. He darts close and grabs the wrist of a female, writhing and in tears, moaning "ayuda me, ayuda me," and he pairs it with one across the field yelling the same. Another screams "dō shita no," and he yanks it along, kicking and screaming like an errant child, over to a male who weeps those same words.

Helps and yelps ring out as the nightshaded Abaddon separates them into batches, and eventually the humans understand his goal. Their brilliant minds kick in and, group after group, they take turns yelling the word for COME in their newly fractured tongue. Any human that understands a particular warble moves toward the cluster that calls it, and eventually a pattern emerges. A sound off, one tribe at a time. "Halika dito!" "Ven aquí!" "Taeal alaa huna!"

Abaddon pants from his efforts, flicking his tail in orange annoyance and looking around to see if there are any stragglers, though there seem to be none. The humans are all chattering wildly now, so he gives himself permission to step back, leaning against a yew tree and getting a good view of the mayhem Atua just caused.

Why would it possibly...?

As was inevitable, once the immediate danger of incoherence is gone, one of the humans notices Abaddon's stark figure and finally realizes who he is. Eyes flying wide, the female cries out, flailing a pointed finger in his direction and hollering a new word that means him, somehow.

Devil.

He kind of likes it. Others in the woman's new tribe call out in shock at seeing him, the terrible bringer of the great flood.

Abaddon just watches, interested to see when they'll start to run. *Yes, children. Yes, yes. I know. So frightening to see the nightmare Atua has inflicted on you face to face.*

At least they don't seem to have weapons. He's been curious about what would happen if they tried to kill them. They'd fail of course, but what would *he* do?

A few more humans pick up the rumble of shattered words, referring to both him and the damage he'd inflicted in the past, that he's doing again now, that he'll do again forever. They tell one another that *he* pulled down the tower and twisted their mouths, and Abaddon can't help feeling indignant.

Some of the few he'd grabbed and paired together step forward through the crowds, afraid but determined as they near him. Abaddon's nostrils flare, and he stamps his hoof, knowing that he'll now be insulted by the ones he specifically went out of his way to save. He shouldn't have helped at all. He should have let the herd fall into wails of sorrow. He should have...

His thoughts halt as they kneel before him.

Teeth clenched behind his mask, his fake face stares them down, eyes glowing as the kneeling humans gaze at him with blank voids in their minds, saying nothing, letting this moment drag out longer and longer... until they bow, foreheads pressed to the valley grass.

He loves them immediately. Ohhh, it's dangerous how quickly it happens. The epoch-old habit of adoring them grabs hold of his heart with an unkind squeeze.

The other factions gear up into a cacophonous tirade, knowing Abaddon for who he truly is and ranting at those before him who don't seem to care. Those at his mercy revere him with glistening eyes, whispering sweet and silent "thank yous" from their heart to his.

These ones understand it wasn't me. They know I tried to help.

Which is why, when their once-compatriots begin to rally with angry shouts—furious at those prostrated on their knees—Abaddon does the only thing he can think of. He lifts his hand and summons the disgusting power of his creator, rolling the land in a heavy swell and sending the rabid humans sprawling.

His people never look away from his sunspot glare. Instead, their mouths move to call him *Su'mus iv tave qy.* Son of Atua. *Midwanas wo.* Powerful one. And *Satan.* For the last, there is no translation. To the humans, it's just another name for the mighty Abaddon.

He quivers, unsure of what to do. Should he collect a new set of followers? He no longer wants flowers and kisses. He never wants to be touched again. His horns are twisted and dusty like coal, so there's nothing to trim or to care for. He doesn't want their love either, simply because he doesn't want to love them back. He doesn't want to know them as individuals who will die, leaving him aching to weep but unable...because he is not Nox. What could he possibly want from them?

This, he supposes. These people, on their knees, looking at him and not Atua.

Suddenly bathed in a purple light that beams from Abaddon's dark form, the little fools smile. He may not want to love them, but it's already too late. It was too late the moment they began worshiping him. He doesn't love them as distinguishable minds, no, but he loves them for their numbers.

Danger, danger, danger, his dying conscience cries.

Abaddon simply nods at them and steps back, issuing a warning: "Atua wants you for itself, but it is more than happy to destroy you. Love it if you must, but don't trust it." And because he can't help himself, he adds, "Love *me* if you must... but do it in the shadows, for your brothers and sisters will never understand.

"I can hear your minds, children of Noah. Like Atua, I know your thoughts and the evils that live there. Atua won't love you for them. It won't forgive you. It may even kill you—but you can do no wrong in my eyes."

After all, there's no way you could possibly match the blood on my hands. Of the many things I am, a judge is not one of them. To me, none are broken. None more than myself.

Peerless.

He smirks with a self-loathing they can't see and continues his backwards steps, looking at them for a good long while before turning away.

I've ruined something again, haven't I? Atua divided its people by language, and I just divided them by belief, yet again. I suppose I didn't learn from my mistake. He chuckles with unending fatalism.

"My poor children, what have I done to you?"

Though it only makes him smile, resigned above all else.

* * *

The instinct to commit acts of violence is something all of humanity shares. Some are immune to the physical aspect, but those seem to have an affinity for *emotional* violence, instead—and sometimes, that type of damage is worse.

Animals are deadly, but mostly in service to their own survival. Nature is deadly, but it's impartial and has no sentient control. But humans? Humans are far beyond Abaddon in their innate desire to hurt others. No matter how often they feel guilt, they still return to sin again —and in new, colorful, innovative ways. Abaddon may have inspired their urges, but mankind honed them to a vicious point. Those clever, clever monsters.

Yet, they also perform acts of such kindness. Such love. Such bravery. Abaddon finds the ones who are good, yet untouched by Atua, to be the most miraculous of all. They are precious. Rare and lovely. And since their creator isn't wedged into their minds, Abaddon can come and go as he pleases, listening to their rationales for good deeds and checking to see if they harbor secret sins. Often, they don't. It's beautiful.

As much as humans have inherited Atua's evil through Abaddon, they've also been gifted the benevolence it takes from Nal. And make no mistake, Abaddon believes with his whole heart that Atua takes—no, *steals* Nal's unconditional love, meting it out in drips and drops when it wants to feel special. But the humans would be better off giving offerings to their own imaginations than to follow something with so little care for them in return. Even now, Atua unleashes its wrath in unprecedented ways, usually punishing the people who follow Abaddon without shame...though it has no mercy on its own people, either. Even when they only disappoint it the tiniest bit.

...Which is why Abaddon is left standing, staring at a beautiful woman turned into a pillar of salt as Sodom and Gomorrah sizzle in the background, the cries of Abaddon's hedonistic devotees long since burned out of them. He'd like to feel wrath on their behalf—after all, it was his joy in any and all sensations, including pain, that caused their downfall—but he doesn't feel that horrible red glow of anger emanating from his heart. Nor a deep blue. Abaddon just feels the black of loathing. He hates himself. He hates his lack of power. He hates Atua, now and forever.

Hates, hates, hates.

Only then does the red seep in.

I'll find a way to end you. There must be one. Perhaps that's why you tore down the tower the humans tried to build. Maybe you do *have a seat on high—one where you're vulnerable. One where you are tangible, with a soft belly for me to bite into. I will destroy you the way you destroy every-thing else.*

He seethes, grabbing onto his power and letting it settle into the pit of his stomach, raising him into the air. His earth urges him up, pressing on his hooves and blessing his choice to pull Atua from its hidden throne and end it. He is alone in the sky. Alone in the clouds. Alone... until he's not.

Predictable. So predictable he almost laughs.

Nal rushes toward him from above the cirrus and cumulus, her pretty wings keeping her aloft, and her tail healed and whole. Abaddon mentally grabs the air in a vise grip, his teeth bared behind his nightmare black mask as he commands the ether not to let him fall.

"Leave," he says, his voice a low rumble. "I don't want you here." But it comes out so quietly, she doesn't hear him. Did he do that on purpose? Or did his subconscious take over? Did Atua clamp down on his vocal cords? Who knows. The only certainty is that she comes ever onward.

There is no smile on her face. Instead, it's flooded with blue concern. Her heart is devoid of the feverish purple he has remembered every day of his semi-solitude, dreams of their bodies entwining the way humans do at the forefront of his dirty mind. She's grown a bit—an older child instead of a young one, perhaps—but it's not enough; he had wanted her to match Eve. She hasn't fallen that far yet, but he's not sure how to feel about it. Disappointed or proud, which is right?

Both.

Ask me what happened to my face. Ask me about the acid, tear-drawn scar that runs down my body. Ask about the bleeding colors. Ask about my burned skin. Ask me.

Instead, her smile suddenly surfaces, beaming with happiness as she wings closer, flashing a grin of pure gold. "Nox!" she calls, high pitched and happy.

I love you but leave. I love you but go. I am not Nox. I can never be Nox. I am Abaddon, and I poison mankind.

She collides with him, twirling them both in midair as he does his best to keep hold of the particles that lift him.

"Look at you!" she squeals. "You're here! You're in my sky! Are you coming home!?" She ends the question in a rush of hope that breaks his heart.

What do I do? What won't destroy her? Probably lies. Lies of happiness. Lies of loving my life and loving my work.

But it's impossible.

"I can't come back to you," he croaks, refusing his tears. "I never can. My journey will never end. I am stuck here, made to corrupt and ruin, and it's Atua that makes me do it!" he confesses, his last word ending in a sharp and vicious 't' through clenched teeth. "There's no escape from its plan. It will destroy any and all of the humans that love me, love my emotions, love my ways, love my ideas, *and I will never forgive it!*" The speech leaves him like a tidal wave, pouring from his soul, unstoppable as his breaths pull in and out too fast.

Nal looks at him with sadness on her face. "Oh, Nox. My sweet Nox."

Her hands lift up to cradle the rigid lines of his mask, and before he can stop her, she removes it. He has no idea what this part of him looks like. He only knows that the air stings his face.

Ask me about my glowing eyes. Ask me about my blackened, ever-

growing hair. Ask me about the aged imprint of thorns over my cheeks that never heals. Ask me, Nal. Tell me how hideous I am.

With her free hand, she strokes his dark tresses and the crest of his brow, assessing him with a blank stare. Her palms slip up to touch his misaligned horns, and they slough off slightly, letting charcoal dust flutter toward the remains of the burning cities below. "Did the humans do this to you?"

No. Atua did it to me. Your beloved, disgusting Atua.

Eyes sparkling, she smiles at him, wiping away the tears he didn't know he was crying. "Every time I see you, Nox, you've evolved. How are you always so beautiful?"

His eyes sink closed. He never wanted to be touched again, and he still doesn't. Not by anyone who isn't her.

"I hurt, Nal. I hurt so much."

She caresses his heart as it bleeds blue down his body. "Because of Atua?"

"Because of its plan. It plans to have me ruin the humans—but they're so wonderful, Nal. If you only knew them, you'd love them, too." His hand slides up over hers, keeping her warm skin close. "Atua doesn't feel guilty for the pain it's causing; it never has. When it kills them, it doesn't understand how much of its destruction lingers. It doesn't just wound them now. It wounds them for generations."

"But," she shakes her head, "It spares some of them."

Abaddon's eyes narrow as he flashes red, casting violent shadows on her. "It should spare *all* of them. It shouldn't pick and choose. All deserve its love. They are beautiful. They are wonderful."

They are mine.

"I..." she starts, palming her own heart, awash in conflicted colors. "I tell Atua that I can feel you hurting when It punishes the humans, and that the feeling is bad. But Atua can't understand pain."

"It's not that it can't. It won't," he says, scowling. "But I want it to. I want it to hurt and feel guilty and change."

And die.

Nal looks at him, a deep resolve firming up her features. She kisses him then—on the mouth, and longer than she ever has before. He falls into it immediately, but as soon as his lips part to welcome her home, she pulls away, placing his mask back over his face.

"I'll help you." She stares into his searing eyes, unafraid. "I'll go to the humans. I'll learn what pain they have to endure in their short lives. I'll learn their struggles and their joys. I'll know them like you do, Nox. And, once I do, I'll convince Atua to save them."

All time stops.

Save them.

Not spare. But save.

Abaddon's heart stops in his chest. "Nal, no," he pleads, scrabbling at her hands in a panic like he's never felt. "No, no, please!"

She only touches his hair one last time, nodding firmly. "I can do it. Believe in me. I'll save them, I promise." She pulls back, leaving him bereft and desperate, calling after her.

And then the air lets him go.

He can't grab onto it. Did he lose his concentration? Did Nal take away his hold on her element? Did Atua? Who knows. The only certainty is that he's falling, and all he can do is plummet.

"Nal, no!" he bellows after her, unafraid for his own well-being. He's immortal, after all. "They'll kill you! Atua will let them kill you!" His voice almost breaks. He's screaming and howling and begging. "Nal! Nal, *please!*"

But either she doesn't hear, or she doesn't care.

The ground below frizzes into moss atop moss atop moss, building a hill faster than possible, catching Abaddon's prone body in soft sponginess. He rolls to safety, left wide-eyed and scouring the sky for any remaining sign of his beloved, but it's too late. She's gone.

He's done it. It was inevitable, of course. Fate is fate is fate. Abaddon has set off the prophecy: Nal will die for the sake of mankind. And just like everything else, it's his fault.

She'll die, she'll die, she'll die.

...Unless I can find a way to stop it.

Can he stop it?

Hope returns to him, but it's tainted. Vindictive.

Maybe the only reason I was never able to truly defy Atua was because I loved it too much. And after that, I believed its words and imagined myself unable to disobey. But I was wrong, wasn't I? I have more power and control than I think I do, don't I?

A voice whispers inside him. *I guarantee it.*

But does the voice belong to Atua? Or is it just Abaddon's own wishful thinking?

Only time will tell.

NICHOL
NOX

Chapter 6

~SALVATION AND DESTRUCTION~

Abaddon has always listened closely to those who are "blessed" by Atua, though in a round-about sort of way. If they're strong enough in their beliefs, he can't get into their minds, but he can see through the thoughts of those around them. This is how he hears the prophecy that Atua will send to Earth a savior of man...and Nox knows immediately, it will be Nal. She'll be born as a human child, putting her in a situation where death is not only easy, it's inevitable.

He needs to stop it, and to do that, he needs more information, but there are too many human minds to listen in on. Even if Abaddon strains day and night, Atua has thwarted him, giving random figures across the globe just enough connection to call his attention. It's maddening. Even when the humans start collecting the words of prophets onto paper, there is never enough time to read it all, hear it all, see it all.

And so, Abaddon needs to *make*. He needs eyes and ears every-where, and he needs them right now. One missed prophecy and it may be too late. He still *makes* wrong, but if he can get just one thing right, the one thing that matters, it will all be worth it. He needs a vessel.

He tries to make his creation look like Nal if she had grown to the size of Eve, but he was foolish to think he'd ever make anything so grand. Still, she resembles the humans he so loves in their ever-growing numbers, even though her mind is a disappointment. He's never been able to create a higher level of sentience, so she's rudimentary at best. It's not that she's stupid. She's stunted. But she's the best he can do. Maybe the best he wants to do.

Lilith.

He ruts into her just once—one thrust he takes absolutely no pleasure in, feeling like he's defiled his own body—but once is enough. Afterward, she reaches out feebly, using her fingers to stroke his blackened hair, but he bats her away with a vicious snarl.

"Do it again and I'll cut them off," he warns, cruel and hateful, and her hands flop down immediately in submission. He murmurs to her in something that sounds soft but is laced with malice. "Because our children will be born and not made by my ineptitude, they'll have minds that work better than yours. Not that it's a difficult feat."

Abaddon rests his cold hand over her flat stomach. "I will give them the power to dip into the minds of mankind, just like I can, and my seed will live in you forever. You will *make* endlessly."

She doesn't even know to nod, but her stomach grows immediately under his palm, that working womb the only thing that needed to be perfect. Not just perfect. Never ending.

Necessity more than kindness makes him seat her on a throne beneath the crust of the earth where he plans to hide his brood. The rocks are kind, and dutifully split themselves into plates and geysers at his command, forming volcanoes and deep caverns, anything to make a place for his children to emerge.

In moments, the first batch cascades from her in a wet slide, mewling and deformed, but filled with intelligence and the ability to grow dim like their father can, ready to hide among the shadows and do Abaddon's bidding.

Abaddon steps back as they slip out in piles, each one shaking off the fluid of birth and growing to a proper size with an agonizing stretch, crying out, just once, before staring up at him with red eyes and pointed teeth.

When the first one touches him, he kills it without hesitation, and the others learn their lesson. He hates them already, but they are essential if he is to stop Nal's birth.

"Travel to every edge of existence. Listen for humans who have access to Atua. If you can't get into their minds, it's proof of their strength, and those are the ones I want. Any prophet—*every* prophet—is to be brought to my attention. Those, I will follow on my own."

He points at a cluster of his brood. "Stay and teach your brethren their purpose. The less I see of you, the better. Keep your mother alive or I'll slaughter every last one of you. And I won't be quick. I'll flay you at my leisure over decades, and I'll love every minute of it. Pain feels as good to me as pleasure, after all."

He doesn't bother to ask if they understand. Working his way toward the craggy gates of the hell he's created, Abaddon *makes* once more, forming creatures modeled after the hounds he'd once liked. Loyal and true to the very end.

"Guard my domain," he commands them, and they have just enough intelligence to grasp the concept. They snarl and drool venom, and he is satisfied. "Let no one in, man nor beast. Only the things I've made belong here. My bitch, my spawn. No more."

He wants to bathe and get her off him, but he'll wear the scarlet of her maidenhead awhile yet, if only to prove to himself that he'll do anything. Absolutely anything.

I won't let Nal be born. The only way to save her is to think like those clever humans and smash the walls built around what I thought I was capable of.

If I'm to be evil, let me be evil.

* * *

His effects ripple worldwide, for he is Abaddon, the doom of mankind. Suddenly, and without reason, females are made less-than.

Some societies don't allow this, but most do, relegating them to the weaker sex, only good for breeding, just like the woman he himself had made.

His deep desire for Nal after her last kiss has given males a taste for younger and younger mates as well—some barely women, some not yet women at all. Those small, frail bodies...

Abaddon doesn't hate these men for their newly acquired sin. Their evils are just a mirror of his own desire for his pure, perfect other half, after all. A side-effect. It's not their fault. It's his. It always is.

That's not the only thing, either. His demon spawn and the way he uses them—without love, without consideration, without mercy—has given birth to something mankind calls slavery. The strong and powerful dominate others, relegating their kin to mere worker bees who labor under cruel conditions, beholden to the whims of their masters. Just like Abaddon's children, they are a means to an end.

He's not sure he cares. He is single-minded in what he wants to do, everything else be damned. Especially him. He's no better than Atua now, losing the moral high ground...

Because he's about to inspire genocide.

On purpose.

Pharaoh's soothsayers are twisted in the way they understand Atua, Abaddon muses, sitting in the lap of a towering Osiris statue and feeling the cool, polished stone beneath his fingers. *They attribute its might to a pantheon of fiction, not seeing Atua for what it truly is. Why would it come to them of all people? This must be a trick. Another distraction.*

And yet, the soothsayers perform small miracles, proof of their connection to Atua. It's the only reason Abaddon listens long enough to hear the divination he seeks.

Nal is prophesied to be born a male, but it doesn't bother Abaddon in the least. Her sex is irrelevant; it's her soul that matters. No matter what she becomes, human, beast, or bird, he'd still revel in every moment of her existence. But that would mean she'd have to be born, and he will never allow that to happen.

* * *

With fine linens and kohl-lined eyes, Pharaoh scoffs at his 'sacred' sycophants. "I will not heed your warnings. My lineage will remain untouched. No slave can humble the rule of the Gods."

Seti includes himself in that tier of importance since all Pharaohs, no matter what dynasty, consider themselves deities. Abaddon almost gives himself away by snorting at this ridiculous vanity, but there are more important things to do.

Watching as Seti sends his soothsayers away, Abaddon lurks around the dark corners of the king's chambers. As this ruler of men sits unattended on his throne, Abaddon sneaks into his mind, a comfortable place of self-importance so deeply rooted it's only a matter of course.

Darkness personified, Abaddon whispers, "You must end all who might be mother to this loathsome child. That slave will come to steal what's rightfully yours, so saith the Gods. You would do well to heed their counsel."

Grinning to himself, unseen, Abaddon stands beside the great Seti, driving him to distraction. The adorned man strokes his faux beard and considers Abaddon's words as if they were his own thoughts. As far as he knows, they are.

Abaddon continues his flattery. "There are none above you. You are the morning and the evening star," which is a lie and an insult to his namesake in the sky. "Eliminate those of childbearing age. All of them. Prove to the Gods that you trust their warnings."

Seti meanders a bit, mulling over these wise words as Abaddon follows close behind, his lips forming a small smirk while he slips behind Pharaoh, hidden in the shade of the alabaster pillars that line their path. Once Pharaoh reaches his balcony on high, the human regards the work being done below, witnessing the slaves' exhaustion, pain, and strife firsthand...and then calculating. Abaddon hears Seti's thoughts plain as day as if he's speaking them aloud.

The Hebrews are too numerous, it's true—but without the women, there would be mass depletion in the coming years. No new assets born until the un-bled grow old enough to bear fruit. It would be a grave error to destroy my life-givers when all I need to do is cull the herd. Cut down the budding males capable of violence. It should have little effect on yield, this way. Women can lie with any man. I'll simply breed them differently. Instead of one-to-one, I can pair them one-to-many.

Abaddon's muscles go rigid, and he grits his teeth.

Seti nods, the thought like a stone. "The male children of a generation, then. Work may slow as the current stock ages, but it is a sacrifice I'm willing to make," he tells himself. "This will satisfy the Gods."

Abaddon could kill him. He wants to kill him. He reaches into the man's mind again, but it's to do more than just listen. More than speak. He tries to take hold—something unprecedented. His hand is invisible before Seti's face as he tries to force the man to do his bidding. If Abaddon's powerful, all-seeing children obey his will, then this conceited, insubordinate, arrogant king of men will, too.

"You will take the mothers." Abaddon growls the command behind his mask.

Eyes opening wide, Seti's mouth falls slack, his face a blank stare. "I... I will..." he trails off, and Abaddon's heart takes on an eerie new glow. *Indigo.* The desire to overpower.

"The *mothers,*" Abaddon repeats through his teeth. "You will not allow these children to be born." He presses his will into Pharaoh's body, trying to brand his thoughts onto the man's consciousness, to take him over completely...

But it doesn't work.

As if coming out of a trance, Seti shakes his head, rubbing his temples. "The male children..." he says again, unsure, but unmoved. Eyes narrowed, he frowns. "And the male children only. So let it be written, so let it be done."

Dumbfounded, Abaddon stands thwarted by a mere human. A weak and feeble-minded *human!*

Without warning, Atua's presence floods him, filling Abaddon with a deep hatred at its unwelcome intrusion. It mocks him with two simple words:

Free will.

Then I *will kill the mothers!* Abaddon mentally screams at his creator. *If Seti won't give the order, I'll take matters into my own hands!*

My child, have you ever killed a human?

Abaddon bites his tongue so hard it bleeds, and he revels in the metallic tang.

That is a power I will not grant. You can whisper, but you cannot control. You can inspire, but you cannot force. And you can never kill them.

"Because that job belongs to you?" he retorts bitterly, loud and unheard in the now-empty hall of false Gods, enormous stone monstrosities towering above his head. Atua replies with a simple:

Yes.
But fear not, sweet Darkness. My songbird's birth is still in the future. Listen closely to the child who survives your massacre. You'll know him when he comes—as will all of Egypt. He will reveal the prophecy you so desperately seek.
He will also teach his brethren My requirements for mankind. The obedience I desire. You will then know exactly what I will judge them for, my son. And in knowing, you will inspire them to go against My commandments. My punishments will then be earned. Deserved. Just. The corruption you sow will absolve Me.

"Why do you do this? What reason could you possibly have?"

Eternity is long, beloved.

Abaddon sneers beneath his black mask. "What does that mean?"
...To which there is no reply. Seething, he screams the words again, then bellows them for good measure.
But Atua remains silent. It has said its piece.

* * *

The irony is that she's born under his star. Abaddon tried to sic a local ruler on the women again, the same way he had with Pharaoh, and with the same amount of success; none. All hope is lost. He weeps for the first time in a very long time, unable to stop for what feels like years...until one of his brood tells him of her.

It makes sense. Of course, Nal would be a prophet. Even more, she's a *child* prophet. Special and singular, she teaches not only of Atua's will, but of the power of benevolence.

To say he falls in love again doesn't come close. It's more intense than that. Inexplicable. All-encompassing and obsessive. Her deeply instilled connection to Atua separates their minds, keeping him from whispering his adoration, frustrating him to no end, yet despite the temptation, he refuses to alienate her by appearing openly among her throng of supporters. Instead, he resigns himself to watching. Endlessly. Always. Even in her slumber, he will not rest, taking in every small puff of breath that leaves her pretty mouth.

Rumors say she's a boy. Of course, they do. Women are too weak to speak for the Gods according to the rule of law. It doesn't seem to bother her, though. She prefers to be Nobody from Nowhere and is smart enough to know that most rumors are outright lies or half-truths at best.

Abaddon's not immune, either. The latest stories say his Hell is a place of torture, a place where his demons inflict horrific pain on the sinful just to enjoy watching them writhe. It's a nightmarish tale parents tell their children at night to make them behave, and it works. For a while.

The truth is that Abaddon *has* begun to inherit the souls of sinners, though he has no idea how or why. He does nothing to them—no hot pokers in their eyes or bees in their bellies—but they are trapped, unable to leave his realm. He's tried several times to release them, but to no avail. They're...unsettling. Even his hated children steer clear of the lost spirits because all they do is weep, remembering their past deeds with wailing and gnashing of teeth. Abaddon need not punish them. They punish themselves. It's fascinating. Terrible, but fascinating.

* * *

One day, while watching his beloved snooze in the shade of a tree, Abaddon asks, "Are there more souls where you come from, Nal?" Though that's no longer her name. He doesn't care about her new name. She is as she always was, whether she knows it or not. Even though she doesn't glow anymore, Abaddon can still feel her joy and love for everything.

She snores for a moment, ensnaring his heart with wanted thorns as she turns to face him in her slumber. He tells himself it's by instinct, not by chance. No matter her name, race, or face, they are meant to be together. Good and Evil aren't at odds. They exist to bring balance. To keep the cycle spinning. Life and death. Day and night.

"One needs the other, doesn't it?" he murmurs, wanting to touch her oak brown hair, but afraid to wake her. He is nothing but gentle now, happier than he can remember, and he prays that it will keep the humans at bay. "Atua may try to separate us, but you will always be with me. You told me once that there was no belonging between the two of us, but that's not true. I belong to you. I may have been made first, but you've owned me from the moment you were created."

He doesn't think about her end. He only thinks about now. It's the only way to stoke the golden beam of love amidst the roiling vortex inside him...and my, does it shine.

She stretches and lets out the tiniest grunt, her earthen bedding leaving something to be desired.

"I could give you riches beyond your wildest dreams, Nal. I could make you a queen." He smiles at her, gentle, soft, and all-knowing. "But you wouldn't want that. That's not what you're here for." He does touch her then—a lock of her hair that's gone astray, splaying over the shaded grass. She wears it down now, and it's gorgeous. He doesn't dare pick up the messy strands, but he presses his fingers to them and sighs a lovely sound, as if he was her Nox again. Her constant presence makes him *feel* like Nox again.

* * *

She grows older and begins to wander the land, almost aimlessly, with Abaddon trotting unseen in her shadow. His Hell may be multiplying with the trapped souls of sinners, but Nal inspires many to reach for the goodness inside them, ensuring they'll never end up in his realm. It's a noble cause. She touches their hearts through love rather than fear, teaching them how to deal with guilt in a whole new way. A softer way.

Repentance.

It's a cycle of sin, guilt, apology, and forgiveness, over and over again until you learn your lesson and change. Ages later, that's still the most important part. But the evil Abaddon has inspired in mankind is an uncontrollable thing, moving in ways he can't anticipate, filling his dark caverns to the brim with new arrivals. There are just too many sins to try out and enjoy. Too many to remember to repent for.

Still, out of all the atrocities they could have committed, it only takes a small incident—lenders and vendors in Atua's church—to set Nal off. It's stunning to watch her scream at blasphemers with righteous anger, to see her flipping tables and ordering everyone out, eyes burning in fury. Abaddon abandons Nox in an instant then, gold turning to violet.

She's corruptible.

Does that mean he can make her his? If he can make her sin enough, if she doesn't repent, can she live in his underground lair when she dies? He'd wave a hand and put Lilith out of her misery in a moment to ensure Nal's place on his throne. He'd adorn it with anything and everything to make sure she knows that, while mankind's worship is fleeting, his is eternal, and he has worshiped her from the very beginning.

But she repents and is forgiven.

It hurts him to see. After all, he never was and never will be forgiven, no matter how much he says he's sorry. His anger and jealousy are pointed at Atua though, for now and for always. He refuses to blame Nal for the grace and power she receives from their unfair creator.

The priests and Pharisees aren't as knowledgeable as Abaddon, however. Aren't as wise. Jealous of Nal's connection, they want Atua all to themselves, even though not one of them can feel its presence. Abaddon's demonic children tell him of their plots, but there's nothing he can do about it. Free will, after all.

His frustration and self-hate deepen as he reflects on his limitations, forcing him to abandon Nal for months on end while he tries to get himself under control—though her absence only makes him more volatile. Interestingly enough, the darker he gets, the holier she becomes. While he rages, preaching to his lost souls that they wouldn't be lost at all if not for Atua, Nal teaches the living that embracing its love will bring them salvation. Bring them home to heaven.

So, there is a heaven, Abaddon realizes, watching her through another's eyes. *If so, I want it.*

The thought is like lightning.

Nal's miracles are becoming stronger. At first Abaddon thought the stories of her power were exaggerated until he tiptoes back to the surface and watches her turn water into wine. Calm storms and walk on the ocean's skin. Multiply a single piece of bread to feed a multitude. Enraptured, Abaddon watches her heal the sick and raise the dead with his own eyes. It's the power Seth had wanted for the humans, oh so long ago.

"Where were you when Cain killed Abel?" Abaddon asks in a reverent sigh. Not one of blame, but one of wonder. "Imagine what good we could have done if you'd only been here from the very beginning."

If she'd been with him, nothing would have ever gone wrong in the first place. He knows this like he knows the sunrise.

Abaddon follows Nal's every footstep and witnesses her mission in all its glory. She travels across the miles, preaching kindness to all that will open their hearts and listen. Better than Atua's blunt, unforgiving commandments, Nal inspires mercy for the poor, for those who mourn, for the meek. For those downtrodden and hunted by society, the sinners and the whores. If anyone should be a God, it should be his Nal. Abaddon worships her after all, so why shouldn't everyone else?

Yet there is something wrong with her. Something even her friends don't notice, no matter how many of them there are. But Abaddon has been watching her for over thirty years now, so he knows each and every one of her tells. He sits, dimming himself at a banquet dinner, tasting the wine on the tongues of her apostles as he focuses on the sadness casting a shroud on her features.

How can no one see this? They must be blind.

When her clan falls asleep, she slips away, and there's no way Abaddon won't follow.

* * *

Nal kneels at a tree in the moonlight, hair lit with a soft glow, hands clasped in front of her as she gazes up into the night sky. Abaddon daydreams of what thoughts she might be offering to the stars...until she speaks out loud.

"I can't."

It's so soft, she might not have said it.

Her eyes glisten and Abaddon gets down beside her, wanting to reveal himself. Removing the visual barrier between them, his thumbs hook under his mask as he takes it off, crisp air still stinging as he waits for a chance to appear before her.

She beseeches something. Atua most likely. "I know what you want from me, but I'm afraid." Her hands worry at one another as she hitches in a concerning breath. Pleading with the moon, her voice cracks. "Will it hurt?"

His heart breaks. "Will what hurt, Nal?"

Startled, she widens her human eyes and sees him for the very first time. She rears back, digging in her heels and pushing away, but she doesn't run.

"Who are you?" she asks, but it's not the whimper she'd made before. It's strong and worthy of the power she wields.

He circumvents the question. "I have many names." If he gives the wrong one, she will fight on premise alone, and that's the last thing he wants.

"Who is Nal?" she asks.

His lips tip up at the corners. "It's a word that means you."

Like Abaddon means me. And Lucifer and Satan and Diablo. Baphomet and Mammon and Mephistopheles. I am many things, Nal, and all of them are yours.

"Will what hurt?" he asks again, leaning closer.

"What happened to your eyes?" she counters, obviously avoiding the topic as she takes in his vicious red and yellow gaze.

Tipping his head to the side, his black hair cascades over his shoulder as he considers his excuses. "I can hear our creator, too. This" —he gestures at his face—"is a sign of my ties to it. My connection is a bit different than yours, but also very much the same."

He pulls leaves between them, dried and crackling, and blows slightly, igniting them into small flames. She marvels at him, making him secretly preen.

"I like your miracles better," he admits, stroking her ego with the truth.

Her eyes bubble with unshed tears and her lips tremble, avoiding the secret that rides the tip of her tongue. Instead, she asks, "Why do you have that glow?"

"Oh, this?" he gestures at his chest, amused. *You used to have one, too. Though never quite like mine.* "It shows how I'm feeling."

"What does gold mean?"

He looks away, shyly. "I'm happy. Happy to meet you." *To speak with you. To hear your voice aimed at me. To have you look at me and know I'm here beside you.*

Though still sad, her guard drops. He just lets this moment exist, trying not to scare her, adding sticks and twigs to the fire to stave off the night's chill. He can't feel it, but he can see her skin is blossoming into gooseflesh with the cold. His earlier instincts were always to protect, and since he's not sure if he should hold her, this is the next best thing. He wants to hold her, though. He'd die a million deaths for it. After all, she's finally the right size.

"And..." She hesitates, licking her lips. "What does purple mean?"

He rests a hand over his heart. "Worry," he lies. "You seem troubled. I'd like to help you if I could." To prove his connection to Atua another way, or perhaps as a means of comforting her, he asks the earth to roll over some dead branches and adds them to their small pyre. Smiling at her, he wishes she knew how much this moment means to him. How much he's dreamt of it. "Are you warm enough?"

She scoots closer to the fire. Closer to him. She looks over with a sheepish smirk. "Thank you."

"It's nothing. I'm happy to help. You and I are sort of the same with the miracles we can do, and it's nice to be in similar company. Our creator has me on a mission and it's... isolating. Sometimes, I feel very lonely."

"But you're not alone," she says, looking at her fingers, fiddling, so much like before. "Because God is always with you." Searching his face for secrets, she asks, "What's your name?"

"Nox," he replies. *For I will always be Nox for you. I would move mountains for you.*

He tries once more, "What's going to hurt, Nal?"

If she minds his name for her, she doesn't say. "I'm on a mission, too. I'm here to save everyone. I think I've wanted to do it for a very long time. Sometimes I feel like I've been preparing my whole life, or even longer, to fulfill my purpose, but the end is coming too fast...and I'm afraid."

She pauses, letting the crackles of the fire fill the air before her sorrow finally spills over. "I...I've asked God if He can let me go. If I can somehow escape my destiny." She wipes her tears with no small amount of shame. "But I have a higher purpose. It's about more than my wants and needs. It's like a promise I made long ago, and I need to see it through."

Abaddon leans toward her, offering amnesty. "What if you could be free of the promise? What if the person you're obligated to released you?"

She looks at him sternly. "Then I'd still do it anyway. My mission is to—"

"Save mankind from their sins. Save their *souls,*" he says disdainfully, his color fading to orange.

She straightens. "Yes."

Stubborn. She's not going to say it, so he'll say it for her.

"By dying for them."

Her limbs freeze in place as if time has stopped.

Abaddon lifts his eyebrows in a gentle challenge. "With no guarantee they'll follow your teachings? With no guarantee they'll learn from your sacrifice?" His tail lashes on the fallen leaves, making a *shushing* sound, and she truly looks at him, her body tensing with discomfort. It makes him frown. "The humans are doomed, Nal. They are beautiful and clever and corrupted and horrible. I love them. But if the cost is your life, saving them is not worth the price."

She moves farther from him and from the fire, suspicion dancing in her eyes. "What are you here for? What's your mission?"

Feeling her distance like an aching wound, he gets angry. "Saving you from yourself! Saving you from a mistake that will end you for no reason!"

She stands up and backs away then, but he's having none of it. His temper is up and she's not doing her job and soothing him like she's supposed to.

"I have a purpose," she almost growls at him. "The people need me!"

"No! They need *absolution*. Atua wants obedience to its arbitrary rules just so it has a right to punish mankind, and that notion has been so drilled into you that you believe the decision was righteous. It makes you obstinate and unmovable. Unteachable. Faithful in the worst of ways! The light needs the darkness, don't fool yourself otherwise. Let go of your faulty ideas of a world without sin. A world of salvation." He advances on her until she stumbles backwards, bathing her in red light. "Do you want to know a secret about your creator? *My* creator?"

He stalks around her as he speaks, but she does not cower. No. Not his Nal.

"The truth is that it's *bored*. It puts us all on this earth to struggle and suffer and kill and die because it is a child with a toy it can't help but throw on the ground. It doesn't care that the toy breaks, because it has the power to make a new one! We are puppets."

She glares at him as he prowls. "I know who you are."

"And who am I?"

"The Devil."

He huffs in satisfaction, nodding at her with a jerk of his head. "You know who I am, but do you know who *we* are? You were made for me.

We are two that are one. We are mirrors of each other. Earth and sky. You are my other half, Nal. My soulmate."

"You're lying."

"No," he smirks, holding his ground. "About that? Never. I'm the reason you exist. I'm even the reason you're *here.* You promised to save the humans *for me.*"

She hisses, "I promised to save them *from* you!"

"Unfortunately, my love, it's all one and the same. Because Atua cursed me, just as it's cursing you. It has planned to kill you from the very beginning. Part of its grand plan." He lunges in, faster than a whip, and snags her by the arm, dangerously close and breathing in her perfect breath. "But we can defeat it. We'd be so much stronger if we were together, stronger than Atua could ever be. That's why it keeps us apart. If you join me—"

She balks, but he holds her firm.

"—if you come home into my arms where you belong, I will give you everything. I'll give you love everlasting."

"Get away from me!" she commands, and he almost feels compelled to do it. She's bursting with that righteous anger again, and oh, how he loves to see the pink blush of fury on her face. His Nal now has feelings. Perfect, lovely, exquisite feelings.

But then one stands out from the rest, and it makes him comply immediately. He knows all her tells, after all. Filling with dread, he sees she isn't consumed with red wrath. Her face is the epitome of blackest contempt. Pure hate.

No. No, not that.

He drops to his knees in supplication, his anger a snuffed candle as a familiar, desperate panic sets in. "Don't come with me then, you don't have to come—just don't die for this. Whatever is coming for you, if you're afraid it will hurt, that means it will. Do you know how hated you are for your excellence? The jealousy everyone feels over your power and connection to Atua? If they kill you, *when* they kill you, they will make it hurt if only to prove a point, do you understand?"

She scowls at him, loathing him with everything she is. "Get. Away. From. Me."

He flinches as if burned. He's running out of options. He needs to salvage this. "What if I'm sorry? What if I repent?"

Shaking her head, she looks at him one last time. "Some things don't deserve to be forgiven."

It's as if she's stabbed him. His brain isn't working as he watches her go. Why is she always going away? Why is she always leaving him?

Afraid to follow, afraid to stoke her hatred, he simply calls her name over and over, though it's no use. Abaddon's wails turn to snarls turn to viciousness as insanity grabs at his ankles and pulls.

* * *

I need to stop her, I need to stop her, I need to stop her, pulses through him. If she's afraid of the pain, then she knows something he doesn't. The local religious zealots are gearing up to displace her, and he'd kill them if he could, but his hands are tied. All those who want the Pharisees dead fear their power too much to act on their desires, so no matter how much Abaddon whispers and cries and screams into their ears, he is thwarted over and over by Free Will.

FUCK free will, he screeches silently. *If I don't have it, no one should. It's unfair, unfair, UNFAIR!*

He knows logically that she'll die anyway. She's human. She was born, and so she will die. Now or later, what's the difference? Reason says if she's earning favor by doing this thing, he should just let her have her moment. Perhaps she'll live on in heaven.

But no, he needs time. He needs time to get back into her good graces. She can't die with that hate in her heart. Not for him. He is hers, she is his, so *why!?*

The lost souls of Hell flutter around Abaddon and see his pain, empathizing in a way he's no longer capable of. "If heaven takes her," he sneers at them, "We take heaven." They suffer and stare at him, praying for their pain to end, and he lies to them. He lies and lies and lies.

"If heaven is ours, all its peace will be yours. You'll be reunited with your loved ones. You'll be able to make amends. But Atua won't let you in willingly. Atua will fight. Which is why we have to be ready. If we can take heaven, it will be like going home."

Home. Home to his Nal, where she is small and dreams about him and feels his pain and names stars after him. Where she needs him and he needs her, and their connection is the most perfect thing in the entire universe. Where they are innocence and love personified, as pure as fresh snow and as gold as the sun.

And somewhere is his vast domain, Lilith clenches, spilling out more of his children. Spawn to be used for the slaughter.

* * *

I need to stop her, I need to stop her, is the line of thought that ruins him. Ruins her. Ruins everything.

Nal's disciple, Judas—the most susceptible of all her followers, yet the one she has the softest spot for—picks up Abaddon's cry and misunderstands. He twists its urgency and takes it in a new direction.

"This is going too far," Judas tells the Pharisees. "She's not the daughter of God, like she claims. These miracles must be false, somehow. She's just a human, no more special than any of us."

Judas hunches while the unseen Abaddon writhes with the urge to destroy him for his lies. There is no outlet for this feeling, and he's going to melt with the heat of his rage.

"We know," those false prophets coo, worried more about their status than about anything to do with Atua. The Pharisees may perform rites and rituals, but they care nothing about actual righteousness. Hypocrites, all of them. "We can stop her—"

"Speak with her," one softens. "You know the Romans do not care for our kind, nor the spectacles she woos the crowds with. She is foolish. Ignorant. Once she understands the position of the church, she'll see how insane all this is."

Insane? I'll show you insane, Abaddon froths.

Judas cringes, weak and worthless. "You'll hurt her."

"We won't," the liars vow. "We are also ones who follow God. Thou shalt not kill, remember?"

But you don't plan to kill her. You plan to have others do it for you. Loopholes, loopholes.

Judas is considering. That bastard betrayer is actually considering! But it's only when they bring out the silver that the man is truly swayed.

"You don't even have to keep it for yourself. You could give it to the poor. This is just a fee for your service and it's all for the greater good," the Pharisees tell him, as if they knew what goodness is. "Caesar is volatile. She's putting everyone in danger. This is bigger than her. Bigger than any of us."

It's only after Judas gives Nal up and they toss his coins to the ground that the man realizes he's been used. Tricked. The Pharisees' persuasion has turned to mockery as they refuse to even touch him, making Judas collect his blood money from the dirt. Yet the man still makes no effort to stop it from happening. Instead, he does what Abaddon never had the chance to.

He kisses Nal goodbye.

And she knows. Either by instinct or divine revelation, she understands exactly what her friend has done. She puts on a strong front, but Abaddon sees the depth of her pain. He always does.

When she's taken by the mob who once revered her, Judas finally understands what this means. What they'll do to her. A friend he's shared countless meals with and listened to for hours upon hours. One he believed in...until he didn't.

And now she's about to be crucified.

Judas knows it's all his fault. The betrayer's tormented sorrow knows no bounds then, and the man is lost...which is why when Abaddon leans close and hisses the words, "Kill yourself" into his mind, that's exactly what he does.

* * *

Abaddon thought his empathy was dead, and maybe it was, but Nal brings it back to life as he watches her agony. Every lash across her back, every nail between her bones, every thorn upon her crown. He'd had thorns rake over his flesh once upon a time, and he knows the pain of it...but the lance. When she is lanced, he *screams.* And when the inevitable end begins, the earth obeys him.

Humans tremble—not out of fear, but because of the ground rumbling beneath their feet. Nal's sky darkens as her head dips ever lower, and Abaddon only needs to swipe one hand to the side to tear a crack through the dust. Still, lepers brave the shaking earth to dive in and sample her blood, healing themselves even as she fades, taking every last miracle from her sagging body.

And when she finally dies, the once-Nox breaks his promise. His eyes burn red tears as he grabs hold of the sky—Nal's domain—and swirls it into nightmare clouds, lightning pouring down in unending swaths of white fire, ripping apart the land.

Die, Abaddon demands of everything in sight. His children, the only thing under his control, curdle instantly, yet the humans only hold each other, suddenly filled with nobility and bravery and care and self-lessness.

It's laughable.

Another blare of white light zigzags, drawing a curtain through the humans he can't kill, but can ruin with terror, burn and scar with trauma. There is no ending his howls as the sky turns black, the thick, tumultuous clouds hiding even the tiniest pinprick of light. The humans cry out for mercy, but Abaddon has none. Crags burst up out of nowhere and the humans roll down, skittering over pebbles that skin their knees and break their bones but will never do enough damage.

And then, a single beam of sunlight penetrates the thunderheads. It's nearly blinding, and it shines its brightness down on one thing and one thing only.

It lights up Nal's cross, casting her limp body in chiaroscuro.

A dove flutters down, landing peacefully by the woman who was an angel, who once created its ancestors, who loved them just like she used to love Nox. Abaddon's wrath breaks and he goes to his knees, gasping in breaths that will never slake his thirst for air. He stares at the dove, and it stares back at him.

She's soothing me, isn't she? Is this forgiveness? Has she gone to heaven and remembered who I am, finally deciding to pardon me from her hate?

But when daylight blesses the valley, it leaves the sole figure of Abaddon under a shroud of black darkness, as alone as he has ever been. Her light and goodness is out of reach. Maybe it always has been.

His bitter laugh drags the last shred of sanity from his mind, and the earth takes him. Like long ago, it has mercy and swallows him up, pulling him down, down, down. Far past his Hell-home, far past his caves of the lost. Into the heat of its gravity well, Abaddon sinks, his body burning but his mind like ice. His skin flays red, the remains of his horns turn to onyx, and his heart bleeds only black.

There's no saving him. No forgiveness. No love. There's only overthrowing the one who ruined him. Who ruined *her* by making her something she was never supposed to be. His Nal would have never rejected him. *His* Nal forgave everything and told him he was beautiful. That she loved him! Forever!

No, that thing he met may have had Nal's soul, but it was polluted by the sins of humanity. Does he hate her? No. Only himself. Does he still want her? No. Never again. She is fake. He wants the real Nal. *His* Nal. And to do it, he'll destroy earth, mankind, and everything. He'll bring about the Armageddon he never wanted and rip a hole through heaven's gate.

And if she fights him?

Well.

He'll have all eternity to kiss and make it better, won't he? If she is the sun, he is a black hole. He'll suck anything and everything into himself, eventually. Even her.

"And then we'll finally be together. There will be no escaping anymore. No fluttering away. No distance. No rejection. I will come home at long last, just like you've begged for ages. It doesn't matter if you want me or not anymore, sweetheart. I'm coming for you. After all, you're mine.

"And it's time you learned that."

SOULMATES
& SILENCE

Soulmates and Silence

~YOU DID THIS TO YOURSELF~

Unicorns. Throughout the lands, they are regarded as the most mystical and majestic of all creatures. Bodies like white stallions, muscular and powerful; strands of golden hair that catch the light with rainbow hues; and singular horns that swirl in a glittering spiral, a holy, sacred artifact said to cure even death. These creatures are considered purity itself by all who know their name. Something that draws in the most delicate and innocent of maidens. Creatures people hope and pray to see.

Silen, a young man of light brown hair and lighter blue eyes, knows a fantastical beast such as this—was practically raised by him. Koti, one of the most ancient and renowned of all...

Too bad he's such an asshole.

If you hadn't left me behind again, this never would have happened in the first place! Silen thinks, the words holding little barbs he'd like to rake his friend with. Shoving roughly, Silen pounds his comrade's haunches to no avail, yanking strands of the creature's hair out to annoy it if nothing else. Unfortunately, it doesn't matter how strong he is; the beast doesn't budge. It doesn't matter how much sweat he works up as he shoves; the unicorn's heavy frame is like a soft stone to beat his body against. Silen's staccato, nasal puffs of effort merely make Koti roll his beautiful eyes.

"Why take it out on me? " Koti says. "You did this to yourself. I tried to save you, but noooooo, you had to go and be all...you about it!"

Silen silently lances Koti with the thought: *You're the one that taught me to BE like this!*

Gesturing to his chest with his eyebrows up, he sneers, saying nothing, though the unicorn catches his drift anyway.

"Unequivocally. Your. Fault." Koti lets out a snort. "Out of everyone to irritate, why did you have to pick Ambek? He's the most powerful fairy spirit in the forest! Not to mention he has a legion of sycophants. You're lucky you made it out alive." The glorified horse kicks backwards, missing Silen's shin by an inch. "You think because you're with me, oh mortal man, you can do anything you want? Steal from people? Stab at people? Emotionally slap people until they cry like babies?" The unicorn glares at him with one, shiny eye. "Because you absolutely *can!* But only when I'm there to teach you how to get away with it *properly!*"

To this, Silen only puts his face in his hands, scrubbing at his eyes. He hates this most recent turn of events in a lifetime of...well...events. Though, as usual, Koti is right. It was his fault. After all, earlier that day...

* * *

The forest was beautiful. Some said "enchanted"—and they were absolutely right. The woods were filled with a number of magical creatures. Satyrs and nymphs. Naiads and dryads. Beasts both beautiful and terrible, awe-inspiring and oh-so-preciously rare. Though perhaps, to Silen, they may not be nearly rare enough, given how many of these stunning specimens posed an immediate threat to his personage.

Beyz, an overlarge troll, approached with spittle drooling from his fanged mouth, lips curled in a menacing smile that would make any good henchman proud. Silen leaned backwards just in time to avoid the spiked club that Beyz swiped his way, feeling the breeze of it on his neck. Any closer and he'd have bled out on the pretty tulips, something he preferred to avoid.

"Hey, hey, hey now!" Silen shouted. "What's the point in that?"

Ambek, the revered leader of this motley crew, scowled. "The point is that I am insulted. You are insolent, vile, and have no respect for what's mine."

"All I did was pee on it!"

"It was my WIFE!"

"And she's a *tree* most of the time! How was I supposed to know? What else am I supposed to pee on?! The grass?! You *eat* the grass!"

That only made Ambek seethe. He jumped higher up on the craggy stone directly before Silen, looking down as if ready to eviscerate him... yet somehow Silen barely noticed. He was too busy muttering to himself in thought, scratching his chin.

"Though I suppose everything else pees on the grass, what's a little human mixed in? Maybe you've developed a taste for it over time? Is it salty, like sweat?" Looking up, he declared a mental victory, as if he'd solved one of life's great puzzles. "If you prefer it that way, I promise to pee wherever you eat!"

Beyz took another swipe at him.

Silen ducked. "What! It's seasoning!"

Ambek hollered in frustration, the spines on his back standing on end, resembling red fire. His narrow wings fluttered but he didn't fly, proof that he'd rather let his minions do his dirty work. Ambek's wife, the urine-soaked nymph, sat beside him with wide eyes, clutching at his hooves and looking the epitome of leafy innocence, though Silen knew better. This isn't the first golden shower she'd likely indulged in.

Another minion swooped in on the offensive. It was a sassy faun that lurched forward this time, teeth out and ready to snap—especially dangerous given that fauns were *not tall*. Silen backpedaled, clutching his groin to protect what was rightfully his while the mini-brute kept advancing, leaving Silen no choice but to roundhouse the poor bastard in the face, knocking out one of his weaponized front teeth in the process.

A silence fell over the glade as the faun spat out the obliterated tooth, root and all, and once the thing was done bouncing across the pebbled dirt—*ping, ping, pa-ping*—everyone turned in slow motion to look at Silen.

"First blood," someone whispered.

Silen's entire body went rigid. "Well, if you didn't try to eat what belongs to my soulmate someday, then this wouldn't have happened, now would it?"

Everyone stared, fists clenching slowly. Dramatically. Knuckles cracked and teeth grinded, sending Silen's runaway mouth off into nervous, one-sided banter.

"I mean, how would you like it if I nipped off *your* bits!? Not that you have big bits, you being tiny you and all... I mean, if anyone has big bits here, it's Ambek. He's like a stud in rut, and I mean that in the nicest of ways, other than the fact that looking at him is mildly terrifying because it swings in my direction when he walks. It's like, if I got close enough, would it pendulum and touch me? Because I don't know if I could handle that, emotionally. I might need to have a good cry about it. I'm just not that kind of guy. I mean, I'm the *crying* kind of guy, just not the touching-huge-bits kind of guy."

Some random henchman broke into a laugh and everyone else had to stifle a snicker, even the one-less-toothed faun. After all, a forest-wide truth was known. No one wanted to be whapped by Ambek's male parts. Sometimes—most of the time—not even his wife.

The fairy spirit only needed to raise an eyebrow for everyone to settle into coughs of discomfort, though their mouths still twitched in barely contained amusement.

"While I appreciate your backhanded praise for my under-carriage—"

The crowd snorted again, lips trembling as they reigned it in.

"That doesn't mean you've been saved from my wrath. All it means is that I'll kill you quicker. A reward for your compliment."

With a waggle of Ambek's fingers, the advance against Silen came again in earnest. Clubs, teeth, claws, the whole of Ambek's horde descended on him with a detached vengeance. Nothing personal. Just another job to be done for the most powerful spirit they knew.

Silen wasn't much of a fighter, but a dodger? That was where his true strength lay. His muscles were wiry and his form slender, making it easy to tip this way and that, slipping between his enemies, sucking back to avoid a taloned swipe through the air, and lunging to the ground for a quick roll between Beyz's tree-trunk ankles. Still, they closed in, and Silen got pushed ever closer to a thicket of brambles, the burrs of which were tipped with a long-lasting poison that would leave him itching in the most unsightly of places. A must-avoid kind of plant.

Please don't let it ruin my day, he thought.

A whinny of salvation peeled out in high pitched notes as Koti, that marvelous son of a magical mare, leapt over not only the pricker bush, but over Silen's head, landing stoutly between him and the gathering of henchmen. The beast stabbed his horn forward in a gesture that was quite clear: *Come closer and I will gut you.*

Still clutching Ambek's legs, the nymph's hand flew up in rapture as she stated the obvious. "A unicorn!"

"Yes, dear, we all have eyes," Ambek said.

Koti puffed air out through his thick lips, making a rumbling sound as his horn threatened. "This human is under my protection."

Everyone blinked, confused. It was unheard of. A precious unicorn and a mundane man?

Ambek, nearly dazed with the idiocy of it, asked, "Why in the name of the forest would you—?"

"I'm charming," Silen cut in from behind his friend's rear. "And hilarious. You think so too, I know, you're just being shy because you're mad at me. Though, in all honesty, it should be your wife that's mad at me. Unless she liked it."

Koti responded with a flick of the tail that effectively slapped Silen's mouth into stillness, though he was otherwise unfazed. It was only when Ambek chuckled, a dark look on his face, that the human got his first chill of fear.

I'm dead, aren't I?

The spirit took a seat next to his wife on the high rock and hummed in contemplation, eyeing Silen with a malice barely hidden under his smile.

So dead. Dead eighty times over. Harpies-eating-my-insides-for-all-eternity dead.

Ambek looked haughty. Eyebrows raised and lips quirked up at the corners, his wings gave another excited quiver. "Since you're so *charming,* Silen of the River, why don't I go ahead and give you an opportunity to prove it? I propose a wager."

Koti grunted. "That doesn't sound ominous at all."

Ambek slid his hand around his wife's shoulders, bringing her close and kissing her fall-colored hair. "You mentioned a soulmate. You have a mark, yes?"

From behind Koti's tail, Silen lifted his tunic. Just over his navel was a red swirl, something like a spiral. He wanted to find the person who owned a matching symbol with his whole heart, but at this point, feared that he never would. Not unless he walked up to every girl he saw with his shirt hem to his chest, baring his belly, which would be the worst kind of attention-seeking possible. Even Silen had his limits.

Ambek's smile was sly. "Then we have our wager."

"Say again?" Koti asked, his horn still lowered and ready to go.

"I'll be making your ward live out his namesake. Silen shall become *silent.* I am taking his voice."

Both Koti and Silen tipped their heads to the sky with groans.

"Whaaaaat?!" balked the unicorn.

"Whaaaaat?!" balked the man. "But I sing like an angel!"

"You sing like a crow," Koti corrected, "but I'll be even more irritated if you're mute."

"See?!" Silen gestured at his friend. "Do you really want to annoy a unico—"

And his voice dropped to nothing.

Absolutely nothing.

Silen grasped his throat, mouthing words that wouldn't come with wide eyes. It was like an emptiness took over his insides. With both hands, he patted himself, filling with terror as he looked to his friend for guidance. Koti stared at him for a minute before rearing his head back and yelling, "Ugggghhhhhh!"

They both stomped their feet in an arrhythmic pattern, tearing grumpy holes in the ground, hooves and boots kicking up clots in their shared anger and depression.

With a snort, Koti said, "Fine! What's your game? I assume he gets his voice back if he meets your demands."

"Of course! And I'm a spirit of my word. I keep all my promises." Ambek gestured to himself like he was somehow all the more benevolent for it. Silen gave him a rude gesture with his finger but did it behind his friend's rump to avoid any further repercussions.

With his hand towards the clouds, Ambek smiled. "It's a full moon tonight. A time for lovers, is it not? Let's give *Silent* a chance to seek out his fated companion. If he finds his soulmate by the next full moon and earns a kiss of true love despite losing his...*charm*, all is forgiven."

"His soulmate?" Koti asked. He bared his teeth in that weird way only horse-like creatures could, his upper lip lifting strangely. "Not just a lover, but one with his *mark?!*"

"That's the wager," Ambek said with a shrug.

Again, the unicorn stomped with an "Ugggghhhhhh!" directed at the sky.

* * *

Startling Silen from his inconvenient flashback, Koti grabs the man by the leather of his tunic and whips him aside, landing him rump-first in the grass. Grumbling, the unicorn plods close enough to hover over him, casting ominous shadows.

"If the concept of idiocy could grow a face, it would look like yours: slack-jawed, dirty, and with its eyebrows lifted all the way up to its hairline in everlasting surprise."

Silen hefts himself up, getting back in his friend's space without fear. He has So Many Comebacks for this mythical prick of a horse but is unable to spit any of them. It's enraging! If his hands could wrap around Koti's neck, he'd throttle this amoral immortal.

Still, without Koti jumping into the fray, this could have gone so much worse. In fact, if not for his friend, Silen's entire *life* would have been...well, unlivable, really. Koti hasn't just saved him once or twice. He's been saving Silen for as long as he can remember. And even during those times when Koti is the one actively, purposefully getting Silen into trouble, he's always there to help get him out of it again.

This will be no different. Koti has never abandoned him. Never will. Silen believes in that the way he believes in the sky.

I can't stay mad at you. Silen thinks at his friend, going from gesturing rudely towards his face to petting his muzzle, trying to soothe their mutual vexation. Koti tolerates it for only a moment before pulling away.

"You have the weepy eyes." Koti grunts. "Don't with the eyes. You know how I feel about the eyes!"

Silen loves his friend. His comrade. His mentor—if a unicorn could qualify as such a thing.

"I said stop!"

Holding his hands over his heart, Silen spreads them and signals love flowing from him to Koti, the action intended to annoy the unicorn more than anything else. Silen then begins to do a mock dance of appreciation and kinship, though it probably comes off as a mental illness of some kind.

Not too keen on body language, Koti rolls his dewy eyes. "I already hate this. Don't move."

The unicorn points his magical spire directly toward Silen, whose hands go up in immediate surrender.

"Don't be stupid," his friend hisses, backing him up until Silen's rear end hits a tree. He squints his eyes shut, preparing to be dispatched for no reason whatsoever, until Koti's horn taps against his forehead. He feels a sudden pulse in his brain, a heavy *thump,* and the sensations around him become...*more.* Head swimming, Silen goes to his knees.

"Yeah, it'll do that," Koti says, as if it was an everyday occurrence. "Give it a minute."

A minute? Silen thinks. *My mind just popped!*

"It didn't pop," Koti says. "I just connected our souls on a deeper level. You're magical, I'm infinitely more magical; it was easy. This forest ebbs and flows with a never-ending pattern of enchantments. Now, you can finally see. Hear. Experience its richness."

Silen looks at his friend, eyebrows knit. *Did you just hear my thoughts?*

"Out of everything I just said, that's all you came away with?" Koti blows out a puff of air and straightens, looking back over his withers towards the tree line. "We have to find your match. Normally one is born close to the other, but that doesn't guarantee your families don't migrate."

Silen sulks, feeling his old hurt. *Too bad I don't remember the name of my village. It would have been a good starting place.*

"Yes, well. We can traipse around the area where I found you. Stir up some old memories."

Silen doesn't need words this time; he just makes a face.

"If she's your soulmate, chances are that she's waiting for you and not married off to some other unwashed male. Perhaps she's still unattached and innocent. Adults will throw their virgins at the woods if they hear I'm prancing around. We can spirit a few away and see what comes of it."

Silen narrows his eyes in reproach.

"Don't you start with me." Koti is never one to be moved by morality.

If you have to trick her to come to me, she's probably not my soulmate.

Koti pokes his horn against Silen's belly a little too hard. "We'll just look for one of these. Some ladies wear their bodice hems high and their skirt waists low."

Tantalizing, but I don't think any virgins they throw at you would dress like that. Besides, I like a hint of bashfulness in my woman.

"Says the man who's never even had a woman."

Silen crosses his arms and scowls. Being soulmated comes with consequences. If you try to...*pair* with the wrong person, not only is it revolting, but it hurts to even try. His teenage years taught him that much.

I'm just shy, he thinks.

"Says the man who exposed himself and pissed on a nymph."

Mistaken identity! Silen lifts his hands before letting them clap back down against his thighs. *So, what then? We just go around the woods hoping for naked women?*

Koti's tail twitches, flicking a fly off his hock. "No. We do it my way."

Silen sighs. *So we're spiriting away a damsel.*

"Damsels, perhaps. Plural. It's the easiest way." Koti's eyes glisten. "And the most fun."

Silen's silent groan cannot be overstated.

eep

Chapter 2

~THE SEARCH~

The first one punched him dead in the face. Silen should have realized leaning against a wall on the edge of a town, grabbing a girl's wrist, and trying to silently lure her into the woods was a bad idea. The girl knocked him on his ass and some man-meat of a husband gave him a few rib kicks for kindness' sake.

The second time Silen tried to beckon some maidens his way, he was smarter about it. He'd gotten (stolen) a flute and proceeded to play it (badly) on the outskirts of town. Over the course of the day, it drew the attention of three different women who knew the instrument well enough to consider him a nuisance, all of whom wandered over to tell him off. Unfortunately, they were all well past marrying age. One did, however, try to teach him for an hour or so before she realized she was wasting her time with a mute, waved her goodbyes, and abandoned him for dead in the alleyway. Still, Silen was happy to have a rudimentary tune or two under his belt. If he couldn't speak, maybe he could at least blow shrieking whistles at people.

The third opportunity came upon Silen and Koti in the woods. A young woman approached as if angry, thrashing her way through the underbrush in crunches and crackles until she stood before them, blocking their path. She glared and cocked her hips, telling Koti she was as pure as the driven snow, and it was about damn time he finally went about finding her. It was the strangest confrontation.

They wondered if the soul bond had called her to Silen somehow. Was she the one? The unicorn glanced at Silen in sympathy knowing that she was repugnant. Not her looks so much as her personality. She had a way about her that made you want to claw your own face off. Upon meeting her, Silen prayed she'd either be driven away by wolves or eaten by them. He'd rather lose his voice forever than be bound to something like her.

Koti told her in beautiful language that they were looking for the most innocent maiden in all existence, one with "The mark of the goddess on her navel," and if she didn't have it, to please step aside. The woman, true to form, insulted them in seven different ways—none of which they'd ever heard before—then kicked Silen squarely between the legs, and ran away in wailing tears. Apparently, she didn't have what they were looking for.

Word spread throughout the village that a unicorn was searching for an innocent with a soulmark on her belly. At first, that seemed like it could only be a good thing; the more who knew, the closer Silen was to ending his search on a happy note. Unfortunately, however, when scores of supposed-virgins tramped out in the morning mist, Silen realized that notoriety wasn't always all you'd hoped it would be. Many of the contenders had painted squiggles on themselves in a poor attempt to get the unicorn's attention. It made Silen ill to see how many were willing to pretend to be soulmarked, given the pain it had brought him throughout his life. They treated it like it was an honor instead of a curse. There were blue marks, green marks, purple marks, marks drawn with blood, all flaunted like jewels in the shapes of circles, triangles, squares, and stars.

Only one had a red spiral, and Silen nearly died of shock when he saw it. Going closer, though, he knew that the girl wasn't the right one.

Something in his gut rejected every piece of her. Hearing his thoughts, Koti asked Silen to touch the girl's mark to see if it glowed...and of course it didn't. It rubbed off and every one of her pores made Silen's skin sting. The girl trudged away in shame then, along with every other woman in the forest clearing. They all knew that, no matter how much they painted themselves, they could never glow.

It was time for the next town.

* * *

Now, Silen mopes as he sits picking grass and eating the thicker stalks. They taste both sweet and bitter at the same time, though only the sweetness stays on his breath. To ensure his teeth stay healthy, he chews them for longer than he needs to, having learned from Koti's example and scraping them clean. He has the best teeth out of any human he's ever met and is quite proud of them. It's one of the few silent charms he has, one he plans on using to his full advantage once he meets the girl of his dreams. Who doesn't like a nice smile? Will his soulmate have a nice smile?

I never realized how badly I needed her until now, he thinks.

The unicorn stands beside him, also enjoying a nibble, pulling out purple-headed clovers in clumps at a time. "Liar. You've always been obsessed. Longing to find her. Dreaming of her. Going off on tangents about how it would feel to copulate with her."

I know, but this is different. Every sunrise I wake up with such hope and every nightfall it dies a slow death. It's like...

"Like waiting for your parents all over again?"

Something heavy weighs down Silen's chest, making it hard to breathe. Without being able to run his mouth ad nauseam, he's mired in a swamp of thoughts with no hope of distraction. It's always better to play the fool than realize you are one.

At least I have you, he thinks at his friend.

The unicorn *hmph*s, getting down on his knees and resting beside

Silen. "I will never leave you. Even when you die, I think I'll bind your soul to a rock so I can keep you." Koti wrenches more grass from the ground and talks with his mouth full. "Don't give up hope just yet. If we haven't found anything by the time the moon hides and the sky turns black, we'll start thinking of other options."

What options?

"Begging?"

Silen snorts. *I can't see you begging for anything.*

"Who said it would be me?"

With an expression that's supposed to be accompanied by a groan, Silen lays back in the greenery, letting its scent soothe some of his worry. He belongs here. He belongs in these woods with this beast. If futures were written in the stars, this was the one meant for him, voice or no. Soulmate or no. Though the thought hurts.

Am I destined to fail?

"There's no such thing as destiny. Our fates are our own." Koti nuzzles Silen's foot for the briefest of moments. "Even stupid fates like yours."

Silen's chuckle makes no sound, leaving the empty air to the symphony of crickets. After shoving his friend for no reason, patting his flank, and dusting off a few fireflies, Silen rises with a stretch, heading off to the lake for a drink and to the trees for his personal relief.

"Make sure it's not a nymph this time!" Koti calls. "Or they'll curse that tiny trinket dangling between your legs, and at that point it'll disappear!"

To which Silen makes a vulgar gesture over his shoulder.

Ambling toward the lake, he looks down at his crotch and sulks. Koti is an idiot. It's definitely a normal-sized trinket.

* * *

The lake is beautiful. The waning moonlight dances on the ripples, a tiny spectrum you can glide your fingers through. Silen finishes his business with no repercussions, the tree being only a tree, and moves on to take a drink. Without talking a mile a minute, he's less thirsty than usual, which means he has to fill his waterskins less. Fewer trips back to the place where, long ago, he became his true self instead of the little boy who was starved for affection.

Sauntering from oak to birch, his brain trips over unfortunate memories—ones he wishes he didn't have but does anyway. He's lost in them when, suddenly, a slosh of water a little further offshore catches his attention, causing his steps to slow. His senses go on high alert, knees going wide and hands coming up defensively. His ears search for sound. One never knows what's waiting around the corner, and without Koti to protect him, there is very little dodging that will save him from a wandering bobcat, bear, or banshee.

Peeking around the trunk of an ancient willow, he spies a human figure bathed in pale blue moonlight. A female figure. She lifts water and runs it over herself, cleaning her naked body. Her long, black hair is wet and drags down her back, covering her rear from view, though her hips curve visibly. Her shape is stunning. Gorgeous. And when she turns in his direction, his eyes drop from her face to her breasts to her belly...where a red spiral lies.

Everything in him trembles. Silen had thought he had both pride and shame about his mark, very rarely showing it, but that thought drops from his mind like a falcon towards the treeline.

Wrenching his shirt up into a whorl over his ribs, he crashes into the water, wanting to call out to her, but absolutely unable. Her wide eyes, colorless in the dark, lock onto him before she covers herself in perfect shyness, letting out a gasp of shock.

She spins away as he approaches awkwardly, splashing and almost losing his balance twice, trying to show her what she's likely been looking for her whole life. It isn't until her scream splits the night air that Silen stills, unsure of what to do as she clambers, trying to escape.

She can't do that. Why would she do that? He needs her. Doesn't she need him?

KOTI! he screams silently. *KOTI, I FOUND HER! SHE'S RUNNING AWAY!*

On the bank in the mud, she scrambles to get her clothes on. Silen can't help but watch every movement, petrified and unable to drop his gaze. He knows only one truth…she doesn't want him.

Without a moment to waste, his heart breaks into pieces.

That's when Koti steps up in all his glory. The moonlight kisses the golden hair of his mane, glowing and ethereal. His horn twinkles as if reflecting the stars. Fireflies frame him in majesty. In times like this, even Silen is in awe of his friend. It's showmanship, pure and simple. A carnival trick. But damned if it wasn't effective.

"Hush, maiden, my friend and I will do no harm to you." Koti soothes her with the softest of whispers. It carries through the night with the power of his magic, throbbing as if he's speaking inside of you somehow. Silen's arms turn to gooseflesh.

With a cry, she drops to the ground in supplication as she stares at the unicorn, covering her mouth with both hands in obedience.

"You need not fear me, child. I only come to those who are worthy."

Liar, Silen scolds. Koti eyes him for only a moment before getting back to work.

"Sweet one, do you know why we've found you here tonight?"

His soulmate shakes her head while still clutching her mouth, trying to keep quiet like she was told. She quivers with emotion and Silen wants nothing more than to comfort her. Hold her. Everything he's ever needed in life has narrowed down to this one pinprick.

"We've found you because we need you for our quest."

"Q-quest?" she asks, and Silen's heart aches. She even sounds beautiful. Musical. He's swooning. His knees might let go and he might drown.

"Yes. My friend had his voice stolen by an evil fairy. We need your help to restore it by the next full moon."

"How could I possibly help? I'm just a—"

"Tell me, innocent one. Do you have a soulmark?"

From behind, Silen wants to see her face. He wants to watch her lips as they move. As it is, all he can see is the small, side to side shake of her head.

She asks, "What's a soulmark?"

Silen's blood runs cold. *She has one, Koti. I saw it.*

"There are people in this world blessed with magic, born with a soulmate—their perfect love match. If they can find one another, only then will they know true happiness. Without their soulmate, they are but half a person and live out their lives with an emptiness they can't explain. These people are marked on their skin. Special patterns in special colors. And if your soulmate touches the mark, it glows. Do you have something like that on your body, child? Your belly perhaps?"

The woman puts her face in her hands, muffling her voice as she speaks formally. "It's not permitted for me to look at my own body, oh honored one. Otherwise, I am filthy. Sullied. My body is meant for my husband alone."

Silen's mouth goes dry. Still hip-deep in the water, his hand clenches harder around his now-sopping clothes, looking at his friend as jealousy burns him.

"Are you promised, young maiden?"

"Y-yes..." she stammers. Silen wants to scream. "B-but I cannot bear to be near him. It breaks my heart and it's like my skin stings when he touches me. But he is wealthy, and I have been raised for none but him. My parents will not be moved no matter how I beg. So, I...I ran." She bows, forehead to the ground. "Please do not punish me. And please do not tell me to go back. If you insist, holy one, I will...but—"

"What is your name?" Koti asks.

"Saelle."

Silen and Saelle. Even their names go perfectly together.

"Saelle, destiny brought you to us."

What happened to 'There's no such thing as destiny?' Silen snarks.

Koti tosses him his best *Shut up* glare.

She shakes her head in confusion. "But I don't have a mark."

Tell her she does. Tell her she's mine. Tell her that it won't burn when I touch her and that I'll only bring her joy for the rest of her life. Tell her I'll love her until the end of time. That I'll do anything, give anything, be anything...

But Koti only says. "It doesn't matter. You are meant to help us find Silen's soulmate. Will you help my friend, little one? Will you help *me?*"

How could she possibly refuse?

She ventures a look over her shoulder at Silen, fear still drenching her features. "He's terrifying."

It's like she stabbed him. He staggers under the weight of her rejection.

The unicorn only chuckles, tossing his mane. "Yet if you heard him speak, you would only laugh. And if you heard him sing, you would laugh even harder."

Silen's eyes snap up as he glowers at his friend, though the girl's lips suddenly tip up into a small smile. In the space of a moment, she completely relaxes. In fact, the whole forest is suddenly brimming with a sense of safety and sweetness.

You're doing this, aren't you? You're tricking her. Bewitching her.

Koti only stands straighter, no doubt proud of himself, self-righteous as always. Mischief gleams in his beautiful eyes.

This isn't going to go well, Silen warns. *When she realizes, she'll only hate us.*

He is summarily ignored.

"So, will you come, little one?" Koti asks. "Aid us in our quest?"

She nods, looking up at the unicorn with such reverence and hope that Silen feels a deep twinge of guilt. Sealing the deal, Koti nuzzles her sweetly.

"And if we succeed, fair maiden, I promise to protect you for the rest of your life."

Because we're bound, and she'd be with me. You manipulative bastard.

Though, whether Silen likes it or not, it seems that's exactly what Saelle needed to hear.

* * *

Sleeping is an awkward arrangement. Silen normally leans on Koti's flank, staying warm in the night's crisp air, but Saelle wouldn't come within ten feet of him, and so exceptions have to be made. With nothing but innocence and gratefulness, she cuddles against Koti's shoulder while he tells her of their quest, wrapping his head around, breathing warm air on her knees, and keeping her in comfort. Silen is jealous for more than one reason.

Meanwhile, he lays with the one small, rolled blanket Saelle had pilfered from her family before running away. He soothes himself with the thought that, even though she doesn't want him, she obviously doesn't want anyone else in particular, either. If it stung when she touched her intended, it's further proof that she did carry a soulmark and not just an ownership branding or a very oddly specific tattoo.

He can't sleep knowing she's right there. His arms ache to hold her. His lips beg to touch her skin. Anywhere. Everywhere.

He straightens out on the damp grass and presses his fists against his eyes, mouthing something that looks like a gripe. His brain pulses the word *Unfair!* It's one thing not to have her at all, but a completely different thing to have her so close, yet so far away.

He tries to think of how to woo her, but his words are gone. If Koti didn't appreciate his interpretive dance, she certainly won't either. She'll probably scream and run away from him again.

Cursed. I am forever cursed.

Koti huffs and Silen gives him the side eye. Quietly, the unicorn hisses, "Stop mind-whining at me."

Silen sits straight up in irritation and gestures to his chest, mouthing, *How am I supposed to feel?!*

Koti leans his neck forward toward Silen, trying to speak softly so Saelle can stay in the land of dreams. "Be grateful; she's here! We have what we need."

You believe me, then?

"Oh yes. You've never been this utterly stupid before. And I say that knowing you've been stupid your entire life."

Petulant, Silen wraps his arms around his legs. *I'm not stupid. I'm lovesick.*

"We'll just make her fall in love with you."

She's supposed to be in love with me already. And how could I possibly make her see me that way? I can't tell her how I feel.

"I can speak for you. Tell her all your snide comments and moronic jokes."

Silen lifts his eyebrows at the unicorn, one significantly higher than the other.

"No, you're right. That would make me sound like a fool."

And if you make me sound like you, pretty words and sweet sonnets, she'll fall in love with someone who's not me. Someone who doesn't even exist.

"I know literally no sonnets. Blow your flute at her."

Now that's a way to make her run.

"No worse than your singing."

Silen tosses himself on the ground again. *I hate you. You're miserable.*

"You love me. I'm your savior. And I will be again. I'd take your incessant bleats over this soundless boredom any day."

Aww, it's almost like you complimented me.

"Well, I'm going to have to do it more often over the next few days. I already hate it. I'll have to tell her stories about you, too."

Well, that won't go well...

"I'll edit. Be selective."

No. Better to tell her everything. Perhaps she'll be charmed by my failings as much as my wins.

"What wins?"

Now you're just being mean.

They look at each other in mutual amusement.

"Get some sleep. I'll lull you. We need to be fresh tomorrow."

With that, magic seeps into the air and Silen's eyelids get heavy. There are many benefits to being tied to a mystical being. Magic is definitely one of them.

* * *

Silen wakes up to Saelle humming and the grin that spreads on his face can only be described as dopey. She's picking through the bushes looking for berries...BUT UNFORTUNATELY THOSE BERRIES ARE POISONOUS!

Silen launches up and barrels towards her, waving his hands in a *No, no, no!* gesture. Blundering in a panic, he snaps a pile of dry twigs beneath his feet, surprising her and making her whip around in what looks like abject horror. She screams at the top of her lungs and dodges, putting the bush between them in one rapid leap, making Silen *No, no, no!* again, but for an entirely different reason.

Koti snorts himself awake and puts on his best mystical voice. He sounds sleepy and mostly disinterested, her wails giving him no concern. "Sweet one, what's wrong? What frightens you so?"

Her finger jabs in Silen's direction. "Him! He attacked me!"

Silen flings an open hand toward the bush. *She was going to eat from it! She doesn't know any better!*

The unicorn flicks his eyes between them. Getting up awkwardly— front legs first, then hopping up on his back ones—he steps towards the shaking woman. "These berries are poisonous, little one. Silen was only trying to protect you."

"Well, why didn't he just tell—" She stops and looks at him.

Hands on his hips and mouth tweaked in annoyance, he shakes his head and taps his throat. *No luck, pretty girl,* he thinks.

"Oh..." she says, at least having the wherewithal to look sheepish. "You can't talk. I overreacted, didn't I?"

After a long-suffering sigh from her unrecognized soulmate, her outburst is forgiven with no need for an apology. Though she does give one...

"I'm sorry, oh holy one. I shouldn't have disturbed you from your slumber." She bows before Koti, and his back hoof paws the ground in irritation.

"You needn't speak so formally to me, fair one."

You're speaking formally to her, Silen thinks. *Besides, it's probably what her parents taught her.*

"It's the way my parents taught me," she says. "I must always be respectful."

Unless she's yelling about me, apparently. No small amount of irony there.

Koti decides to drop his high-and-mighty act. "Just talk like you do with your friends."

She was probably secluded to ensure she didn't find her pair, especially if she was promised to another from birth. She probably only had maids or something.

"I'm sorry, I didn't have any friends. And if I acted improperly or confided in the staff, they would report my transgressions to my parents. In my life, the one I've spoken most freely with is you."

"Freely?"

Because she confessed she didn't want to get married and that she ran away. It was probably a desperate act on her part.

Koti rolls his eyes and looks at Silen. "Will you shut up? How do you know so much?"

Silen knits his eyebrows. *I...I have no idea.*

"Don't tell me I've made you clairvoyant, because that would be an absolute nightmare."

Silen facepalms. *Do you remember when I ate those mushrooms and thought I saw the future?*

Laughing, Koti says. "Oh, that was hilarious. I would have kept sneaking them into your food except you wouldn't stop throwing up."

That was YOU? Silen asks, stomping over and shoving his friend's high shoulder in frustration.

Pulling further away with a cringe, Saelle looks back and forth between them. "Wh-what's happening?"

At least she didn't put 'My lord' or something at the end. Baby steps.

Koti simply says, "I hear Silen's thoughts."

As if it would help, she throws her hands over her head in self-defense, apparently not wanting to be spied on, all while staring at the unicorn with wide eyes. It's insanely adorable.

Chuckling, Koti says, "No, child. I can't hear *you*. Only Silen and I have a special bond."

Mouth dropped in shock, she lowers her hands and clasps them together as if pleading with the unicorn to reconsider. "How can that be? He's so violent! He just hit you! That's sacrilege!"

Koti rears a hoof back and clips Silen on the thigh, making him step back at a quick pace before falling completely over.

Ass!!

Koti whinnies happily. "Oh, believe me, if he's violent, it's only because I've taught him to be. I raised him."

Saelle visibly twitches. "Why would someone as precious as you raise a lowly human?"

He should be insulted, but Silen can't think beyond the throb in his leg. *That one's going to bruise.*

"He's not lowly. He's magical as well. All those who are soulmated are. That's not why I raised him, though. It's because he's brave. Reckless. And because he has a way about him that makes me laugh. As an immortal, I tend to not hold on to fleeting things, but his company has proven to be worth the heartache I'll suffer when he dies."

If I die, it will be because you killed me, Silen gripes, rolling around on the ground a little. Koti doesn't correct him either, the sadist.

Saelle eyes Silen warily with her pretty mouth pursed. "Alright. If you trust him, then I will try to as well. But please, if you would ask him not to touch me. I'm meant only for my intended."

Ask me yourself! Silen pouts. *And I am your intended!*

"You're thinking of him even now?" Koti asks.

She considers, her eyes turning sad. "Not the one my family chose, but there must be someone out there who's meant for me. Someone I can love with my entire being. Someone I would love so much, it hurts."

Silen's heart throbs. *Me. It's me. How can I make you understand?*

"Do you read?" Koti asks. "I have a feeling I don't know as much about soul bonds as I'd like to. It would help us find Silen's true mate."

Nodding, she seems shy. "But there is no library where I'm from…"

"Oh, we don't need a village library. We need an occultist library."

Silen wants to groan. *Please, no. Not her. I hate her.*

Meanwhile Saelle shrinks like a mouse under the eyes of a predator. "But our souls will be eaten!"

"Not at all. We will, however, likely have to listen to a painful rant at Silen's expense. Come." Koti turns and lowers his neck to nudge Silen off the ground with his muzzle. To be fair, Silen is milking it at this point. "The witch we need is only a day's walk from here. She always refuses to read her books to me, says I'm too powerful already, and she hates Silen. He told her where she could stick her black magic and she didn't like it much. She cursed him with a rash for eight days."

Silen stumbles up and scowls at his friend. *What happened to being selective in your storytelling?*

"You told me not to," Koti reminds, flicking his tail.

Saelle looks at Silen like he has the plague. "It's not going to come back, is it?"

"Oh, no. We found a good witch who dunked him in enchanted milk."

She...giggles. Ohhh, Silen would get eight million more rashes if it meant he could hear that sound again...

Though the fact that it was his first impulse disturbs him.

Chapter 3

~THE QUEST FOR WHAT YOU ALREADY HAVE~

Madge's house is like a bunch of broken angles slapped together. It always looks like it's about to fall in on Silen's head, and that's only one of the hundred reasons why he hates coming here. Yet here he is. Again.

Casting one last sigh at his friend and unwilling soulmate, Silen walks up to the ramshackle door—cracked in some places, mossy in others—and knocks. There's a muffled sound of something tipping over and a grunt of displeasure from inside. He can hear the witch stomping closer before she flings open the door, regarding Silen with narrowed eyes.

"No," she says, and the door slams in his face.

Silen turns to look at his friend and gestures at himself with his eyebrows up.

I'm shocked, Koti. I'm hurt.

He's sarcastic, that's what he is.

The unicorn shakes his head back and forth, flipping his mane from one side to the other with a sort of *pfft* sound. Silen moves aside, and

Koti uses his horn to stab at the door with a dull *thunk*. His spire embeds itself so deep that the unicorn needs to wrench his head to pull it free.

There is an "UGH" from the other side, and the slab of abused wood opens again. When the witch sees Koti this time, her exasperation only gets louder.

"I said NO!" she says again, outright *whamming* the door and making the unicorn have to rear back a step to avoid his horn getting snapped.

The pair of friends look at each other, at a loss for words, though history tells Silen that Koti is likely considering one of two options. Violence, which won't get them what they want, or enchantment, which Madge would be expecting, so it won't work.

Instead, a small "Ahem," turns them both around. Saelle looks at the ground, hands wound together behind her back and looking utterly embraceable. "I...I could try. If you want. Um, I mean, if she won't eat my soul."

Charming. She's so ridiculously charming. And oddly brave.

Stepping up, she avoids Silen entirely, sliding along Koti's flank and keeping the unicorn between them. Her knock is so quiet, even they can barely hear it, but it becomes a stronger rap-RAP-*RAP* as time goes by. And Saelle doesn't stop either; she knocks for about a full minute before the door yanks open again.

The witch sees all three of them looking at her expectantly. Madge is a pudgy thing, filled with more venom than you'd think for one with a face as carefree as hers. Her hair is a puffy tuft of unpleasant knots and her clothes look strained to the point of bursting. This time, it's the witch who sighs as she takes in the girl, toes to crown, before literally *taking her in*. Madge grabs Saelle by the arm and yanks her inside, banging the door shut one last time and locking it for good measure.

Silen's about to have a conniption.

Koti steps back just as quickly as Silen does, though Silen trips over himself and lands painfully on his spine. It doesn't slow his progress. Flipping over, he scuttle-crawls to Madge's single, overlarge window—nearly waist to ceiling—trying to avoid getting clomped on in the process. Koti curses under his breath as his human slithers between his legs and wrenches himself up, streaked with dirt, to look through the warped glass pane, likely left open to let the breeze through.

Saelle's eyes are wider than Silen has ever seen, and she looks shrunken into herself as Madge walks around her appraisingly. Silen's mouth moves in the shape of insults that go nowhere as he gestures wildly. Koti only hooks his head through the opening.

"Now what could you want with our lovely damsel?"

Madge hums. "I'm trying to figure out how you managed to get a damsel in the first place. Is she bewitched, kidnapped, or stupid?"

Silen's gestures level up in vehemence as he tries to thrust his body through the window. Koti knocks him back onto the ground again, keeping things civil.

"She's an innocent," the unicorn says—which isn't a no to any of the accusations.

Madge harrumphs. "Girl, why on earth would you follow this lot through the enchanted woods? It's a miracle you haven't been eaten or defiled in some way."

It makes Saelle *eep*. When Silen pulls himself up to look through the window again, he can see her trembling. "I'm h-here to help the man find his soulmate."

"Man?" Madge asks, tossing Silen a look over her shoulder. "You mean this overgrown child?"

"His name is"—her pause is far too long for his liking—"Silen. H-he needs to find his soulmate before the full moon."

"Oh, yes. The forest is abuzz with the news. Ambek took your voice, boy? We should all thank him for his generosity, though I suppose your stubborn stallion has a problem with it."

Koti chuckles darkly. "You know me too well."

"That vow you made to this child is a curse, unicorn. He's always been a curse."

Those words, an echo from long ago, hurt Silen in a way he can't even begin to explain.

Koti shoulders Silen, almost knocking him over as he tries to reassure him in his own brutish way. "Now, now, Madge. Though I've *intensely* regretted his presence from time to time over the years, he's my favorite thing on earth."

"Being a deviant is your favorite thing on earth."

"Close second, then."

Madge still walks around his soulmate in circles, judging her worth. "Virgin, are you?"

Saelle couldn't glow redder if she tried. "Y-yes."

"Soulmated, yourself?" Madge asks with a knowing nod, likely feeling Saelle's tiny thread of magic in the air.

"No, ma'am."

With her brows up, Madge slides her eyes over in Silen's direction. He can only bite his lip in a feeling of utter loss. Every rejection stings worse than the last.

Madge must understand the look on his face because she murmurs, "Well, now...that's interesting."

"We'd like to look at your book on soul bonds," Koti says. "There's something I need to understand."

"You've been trying to get a hold of that book since the boy's Adam's apple bloomed. I said no then, and I say no now."

Silen watches as Koti nods slightly towards Saelle with meaning. "You know that being without their pair can leave them empty their whole lives." Looking at Silen, he adds, "And rejection can drive them mad."

Madge looks between the star-crossed idiots, picking up Koti's innuendo even as Saelle is none-the-wiser. Her lips purse as she stares at Saelle, tapping her arthritic finger over her cheek. "You want to save him, girl?"

"Only because K-Koti asked me to, ma'am."

Silen outright winces, wrapping his arms around himself. Madge looks at him with sympathy for the first time.

"Well then, let's help your evil unicorn and his orphan brat."

Madge sidles over to one of her large bookshelves, floor to ceiling with cracked leather tomes and rolled up, delicate scrolls.

"Ma'am...why wouldn't you let Koti read the book before? He could have—"

"Could have eaten even more of my pages, that's what. You can give a unicorn an amazing brain but that doesn't make him any less of a moron."

"It was delicious!" Koti protests.

"It took me two days to make the ink, a month to press and trim the paper, and just as long to illustrate alongside my perfect handwriting. Never mind the precious knowledge I couldn't recall from my original script once you chomped it all away. You can go to the underworld and rot, you horrid thing."

Even Saelle looks at Koti with a reprimand written on her face.

Madge climbs up a few steps on the ladder that leans against the wall, making small groans on her way. It's all a show. Madge looks decrepit, but she's spry and wily. She's chased Silen down and thwapped him quite recently. Despite their bickering, Koti likes her. Or likes using her. Or annoying her. Silen can never tell which one. Silen, however, is more than a little afraid of her—and for good reason. She's terrifyingly temperamental.

"Ohhhkay, girlie." Madge pulls down a thin, flimsy book. Either there's not much known about soul bonds or not much to tell. Given how long Madge has known he was soulmated, Silen wouldn't be surprised if she'd torn out half of the pages just for spite. The parchment looks perfect, unmarred, as if it was written and put away never to be looked at again. "Can you read, little miss innocent?"

"Saelle, please. You can call me by name if you prefer."

"If I prefer..." She snorts. "Who in the hells taught you how to speak?"

Silen's hackles rise on Saelle's behalf, and Madge sees every one of his hairs stand on end, testing his reactions with malignant amusement.

Saelle shrinks again, worrying her hands together. "M-my parents. And yes, ma'am, I can read."

"Parents are overrated." Madge flutters the pages of her thin book, squinting at the blur of words until she finds what she's looking for. Handing it over, she tells Saelle, "This is what you need. Read it out loud so your reverse harem can hear."

Not understanding the reference, Saelle just blinks at them and stands straighter, clearing her throat as if she wants to make a good impression. She squints and bites her lip, so alluring Silen just wants to kiss her.

"Soulmates are bound for all eternity. Even if one dies, its spirit will linger close until its pair passes as well. Once the pair's connection is completed by touching each other's marks, only then will they know peace. Soulmates who cannot find their pair, are forced apart, or are rejected by their mate often lose themselves to life-ending sadness or insanity. Only the cruel would keep one away from the other.

"Though unusual, soulmates can pass by or reject each other if they do not both individually trigger the bond they share. Every soulmate recognizes their pair in a different way. Some only need see their soulmate to know. For others, only touch will spark the connection. Still more must hear the voice of their soulmate for their flame to ignite. Each of these reactions seems immediate and never ending."

I knew at first sight, Koti. I saw her and immediately needed her. I knew I would die for her. Suffer for her. If she loves me back, I think I'll explode.

"Once the pair ignites their spark, their magic will truly begin. Pairs are flooded with good luck. They will never fall ill, their need for physical things like food and water dwindles, ensuring they never go hungry or thirsty, and their lives become long. Some are recorded as living as many as two hundred years."

Koti whinnies quietly as the corners of his mouth tick up. "Ooh. I get to keep you for longer, do I?"

Silen's sour mood lightens a little.

"And their luck seems to continue on for at least a generation, their often-numerous children knowing nothing of hardship."

Silen brightens a bit more, a small smile curving his lips as warmth spreads through his body. *Often-numerous, you say?*

Saelle's face goes red as she stammers, "And wh-when their bodies come t-together..."

And now he's *really* interested.

Madge plucks the book from Saelle's hand before she can turn the page. Eyeing Koti, she asks, "You get what you needed?"

"Yes, that had the missing piece."

Saelle looks at Silen with fear in her eyes. "Oh no...what if he has to touch them? He'll traumatize people if all he does is go around fondling women!"

Silen facepalms and Madge laughs harder than he's ever heard.

"Traumatize? More like they'd take his hands off as soon as he tried. No, child. Knowing Silen, he'll know her on sight. The trick is how to get that unlucky girl to see him for what he is, as well. Especially if she's a prude, like you seem to be."

"You don't know the half of it," Koti agrees, only to have Silen shove his friend's long face.

Madge crosses her arms and stares Silen down. "I'm sure he'll find a way to catch her eye. That one is desperate for attention. Being abandoned makes him overcompensate for all his shortcomings. Or try to, anyway. And fail most of the time."

Saelle turns to him in worry and Silen shrinks under her regard.

Madge keeps twisting the knife. "Anything and everything to get someone to look at him, like his parents wouldn't."

The meanspirited hag. Silen's old hurt rages, putting a vise on his chest.

Koti's gaze turns into a glare as he stares down the witch. "That's enough."

"I'd have left him behind, too," she continues heartlessly. "Seems one needs an eternal life and a century or so of boredom before they'd waste time with this brat. I'm sure he'll be forgotten minutes after he's gone."

Madge always hits his soft spots, trying to get back at him in their never-ending game of one-upping each other. But this is too far. Everyone rejects him, but never Koti...though after being left behind so cruelly in the past, Silen knows that deep-seated fear will always remain.

Don't ruin this for me. Don't make me feel like just a stone to trip over in his long life. Like a momentary chore or a burden. I can't bear it.

Silen clenches his fists and looks away, unable to handle these pointed words without the ability to fight back. Normally he can hold his own, but he has no words to hold her at bay, and she's loving every minute of it.

"Perhaps it will even be a relief when he dies. After all, he's only ever been an annoyance and an embara—"

"Stop it right now!"

It's a loud whip crack that fills the air, silencing the witch...but it wasn't Koti this time.

It was Saelle.

Looking up, she's standing between the witch and the window, effectively blocking Silen's view. Saelle's arms are held out protectively, even though Silen knows she's terrified.

"There's no need to be so cruel! Can't you see you're hurting him?"

Silen stares at his soulmate's back. At her dark hair as it draws a straight line down her body. At the flow of her skirts as they barely cover her ankles. She backs towards the window, getting closer and closer until he can almost smell her sweetness. He's dizzy with love for her, letting it eat him from the inside out.

"You can...you can curse me if you want," Saelle says, "but I won't let you abuse someone who's already in pain. It's not right! It's evil!"

Madge's voice drops to a deadly timbre. "Careful, child. I know very well what evil is, and I can show it to you. Perhaps you're too young to know the difference. I'm more than willing to be your teacher."

A true threat. This situation has just gotten dangerous.

Saelle stumbles back with a gasp, ominous magic crackling like static, and Silen has had enough. His soulmate is close enough that he can loop a hand around her clothed waist through the window, yanking her outside and placing her respectfully before she can react, careful not to brush her skin and upset her. Perhaps that's her trigger to acknowledge him, but she doesn't want to be touched... Silen will have to woo her first, somehow. He can't hurt her. He won't allow himself. She's finally shown him the first rays of her kindness, though, and for today, that's more than enough.

He sees Koti nip the shoulder of her dress and pull her into a stumbling run as the unicorn trots them away, making an escape from Madge's temper. Her flares are vicious, and Silen has the scars to prove it.

* * *

Dinner is simple fare. Koti calls down a colorful bird with his magic—a pretty, plump thing—and stabs it to death. Saelle looks like she's about to pass out when it happens, which is downright adorable. Last night's fare consisted of dried, pre-prepared food stored in one of Silen's nearby hidey-holes. He's like a squirrel sometimes. From this point on though, they'll have to make do with what they can find out on the trail. She'll have to adjust.

They're about to go beyond Silen's normal forest radius into the unknown. The three towns they'd already visited lived on the periphery of his experience, and Madge's was the farthest he'd ever gone. He doesn't know what awaits them now, and it makes him uneasy.

Looking at Saelle, he knows his poor soulmate has it worse. She's left behind everything she's known—everything she's been groomed for—and has fallen prey to a sacred, holy beast, one who is not as benevolent as she'd been led to believe. One who she's now heard curse more filth than should be possible, seen mildly abuse Silen as a part of his daily routine, and who took her to a moody black magic user for a quest that's, at best, an exaggeration and, at worst, a lie.

If Silen had his way, he'd just tell her the truth. But for all his faults, Koti is wise. If he thinks Saelle needs to connect naturally for this to work, Silen will stay the course. Still, she's outright drowning in new experiences, and Silen worries for her. Which is why, when she looks like she's about to be sick as the bird sinks down an inch or two on Koti's horn, Silen takes pity.

Scanning the boughs in the dark as she quietly voices her disillusionment, he sees a sleepy bees' nest. Taking out his flute, his minimal training at the ready, he goes to stand beneath it.

"You're going to get stung," Koti calls over.

Silen looks back just in time for the unicorn to chant something guttural that makes all the feathers burst off the bird with a loud *poof.* Saelle screams, jerking back as downy fluff seesaws in the air.

"Oh, I'm sorry, did you *want* to eat the blue part?"

Silen shakes his head and rolls his eyes at their antics. Bringing his hands up, he presses his fingers over the instrument in what looks like the right pattern and takes a deep breath.

The first note is a shriek that surprises even himself.

"What are you doing?" Koti asks.

I'm trying to make them leave. I want some honeycomb for Saelle.

His friend chortles. "Yeah, I'd like to see you try."

Don't worry. I've got this.

...is what he hopes, anyway. In truth, he has no idea what he's doing. Positioning himself again, he blows a sweeter chord this time, letting his fingers dance in the pattern he was taught. There are a great many things that Silen will never do by intuition, but once you teach him, his mind is a painter, capturing the image in brush strokes that will never fade.

Saelle comes to stand nearby, preferring Silen's music to Koti's poultry dismemberment using his hooves, horn, and teeth. The bees are waking and starting to wander out of their hive, making a shimmering cloud.

If I'm magic, let me be magic, Silen thinks, switching to the second tune, the more lively of the two by far, and adding in new notes with his own flair for texture.

It's working! The bees are blooming around the nest now, their buzz becoming a writhing thrum. At this point, he just has to will them away into the distance.

He just has to...

Koti, what do I do now that I've woken them up?

His friend laughs. "Suffer?"

Silen lowers his flute to turn around and glare at his friend, but the moment the music stops, the bees launch. Silen's silent scream is wide-mouthed and undoubtedly worth seeing as he snags Saelle again, by the hand this time, and tries to drag her along. The moment their skin touches, however, he goes to his knees in a jolt of painful pleasure, one that whites out his mind.

It makes sense. He saw his soulmate and his entire field of vision narrowed in on her. He heard her voice, and his knees went weak. Now, skin to skin, he wants to worship her. Devour her.

Mine. Silen's heart begs as he looks up at her like the goddess she is.

And then he sees the imminent threat of the swarm behind her. There is no time. He pulls her arm heavily, landing her on the soft ground before draping himself like a blanket of protection over her as the hive descends.

Wait—*descends?*

They're HORNETS! Silen realizes, stings prickling along his back as Saelle wriggles in a panic beneath him, crying out her distress.

"Be still, girl!" Koti yells. "You want to be stung, too?"

She goes limp beneath him as Silen's back lights on fire with dozens of needling stabs. His neck. His scalp. His soundless ouches get him nowhere, but his huffs of air in Saelle's face warn of the massacre above.

"You idiot!" She hisses. "Fool! Moron! Stupid! Masochist!"

All of which may be correct. Still, he manages a shushing sound as he trembles above her. After what feels like hours when it was probably less than a minute, Koti says, "That's enough of that," and the bees disperse. It was that easy.

Silen rolls onto his hip, releasing his soulmate and panting with his face pinched in pain. Saelle doesn't run away this time. No, not at all. She hauls back and *slaps* him. A nice, good, whip crack that rocks his jaw to the side.

Maybe he is a masochist.

"You know," Koti says, "you may want to consider that Silen has your best interests in mind."

Saelle is too busy to consider much of anything, focused more on glaring at Silen in fury, her lips pulled into an endearing sneer.

With a sigh, Koti turns to Saelle. "You were sad because I killed something—which I did specifically so you could eat, by the way, so the blood is really on your hands—and Silen just wanted to get you honey to sweeten that sour moment. Yet here you are, still sour. He was being kind. And, if you haven't noticed, this is the third time he's saved you. From stinging bees, to poison leaves, to dragging you far away from magical misdeeds. He is a knight in shining armor, child, he just does it in true Silen-style."

Koti clip-clops closer. "Let me see," Koti says, and Silen obediently takes off his tunic, Saelle spinning away with a fevered blush. Irritated, he pats his belly, right over his mark, and mimes throwing the goddamned thing at her, scoop after scoop of soulmark.

Koti hisses between his teeth when he sees. "That's over two hundred stings!"

What? Silen knits his eyebrows at his friend. *No it's not...*

Still, Koti goes on in the most whiny, coddling voice he's ever heard. "Those look so terrible! Oh! It must hurt so much!"

Seeing Saelle's shoulders sag, Silen eyes the unicorn. *I know what you're doing...*

"Ack! There are even still stingers left in there! Oh! Oh! It's swelling up so fast! I'm almost glad you have no voice, or I know you'd be howling. Your face looks like you're crying, too. Oh, no! Saelle, he's crying all because he wanted to help you and instead you slapped him and now he's going to die from bee stings!"

"DIE!?!" she cries out, her hands going to her face in horror, still turned away.

You evil, glorified horse.

"But I'll save you, Silen. I'm the only one who can. Quick, before your throat closes! I know how allergic you are!"

At that, Koti gently touches Silen's back with his horn and the stinging pain melts away, imaginary crisis averted. Silen can't help the sigh that leaves him as he flops belly-down on the grass in relief.

"DID HE JUST DIE!?!?" Saelle wails. "WERE YOU TOO LATE!?!"

Why is she so cute?

* * *

The crickets are singing and the growling prowls of griffins hover around the protective bubble that Koti keeps them nestled in. There is a never-ending blue fire in the center of their charmed barrier, smokeless and lovely, keeping them warm as fall turns the leaves into golds and reds.

Silen pretends to be asleep, secretly staring at what's left of the moon as it slits down to blackness. He's cuddled into Saelle's old bedroll—which, for all intents and purposes, is now his. At night, she stays tangled around Koti, still loving him despite his obvious flaws. Silen can sympathize. He feels exactly the same. It's likely he even loves Koti all the more because of them. It's heartwarming that his soulmate and he share that...though it might be the only thing they have in common.

Tonight, the other two are awake and chatting while Silen lays still. Saelle is braiding Koti's hair, weaving dandelions in, but Silen is too lost in his own misery to enjoy their warmth. The book's words haunt him. It had said soulmates' bonds can be activated by sight, touch, and sound. Saelle has now seen him and touched him with no changes...that only leaves his voice, the one thing he can't give her. That means all is lost. She won't fall in love before the moon shines bright again, his voice will be forever gone, and he'll crumble from wanting her.

He curls around himself tightly, ignored by his traveling companions as he tunes in to their conversation. Koti knows he's awake, of course, and paying attention. Perhaps that's why he changes topics.

"Why do you hate him so much? Silen, I mean," Koti asks her.

"I don't hate him. I just...I'm scared of him."

"But why?"

There is a pause. "Even without being loud, he's loud. His hands are always moving. He's always running around. And he looks at me in this way that's...intense. I don't know what to do with it. No one I've ever known is like that."

Koti hums a sort of agreement.

"How did someone like you come to take care of him? That black witch was saying so many mean things. It seemed to hurt him. I couldn't bear it."

Koti snickers. "She was right about one thing. Unicorns are both revered and immortal—thus two things become true. We can get away with a lot...and we are also very bored. Silen's and my relationship exists because of these two truths."

Yes. Silen remembers the day they met quite well. It was the day he found out what a true ass Koti could be. Yet it was also the day that his best friend saved his life.

* * *

Silen was no more than seven, lost in the woods, staring at the bank of the Az river. His parents left him behind with vague promises to return...yet hadn't. Two days had passed since then. Silen's face was a mess of tears and snot that he rubbed at constantly, sniveling and truly coming to understand that no one was coming back for him. Soul-marked children were considered bad luck, after all. They aimlessly searched for their other half until death, dragging down the family with their worthlessness. And that's exactly what Silen was. Worthless. Thrown away. Abandoned.

His possessions had whittled down to only an aching heart and his satchel. Made of shabby cloth, the bag hosted two things: the embroidered shape of his red spiral with the word "soulmark"—a warning so that would-be do-gooders would know of his curse—and any food he was strong enough to carry. He didn't know his way home. He didn't know how to forage. The only thing Silen knew was that he was going to die there. He didn't want to die.

In that sad, resentful moment, he decided to eat his food slowly. To take tiny bites until he could find a village. If he just proved he was a good boy, that he had worth, then maybe someone would take pity on him. He just had to make every morsel last, apple by apple by precious—

And that's when a unicorn snatched his satchel and yanked. The strength of it nearly tore Silen's shoulder from the socket, but his skinny frame served him well, letting him cling and dangle as the mythic beast shook its head, trying to fling him off.

"Let go." the creature said through gritted teeth, but no. Silen had lost enough that day.

With more fury than he'd ever known, he hooked his young fingers into the unicorn's nostrils, causing it to rear back with an uncharacteristic bray. Clenching his stomach quickly, Silen pulled his little knees up and worked them between his pack and the creature's chin, launching himself up to grab the thing's spiraled horn. Both that pointed spike and the creature's chomping teeth were the most dangerous weapons it had, so the boy hiked up onto the animal's face and crossed his feet together under its jaw, clamping on as the unicorn reared and bucked, taking off at a gallop. With cinched eyes and a vise-like grip, Silen rode through the forest, bumping and bouncing but never letting go.

"GET OFF!" the thing yelled, and Silen heard his pack drop. Opening his eyes, it had fallen far behind them. He needed it, but if he let go, he'd be trampled. Or stabbed.

Clamping his knees higher, they dug into the unicorn's large eyes, making it shriek a whinny and stop short, lashing its head back and forth, temporarily blinded by skin.

"I won't let you kill me!" Silen yelled, squeezing his limbs to hold on with all his might.

There was a rough huff as the unicorn flung its head in rough jerks. "Let me go, child!"

"No!"

"I said, Let. Me. GO!"

"You think I'm stupid, you oversized donkey?!"

"What?"

"You demon! You thief! You ugly thing! Half-brained idiot! Evil-eyed horse!"

There was a pause as Silen's muscles started to tremble with fatigue. The unicorn...chuckled.

"No one has ever spoken to me like that."

"Because they're scared of you!" Silen yelled.

"Because they worship me," the beast corrected.

Silen jabbed his knees into the creature's eyes again, making it wince and step back a pace. The boy grit his teeth in effort. "Then they're all crazy."

There was a deeper laugh this time. "You know, it's only a matter of time before you fall off on your own."

"Yeah, and it's only a matter of time before I bite you. I have sharp teeth, I swear! And if you kill me, I'll haunt you for a thousand years!"

"A thousand years is nothing to an immortal." The creature twitched its neck again, thudding its front hooves against the dirt as it hummed in thought. "What's your name?"

The question took him by surprise. "S-Silen."

"I am Koti. A human's life is short, and you seem entertaining.

Instead of stomping you into mush and being haunted, why don't I just take you with me?"

"Mama says you mustn't tell lies."

"Why would I lie?"

"Because no one would want someone like me! I'm soulmated! I'm cursed!"

"Ah, so you have some magic in you. All the better."

That gave Silen pause. No one had ever taken the news of his curse without rejecting him outright. Being young, hope found him quickly, making him dare to ask, "You won't throw me away?"

That warm chuckle came again. "Child, if it makes you feel better, why don't I vow to protect you?"

"Why?"

"I've really got nothing better to do."

"You'll take it back."

"Impossible. I've already said it. I'm bound by it."

Silen sniffled, letting those words sink in. "Y-you like me?"

"I would like you more if you got off my face."

The unicorn shook its boy-covered head again, and this time Silen almost flew off. Lowering his neck, Koti brought Silen close to the ground, and he couldn't help but let go.

Landing on his rump, he cringed in anticipation. Instead of getting gored, though, he felt the creature mouthing his head...it got spit all over him, but he believed it was meant to be a kindness. And it was.

"You'll protect me?" Silen asked.

"Your whole life."

"You won't ever leave?"

"Not even if you want me to. You're so reckless, it's charming. But I *am* eating all your apples."

* * *

Even now in his misery, the memory makes Silen smile.

Saelle shuffles, cuddling closer into Koti's side. "The witch says you'd be lucky to be rid of him. That he's an embarrassment."

"He's hilarious. And brave. I wasn't lying when I told you he was a knight in shining armor. He gets himself in trouble—a lot—but most of the time it's because I trained him wrong as a joke."

Saelle's giggle is like music. "You are a horrible thing, aren't you?" There is another pause, followed by shuffling sounds. Silen has to struggle not to look over his shoulder and see what they're doing. "I know what it's like to be unloved. I may not have been left behind, but from the moment I was born, all my parents could think of was how to give me away. I think I can understand his loneliness a little bit."

Silen wants to cry. He really is a crier.

"We need to find his soulmate," she states firmly. "I don't want to see him sad like that ever again. If he's as kind as you say he is—"

"Kinder," Koti corrects.

"—then he deserves happiness."

So, give it to me, Saelle. Please see me. Please love me. Even if I never speak again, I need you to be mine.

"But," she continues, "how can we find a soulmate? Where do we even look? Do you think he'll know her right away?"

"Silen will know her on sight. Maybe he's already met her, but her side of the spark hasn't ignited yet."

"Oh, how terrible would that be? That would mean you'd left her behind already."

"No," Koti sighs. "I would never let that happen."

It's Saelle who hums now, a sound of happiness. "You really do love him, don't you?"

"And I'll love his soulmate. And his children. And his children's children. Unless they're idiots, in which case I'll abandon them immediately."

You damn bastard.

Koti snickers to himself. "But I believe his soulmate will find him, see him for who he is and adore him. It's only a matter of time."

There is a heavy sigh. "I hope so. I'd like to hear his voice one day. You said he's a singer?"

"Not at all. But that doesn't stop him from trying. Like I said...he's brave."

Om
nom
nom

Chapter 4

The town in the valley below looks pleasant and quaint, making Saelle feel homesick. Not that she ever wants to go back again. More and more, she's realizing that she didn't belong in that cold home with such cold people. She lived her days either numb or aching with sadness. Out here, though, she's never felt so many wondrous things all at once. Amusement and irritation, fear and elation, and she even found a fiercely protective side she didn't know existed, a special sort of bravery. Saelle—the timid girl raised only to be sold off to the highest bidder—is now an agent of destiny off on a noble quest. She has stood up to a black magic witch, traveled the wilds of the enchanted forest, slept under the stars, and done so while in the presence of a legendary unicorn. One that's beautiful. Regal.

Too bad he's such an...ass.

Even thinking the word makes her blush. Koti's vocabulary must be rubbing off on her.

She loved him immediately. Koti is charming and powerful. Everything she'd ever thought a unicorn would be as well as everything she thought it wouldn't. It's a shock to her sensibilities—but after a lifetime of monotony, the feeling of being taken by surprise is more than just welcome. It's exhilarating.

So is looking at the little dwellings below, nestled a short distance from the bottom of the waterfall they now stand atop of. The water rushes past in whitecaps, producing a fine mist that hovers over the din of the pounding falls. The height here is dizzying, but Saelle is not afraid. Koti is with her, after all. And...Silen as well, the man her quest revolves around. He seems to want to protect her, too.

Saelle looks at the thatched roofs and the winding roads, wondering if Silen's soulmate lives within those village walls. Is she wandering around a marketplace, buying flour and herbs for dinner? Does she have brothers and sisters? Is she wealthy? Is she a street beggar or a service girl? Is she beautiful like he is, or is she plain? Is she sweet? Is she smart?

"Koti, what exactly am I supposed to do? It's not as if I'll know who his match is when I see her."

The unicorn *pffft*s with his ample lips. "That's for damn sure."

She looks at Silen who only lifts his eyebrows at her with a half-smile.

"But it's written in the stars, child. When the time comes, you'll know what you're supposed to do. I'm sure of it."

If only she had Koti's confidence. She'd like to help Silen find his happiness, truly. Sometimes he looks so sad. So full of...yearning. She'd read books with feelings like that in her collection at home. Fairy tales of princesses and knights separated by class, secret lovers separated by the foretelling of the heavens, enemies who looked in one another's eyes and saw home, even though it could never be. Saelle wanted a romance that felt like that. A constant draw towards her intended, as if the sun rose and set because of them alone.

Her real-life betrothed was nothing like that. He was old and gaunt; his smile seemed to contain a vile slickness that made her afraid, like every glance he gave her was a silent warning of things to come. When he set even a finger on her skin, every inch lit on fire in the worst of ways, no matter where he touched her. He always misinterpreted her gasps of pain, her small whimpers, and would look at her as if he was both hungry and feral at the same time. He'd whisper the word, "Soon..." and it always felt like a threat more than a promise.

She shudders at the memory and Silen takes her hand, pulling her back from the cliff face, *tsk*-ing at her for getting too close. He's over-protective. Likely because she's the one who will help get him what he needs. The man is obviously longing for his mate, not to mention getting his voice back. Saelle knows what it's like to be voiceless, having to keep her personality in a bottle all these years. Speaking so freely now, she can't imagine ever losing the privilege again. With Koti's divine influence, she's never been more mouthy in her life, and it's wonderful.

If Silen was raised with this magnificent beast, no doubt he must have the same unruly tongue. She'd like to hear it one day. In fact, she has a deeply rooted desire to hear his voice more than anything. It must truly be her destiny to help him if she can wish this hard for something. The feeling chokes her sometimes. Whenever the man gestures frantically at his unicorn friend, screaming silent words, Saelle's insides clench. Ache. It's enough to bring tears to her eyes.

"So," Koti sighs, "I guess I'm going down there."

Silen slaps the unicorn's haunch and swivels his finger in a circle, indicating all of them.

"No. It's too slow." But there's something smug in Koti's voice. "You two should stay here while I scout. If there's something interesting, I'll come get you."

Silen's eyes are wide as he gestures between just himself and Saelle now, back and forth so fast it blurs. The unicorn only chuckles.

Saelle's asks, "But Koti, how can I help you find anyone if I'm not even—?"

He tosses his mane. "You'll do your part; don't worry about that. You'll keep this writhing dolt over here busy, so he doesn't do anything stupid."

Saelle's mouth drops wide and Silen makes an indignant huff, tossing his hands in the air and letting them clap back down at his sides.

"Just me and him?" she squeaks.

What's she going to do now? Everything that she'd been bred for slaps her in the face, reminding her to *never under any circumstances be left alone with a man!* Her true love is out there somewhere! What if he thinks her impure and passes her by after something like this?

Koti can't read her mind, but even if he could, it's likely he wouldn't care. Instead, he tosses her a wink with a perfect, glinting eye and whinnies, rearing back and *DIVING* over the cliff and down the waterfall.

A shriek tears from Saelle's throat as she drops to her knees and scrambles to the edge, only to find Koti galloping through the air down towards the valley, his feet silently hammering...on the top of a rainbow. An arc of color traces the wind and he rides it as if it were solid ground, his muscles flexing beautifully as his mane and tail flutter behind him. She gasps, clamping her hands over her mouth in awe until something catches the corner of her eye.

It's Silen. He's pacing back and forth, gesturing in a rough rhythm, no doubt cursing out the unicorn in his mind. His fist raises, middle finger up. He bites his thumb and flicks it in the unicorn's direction. He fans his hand across the bottom of his jaw as if blowing a venomous kiss. She knows what none of it means. His lips even move, he's so frantic, and Saelle can...she can make out the shapes of words! Things like 'damn you' and 'stupid' and 'what' and 'wrong with you.' Silen's teeth are bared in between mimed phrases. Saelle can't hear a thing over the roar of the falls, but she wonders...

Lashing out, she grabs his wrist and pulls him farther away before whirling on him.

"Say it again!" she urges.

He looks confused and annoyed. Frowning, he shakes his head back and forth and taps his throat again, his ever-present reminder that he can't speak, as if she was a simpleton who'd forgotten somehow.

She grunts, hands on her hips. "I mean move your mouth. Maybe I can read your lips. Just now, I thought I could make out some of your words by the way you—"

But she can get no further. He grabs her hands faster than anything and his mouth goes a mile a minute, babbling so rapidly that anything intelligible fades away into a series of facial flutters. She hears "s"s, the clicks of "k" sounds, and "t"s—all of which come more from air and tongue than from vocal cords—but it's all too fast.

"Wait! Stop!" She tugs herself away and she's never seen a person deflate so fast, his excitement falling away into something terrible. Her heart aches for him, it truly does.

She starts nervously braiding her hair into black plaits, looking over her shoulder and wishing for Koti, already uncomfortable with both her emotions and Silen's. There has to be a way to understand him.

Why does she always feel so strongly about this? Maybe her purpose isn't to help him find the right soulmate... Maybe it's to help him learn how to communicate so he can woo his pair once he has her. Perhaps his soulmate is activated by sound, so he'll have to find other ways to make her fall in love.

The feeling solidifies in her mind as utter truth.

"Can you write?" she asks. He shakes his head. Crinkling her nose, she supposes it makes sense that a wandering man would never have learned. Even if Koti knew how, what was he going to do? Hoof print letters into the ground? He doesn't seem the type to put in such effort. "Well, I can fix that. I'll teach you."

Silen downright glows.

She starts to pace. "Until then, maybe we just start slow. Say something simple."

He blinks at her. His mouth opens slightly, then his tongue touches his teeth before his lips make a circle. Something like Aah—lll—oh.

"Hello?" she guesses.

He's so excited, he grabs her again.

"Stop that!" she hisses, pulling away. "You're always so...ugh!"

He's properly chastised. Still, he seems hopeful.

She regards him, narrowing her eyes. "Say the word yes."

He mouths it, and she embeds the movement into her mind.

"Say no."

He does, but then shrugs, nodding his head first and then shaking it, pointing to himself as if to inform her that he can already get that point across on his own.

"Yes, yes, I know. But I...I want to learn the way your mouth moves. I need to."

His whole face lights up pink. There is a beat where he stares at her for way too long with his pretty blue eyes before he mouths something that looks like 'I love you'—which can't be right.

Saelle's got a lot of work ahead of her to solve this visual puzzle. Fussing with her hair, she tries to decipher his word-shapes, *hmm*-ing. After a moment, Silen sighs visibly, his chest puffing up with an exaggerated amount of air before it rushes out in a *fwoosh*. He flops down onto the crunchy leaves of the forest floor with a drawn-out snort of frustration, putting his face in his hands and sighing about eight more times. She doesn't blame him.

Sliding over, she squats down, wrapping her skirt—more worn and dirty than should ever be allowed—under her knees as she looks at him. He seems crushed. Sunset is coming, and Saelle knows that there will be no moon tonight. Silen's time is half over, and they've only just now come to another village of hopefuls. This must be excruciating.

They just exist in the same space for a minute. Eventually, though, Saelle's curiosity niggles at her.

"Are you thinking about your soulmate?"

He nods somberly.

"Do you think about her often?"

He looks at her with a softness to his eyes. Slowly, he mouths the word 'Always.'

It does something to her insides. Her chest seems to twist, and her stomach follows suit.

"Does it hurt?"

His lips shape the word 'yes.' He seems so vulnerable, and she doesn't know what to do with the emotions it stirs in her. Looking away, she laces her fingers together, her heart racing. He leans in and ducks his head, catching her eyes even as she stares at the ground.

'And no,' he manages. Resting his hands over his heart, he clutches at his shirt.

'I' he tries.

'Feel.' He leans just a little closer.

'Love.'

That last word is clear as day. The breath that pushes past his lips gives it a slight sound, and Saelle is electric when she hears it. Her heart throbs and every part of her gets hot. She has read about this feeling. She's not supposed to have this feeling. Not for a destined man.

She stands up and starts braiding and unbraiding her hair again. "I'll help you find her. I have no idea how I can or why I can, but I won't give up. Even after the moon waxes, if we haven't found her, we'll keep looking. You don't need a voice to make her fall in love; I'm sure of it. You can have a happy life together, just like it said in that witch's book. Luck and longevity and numerous babies!"

Her mouth runs on its own at that point, babbling reassuring and hopeful words. He's grinning at her, perhaps laughing, but the more she speaks, the better she feels. She'll take this sudden, unwelcome longing and point its energy at something to do instead. That's her way. She used to embroider stitched words of sadness before hiding them in other loops and making beautiful works of art. She used to have singing lessons where she would channel all her loneliness into sweet arias. Now she'll take her sinful thoughts and throw them into dedication to Silen's cause.

"Let's prep for camp!" she says, way too loud. "I'll get the firewood!"

Before Silen can stop her, she ducks into the brush, weaving and looking for the kind of branches that snap under her feet. Even Koti's never-ending blue fire needs sticks to get started. She just needs to find the dry ones and ignore her burning eyes.

She can do it. She can focus. She can bury her feelings, just like always.

She's good at that.

* * *

"The letter 'R' can be a little tricky in uppercase: a bubble, a straight line, and a diagonal one," Saelle says, drawing with a stick in the dirt. She'd gotten a huge pile of them for the fire, but this is the best one for writing. Nice and pointy.

Silen sits staring at the lines with their little ramps of sod pushed out to either side, making rich brown ridges along the letter's shape. He's chewing methodically, having found them fruit and a few vegetables. Saelle misses seasoned dishes, piping hot from an oven versus eating things raw or roasted on a spit, but she wouldn't trade this new life for a world full of delicacies.

Silen pokes his finger into the dirt, giving the letter a try in one stroke. It comes out backwards. He tries again, wobbly and unsure, but the more times he writes it, the more perfect it looks. The ground around him is littered with letters now, and even when Saelle brushes it all away periodically to start from scratch, Silen remembers them all with no issues. Once he gets it down, he gets it down pat. He can even spell his name already, having asked her for the 's' sound with a soft hiss. For as unintelligent as Koti claims he is, Silen's proving that sentiment wrong with every beautifully shaped letter and silently phrased question.

Saelle wipes the ground bare again, giving them more space to practice. Grinning at her, he takes the stick and turns away, doodling off to one side where she can't see. When he turns back, he beams at her. She lifts up to peek over his shoulder and sees:

SAELLE

written perfectly with a little spiral drawn on one side and a moon on the other. It's very pretty. She smiles back at him, eyes crinkled with amusement as he gestures at it a few times, no doubt proud of himself. As he should be.

"I wish I could teach you how to sing the alphabet," she says. "There's a whole song to help you remember it."

Puffing the hair out of his eyes, Silen stares at his lettering, brows knit as he pouts, drawing more spirals around her name.

"Do you want me to sing it for you?"

A smile blooms on his face and he nods, curling his arms over his knees and looking boyish. Adorable, really. Saelle hides her blush well and clears her throat. It's a simple song, too simple to be impressive and almost silly to sing to a grown man, so she sings only the notes and not the embarrassingly infantile words.

It comes out slow. Sweet. Somehow, from her heart, the childish tune about childish letters becomes something lovely—though she's not really sure how she's managing it. At the end of the song, Silen takes out his flute and twirls his pointer finger in a downward rotation. She thinks it means *"again."*

Under the moonless dark with nothing but firelight, she sings and Silen plays. He's clumsy at first until he truly understands which notes come from which presses of his fingers, but once he gets it, their sounds twine together and cascade up to the stars. Soon, Saelle starts singing other things. Lullabies and bard's songs. Each time, Silen listens to the first verse and chorus before trying his hand, picking up her notes lilt for lilt as they make something beautiful happen together.

Her heart is so full. How could she have missed out on a life such as this until now? How can just a few days be making up for everything that came before? She doesn't know. All she knows is that her voice catches as her tears come, and eventually her song fades away. Silen doesn't stop, though. He leans his head on her shoulder—such a simple reassurance but so, so meaningful—and keeps playing. They're new songs now, perhaps ones he's heard before, perhaps ones he's made up. As she cries harder, he only nuzzles in, letting his song fill the nooks and crannies of her heart.

That's when a growl cuts through the night, followed by a cat-like snarl as something lunges towards them, pouncing off a tree trunk as it attacks.

Silen shoves Saelle away, rolling her to the other side of the yellow fire before he jumps up, holding both palms out and trying to keep the beast at bay.

It's huge—with the body of a lion, great wings tucked tightly along its sides, and a curved, pointed, scorpion tail hovering above. It stabs the thing down, Silen pulling back just in time to avoid it. Gesturing at himself now, he waves at the creature's face and snaps his fingers as if to get its attention. It sniffs for a moment before padding forward, seeming to watch the fire flicker its light over Silen's features.

With a growl, the creature shoves Silen aside and leaps over the flames, headed for Saelle this time. She screams and pushes backwards with her heels, scraping her rear over a set of roots and getting tangled in her dress as its fangs come ever closer.

Manticore, she realizes, knowing the monster from her stories.

She's going to die.

Silen throws himself between it and her with his arms held out protectively, trying to back the beast down.

"Out of my way," it hisses, punctuating its sentence with a flick of its forked tongue.

Silen only shakes his head and widens the span between his hands, making a wall between the monster and her.

A taloned paw swipes at him this time, faster than quicksilver, raking against his flesh and knocking him away, but before the beast can step even an inch closer, Saelle hears—

"JERRY!"

The beast freezes, and...groans?

Koti canters up, winding through the trees and pointing his horn at the manticore's face. "What in the seven hells is wrong with you, Jerry!?"

The beast—Jerry?—rolls its eyes. "I didn't eat your boy! I didn't!" Its voice is muffled with teeth.

"Yes, but you were about to eat my girl!"

Jerry's head lolls to the side and it flicks its tongue. "What, are you starting a human collection now?"

"Maybe." Koti's horn drives closer and the manticore flinches. "Maybe I'll breed these two and start a colony of children. Ones you absolutely Will Not Eat."

"You're no fair," Jerry whines, lashing its curled tail, the spike dripping with venom. "I'm hungry! I haven't eaten for days!"

With a few grumbles under his breath, Koti stands down. "What? You want me to get you a rabbit?"

"Look at the size of me now. You think I'll make do with a rabbit?"

"A deer?"

Jerry considers.

"I'm not luring in another human, if that's what you're getting at."

The manticore sulks—an expression Saelle didn't know such a beast could make. It repeats, "No fair."

Saelle looks to the side to see Silen on the ground, holding his ribs and panting with red seeping through his fingers. Blood...and a lot of it.

She gasps, and Koti looks over quickly, seeing his ward on the ground before squeaking a horrified, "JERRY!"

The beast looks over as well. "Oops."

"JERRY!" Koti yells, this time low-toned and angry.

"He wouldn't let me eat her!"

"OF COURSE, HE WOULDN'T LET YOU EAT HER!"

Koti stomps over to Silen who is trying to get up and failing. Everything in Saelle hurts. She wants to scream.

Silen rolls over with a grimace and Koti mutters for him to "hold still" before touching his horn to the wound. Silen hisses in pain for a quick second before sighing in relief and collapsing back, shooting a daggered glare at the manticore.

Incredulous, it repeats, "You wouldn't let me eat her!"

Koti turns on the animal. "Shall I take your tail again?"

Jerry backs up, stepping into the fire and not minding one bit. "You wouldn't."

"Oh, I absolutely would."

"But it takes months to grow back! And even then, it's a baby tail! A bee stinger! It will take me a year or more to get it like this again." Jerry looks lovingly over its shoulder.

"Then memorize her face. Get it embedded into that tiny brain of yours, so this never happens again."

The thing huffs, stepping up closely to Saelle. She squeaks with fear but is otherwise frozen. Jerry's breath snuffles as the monster stares deep into her eyes. Sitting back, it tips its head to the side as it regards her.

"Fine. I know your scent, your eyes, and your aura. I won't eat you. And I won't eat the babies you and Silen make."

She blanches.

Jerry turns to Koti. "Satisfied?"

Koti's nostrils flare. "And?"

Lashing its tail once more, Jerry looks at Silen, who still holds his side, glaring. "Sorry, whelp. I won't do it again."

Silen makes that same gesture with his fist where his middle finger sticks straight up.

Koti chuckles. "No harm done, then."

Silen's eyes shoot up to his unicorn friend before angling that same pointed gesture in Koti's direction. It only makes the unicorn laugh harder. Saelle really wishes she knew what that meant.

* * *

They mucked about town for two days, leaving Koti in the woods and only coming back to sleep. The unicorn had brought them a purse filled with coins carried in his teeth but when Saelle tried to ask how he got it, Silen simply took her by the arm and shook his head. A clear indication not to ask.

With the money, they bought Silen a new tunic, his previous one having been shredded up the side. He also snuck away and came back with pastries for her which she gobbled up, tossing her manners far, far away. He smiled at her then, and her heart skipped a beat. Without hesitation, he handed her the whole package of treats, and when she offered him one, he just nipped a bite from the piece in her hand, making her feel like she was going to melt into a puddle on the ground.

"You're a scoundrel, you know that?" she says, watching him chew.

He ticks his eyebrows up with a grin, a familiar expression he makes when he's pleased with himself. His mouth shapes *'Who? Me?'* and she shoves him away a bit. Somehow, she doesn't mind touching him anymore. It comes naturally. Perhaps, if she meets her intended, she'll have to tell him that she and Silen are like brother and sister—though she feels like anything but.

"So, where's left to look? We've gone to every tavern and inn asking about cursed girls with soulmarks, we've visited the farms and the local alchemist...anywhere else she might be hiding?"

Silen's smile turns melancholic. Small. Almost dejected. He always gets sad when Saelle talks about his soulmate. It's this reaction that helps her keep her growing feelings for him in check. He needs his true mate so much more than just some random girl he found in a lake.

Saelle wonders what will happen to her when this is all over. She gets teary-eyed but hides it well by pretending to get sweets stuck down her throat, earning Silen's concern as he pats her heavily on the back. It feels...nice. It might be worth really choking if it means he'll fawn all over her like this. She finds she likes his eyes focused on her.

But guilt creeps into her gut. "So, where else?"

Silen shrugs and points to the village gate. He puts his hand on his forehead and pokes a finger out, symbolizing Koti's horn. They've come up with quite a few hand signals now, communicating in their own way. It's still not enough, though. She wants him to get his voice back. She wants to listen to him for hours.

With a nod, she agrees to leave, and they begin to work their way through the crowd. She's noticed that Silen seems to duck every woman he approaches, trying his best not to touch them. Perhaps that means he's trying to keep himself pure for his intended as well...though he does touch *her* all the time... Maybe he doesn't count Saelle as a woman. It's a bitter thought.

"When...when you saw me naked in the river," she starts. He all but lights on fire, his face turning a furious red. She blushes too, but she still has to ask, "Did you find me beautiful? I've never looked at any part of myself, not even in mirrors. I don't know how I compare with all the pretty ladies around us. Am I...fair?"

He turns and takes her cheeks in his hands, bringing her close and gazing at every part of her face, watching her mouth. She aches at his sudden caress. Her heart, her lungs, her mind. They're so close together, bodies almost touching, and she just wants to fall into his arms.

Wetting his lips, Silen nods, the breathy shape of 'yes' making her tingle all the way down to her toes.

"Do you think a man could love someone like me someday?"

He presses his forehead against hers and she breathes him in. He smells like rain and new leather. She can only hear the airy whisper of his breathing as he mouths words she cannot see.

"Do you think someone could love me now?" she asks, her eyes slipping closed.

He nods against her and nothing else exists in this world.

Nothing but guilt.

She backs away. "Thank you. Sometimes I'm afraid that there's something wrong with me. That I'm not attractive. The man they betrothed me to was neither friendly, handsome, nor young, so I always wondered if someone else—someone my own age—would even find me desirable. Worthy."

He tries to take her hand, but she slips away. Giving him a sardonic smile, she says, "I won't pretend that I'm happy you caught me in such a compromising position, but I am grateful for your kindness. It gives me hope. And if that's the way I had to meet you, I'd do it over and over again."

He gets that special look on his face and mouths, 'Me, too.'

That will have to be enough.

* * *

At the edge of the forest outside the village, Silen makes his excuses —a different hand gesture that makes her cover her eyes in humiliation. He pokes a finger out from between his legs, a reference to having to go to the bathroom. It means he's about to leave her alone, but she's not about to tell him no. It always takes him a long time, though. She's peeked at him only to find him clothed, shaking trees with a frown before moving deeper into the woods to try another. She has no idea what that's all about.

People are milling towards the village from the path through the woods, some carrying what they've successfully hunted and others carrying goods from nearby towns, whispering about seeing a unicorn. None of their companions seem to believe them, but Saelle smiles knowingly. Koti likes these rumors to spread to see if he can lure out more maidens. So far, they've had no luck.

Saelle hears a loud *psst!*

Behind a thick maple tree stands a pretty girl with dark skin and large eyes. Her hair is jet black, kinked with curls, and it shines almost blue in the light. Her skin seems to shimmer, as if she's dusted with tiny crystals. Her lashes are long and heavy, framing her eyes like kohl. She is undoubtedly the most gorgeous woman Saelle has ever seen.

"PSST!" she calls again, waving Saelle over towards the tree, looking around nervously.

Confused, Saelle approaches. "Me?"

"Yes, you!" the stranger insists. "Would you please come here?"

And why wouldn't she? Closer now, the woman pulls Saelle over, hiding the two of them behind the knobbled trunk. She whispers. "Are you the one traveling with the soulmated man?"

Saelle's mouth goes dry. "Yes..."

The woman's eyes are star-filled and glittering. "Because...because I think he might be my pair."

Stomach sinking to the ground, Saelle weaves a smile on her lips and tries to sound excited. "Really?"

Nodding, the woman leans closer, whispering. "Do you know the shape of his mark?"

Saelle shakes her head.

The woman looks crestfallen. Picking up the hem of her bodice, she shows a red twirl—a spiral just over a round, shallow divot in her belly. "This is mine."

Koti had asked Saelle if she had a symbol there. Silen's always drawing spirals on the ground, as well. Could she be the one?

Saelle's blood turns to ice in her veins. "W-wouldn't you know immediately if he was your pair? Why are you unsure?"

"I saw him and didn't get that spark the legends tell about, it's true, but I've never heard him speak or touched his skin. That means there's still a chance, right? He just seems...*alluring* to me. I can't stop thinking about him." She presses her hands to her chest as if feeling her heart race. "You're not...in love with him, are you? You look at him like..."

Swallowing heavily, Saelle shakes her head, willing herself not to cry. "No. We're just good friends. I"—she hesitates—"I think you may be the one he's been waiting for." She takes the woman's hand. "Come with me. I'll introduce you. We've been searching for you for a long time."

But the woman pulls away, wide-eyed. "But what if I'm wrong?"

Saelle knits her eyebrows. "Then you're wrong. They've come across many women who were wrong."

"They?"

"Silen, the man you seek, and Koti the unicorn."

"He has his own *unicorn?*"

For some reason, that bothers her. "Koti is owned by no one."

Clenching and unclenching her hands in irritation, Saelle changes tacks. "What's your name?"

"Jessame."

She smiles halfheartedly. "How pretty. It's like a flower."

"And you?"

"Saelle."

"And his name is Silen?"

Saelle nods and the other woman swoons, leaning against the tree with a look of pure joy taking over her face. All of a sudden, Saelle wants to hit her.

Gritting her teeth, she says, "Even if you're not his pair, I'm sure he'll be respectful." Or he'll give her one of those perfectly rude hand gestures. "I can introduce you. He'll be back in just a—"

Jessame waves frantically, her beautiful curls bouncing. "No, no, no, please! It's not just about 'what if he isn't.' What if he *is?* My whole life will change! I don't know what that looks like or if I'm even willing to risk it. I don't know who he really is and I'm...I'm scared."

Saelle would growl that *she's* not scared of a *perfect* man like him, but she actually had been at the beginning. That was before she knew him, though. Before she...

But Silen has a deadline. He can't afford to wait for Saelle's jealousy to ebb, nor for this strange woman to cough up some courage.

"There's no time to waste. We're searching for his true soulmate, and we won't stop until we find her. We only have until the moon is full."

"Why?"

"A powerful fairy stole his voice away. Only if his true soulmate kisses him by the full moon will it come back. But even if it doesn't, he still needs to find his pair as soon as possible. He's so... *sad* without her. He needs her."

The woman looks at Saelle with such heartbreak. "I know how that feels." She rests a hand on Saelle's arm, and it stings. She hasn't felt this kind of pain since her betrothed or her housemaids touched her. It sets her on edge. Jessame asks, "Can I just stay close for a little while? Watch you all and see what kind of man he is? Maybe you can sneak away from time to time to tell me a little bit about him. Perhaps it will help me be brave."

"Okay..." Saelle agrees reluctantly. "But in the meantime, we have to continue our search, just in case you're not the one. Are you sure you're willing to follow us, though? Won't you be missed?"

Jessame looks wistful. "Those who are soulmated are cursed. People don't take kindly to those with marks." Looking around, she waves her arms back and forth, gesturing everywhere. "I live in the woods. I love it here. I can't imagine living anywhere else, now."

Saelle imagines Silen must feel the same. She swallows her misgivings. "All right. When I'm alone, I'll find you. I haven't known him for very long, but I'll show you that he's not someone to fear—whether he's your soulmate or not."

The woman's bright smile is breathtaking. "Thank you! Oh, thank you so much!"

There is a sharp whistle closer to the road and Saelle ducks out to see Silen looking for her in the distance.

"That's him. I have to go."

"Yes, yes of course!" Jessame urges her on.

Saelle turns over her shoulder one last time. "Are you sure you won't come see him now?"

Biting her lip, the woman gazes at the sky. "I promise that, if Silen doesn't find the one meant for him, I will find the courage to face him by the full moon. If I kiss him, I guess I'll have my answer." She pauses. "Are you sure you're not in love with him? You seem—"

"I'm destined to help him find his soulmate. I'm protective, that's all."

They share a smile. With that, Saelle turns on her heel and walks off towards the man of the hour. The one she's going to have to lose, no matter what.

Too bad she never had a chance to have him in the first place.

Chapter 5

Six days went by like that. Horrible, terrible days. They visited two more towns, but instead of the lighthearted moments she and Silen had shared before, she began to distance herself from him. Whether it was to protect her own heart or reassure Jessame, she didn't know. All she knew was that the woman haunted their every step. Any moment Saelle had to herself was usurped by the woman's pining and fear. At this point, Saelle wanted to throttle her.

The moon was almost full. Sometimes, Silen would look at her and his eyes would fill with tears. She knew it was because she was failing him. It was breaking her heart, and at night, she would cry, too, wrapped over Koti's back while Silen slept on the unicorn's other side.

"Trust destiny," Koti would whisper to her. "Whether you know it or not, it's doing its job."

Saelle wakes up with an idea the next morning. If Jessame is so afraid, *Silen* needs to be the one to lure her out, not Saelle.

Before Silen even blinks awake, she rushes over and flips him from his belly to his back, startling him into rearing away with a comical, silent scream.

Saelle's words are frantic as she points at the dirt. "Can you try to write something for me?"

He nods, bleary-eyed and disoriented.

She grabs his shoulders tightly and lets a pained smile unfurl. "Good."

His face knits into concern, his mouth dropping open to question her, but she places her fingers over his lips to keep him from shaping any words that might stop her—make her want to throw destiny into a ditch to wither, so long as it keeps him by her side. At her touch, his eyes flutter closed, and she desperately wishes he'd kiss her. In a sudden, sweeping fantasy, that's what she imagines his expression means. It's what she imagines he does. What he'd keep doing until she made him stop...which she never would.

"Write *Jessame,*" she whispers.

Silen's eyes fly open, and his brows pull together. He looks...suspicious. Lifting her hand from his mouth, she merely points at the dirt again.

"Please."

Confused, he leans to the side and writes:

JESIMAY

Close enough.

"Now, draw something romantic. Stars. Moons. Oh! More spirals! You draw those around my name all the time!"

His eyes search hers, flicking back and forth between them as he shakes his head, incredulity written all over his face.

"Please," she begs. "I need you to listen to me. There's a woman... Jessame...and she's so beautiful, Silen. The minute she saw you, she wanted you. She's been following us. She's afraid of connecting with you, but even so, I see her and know she longs for it. I think she's your pair."

He shakes his head no again, harder this time. Stubborn. Angry, almost.

Saelle leans in close. "Please trust me. You have to try. Tomorrow is the full moon! You're running out of time!"

Lips pursed and eyes narrowed, he rakes his hand through the dirt, scrubbing out Jessame's name, instead writing:

SA

before Koti approaches, casting a looming shadow.

"I told you not to do that," he scolds.

Silen doesn't look up. He stares at his writing in tight-jawed fury.

"You need to let this happen on its own or it might not work. How many times do I have to say it?"

Silen scrubs his eyes and glares at Saelle, making her nervous. She doesn't know what Koti is talking about.

Silen's lips move. 'Show. Me. Jes-i-may.'

With a gulp, Saelle nods. "Follow me but stay hidden. She's afraid. She promised she'd kiss you by tomorrow, though, so don't worry. But it will be so much better if you win her over first."

Silen shakes his head and turns away from Saelle, but she catches him by the cheek and pulls him to face her again.

"I believe in you. I know you can do this."

After all, you did it to me.

He looks at her in that soft way again, and her eyes water. How is she ever going to let him go?

"Can I...can I still stay with you—with both of you—after this is all over?"

Silen's hand wraps over hers as he leans into the palm of her hand.

'Don't. Ever. Go.' he tells her in his special way, and soon, she'll be able to hear him. The thought makes her tremble as he looks at her with half-lidded eyes.

'Show. Me.' he says again.

And she will.

* * *

"Jess!" Saelle hisses as she works her way through the trees, leaves crunching beneath her feet. The forest is dense here, bushes and bark so close together some of them nearly grow into each other. "Jess, where are you?"

In a moment, the woman ducks into sight, her beauty radiant in the mid-morning sun. She smiles, wide and sweet. "How is he today?"

"He wrote your name. You should have seen it, Jess, he did it almost perfectly; he's learning so fast."

Jaw dropping, Jessame's pupils dilate and her pretty eyes budge. "You didn't actually *tell* him about me, did you?" Saelle nods and the other woman bites her thumbnail in concern...before cursing something nasty under her breath. "Why would you do that?"

"Tomorrow is the full moon! And even without that, when you're spying on us, can't you see how hurt he's been, looking for you?"

"Why do you even care? Is it just because it's your job to help him? Your destiny?" Jessame sneers.

Saelle can only blink at the woman's reaction. "You...you act like you don't *want* to meet him."

"Because she doesn't." Koti steps out from behind a tree and Jessame spits another few choice swears. The unicorn stares at her pointedly. "Silen thought it might be you. Foolish not to bother to change your name, Jessame. Did Ambek send you?"

"Ambek?" Saelle asks. "Isn't he the fairy spirit who took Silen's voice?"

Jessame outright growls at them. It's then that Silen steps into plain sight, leaning against the knotted bark of a willow with the deepest scowl Saelle has ever seen.

"My friend has words for you," Koti tells the other woman. "The first of which is to get out of that ugly form."

"Ugly?!" Saelle balks.

Jessame only sneers. "Fine." She passes her hand over her face, and it changes to shades of red, long antennae growing from her forehead in pretty, elongated stalks. Rolling her shoulders, wings flutter out—iridescent fairy wings—and her shimmering skin starts to flicker beyond her, casting a halo and making her glimmer.

Silen flips his hand forward a few times and mouths the words 'Go. On.'

Clenching her fists with a huff, the woman shrinks down to a tenth of her size, fluttering in the air.

Saelle goes white. "You mean this was..."

"A trick," Koti finishes for her. "A distraction. This is cheating, pure and simple, Jessame. Didn't Ambek say he's better than this?"

Silen just looks at his friend.

"No, you're right, he didn't." Koti steps closer to the fairy flitting around in the air and snaps his large teeth at her. The squeak she makes is borderline adorable as she flies backwards a little, barely escaping him. "I could eat you right now, little one. You'd be crunchy, I guess, though probably sour."

The sprite *pttttth*s her tongue. Her voice is much smaller and higher pitched as she says, "Well, I hope your little fleshling never speaks again! He shouldn't even be allowed in our forests, Koti, you know that! It's a sin! Humans are an abomination! A waste! Ambek shouldn't have taken his voice, he should have taken his *air!*"

And Saelle sees red. Whipping back a hand, she *slaps* that damn fairy to the ground and uses a foot to pin down her small body.

"How dare you!" Saelle grinds out through clenched teeth. "Should I crush you now or let Koti do it?"

Voice silken with dark, vindictive pleasure, the unicorn says, "By all means, Saelle. Show no mercy."

She's never been so angry. "You tell the...the *bastard* you work for that Silen is worth ten of him! That he's better than any creature in these woods! And he's *definitely* better than *you!*"

With that, Saelle hocks back and spits something vile down onto the fairy, uncaring if it cloys her wings and never lets her fly again. Looking at Silen, he stares at her like she's a hero.

Flipping her hair, Saelle removes her dainty, scuffed shoe from the little traitor with a *hmph*, and storms away, pulling back as far into the forest as possible...before bursting into tears.

* * *

Saelle hides herself behind wide, green fronds that stick up from the ground in straight lines. They are starting to crinkle and brown at the edges as they fade, but their serrated leaves are enough to keep her out of sight for now. Her tears are heavy, but she holds back her sobs. She doesn't want to draw attention to herself and make this any worse than it already is. Instead, she stares out at the lake, watching the sun reflect off its surface, trying to take in the sounds of the breeze and the soft, quiet rustling of the forest...until Koti reaches in with his wide teeth and starts shredding the greenery, munching it up in big mouthfuls. He doesn't say anything, only looks at her as he chews, his flat teeth mashing and smashing in crunching chomps until he rips up another bite.

She breaks the silence. "It's my fault. I wasted so much time thinking she was the one."

Koti snorts. "Did you, though?"

A dark cloud falls on her face. "I hated her. She was a nuisance. She..."

"Got in your way?"

And Saelle doesn't know what to say to that.

Splashing sounds start off at a distance, and she peers around the leaves that shield her. Striding into the sun-dappled ripples is Silen...

Completely unclothed.

She *eeps* a little bit before slapping her hands over her mouth, thankful he's at a distance. "What is he doing!?" she whisper-yells.

"I told him to go cool off. I've never seen him so angry."

"Who wouldn't be angry? It's almost time and he has nothing!" She tries not to look at his nudity, no matter how her eyes are drawn to it. "I was destined to be the one to help, and I've failed him."

"There's no such thing as destiny," Koti states plainly.

She looks up at him and blinks. "What? But you said—"

Koti ruffles his mane and scratches his horn over his leg. "I lied."

"What? Why?"

The muscles in the unicorn's flank twitch as he flicks his tail. "I do that."

Inadvertently, she looks at Silen again, taking in his form before realizing what she's doing, and turns red from her collarbone to the tippy-tips of her ears. "Wait... Does that mean his voice isn't—"

"Oh no, that part's true. Otherwise Jessame wouldn't have sucked you into her scheme."

Saelle has no idea what to do with this conversation. Meanwhile, Silen is scooping water over himself. His rear is covered in the water's depth, but the lean muscles of his back are visible from where she sits. When he wets his brown hair, it's much longer than normal and drags over his shoulders, turning darker in color—almost earthen. He has lines where his tunic usually lies over his skin, his arms a rich tan while the rest of him is pale in comparison. His shoulder blades arc as he moves his hands, scrubbing himself in slow circles. Now more than ever, she admires how beautiful he is.

Turning away from the angle of the sun, he runs water over his chest now, a frown embedded on his face. His fingers slide down over something red low down on his belly...a spiral. That must be his soulmark.

"Jessame had a mark just like his."

"*Pfft.* A fairy trick."

"What's that little hole?"

Koti's head lifts. "You mean his belly button?"

"Is that what that is?" she whispers.

"You don't even know what a *belly button is?*"

"I—I've never seen one!" she stammers, embarrassed.

"Stupid woman," Koti grunts, ripping up some more leaves. Mouth full, nearly ruining his words, he adds, "But lionhearted, nonetheless. Not everyone would have the guts to manhandle a fairy. Now she's going to sew your lips shut in your sleep."

"*What?!*"

He just looks at her. "Another lie. You'd better learn to tell the difference or you're going to have a terrible life."

Saelle pulls her face into a grimace before looking back towards Silen, letting the quiet settle in once more. "What are those other marks on his body?"

"Scars. He's always getting himself into trouble."

She squints, trying to see them from so far away. "There's the slash from Jerry." Three heavy stripes lay over his ribs. More faded purple lines and pock marks cover him. "What are those circle ones?"

"Those?" Koti says. "Those are from when he annoys me. I stab him sometimes."

She turns and glares at him, but the unicorn pays no mind. "How can you two possibly be friends?"

"It's one of life's great mysteries."

Shaking her head, she keeps staring, entranced by the man in front of her. There is a sort of heat in her body. A desire to touch his bare skin. Taste it. She wonders if Silen felt this same way when he'd caught her bathing but dismisses the thought quickly. There's no way.

"What are we going to do now?" she asks, on the verge of tears again.

"What are *you* going to do, you mean."

"Me? If there's no such thing as destiny, I have nothing to do with it."

Koti grimaces and mutters under his breath. "I'll stab *you* next." Louder, he says, "You're in love with him, aren't you?"

Her chest tightens. "I'm not his pair."

"Does it matter?"

"It matters if he wants his voice."

The unicorn hums in thought. "I think that, more than anything else in this world, Silen just wants to be loved." Koti looks at her. "Even if that means getting stabbed from time to time."

Turning back towards Silen, Koti says, "Love hurts. It's annoying. It's foolish. It forces you into terrible, long-lasting decisions and saddles you with unimaginable responsibilities. Takes all the predictability and stability in your life and swallows it whole. Love disturbs your peace of mind and replaces it with an endless amount of heartache. Robs you of all your perfect privacy and steals your sweet solitude. You make senseless compromises that anyone of sound mind would laugh at you for. You let it in, just once, and it changes you forever." Then the unicorn smiles, still staring at his ward. "But I wouldn't have it any other way."

With that, he comes closer and mouths at Saelle's head, his lips doing a weird dance and wetting her scalp. It's upsetting—but also comforting, in a way.

"Do what you think is right, child. If destiny doesn't exist, you can only go with your heart."

This time, when she looks out, Silen catches her lingering gaze and dunks into the water with a crashing splash, waving his arms defensively before covering his chest in shyness. His mouth moves rapidly, blabbering and jabbering at her in complete silence.

Saelle's never laughed so hard in her life.

* * *

The sun is setting, and she can't bear it. The moon already hangs in the sky, only the tiniest sliver missing, ominous and terrifying. She'd always looked at the moon and dreamed of a better life, but now she feels like it's cursing her. She's a bad person. Selfish.

But brave.

She wants to be Silen's soulmate. She wants to have him fall to his knees before her and lift her skirts, finding a mark just like his and dusting kisses over it, possessing her just like she wants to possess him. The longing almost chokes her.

Twilight is setting and she's been gone too long, but she's had a difficult decision to make... One that will mean defiling herself.

Grabbing her dress in her hands, she decides to see, once and for all, if she has a mark. She's rejected the man she'd been betrothed to, and the idea of any future love only brings thoughts of Silen to her mind. She wants no other. That means there's no one to keep herself unsullied for. If she does have a soulmark, Silen won't care that she saw it first; he'll only care that she has it. Besides, looking at herself may be impure, but it can't be any worse than staring at Silen's naked body, spying and indulging her craving for him.

Her skirts go up over her ankles, but that's not enough to shake her. It's something she'd already seen. Something unavoidable, really. The rest though...

Over her knees the tattered clothing goes. They are covered with purple marks—bruises, most likely. Questing and sleeping outdoors isn't always the softest thing for your body. Her thighs are pale, downy white hairs laying over her skin. As she comes to her underthings, she starts to tremble with fear. Jessame's words come back to her in the reverse. It's not, 'what if she's his soulmate'... it's, what if she's *not*. What if her stomach is bare, mundane flesh with no magic to be seen? All would be lost. Tears well in her eyes as she lifts her hem ever so slightly up...

But a rustle in the bushes makes her let go of her dress entirely. Silen peeks around a large, frizzled bush, likely looking for her after she's been gone for so long.

She must seem a mess, because the first thing he does is step close and take a hold of her cheek, swiping a thumb over her tears, wiping them away.

His lips shape the word, 'Why?'

And her tears fall harder. "You're so sweet to me. Every moment of every day, you make me feel like I'm someone special. Someone who matters. These past weeks, I've been trying to live my life to help you— but I've failed. Yet you still come to me like this, indulging me when I'm not even your soulma—"

Just like she did, he places his fingers over her lips, shushing her with soft, airy sounds. She's going to faint; her heart is beating so fast she feels lightheaded. Taking his hand in hers, she laces their fingers together and takes a deep breath. It's now or never.

"I love you," she blurts out. His eyes go wide, but before he can reject her, she lets her thoughts rush onward like a roaring river. "I know that I can't give you your voice back. I know that I'd be stealing a life of luck and longevity from you. But I'd try to make you as happy as I possibly could for as long as I'm alive! I would do *anything* to make your sacrifices worth it. Please, Silen. I'll give you my soul! I'll give you children! I'll be anything you want...just please..."

The way he's looking at her is melting her insides. His eyes are half lidded and his lips part as he watches her mouth move. As she speaks, one of his arms wraps around her, caressing the curve of her back, making her unable to think of anything but him. His name is the only word she has left as he draws her closer, letting her breast lean against him. Still holding his hand, she presses his wide palm over her pounding heart.

"Even if I'm not your soulmate, this is yours. It aches when I see you. It weeps when I think of you ever going away. My heart beats for you, Silen. Only for you."

And she goes up on tiptoes to kiss him. Filled with hope, it's the softest of caresses, the briefest, most chaste brush of their lips...but he *moans* at their touch. With that sound, everything in her goes haywire, making her gasp his name against his mouth before he dives in deeper, curving a hand around the apex of her neck and pulling her in as he takes over her senses, kissing her hard and long, warm and frantic, as if she'll disappear if he ever lets her go.

"You *are*—" He pants over her lips. She's going to explode. Every sound he makes is a beautiful agony. "You *are* my soulmate."

He lifts his tunic up and off, tossing it to the ground and pulling her back in immediately. Taking her hand, he drags her fingers over his hips and up, up, up over his mark. A flash of yellow lights up between them as he glows. It's as if his whole body ignites as he cries out, making her a vessel of raging need.

"Let me touch you. Please, Gods, Saelle, let me touch you."

Possessed—crazy, maybe—she hikes her clothing up again, higher and higher, all shame be damned, and the feeling of his calloused fingers over her soft parts makes her breath stutter.

"Yes," she whispers. "Please."

With a rumbling purr that makes her knees weak, he slides his thumb against her skin...

And the world bursts into color.

Looking down, she's the same as he is. The exact same. Together, a sweet light pours from them both, wrapping them in magic and perfection. Laughing a little, she dives in and takes his mouth again, needing him more than anything she's ever needed in her life.

Pulling away slightly, flushed with desire, he tips her chin up to stare at him. His baritone makes her quake. "Now I can tell you all the words I've been dying to say. The first being...you're mine. From the moment I saw you, I knew you were mine. Thank the stars you love me because I would die without you. I would break into a million pieces."

Saelle grips his bare shoulders, holding him tight as she swoons.

Impossibly close, he tells her, "It's not enough to say I need you. I don't have words to describe my want,"—his lips graze hers—"my desire,"—his fingers caress her mark again, and she whimpers—"my longing for every expression on your face, every adorable word, every insecurity you've admitted and every ounce of kindness you've shown me." He smiles, dimples gracing his cheeks and making her heart flutter. "You are so fearless sometimes, yet here you are vulnerable and soft. You need love just as badly as I do...and it makes me want to swallow you whole. Even when you were rejecting me, I could think of nothing else. You've taken me over. Without you, there is no air. No light. No sound. Without you, Saelle, there is nothing."

He caresses her face, and all is right with the world. It doesn't matter what she comes from or who she's been; it only matters that she's never going to be alone again.

And her glowing spiral burns ever brighter.

* * *

Koti canters and bucks, annoyed as much as he is charmed...until his hair gets yanked.

He whinnies his irritation and shakes his head, trying to get the damn thing *off* already, but she giggles, wooing him just as easily as she pisses him off. Why is he like this? Out of every unicorn in the world, why does *he* have to be the one obsessed with humans?

Well...not just any humans.

Silen's firstborn still tries her hand at riding him, even though Koti wants none of it. No matter how much swearing and shouting he does, the little girl is uncowed. Fearless, just like her mother, only reincarnated as demon spawn. One he already knows he'll defend to the death.

Saelle comes out of the cottage with another babe at her breast and a third toddling around her ankles. When Madge's book said *numerous children,* it did not lie. Stupid goddamn book. His humans breed like rabbits.

"Kirana! Stop bothering Koti or he'll bite you!"

"I absolutely will!" he mutters at the child, looking over his shoulder and clicking his teeth as he nips the air. "And you'll have deserved it!"

"Eeeeeenough of that," Silen chides, dropping his pack and jogging up from the path. He grabs his little one and lifts her off, patting Koti's flank as if it would make him feel any better.

It does...

But that's not the point!

Silen *tsks*, setting his offspring down and poking her nose. "What have I told you about Koti?"

"That he's evil," the girl parrots.

"And?"

"And he'll stab me to death."

"And?"

"And he's your best friend."

"So you need to love him with your whole heart," Silen adds. It's that last part the whelp seems to have trouble remembering.

"Child," Koti infuses his voice with the most dulcet of tones, "ride me again and I will stomp you into a painful, bloody pulp, bring you back to life, and do it all over again." At that, Koti mouths her head, making her laugh as his lips slop at her. "Also, I love you, you vicious thing."

"Love you too, Uncle Koti!" She grabs his muzzle, not knowing any better, and squelches a kiss against him, making him groan. Job well done, she darts off to go terrorize something else. He and Silen just watch her go with varying looks of satisfaction.

"She's so adorable," Silen gloats.

"Yes, well, you think your whole brood is adorable."

"He's not wrong!" Saelle calls over before leading the other two little ones back into the house.

Koti hates it here. They've settled down and no longer travel the woods with him. Now, if he wants to see them, he has to lower himself to something as insulting as a *visit*. Sometimes even eating this vile and delicious thing called "hay." When he considers it an offering of worship, though, it makes him feel a little better about it.

Silen casts him a look out of the side of his eyes. "Do you want to be brushed?"

Koti stomps, indignant and put off, snorting and pounding the ground with his hooves. "Of course, I do! Why even bother asking?"

With a chuckle, Silen shoves him. "I'll go get the brush."

"And braid my hair!" Koti demands.

"Yeah, yeah," his human gripes.

Gods, he loves them. He wants them to live for a very, very long time. And thanks to their magic, they most definitely will. It was worth picking up Silen, that lonely little soulmated boy, once upon a time. Every moment with him has been a moment Koti will remember for all eternity. This family has changed him, stealing away his boredom and giving his life new meaning, a gift he'd never thought possible. With them, he has found happiness. A life filled with laughter, adventure, annoyance, aggravation, and love. Not as strong as soulmates' love, perhaps...but strong, nonetheless.

Nothing could compare to Silen and Saelle's connection, after all.

It was written in the stars.

The End

Afterword

Writing is truly an addictive thing. Diving into characters and finding their personalities, giving them trials and hopes, building a story around them—it's truly one of the most satisfying things in my life. It ranks right up there with being a mother and a wife, because I'm creating, comforting, supporting, and making people happy, all just by setting pen to paper.

Also making people sad. Don't forget that part.

Trying to take these fairy tales and legends and morph them into something new was incredibly fun. Originally, I'd written Sympathy for the Devil, but I hadn't known what to do with it. I loved that piece so much, controversial as it is, and wanted it to have a home. Enter the 321...Write! Discord group. Many of us were contemplating collaborating together on an anthology that would bring fairy tales into the modern world. Apparently, I was incapable, because what resulted was Soulmates and Silence, which is not what I'd call modern in any way shape or form.

The project disbanded, as everyone got very busy, but now I had these two stories on my hands with no home. Plus, I had the smack in my face that I never actually took a fairytale and made it contemporary. I decided that, if I can't do an anthology with friends, it doesn't mean I can't do a collection of short stories with me, myself, and I. Thus, For the Love of Coffee made its way into the world—as did its many mugs. In fact, my beautiful sister-in-law bought me a mug that says, "You're never alone if you have inner demons," just like the one in the story. I was flabbergasted and overjoyed. I will now have hot cocoa in that mug for the rest of my life.

Capping everything off was really difficult, however. I'd had an idea for Pinocchio, but I couldn't bring it to life. I couldn't even get past an outline. My concept was simply that. A concept. A fleeting image in my mind. It had no substance or bones, and so I thought my project was dead.

Enter sticky notes.

Whenever I have a random idea for a story that pops into my head, onto a sticky note it goes, and it's subsequently shuffled off into a multicolored mess to be picked through at my leisure. Desperate, I dug through the stickies and happened on something I never even remembered writing down. (Which usually means it came to me in a dream.) It was the exact plot to Symbiotes, minus the froggy-kiss at the end.

I'm just going to put it out there—I cannot overstate how essential stickies are to my slush pile of stories to write. They are a host of cool lines, concepts, characters and more. Without those things, I would have lost every scrap of thought. My mind is like a steel sieve.

One last note before I run away: Thank you so much to Nikki on Twitter who walked me through the Hawaiian lifestyle and showed me more Pidgin than I could shake a stick at. Iokua's entire voice is laced with your love and the culture sharing you did with me. I couldn't have done it without you.

Quick trivia!

When I need to come up with names for characters, I often google-translate words that represent the characters into various languages to see what I like. Many of the character names here were selected in that way.

- Ati si tana: Ewe for "reptile"
- Isi: part of the word for "stubborn" in Igbo
- Madax: part of the Somali word for "stubborn"
- Hisk: Kurdish for "stubborn"
- Ren: Danish for "pure"
- Mak'ur: Armenian for "pure"
- Onye: Part of the word "teacher" in Igbo
- Soghun: Armenian for "reptile"
- Kendani: Armenian for "animal"
- Uzh: Armenian for "power"
- T'ever: Armenian for "wings"
- Gishatich': Armenian for "predator"
- Nal: Tamil for "Day"
- Nox: In Harry Potter, they use this word to put out a light

- Atua: Samoan for "God"
- Midwanas wo: Sithspeak for "Powerful One" (Thank you Star Wars)

Thank you to those who have experienced these stories alongside me. I truly hope you enjoyed your time.

About Me

Nichol (Ashworth) Goldstein
Writer / Illustrator
www.nixcomix.com
Twitter: @Nixcomix | Facebook: Nixcomix
Tumblr: Nixcomix1 | Instagram: Nixcomix1

You know those people who quantify their self-worth by the amount of work they produce? That's me. I just described me.

I started writing novels on May 18th, 2020. As of June 2023, I've written seven books, several short stories, and have a litany of ideas in the pipeline—including a sequel to my most popular book: ALL'S FAIR IN RUTS AND HEATS! I'd really love it if you followed me on social media as more published work comes out.

As an aside, I used to be a comic book writer/illustrator by trade, so I've also created over eighty fully illustrated art pieces to support my stories, as well as a whole damn comic strip and several chibi-comics. I need to calm the hell down. This is a bit much. Still, I hope you enjoyed the artwork included in this book.

Be sure to follow me to see more of my doodles, paintings, and snarkasm™.

And thank you, every one of you, for reading.

The war is never-ending. Morale is non-existent and magic stains the sky as dragon riders spiral, trying to take down the raging soldiers of the Dominion. The people are exhausted. The battles need to end. But how? The hate between the factions is just too strong. Unless...

When Reyanne, the White Mage of the Separatist movement, goes head-to-head with her arch nemesis Zanthrand, the Dark Moon of the Dominion, many choices abound. You, dear reader, hold their fates in your hand. Choose your path and choose wisely. Can you end the forever-conflict? Can you bring these soul-bound sorcerers from enemies to lovers? Or will your choices doom them both?

Good luck, my friend. It's all up to you.

Also by Nichol Goldstein

ALL'S FAIR IN RUTS AND HEATS

Omegaverse, Dark Romance - Heat level: 4/4

After defense attorney Caleb Reed is trounced in court by a rookie lawyer - an Omega no less - he knows one thing and one thing only. Ari Jacobson was meant to be his mate... whether she wants to be or not.

With everything he's done, can Caleb go from enemy to lover, or will his blind obsession destroy them both?

Tags: Rape/Non-con elements, Alpha/Beta/Omega dynamics, Emotional manipulation, Stalking, Praise kink, Violence, Suicide, Angst, Bittersweet HEA.

www.ingramcontent.com/pod-product-compliance
Lightning Source LLC
Chambersburg PA
CBHW070622300726
48975CB00006B/1891